Requie... Goddess

by

A.C. Vincent

The Conrad Press

Requiem for a Goddess
Published by The Conrad Press in the United Kingdom
2024
Tel: +44(0)1227 472 874
www.theconradpress.com
info@theconradpress.com
ISBN 978-1-916966-19-2
Copyright © A.C. Vincent 2024
Typesetting and Cover Design by: Levellers
The Conrad Press logo was designed by Maria Priestley.
Printed and bound in Great Britain by Clays Ltd, Elcograf
S.p.A.

Oh God, I could be bounded in a nutshell and
count myself a king of infinite space.
William Shakespeare.
Hamlet, Act Two, Scene Two.

This book is dedicated to

My dear sister-in-law, Antonella Greenstock
April 3, 1969, to February 24, 2022.

A beautiful face, a beautiful heart and a beautiful soul. Loving and loyal wife to Tim, loving mum to Christian and Danilo. A caring lady who loved her family and friends, Italy the country of her birth and England her adopted home. Champion of all creatures great and small, talented artist. Deeply loved and equally deeply missed by all those she touched in life. God Bless.

For my dear wife Shel and for Mark and Tanya, Gary and Ruth, Steph and Patrick. My grandchildren, Georgia, Katie, Matilda, Hugo, Jack and Emily.

To Frank-John Hutchins, staunch supporter and lifelong friend and for his patient wife Wendy for putting up with both of us.

With thanks to my lovely friend Rekha Mitter for allowing me to use her name and certain aspects of her life in the creation of this book.

My daughter in law Ruth B, for always pushing me to keep writing.

Last but not least, Big M, my friend since school days.

It was a very standard old brown case banded in wood the type of which is often seen in antique shops these days at exorbitant prices.

Rummaging through an assortment of various bits and pieces. A pair of hobnail boots, a pair of gaiters, a pipe rack with various pipes. Some old letters or as it turned out bills for animal feed or cattle and sheep bought and sold at Tavistock Market. A couple of old used shotgun cartridges, still with a faint whiff of cordite about them. I was, it seemed, getting nowhere fast.

With the sudden hard realisation that I was running out of luck, I shoved everything back inside the case. My somewhat rough manner in doing so dislodged a piece of material from within the left hobnail boot. I was about to shove the round cloth back inside the boot and in doing so, turned it over in an act of desperation, as if this dusty black fabric could in some way be of significance.

Imagine my utter surprise and delight, when I found to my complete astonishment, that the other obverse side was alive with colour.

A long slow exhalation of breath left my lips. What I was looking at I was sure was a badge. It was roughly three and a half inches in diameter, but it was the vibrancy of the colours that startled the eye. Surely this was in the same condition as the day it had been put inside the boot.

The background was a deep indigo, rich and full as a late twilight, even possibly bordering on violet. Overlaying this was what I took to be tiny circles in an intense gold braid. Along the bottom edge stood lettering, again in Latin and stitched in vermillion red. The Latin inscription was as follows, 'Nostrum celum Innocentes tuebitur.' Even my weak Latin skills could interpret those three words, 'Our Heaven Protects the Innocent'. Surely, I had hit on something of some significance, was it the Fates that had brought me to this point?

Usually, I bored of things quickly and moved on to the next shiny object of amusement. This was different. A voice inside my head told me to carry on and find out more, far more to this note and to the badge, there must be. I decided

9

to keep my discovery to myself until I had a better idea of what linked these things to my grandfather.

As the weeks and months passed, I was unable to establish any further connection and a brief troll through Tavistock and Plymouth libraries yielded nothing of significance.

1979 arrived, all through that year I kept a steady eye in journals and newspapers, with no real idea what I was hoping to find. The more I thought about the situation, the more deeply it got under my skin. I tried various methods of investigative technique, including talking, almost interviewing, members of the family who were still young enough to remember the old man from a close personal point of view, but avoided bringing my parents into the discussion, without knowing why I was so reluctant to do so.

I asked friends, I asked colleagues at work whilst I continued to look for any reference, written or verbal which might shed some light on my quest, such as it was with an emphasis on 'The Chapter.' That being my only real clue until I could break the Latin code. Seventeen little words.

Now a chance encounter with an old man in the Royal Oak Inn at Meavy, a small village only four or five miles away from my grandad's farm would pay dividends, if only in a quite unnerving fashion.

I was at the bar with a friend when an old fellow called me over to his table. It was a quiet evening and as my friend and I approached him he waved my friend away in what we both considered a rough and rude way. It was unusual as we both knew him well and he was always friendly and pleasant in his manner.

My friend backed off and I sat down with my drink at the table.

'Now boy,' the old bloke said, keeping his head down while his eyes shifted nervously from side to side and having the effect of making me do the same. 'The people you bin askin questions bout. The Chapter. They don't like it.'

His accent was even more 'Dartmoor' than mine and I had to listen closely to understand what he said, but he used the word's, The Chapter.

'They idn takin kindly to it. What youm asking folk bout don't need to be aired in public.'

I smiled because I had been on the wrong end of old farmers and their long-winded jokes, and it had cost me a few pints in the past when it was clear I had fallen for a wind up.

'Tis no laughin matter you silly young bugger,' I remember him hissing through broken teeth, 'the Chapter don't like it. Forget you ever heard of them and burn the note that's my advice.'

Now I had to consider that he had heard about the note. I had spoken to some family members about the note when I had started my inquiries, so it wasn't a secret.

Still, the old fella had mentioned it in context and of course he had used the words, The Chapter.

Try as I might to question him further he would say no more.

I told my friend what the man had said. He was equally perplexed and so we decided that his advice was best ignored but, on the way, back to my friend's house to drop him off, I noted that a car was following. The headlights from the vehicle were dipped, however, if I sped up so did the other car and if I slowed down, then it to slowed as well and kept an average distance of about a mile and a half between us. We watched in the rear view and wing mirrors with fascinated concern.

I dropped my friend off at his house and made my way back home, home for me being a house fifty yards from a local beauty spot called Cadover Bridge.

The vehicle behind kept pace with me all the way back. As I turned into the gateway off the road the lights in the car behind were turned off. I listened closely for a few minutes. I could still hear its engine running.

Moments later I heard it pull away in the other direction. After maybe two or three seconds its headlights lit up the road in the distance. The incident made me nervous, and I of course thought at once of the what the old man in the pub had told me.

11

Rightly or wrongly, I put two and two together and was convinced that I had made four and not five.

After that episode, I decided that I would shut my mouth to all but close friends that could be trusted to remain silent. I was still very

determined to keep up my research and between my work at the quarry and helping my godfather on his farm in the valley below, I had little time to spare to do so.

Once again I seemed to have come to a dead end. The old fella at the Royal Oak was courteous but kept mum about our previous conversation and would be drawn no further.

'You never knaw who's listening my 'andsome,' He told me.

He was right as I was to find that out later in my quest.

1980 arrived and passed without any further developments, although I found one or two interesting bits in old papers that suggested clandestine meetings at various points on the moors during summer. They were vague and were more in the way of visitors who had reported shadowy figures in the night, whilst they were camping. It wasn't much to go on, but I kept the cuttings logged anyway.

1981 was to prove a more satisfying year. I was beginning to compile a dossier of sorts. The badge was now more intriguing than ever, and I set out to try to make sense of what the tiny golden circles represented once again.

On a whim I counted the circles and found fourteen. I could find no relevance to the number fourteen on Dartmoor, nor could I get any further with the Latin phrase. It was what it was but had no historical significance that I could see. I looked closer. Had I missed something, anything. I took a magnifying glass and began a closer scrutiny of the badge under the lens.

Taking my time and an unusual amount of patience, I traced between the gold circles as though I were joining the dots in a child's picture book, with my finger rather than a pen.

I started at the topmost circle and let my finger run down the invisible line to the next circle, then the next and so on.

After the sixth circle in the pattern, my fingernail caught against a raised bit of cloth about the same size as the others.

I got a little piece of cloth and some fabric cleaner and with some gentle teasing, I cleaned away what could have been soot or just dirt to reveal another gold circle and continued to follow the line past one of the circles then another.

Now the line had snaked the other way. Once again, I found another raised piece of cloth and set about cleaning that off as well. This now meant that there were sixteen gold circles currently visible.

I carried on and had almost completed the line when I found the seventeenth and last gold circle. I cleaned it off and as i suspected it was as bright as the day that the badge was created.

It was an exciting moment. Because of my research, I knew that the number seventeen cropped up in some west country legends. Not only that but the golden circles on the badge took on a new look. What if they were not circles, but stars?

The thought was thrilling and more so because I knew that this newly revealed pattern of stars was the earthly image of one of the constellations, woven in a warm beautiful gold thread.

I understood why the pattern had made no sense to me before. It was because three of the main stars were missing. Well, not missing, but had in fact been hidden, apparently on purpose to confuse prying eyes. Why otherwise would a person or indeed persons have that done on an item that was obviously worn with pride on possibly a very important garment?

Now the Latin phrase also made more sense, if it related to the stars, which I assumed it did.

In all honesty, I had also assumed that the item was a badge and now the magnifying glass proved the fact. Tufts of thread could be seen that had probably attached the badge to a garment of some kind. And there was more. Needle holes could clearly be seen around the edges of the fabric.

Sometime later in the year a friend of mine who was a seamstress kindly gave her opinion and confirmed my initial evaluation. She also said that whoever had made the badge was highly skilled in needlecraft.

Returning to the moment in time when the constellation was made apparent by my cleaning off the missing stars.

As I said, it was a moment of great excitement and of relief. It had taken me three years to get to this point and a considerable amount of research along the way, most of which had been misdirected due to my not checking one of two major clues more thoroughly.

How much time I had wasted was all to painfully obvious, but now I was more determined than ever to get as much information as possible in order to follow the two leads, three if you count the veiled threat by the old fella in the pub and it was obvious from his words, if taken as fact and not a leg pull that some form of organisation existed and that they were interested in my investigation.

The galling fact was that I didn't even know. Being tailed by the car may have been significant, or indeed it may have been pure coincidence. Cars were different in the seventies and eighties and most drivers could do minor mechanical bits and pieces to their own vehicles. It was not uncommon for local people to take their cars out on a test run after repairing or fitting parts to a car.

I knew that I needed to keep an open mind and build my dossier on fact, not fiction, hearsay, or rumour.

The new insight on the badge meant that I was certain that I knew what it represented.

That was an exciting moment to say the least. I really wished that I had someone to share all of this with, but at the time, all I had was one piece of documentation and one piece of material. None of this constituted evidence, but if I added in the old fella's warning, then I could be on the right track, to what, I didn't know.

The note was of course equally important and what it alluded too was supported by the badge but there was an immediate way to find out.

Mid-February on Dartmoor is usually the coldest time of year and the most likely to give heavy snowfall. This evening however, it was just icy cold, with a north easterly breeze bringing the temperature down to around minus four degrees.

The heavens were festooned with stars, and it was a moonless night. My parents had gone to bed, so I picked up my binoculars and made my way to the northern fence of the grounds.

It was bitter but a heavy sheepskin jacket and a swig from a hip flask full of whisky warmed my throat and the cheeks of my face as a nervous anticipation set in, and I propped the badge in the fork of

an ash tree and laid a torch on another branch with the beam facing onto

the badge. I looked up to the north, over the tors and found the star Polaris, the North Star. Our constant guide over millennia past.

Previously however around the year, two thousand eight hundred BC, one of the stars in the constellation I was now looking for had been our pole star. So, I let my eyes follow a diagonal path downwards and slightly to the west. I found two of the main stars I was looking for. Then I followed the curve towards Thuban, our pole star of five thousand years ago.

It took a moment to sink in. I looked at the badge and the design match was unmistakable. Lo and behold, there it was. Not the brightest constellation in the sky, even though it's the eighth largest, but recognisable once you found the head of the beast as it were.

The Constellation Draco, the Dragon.

Chapter 2

Mysterious assignation

I was thrilled of course with matching the stars on the badge to the stars in the constellation of Draco, the Dragon and it was a confirmation of fact which I needed to expand on.

It was the early hours of the morning before I got into bed, my mind racing with thoughts that were truthfully, out of this world but now work got in the way and even though I would spend many hours spare hours researching books of all kinds, I still had a living to earn.

The trail went cold and I could not for the life of me find any further connection between the Latin phrases on the note, the badge or the 'Chapter'.

Two things of some import happened in the summer of that year. The first was a missed phone call.

My mother had taken a call from a lady who wished to speak to me. She said she had some information which I might like to be a party to. My mother asked for a number but the woman in question said she was calling from a phone box. She then asked when I would be available and was told to try again later that evening after work.

It was a fortnight before I heard from the mystery woman.

'We need to meet. I can't talk for long as I have limited time.'

I enquired into the nature of her call and asked her name. She told me that she had information that would 'enlighten' me in my quest.

'You may call me Anna. Where and when can we meet?'

A time and place was arranged. I was careful not be taken in and would consider the possibility of a practical joke before I committed myself whole heartedly to believing anything she told me, that was if she turned up for our meeting at all.

In the days before mobile phones became the norm, a phone call held more sway. A lot of people still did not have home phones and if that were the case, it was necessary to walk or drive to a phone box, if you needed to contact family or friends it required some effort.

Our meeting had been set by her for the Saturday of the following weekend. It was to take place at the Warren House Inn at one o'clock in the afternoon.

The pub is high on the moors, remote and in those days, difficult to access without a car. There were no bus services and to take a taxi would have been very expensive.

I would drive myself, but I had no idea how my newfound friend was going to get to our rendezvous.

A long week passed, and when the day came I made my way via Princetown on the Duke of Cornwall's land, through Postbridge and on up past the outcrops of tors and the outlined derelict walls of tinner's huts, tin mining having been an age-old tradition on the moors.

Prehistoric stone circles are also evidenced all over Dartmoor, a sure sign that our ancient ancestors strove to understand the heavens above as well as the earth beneath their feet.

Arriving in good time I found the car park had a dozen or so cars in it. The Warren House itself is settled into the roadside close to the crest of a Tor and at one thousand, four hundred and twenty five feet above sea level, is the highest pub in southern England. At that time of year, it was odd that there was so little trade.

I went in, ordered a pint of mild and took a seat on a bar stool, although it was summer, a fire still burnt in the hearth as it had done for a hundred and thirty odd years at that time, having never been allowed to go out.

There were twenty odd people in the bar at that time including the landlord and myself and a pleasant chat ensued for the best part of ten minutes or so.

Looking around the bar I asked if he had noticed a lone woman come into his hostelry. He said he hadn't. Everyone was with someone it seemed.

There was no sound of any vehicles passing or pulling up. The mantle clock struck one. Someone brushed past me and put a hand on my elbow and I found myself looking into a pair of the most vivid gold-green eyes I had ever seen.

The noise of the customers faded into the background as my new acquaintance guided me to a table in the corner, as far from the other patrons as possible.

We both took a seat and at last I was able to get a closer look at her. She was quite small at around five feet six inches in height. Her skin was white to the point of being almost transparent and so had the effect of making the blood vessels in her neck, breasts, arms, and hands take on a bluish tinge, which was accentuated by her dress in vivid electric blue.

At the time, her hair would probably have been described as platinum blond but was in fact closer to silver. She appeared to be around twenty five years of age and was both pretty and beautiful at the same time. Her eyes dazzled. That's the only way I can describe them. Looking back now, I remember thinking they were green but flecked with gold.

Trying to remain ever the gentleman, I asked what she wanted to drink, but it was obvious that she was not interested in pleasantries, because she ignored the question and got straight to the point.

'You seek answers to questions that should not be asked.'

I was defensive but polite in my reply. 'it's a free world and I can ask whatever questions I want to.'

Anna continued, 'and if by so doing you put lives in danger?'

I enquired how she knew that I had been asking questions in the first place and as for putting lives in danger, what lives?

'We have friends everywhere and they have ears.' Was all she would say on the first point.

On the second point she said, 'There are dangers unknown to you of this world and others.'

She spoke in earnest of that much I was sure. Her expression was sincere as far as I could tell.

It was a strange meeting, not solely because of Anna but because the sounds of the other customers were so muted and distant. As if they were in another room or not even there at all.

'Now I must go' she said and stood quickly to leave. 'Watch the skies.'

I told her that I believed I was entitled to a more comprehensive and thorough explanation and remember her putting a cold delicate hand to my cheek.

'Your Grandfather was of great assistance to us. We should bring you into the Chapter, in time of course.'

A hundred thoughts raced through my brain and I shook my head to clear my mind, closing my eyes momentarily as I did so. In those two seconds, Anna was nowhere to be seen. I walked outside as the noise of the bar returned. She wasn't in the carpark. I walked around the pub. No cars had left or arrived as far as I could tell. I went so far as to ask one of the female customers to look in the lady's toilet for me. She wasn't in there either.

The landlord asked if my visitor had arrived yet. I was perplexed, hadn't he seen me talking to her at the table. I described her for him. He gave me an odd look.

'No' he said as the clock struck one. 'No one who looked like that.'

It has been my intention in this book to stick to the facts and only the facts and try to write this book and from an investigative amateur sleuth point of view.

What I have resorted to in this chapter is to tell you what happened to the best of my memory during that meeting or assignation, call it what you will.

Another reason for me writing this from memory is that I would have more encounters with this woman over the next forty years and so I felt it necessary to give a brief description of her looks and demeanour as well as, as truthful account of the circumstances of our meeting and what was said. This I decided to do to give the reader a feeling for the situation in which I found myself.

You will recall that I said earlier in this chapter that two things of import happened in that time frame. The following chapter explains the second of those and deals with a true incident, which was well documented at the time. It also touches on the incredulous as described by other people and certainly by the authorities.

Many newspapers in the County of Devon carried a story that caused some consternation with some sources blamed for attention seeking, drink, or worse.

I won't go into depth because this is incidental to my story but is a good indicator of what was going on at that time. It was a story of alien abduction and lost time.

Lost time in case you don't know is what the UFO research community refer to, during and after experiencing a close encounter of the fourth kind. That is an actual meeting of a human being with an alien being and abduction of the former.

Late July of that year had spawned a series of UFO sightings and reported abduction and experimentation taking place on the unwary.

Although what I am about to tell you was never reported to the authorities. It was not a close encounter of the fourth kind but of the second kind. It tied in with Anna's words, 'Watch the skies.'

As previously stated, I was working at a local quarry where we mined China clay. The method used is to use high powered monitors, or hoses positioned close to the clay face. The height of the face varied slightly but averaged about seventy feet.

The monitor, in those days, was roughly twice the distance away and one man stood and operated the hose by hand. They were huge steel pipes bent into a loose spiral and reduced by stages from to eight-inch pipe, to one to one and three-quarter inches at the nozzle. They were ungainly to look at, but surprisingly well balanced and easy to move.

A roughly constructed corrugated hut protected the hoseman on three sides and above. The floor was heavily timbered, but the front was open to the elements. A gas burner ring fed by a gas bottle was the only form of heating.

I arrived for work on the morning of the twenty fourth of July nineteen eighty one as usual at around five forty five am for the start of my six am shift. Each shift consisted of a Shift

Boss, Hoseman, Sand Plant Operator and Thickener Process Operator.

I won't go into more detail as to the other job roles. It is unnecessary for the purposes of this part of the story. At this time the departing shift and the shift arriving would meet to exchange information and instructions.

This morning was different as no one was there to meet us. It was unusual but we thought perhaps there had been a breakdown which they were dealing with. We couldn't leave the plants or quarry unattended, so we walked off to our respective workplaces. The plant operators to theirs and the Shift Boss and I into the quarry to drop off our lunchboxes at the canteen or crib hut as it was known locally.

On entering the canteen, we found the night shift boss sitting with a cup of tea. As it happened, he was also a relation of mine so we asked what was going on and he informed us that the hose man had been taken home by one of the plant operators as he was in some distress. When pushed he would say no more on the subject.

Twenty minutes passed with almost no further conversation when a Landrover drew up outside and the plant operator, who had taken the hose man home got out. He was as white as a sheet but would say no more on the subject than the night shift boss would. It was a very strange situation.

We changed shifts with no more being said on the matter and it was agreed that we would keep the incident to ourselves.

Two days passed and the local newspaper ran a story about a UFO abduction about twenty odd miles from the quarry. There were also reports of strange lights seen over Plymouth Sound being reported by fishermen.

The Sound was about ten miles as the crow flies due south of the clay quarry.

A week later we were shorthanded and I changed shifts to help out. I was put on the same shift as the shift that had acted so oddly and about what, I didn't know but was about to find out.

I will refer to them as A, B, D and G. They passed many years ago now but, I still feel the need to protect their identities, though some family or friends might recognise them or this part of the story.

23rd of July 1981, the night was clear, with a waning moon and good visibility to the quarry edges. G told me that he had been on the monitor at around two in the morning. When he noticed a light in the sky heading in his direction. He was used to seeing aircraft heading into Plymouth Airport although the airport closed at about eleven pm but aircraft sometimes used the quarry lights as positioning guides.

Two large orange sodium lights lit the monitor position and clay face. There was another on the quarry road and two at the slurry pump pumphouse beside the canteen, a mile or more away.

At night the quarry was a lonely place. Four men in an area two miles long and approximately a mile and a quarter wide ran the operation. In daylight that number quadrupled with plant machinery and mechanical and electrical staff. The company operated a basic form of radio communication at the time, but it was quite haphazard from the point of reliability.

G continued by saying that the light heading in his direction was a dull yellow and that it increased in size, showing of course that it was growing ever closer. He attempted to call over the radio for assistance but finding that the radio had died he changed batteries but it was to no avail. Then the main sodium lights in the pit went out, followed by the light on the road and the slurry pumphouse and canteen, which he could see in the distance.

At this time A, (the shift boss) was with D, (the sand plant operator). They knew something was wrong because the plant lights and equipment began to lose power until nothing was running. This was also the case with the clay thickener process operated by B.

I tell you this only in order to establish a timeline for context.

Unable to contact anyone, G could only stand and watch. This is what he told me; 'There was a low hum and the air felt like it does before a thunderstorm. The lights grew wider until they took up the whole width of the quarry and more still. It came on slowly and I don't think it was more than a couple hundred feet or so above me. It was like a cloud covering the moon and stars, until I could see nothing but a bit of moonlight up over Saddlesborough Tor (a Tor from which the quarry is cut into, and at nine hundred and ninety four feet above sea level), and a sliver to the west over Cornwall.'

He continued to look me straight in the eye, 'It looked like a massive, flattened teardrop deeper at the front than the rear. With no electric there was no water so the hose stopped it was quiet apart from the hum. I couldn't move. I was rooted to the spot. But up in whatever the hell it was, I could see a figure moving behind the lights as if they were looking out to get a good view. It looked human. I had the presence of mind to look at my watch before the sodium's went out.'

G took a long breath and seemed to shiver involuntarily from his head to his toes.

'My watch showed that it was ten past two. As it moved over the pit, it started to turn north, out towards your house, (My parents' house was half a mile north of the quarry), and then the lights came back on, and I looked at my watch. It was two forty five. I never been so frightened in my life.'

Meanwhile in the sand plant A and D had gone outside to see if anything had struck the power lines.

D told me later, 'We wondered what the bloody hell it was. I never seen anything like it. It seemed to cover this whole end of the quarry and most of the hillside. It must have been at a hundred and fifty to two hundred feet above us because it cleared Saddlesborough Tor with not much room to spare.'

A confirmed the story and added, 'I hope we don't bloody well see it ever again. It was huge. Then it turned North over your place and headed towards Burrator.'

B had left the clay thickener process building, also looking for a break in the power lines. He had seen nothing but the tail end of the craft clearing his building and confirmed the northerly heading he told me after, 'What a pity you missed it, and it went right over your house as well. Then the lights went out, but I could see how much of the sky it blotted out as it moved away.'

Word got around as to what they had seen that night but the lads were reluctant to discuss it any further, even with me or their families.

Putting these men in perspective, to the situation in which they found themselves is simple. They were hard workers. All of them had small holdings and the money they made at the quarry supplemented what they considered to be their main interests. It gave them a regular income which saw them through the hard times.

As for making this story up, what could they possibly gain from it but ridicule? They were very embarrassed by the event and wanted earnestly, to forget it had ever happened.

For the rest of that summer and into the autumn of that year, reports of unidentified flying objects still made column inches in the local papers and stories still did the rounds in the pub bars.

It was not at all unusual to see all sorts of lights in the sky over the moor's night after night. None of which carried the standard safety lights required of civil or military aircraft, and many of which made bizarre manoeuvres of which it could safely be said, that no aircraft of the day or even these days was or is capable of. I kept careful watch on the heavens.

My reason for relating this factual account, is to make clear how many incidents like this had occurred over the moors, and to pose the question, was this what Anna had meant by her words, 'look to the skies?'

Suffice it to say my dossier began to grow ever thicker and reports continued in many newspapers over Devon and Cornwall.

Chapter 3

Conspiracy of silence

Try as I may, I couldn't make head nor tail of the clues I now had in front of me. A note, partly in Latin from some mysterious society. A badge, likely from the same source with a constellation emblazoned on it. Veiled threats from the Chapter via an old man and a meeting with a girl I couldn't now find for love nor money but with an obvious connection to the other three clues.

The first-hand account by four individuals relating a story of some kind of encounter with a UFO, even if I were to believe it with no reservation, could not be tied to the four clues above.

I needed to work with evidence. What I had in my hand, as it were, or what I had experienced myself and could testify too.

Silence had fallen deafeningly around me. It was no good just guessing at things. I must have concrete proof or at the very least a justification to follow a lead and if it came to something, then it needed to be corroborated.

To that end I felt I needed help, and it was a few months later at the start of nineteen eighty two, that I met my now lifelong friend and colleague, Frank. He too worked at the quarry, and it was obvious that we both had a deep-seated love for Dartmoor, its traditions, myths, legends and landscape.

We forged our friendship over that year, and I shared the few meagre clues I had with him, in the hope that he might shed some light on my now five-year-old quest.

Frank and his wife loved walking the moors with their two young sons and so became a font of knowledge for me with regards to the history of the moor. Kistvaen's, standing stones, stone rows, barrow's, all these things which I had seen every day of my life, Frank brought alive with a new way of looking at them.

Now we could set out in earnest to dig into the mystery of the 'Chapter' and what its purpose was. Why it was formed and what end did it seek to achieve? In Frank, I had the sounding board I so badly needed. He wouldn't bullshit me. He would be brutally honest above all else and that was what I needed, a direction to head in and focus to be maintained.

The year went by in a flash. 1983 was upon us and my focus was taken up in a quite different direction. I got married and moved out of my parent's house and brought a house not far away at Cornwood, which is still inside the Dartmoor National Park Boundary.

I share this with you, just to give you some background to how and why this investigation has been so long in the making.

Marriage combined with long hours at work didn't auger well for a continuation of our investigation.

Frank had his boys, I had two stepsons and so the whole thing was put on the back burner, with only the odd sortie into the world of secret societies.

We heard rumours and were offered glimpses, which were either intentional or unintentional. By which I mean Chapter had a mole.

On a couple of occasions over the next five years we were given information which led us in one direction or another, always it appeared we arrived at a place just a little too late. We both felt like Tantalus, always just short of getting that metaphorical drink. The water receding before our very eyes.

Still there was evidence that meetings had been held at one venue or another. We found a couple of pages torn from a hymn book in a local church with what could have been some words in Latin, but it was too damaged to tell.

No one from The Chapter had contacted me to ask me to join their number. Nor had Anna been in contact for help of any kind. 1989 found us still remaining true to our cause and to our quest.

Frustration led us to assumptions, which would be of no use to anyone. All we could do was monitor the papers for stories which might relate in some way to what we were seeking.

Frank and I sat back and waited as we were determined to stick to the facts.

We let nothing deter us from following only the evidence, our own

experiences, (if we were to have any), and first-hand accounts from witnesses such as those of A, B, D and G.

Once again, the fates stepped in to aid us in our difficult quest.Although silence had shut us down for over five years, suddenly we had a break in early in 1990. We had devised a tried and trusted method, which we used when examining the newspapers.

Taking just three local papers, The Western Morning News, The Tavistock Times, and The Ivybridge Gazette, three well respected publications which covered a broad spectrum of newsworthy items.

Over those five years we had checked every page of every paper thoroughly, even down to the personal adds. This was where our lucky streak began.

In the lonely hearts column was an ad which grabbed my attention immediately. It read as follows: *Anna wants meeting of Chapter Seventeen to convene on one eight four, under Michael's supervision.*

The words would mean nothing to the average person in the street, or some lonely heart looking for love.

To those who were involved in The Chapter it was a clear reference to a meeting. An urgent one it seemed. Now all we had to do was break the code. We were sure that this wasn't a job for Bletchley Park, nonetheless it would only make sense to those who knew what those numbers meant so it was still a code that needed breaking.

It was already early March and so it was necessary to hurry along and find out what the number referred to. If it was a date, then it could be any day soon and we would be too late. The term 'under Michael's supervision', was also going to take some cracking.

We started by way of reason with Frank attempting to make sense of the numbers, while I tried to understand the phraseology.

Time went on, a week passed, then another. Sometime around the end of March, Frank was confident that the numbers alluded to a date. He had started with some very elaborate codes, but in the end, he choose to go with a simple, time, day, month formula. It worked, well at least we thought it worked, but we had to assume the use of a twenty-four-hour clock.

The number one gave us one o'clock in the morning, the eight stood for the eighth day of the month and the four gave us the fourth month, which was April.

'Simple but effective,' he said, "providing they use a twenty four hour clock.'

It was now two weeks until the eighth of April. All we had to do was find out where this meeting was being held, then we could observe from a safe distance.

A week passed and I had gone through many a reference book looking up the name Michael. There were of course many, from artists to politicians, from doctors to statesmen and so on. None of which was helping to solve the riddle for us.

Perhaps, we considered it might be the name of one of the secretive Chapters, founding members?

Funny how somethings won't stop nagging at the back of your mind. I pulled out the badge again and looked at words in Latin embroidered on the bottom under the stars. 'Heaven Protects the Innocent.'

Then I looked at the note again, part of which boldly stated, *Protected by the Sanctity of the Church.*

Was it as basic as that? Was it a reference to a church. What about Michael, better still what about St Michael, Archangel, and leader of the heavenly host. Now we had simply to tie it to a church.

Cornwood Church was dedicated to St Michael and All Angels but it was in a village setting and therefore too close to public scrutiny surely? Living in the village as we both did, we knew that any type of secret meeting in the church,

28

wouldn't be secret for long. There were to many houses close by.

I was sure now that I knew where the meeting would be held. The general area fitted Anna's last known whereabouts.

We discussed it at some length and decided that my new guess was in all probability correct and that was the Church of St Michael and All Angels at Princetown which fitted the bill nicely as it was set back from the road with a no houses within seventy yards or so of the main building. It also benefitted from direct access to the south, from the moor. People could go unseen, especially those well versed in clandestine activities.

Had we actually cracked the code? Smug smiles from the two of us suggested that we had but still after all these years we had no idea of what secret was being protected.

Was another long period of fruitless searching about to commence?

There was something else to consider. What would we do with the proof that Chapter existed? Would our knowledge of its existence, really endanger lives, eve own lives?

If we were caught, we imagined the situation could turn nasty, it was a sobering thought. We would proceed with caution.

The eighth of April came slowly and with malice aforethought as both our cars broke down, mine slightly less critically than Franks. We spent a good part of the day getting mine going and by mid-afternoon it was roadworthy again.

Setting off at midnight with a flask of coffee and a small dram of whisky in a hip flask, we headed off into the night, much to the chagrin of our respective wives.

At the end of the road, we developed a flat tyre. The tyre was changed after ten long minutes, and we left the village at fifteen minutes past midnight.

The drive across the moors was uneventful until a Black Galloway's horn took out one of my headlights. The bullock was apparently unharmed having taken a glancing blow to the head as it stepped out from behind a boulder onto the road in front of us.

29

At ten minutes to one o'clock we pulled out onto the road from the church and waited.

We were careful to be quiet as Dartmoor Prison was at the end of the village and the prison was the reason the village was built so many prison officers lived close by, and we didn't want to have to explain ourselves, even though we were doing nothing criminal.

We waited until one twenty am and then made our way up the side of the church, being careful to walk on the grass and not the gravel.

Half an hour passed. It was going on for two o'clock and not a soul was in sight. Had the meeting been cancelled, or had we got the code wrong and thereby the date?

Undoubtedly you will have shared a moment with a friend, when your two tired washed out brain cells are in perfect unison with their two tired washed out brain cells.

'Bugger, it's the wrong church.' We both said at the same time, now realising our mistake, well, my mistake. There was one more Church on the west side of the moors. It too was called St Michael, but St Michael de Rupe. Meaning, of the rock. Very apt, as it is situated at one thousand, one hundred feet above sea level about four miles north of Tavistock at Brentor.

If the secret society, The Chapter was going to meet anywhere, that would be the perfect place.

It was a very beautiful little church, believed to be the smallest and highest working church in England. Even more notable to us, was that it is in an area, that at that time was very quiet and off the beaten track. It was also a long steep hill climb to get up to the church. It would take us about forty minutes to get there.

The drive was steady as we only had one headlight. It was ten past two when we passed through Tavistock and got stopped by a policeman. He let us go with a warning but that delayed us by fifteen minutes.

The last four miles from Tavistock to Brentor seemed to take an age but as we arrived, we saw several cars passing us in the opposite direction. Frank counted seven. Four more were taking the road on to the North.

Now what were we do, go up to the church to look for evidence or pick a car to follow? We decided on the former.

It took us a good ten minutes walk in the dark, from the car park to the church itself. There was no proper path and when we got to the door it was locked. No lights were on and we were totally alone on the Tor except for a startled fox which emerged from the scree of boulders and disappeared just as quickly.

The walk back down the Tor was a silent affair, with both of us very angry with ourselves for committing such an obvious error of judgement missing a vital opportunity at the same time.

Once more however, those three beautiful ladies, The Fates were on our side. As I turned the car around in the car park, I noticed something on the ground. It fluttered a little in the lightest of breezes. I went to investigate while my companion had a nip of whisky from his hip flask.

I picked up a piece of something, which in the one remaining headlight, turned out to be a torn piece of card with a roughly drawn map on it. The fragment that remained was very interesting. It seemed to be part of a map of Dartmoor in miniature, but with most of the southwest missing. All I could see was central and North Dartmoor. There were some points marked with the name of thirteen Tors and someone had written the words, 'new refuge required.'

To say we went wild was an understatement. It was the biggest break we had ever had and was proof positive that there was, indeed, some kind of secret society on the moor's. For what reason we didn't know as yet, but fourteen years had elapsed since I had found the note and the badge.

Now it was as if the time spent on my quest had not been in vain. It was a vindication of what we had been through and more still was a compass which showed we were still heading in the right direction and so it was very personal to us.

More than ever now we wanted answers but were also aware that lives might genuinely be lost, if we choose to take the wrong path, or open our enquiries to too wide an audience. We headed home but kept our findings a closely guarded secret.

The next stage of our investigation was to try to match the piece of the map to an Ordinance Survey map of Dartmoor, that would be our starting point but, we knew that our task would be made easier if only we could find out what the secret was and why it required a refuge. It had therefore to be an object of some kind. What sort we did not know but it was obviously of great value, if not in hard cash, then in some spiritual sense perhaps. That would be a better fit as to why the church might be involved.

We had discussed Anna of course over the course of the years and I wished Frank had met her as his opinion of her would provide a valuable counterpoint to mine. At least the whole 'Personal-Ads' episode had panned out and it proved that this mysterious woman existed. She wasn't a figment of my imagination.

If only I had picked the right church. I may have got to see her again. My wish was to come true but not for a sometime yet.

Chapter 4

Thirteen tors

Now we began to try to build on the piece of map we had found, hand drawn as it was, it still gave us some points of reference.

We laid the ordinance survey map out in Frank's garage on his workbench and began the process of marking out the Tors marked on the portion we had recovered from Brentor church car park.

Beginning with the northern most Sharps Tor at twelve hundred and forty above sea level, which was in northeast Dartmoor.

Close by was Hunters Tor at one thousand and seventy feet in height to the southwest.

Third on the list and slightly further to the southwest was Meldon Tor at a height of one thousand two hundred and seventy fee, which in turn led to Birch Tor at sixteen hundred and four feet and which again was further to the southwest.

Riddon Ridge Tor at twelve hundred and forty seven feet was fifth on the list and a few miles southwest of the previous Tor.

Number six on the map Laughter Tor was one thousand three hundred and seventy eight feet above sea level and, very slightly to the southwest.

Now at last came a change in the bearings on the map and the Tors named changed direction heading northwest.

Seventh was Beardown Tor standing one thousand six hundred and eighty three feet high.

Eighth on the list was Flat Tor at one thousand seven hundred and seventy two feet, to the north-northwest.

Next was Little Kneeset standing one thousand six hundred and sixty three feet in height, then came Great

Kneeset with a height of one thousand eight hundred and sixty three feet.

Tor number eleven was further north northwest again and is the highest Tor on the moor, it's High Willhays and is two thousand and thirty nine feet high.

Moving west-northwest where the list named Sourton Tor as next in line and standing at one thousand four hundred and fourteen feet. The Thirteenth named was Great Links Tor, at a height of nineteen hundred and thirty nine feet and took a heading almost due south from Sourton Tor.

I have included the detail of the height of each Tor as that information will become relevant later in the book.

Irritatingly, we now of course needed the missing piece that had been torn away from the map. It was very frustrating. What the link was between these Tors, we had no idea. We did know one thing that might provide an answer, it was a link but a very tenuous one. They all had prehistoric settlements close by or on them.

Soon we came to the conclusion that it would be hard to fire a gun anywhere on the moor without hitting some prehistoric monolith, stone row, broken kistvaen, barrow or compound wall so for now we gave up that line of enquiry.

There had to be a reason both for the map and a reason for the Tors to be named on it.

Another point in question was had the map been deliberately discarded in order to put would be investigators off the trail of the Chapter?. Was it red herring designed to delay or confuse?

We had to consider that this was a distinct possibility. It seemed that we were destined to chase our tails again. It was becoming difficult to keep any momentum going. What to do next. We could return to the Latin phrases of course but we felt that as we understood what they said, we had no context in which to put them. Again, a dead end loomed before us.

Was the number of Tors relevant in anyway?. Did the missing piece have more names on it. Could there be one, or five, or ten? We were guessing but guesswork was not fact. The ordinance survey map was very helpful as it showed

Dartmoor in two halves north and south but we needed another OS map on a much larger scale.

Purchasing a new map later that week we put it up in Frank's garage and marked the Tors up on it. Now we had a broader view and it helped yet without the missing southwest corner we were still as much in the dark as before so we tried another line of attack.

What of the heights of the tors, did that have any relevance? The only thing that we could see was that they all stood at an altitude of over eleven hundred feet, going up to over two thousand feet. Was that in itself significant?

Again, another question and one without a suitable answer.

We knew two things for sure. Either we needed to find the missing piece of the map, or we needed to find out what the secret was.

Revisiting our reference books but without stumbling on some key piece of evidence to help us on our way, we would be stuck in this limbo. The year was almost over, and Frank and I had both been busy at work and with our respective families, when out of the blue, I had a most unexpected encounter.

I was on the moor at Wigford Down with my German Shepherd dogs. it was mid-November and being around livestock I kept them on leads. It was one of the most unusual times I had ever spent on Dartmoor as it was foggy, but the fog was in columns or pockets then there would be a clear space and then a dense pocket of fog, then another clear space and so on and so forth.

At some point on the hill both dogs began to growl. I thought it odd as they were used to, sheep, cattle or horses and the smells and sounds associated with those animals. It was more likely to be a rambler, but so many years of walking this area had taught me that I was unlikely to meet anyone at this time of year and in this weather.

By now the dogs were really growling and as I walked out of a column of fog, someone was standing with their back to me, and not more than five yards away.

The dogs fell silent as the person ahead turned, it was Anna and although it was over a decade since our last meeting, she looked the same as she had at our first. Anna still had the same silver hair, her eyes were the same green and violet flecked with gold, but the gold seemed more vibrant. I meanwhile had grown a beard and was now in my early thirties.

I remember that she was wearing what might have been described as a uniform of some sort, a red top with black trousers, but sensibly she had on a coat which was unbuttoned even in the chill November air. She had on footwear which seemed to meld into the trousers. I was sure this was not a chance meeting. She wasn't dressed for a moor walk and in truth, she didn't strike me as the kind of woman who liked the outdoor life that much.

How had she found me and more importantly, why?

It was now that I noticed how quiet the dogs were. They stood patiently and with no sign of aggression towards her.

Glancing at my watch I made a mental note that it was two thirty. I tried hard to take in as much of my surroundings as I could including sight, sounds and smells in case they provided any clues as to who this woman was.

Anna was as inscrutable as she was the first time we met. She thanked me for not avidly pursuing the Chapter and thereby ensuring that lives were not lost. She was however aware that I had a colleague now and that we had found a piece of a map.

'What had we done with it?' She had enquired.

I told her truthfully and she was grateful that we had had not made the information public. I told her that was not our intention but added that if she allowed us to learn more from her, 'perhaps we could assist her or the 'Chapter' in some way'.

'That wouldn't be necessary.' Everything that Chapter did was on a need to know basis.

She made it abundantly clear that her role was damage limitation. That what I, or we, had found so far was within her purview to control. She pressed me once again to ask that Frank and I stop our investigations.

36

I replied that if she wouldn't or couldn't share anymore details that we would continue but I promised that we would never do anything to compromise whatever secret she and Chapter were hiding.

'Protecting' She stated firmly.

Although she did go on to admit that in order to 'Protect', certain information and people involved, it was necessary to hide both from the public gaze.

What she was prepared to share, perhaps as a way on sating my need to understand my grandfather's involvement, was to tell me that the Chapter was small in number, there were only seventeen in the whole organisation which had relied on true and trusted friends over the years to support them.

'How many years.' I had asked in hope rather than expectation. 'Forty, fifty?'

'More, far more.'

'A century, two?' I had continued.

Anna shook her head. 'Millenia, no.' She took a moment, 'Eons'.

'Surely, she was exaggerating?' but it seemed not. I was staggered to say the least. Her face remained completely impassive.

I asked again how my grandfather came to be involved.

'He was not a member.' She confided but he was a great help and especially during the years of the second world was.' She went on to say that 'he was a gentleman, I all respects.'

I asked 'how she knew that? Who had she spoken to?

She ventured to say that she had known him personally. I countered that she must have been very young at the time, as when we had first met, Anna had seemed about the same age as me.

That question was irrelevant. 'I didn't matter,' she said.

'How had she found me? I asked her in the hope of at least getting to spend more time with this enigmatic woman.

'Maybe', she said, she would explain the next time we met.

She took a couple of steps back from me and was gone. I shook myself and tried to remain calm and to continue to note sounds and conditions around me. We had spent ten or fifteen minutes together, yet my watch told a different story. The hands passed to two o'clock. The same time as I noted our conversation had started.

Fortunately when I returned to Cornwood, Frank believed me when I told him of my encounter with Anna. That made things a little easier. At least he didn't think I was hallucinating.

We also now knew one more valuable piece of information, and that was the actual number of the members of Chapter. Seventeen in total. That number also matched the number of stars on the badge and in the constellation of Draco. It was another step closer to the truth.

It had been a good day and we had come to another conclusion with regards to the map. What if, we thought, what if it was a match to the badge and the constellation? It was certainly worth a look.

We took a piece of bailer twine (well we were in Devon), and wound it around the first Tor named, Sharps Tor, then tied it to Hunters Tor, followed by Meldon Tor. This began to look promising. Then on we stretched the twine to Birch Tor, thence to Riddon Ridge, (not classified as a Tor but it was named and was certainly high ground at almost twelve hundred and fifty feet in height.

We pulled the twine to the west southwest again and Laughter Tor. West-southwest to Flat Tor. We kept the twine taught and headed northwest to Beardown Tor, then North again to Kneeset Tor and from there a short hop to Little Kneeset. North-northwest to High Willhays, Devon's highest Tor. Then crossed west and slightly south to Sourton Tor. Last on the list was Great Links.

It took a few minutes but it was obvious once the twine was drawn around the thirteen tors, that this was the pattern formed by the body and tail of Draco the dragon or great serpent. All that was missing was the head. Four stars that we would now try to match to the tors on the Ordinance Survey map.

It was one of those real 'eureka' moments. That was it. All we had to do was to follow the line of stars and try to match in the last four stars with the Ordinance Survey.

Now we also had to take a more in depth look at 'Draco' itself. As a constellation, it is the eighth largest of eighty eight recognised. It contains nineteen stars, but only in seventeen of those stars were named historically.

The other two may not have been visible to the naked eye in the past, that is before the invention of the telescope. It would now be a matter of working to an unknown scale. We would chance it though, as the placement of the other Tors, gave us an idea of the distance between the four we considered missing.

We began by measuring the distance between star number thirteen the last on our list and number twelve and this gave us an approximate distance scaled down to match the ordinance survey map between those two Great Links and Sourton Tors.

Put in context against library photographs of Draco, we were able to make our next calculation.

The distance between thirteen and twelve was approximately a quarter of the distance between twelve and what the position of fourteen was. We agreed a scale and applied it to the map to find it took us south-southeast of number thirteen.

It brought us slap bang onto North Hessary Tor, which had been the sight of a BBC FM radio and television transmitter erected in nineteen fifty five for the southwest region. The mast itself being six hundred and forty three feet in height atop the tor, which stands at sixteen hundred and ninety six feet. An interesting discovery and one which was to prove more than coincidental to this story.

Star number fifteen on the map was further southeast again. We were once more thrilled to find we had landed on Crockern Tor the site of an ancient stannary parliament. It stands one thousand three hundred feet above sea level. The next star in the constellation was only one half a degree west of due south. This presented a problem, as when star number sixteen was applied to the ordinance survey map, it didn't match up with a Tor.

In truth we had found a similar problem with Riddon Ridge as it is not described as a tor, but it certainly has large boulders and scree strewn across it and was certainly high enough. At some time in the distant past, it may have fitted the more modern classification of a tor. The nearest to our reference point was one half a degree east rather than west of the imaginary line but it was well apportioned in height and general alignment.

It was Fox Tor, at fourteen hundred and thirty seven feet and bordered to the north by Fox Tor mire, a peat bog and inspiration for Sir Arthur Conan Doyle's, Grimpen Mire in 'The Hound of the Baskervilles.' We would stick with it for now, unless we found a better candidate, which was unlikely.

Number seventeen was easy. Sharpitor sitting to the northwest of Burrator reservoir at thirteen hundred feet above sea level. The more we looked at the bailer twine wound around the pins in the map, the more we were convinced that we were on the right path. It matched neatly to 'Draco' and therefore to the badge.

Now it was time to revisit the first line of the Latin phrases left by my grandad.

'Draco's breath holds the key.' It had stated.

That was all well and good, but without knowing what the 'key' was, or what secret was being protected, we were just a little closer to solving the puzzle but yet still miles away.

What of the second line, *The Universe in a nutshell protected by the sanctity of the Church*? What did that mean to the Chapter?

We knew it to be part of a line from Hamlet. In it he says, *Oh God, I could be bounded in a nutshell and count myself a king of infinite space'.* by which he means, even were he to be contained in a tiny space, the size of a nutshell, he could think he has everything he wants. He is to all intents and purposes denying his ambition. That was how we had been considering the phrase. What if we were on the wrong track?

Frank and I had been looking at that as if it the person reading it was supposed to consider the whole sentence from Hamlet. What if we were to simply consider the first words of that sentence as it was written, 'The Universe in a Nutshell' Does that mean the universe is shaped like a nutshell. If so what type of nut, and why would that information be so critical.

There must be many theories on the shape and size of the universe. So, what would make this of particular interest to a secret society such as Chapter?

It was fascinating work, trying to figure out a logical solution to the puzzle we were faced with. Even if a person knew the exact borders of the universe, it is so vast that we would never reach the ends, or sides for billions of years, and that supposes that one day someone learns how we humans could travel at the speed of light.

The last phrase, 'Beneath the hill, the cave.' Might be a better starting point. All over Devon there were hills with caves in and around them. Many were not strictly caves but overhanging rock's or

sheltered gullies occasionally enlarged by men as protection from the weather, or as temporary hiding places.

Strictly speaking a cave is described as a natural underground chamber. We ploughed through our reference books where there are many chambers or overhangs that maybe described as such but incorrectly so.

We felt that we had hit yet another obstacle so we started at the beginning again and altered our approach to the first line, 'Draco's breath holds the key'.

Our original thought was that it might be a reference to another star or heavenly body in alignment, with Draco. Could it be that we needed to look closer to the earth.

The words clearly stated 'Draco, (Dragon's) breath. After a pause it was decided to look again at the map.

Stars numbered from fourteen to seventeen formed the head of the dragon. So logically its breath might extend a few miles from the mouth. It would now be a case of checking the ordinance survey to look for clues. We would not be short of a few. There were the desolate vestiges of stone quarries from the nineteenth century.

Tin mines and Tinners huts and blowing houses erected in over the from the seventeenth and eighteenth centuries.

Going back thousands of years earlier were the remains of old enclosures for livestock built during the bronze age.

Even earlier evidence of neolithic occupation, stone rows, cairns, kistvaens and the like, any of which may or may not have been used to conceal the secret we were now hunting.

Anna had alluded to 'Eons,' when describing the help that had been offered to 'Chapter.'

As yet we had not yet touched on the relevance of the stone circles and menhirs (if there was any relevance). Still, we had no idea what the secret was, and why it was so important to consider as fact, the word of a woman I hardly knew. A mysterious woman for all that and one that posed as much of an enigma as the secret itself.

Continuing with our investigation, roughly two weeks after my unexpected meeting with Anna, her words, Look to the skies' bore fruit. We had a call from a local UFO enthusiast who said that though the weather had been, as usual unpleasant for November, there had been a break in it a couple of nights ago. We were to cast an eye on the local papers. He would say no more.

Cast an eye we did and on page seven of one of the papers was about three column inches entitled. *UFOs over Burrator Reservoir.*The piece was brief but stated eyewitness accounts had been received telling of strange lights over the reservoir and surrounding moorland. One eyewitness going so far as to say that a craft the size of a football pitch had hovered over the village of Sheepstor and the Tor itself, which lay a quarter mile to the northeast.

We were enthused as once more Anna's prophetic insight had come true. She had been proved correct for a second time. We must follow this lead.

Now things began to slot into place. Sheepstor was well placed in the area we referred to as the 'Dragon's Breath'. It encompassed the distance between Sharpitor and Fox Tor running east to west. From Fox tor to Stall Moor Hill running north to South, and thence Stall Moor Hill above Cornwood to the Wigford Down Cairn Circle above, Cadover Bridge and back up to Sharpitor. Encompassing various farms small villages and hamlets and a good deal of fields and rough moorland.

We held onto our newfound belief that this time we might be firmly on the right path and with some help from our ladies, The Fates, we would find what we had sought for so long.

There were a couple more indicators from a historical point of view which also helped to confirm our belief that Sheepstor was going to prove relevant to our quest.

The first was well documented and it was the well-known, 'Pixies Cave' below the crest of the tor on the southern slope which led down to the village. It's quite small but large enough to fit a man or woman inside. Perhaps two smaller people at a push.

The second and most interesting was that Sheepstor had various names over the years and had that been done down the centuries to disguise its real name. The name gave us pause for thought and a reason the feel very pleased with ourselves. It had taken some digging into but find it we did. It had been known all those centuries ago, back in the late twelfth and early thirteenth century as 'Skytelestor.' I could find no meaning for the word, but interestingly if you just break it down, this is what you find. Sky (the sky), Tele (at a distance), Tor (tor). Not earth shattering but in keeping with our current path of enquiry and we felt, oddly coincidental?

If you write it as Sky at a distance tor it begins to bring in that celestial connotation with Draco. When added to what we were to find out later, it was bound to cause ripples, which might one day be felt around the world.

Chapter 5

The black vault of heaven

The stars have always been a draw to mankind over millennia and so we wondered if anymore Tors had names with celestial ties to them. So we checked then double checked, and then did one more sweep through our books. Nothing. The only Tor referenced with a name change to it was Sheepstor. It had been called a few other names as well, but why this Tor and this one only?

We knew that it had been named Sitelestorra, Scheitelestor, Sytelestorra, Shippistor, and so on and so forth. Why had it been known under so many different names, was to obscure it in some way? Sixteen previous names plus its current name made seventeen, and there it was again, the number seventeen had presented itself before us once more.

Was there something in the number worthy of our attention? We knew that it was the seventh prime number, that is a number only divisible by one and itself and the only one made up of four consecutive prime numbers. Also, the total of those, two, three, five and seven is seventeen. The seventeenth card in the major arcana of the Tarot Cards is 'The Star'.

More coincidentally, in Arabic, it links to the term 'Night Journey.' It is also sacred in Hebrew, meaning 'complete victory', another interesting fact is that it was on the seventeenth day of the second month that Noah's flood began, and on the seventeenth day of the seventh month when the Ark came to rest.

The link to the Ark also was to prove indicative of yet another clue.

We really felt that the number itself was pointing us in the direction of an association with whatever the secret was that 'Chapter' was hiding. There are other links to the number seventeen, but we found many of these to be spurious, so would a further look at the constellation Draco help us in anyway.

In myth we encountered a problem as there are various stories associated with Draco. In earlier times he was one of the titans who had attempted to evict the Olympian Gods. For his rebellion, he was flung into the heavens by Athena and remained there to this day.

In another myth he was slain by Heracles during his eleventh labour to secure the Golden Apples of the Hesperides and placed in heaven.

Yet another story references was the Dragon who guarded the Golden Fleece, made most famous in the story of Jason and The Argonauts. Jason poisoned Ladon with Medea's help and stole the golden fleece.

As with many Greek myths, wonderful as they are, there are slightly differing versions involving heroes and monsters. It was proving difficult to pick one solid storyline to follow.

The end result would be the same though, the constellation was certainly named after a dragon, or serpent. What if we changed tack a little and used a serpent instead of a dragon. Serpents and dragons have often been the subject of mild confusion over the years, as have Wyrms, another type of great snake, or serpent (a sub-order of snake), or dragons.

Wyrms have been present for centuries in the Norse Saga's, Old Germanic Tales, Celtic Stories and English narratives.

The White Wyrm was carried on King Harold's standard at Stamford Bridge and Hastings and was the symbol originally of the West Saxons and later of Anglo Saxon England. It survives to this day, but now in the form of the 'Wyvern' on the flag of Wessex.

We knew also of the myth of Ouroboros, the great serpent who surrounded the universe and is depicted eating his own tail. It was an ancient symbol for the circle of life. Of birth and rebirth and was a well-known character in Egyptian Iconography, representing fertility and continuity of life.

That was all very well and good, but it had no influence on our investigation at the moment. Once again, more clues led to more questions and very few answers.

What we needed most was the secret kept from us and the world at large.

On most nights, when the Dartmoor weather allowed, I would stand in the garden and look to the north, and to the constellation that had taken over my life to such a degree. The nights with no moon were always the best. As a constellation, Draco is not the brightest in the heavens. It was always those times that troubled me most. What were the two of us missing?

1991 one rolled into 1992 and suddenly and seemingly without warning. Another five years passed, and it was 1997. We had not slackened at all in our investigative efforts, but no other clues had been forthcoming.

We watched the skies, but as more and more light pollution poured out of Plymouth and its satellite towns, the darkness became less intense. It had been twenty years since I had found the note and badge left, presumably by my grandfather, in one of his books.

The dog days of summer were passing. Named for the dog star Sirius, otherwise known in Latin as Canis Major, (Big Dog), and in myth was one of Orion's hunting dogs. Always at its brightest in late summer, July and August. It was thought to be responsible for the intense heat of those months.

It's known long since of course that at over eight light years from earth that this is not possible. It was just yet another phrase used from myth and legend that we tend to use so carelessly these days, with little regard for their true meaning.

Visiting Sheepstor we had made our way to pixies cave which was as cramped and uninviting as any cave could be.

We struggled to see what could have been hidden there. It was unlikely that any secret meetings could have been held there. We searched around for other clues and that led us to a find of sorts. Having already gone into a little detail regarding the stone rows and circles which litter Dartmoor.

It was not our intention to go down that path but then as often happens a few days earlier I had come across an interesting passage on a marvellous book written about the moors. Which I felt was worth us checking on in person. It involved a stone row called the Nine Maidens at Belstone Tor several miles northeast of Sheepstor.

Strangely, the book had stated that it was originally called the seventeen brothers and there was that number again.

When we took a closer look on the ordinance survey map, Belstone Tor stone row leading away from the Seventeen Brothers is in direct southwest alignment with Sheepstor Stone Row and wouldn't you know it, they are seventeen miles apart.

Another interesting fact is that the St Michael's ley-line runs from Land's End in Cornwall to Hopton on Sea in Norfolk.

This line dedicated to the Archangel St Michael, slayer of Dragon's (Satan), runs right through St Michaels Mount Cornwall, St Michaels Church on Brentor (previously mentioned in Chapter Three), the Seventeen Brothers Stone Circle and then on through Cadbury Castle, Glastonbury (St Michaels) Church, Avebury Stone circle, Bury St Edmunds etcetera but by circumstance or design?

Why had it been renamed as the nine maidens and by whom, and for what reason?

Seventeen Brothers was a more realistic name as there are seventeen standing stones, one of which has fallen. It was as if in years past, someone or some group, cult, organization had decided to obscure the number.

It had to be said that there was something odd about the continuing reference to the number seventeen.

Frank had noticed another oddity with some of the stone rows on the moor. Although they were often classed as burial sites and of course many of them were. Some had astronomical links as well. It was now that he brought the Staldon row to my attention.

It is possibly the longest prehistoric stone row in the world, almost certainly the longest in Europe at three point four kilometres of two point one miles and is positioned just to the northeast of Cornwood.

The length and the number of stones vary slightly from source to source, some put the number to as many as nine hundred and twenty two. This row should not be confused with Stall Down Row, which is much shorter and has sixty two stones in it, of which seventeen are laid down.

Once more the number seventeen so now we looked at in more detail at the Staldon Stone Row.

Again, we were amazed. New information put the stones counted in the it as many as nine hundred and yes you guessed it seventeen.

It starts at a stone circle to the south known as 'The Dancers' and ends at a ruined Cairn on top of Green Hill. Where the northern and southern ends terminate cannot be seen, one from the other. Also, the peculiar way in which it snakes across the moor is strange as in most of the others, the termini at both ends are visible from each other and infuriatingly failed to aid our investigation.

Why we persisted, God alone knew. However, it was now a matter of dogged determination. Even if we never found the answer, we would continue trying.

We still had our jobs to go to and our own families to love and support as they grew, and grandchildren began to appear on the scene. It left us less time for our deliberations, but we stuck to our path at every spare moment.

We lost friends due to illness, death and just the normal parting of ways, but we also made new friends, one of who would prove invaluable in our quest for the truth. One who proved to be immensely sensible, loyal and entirely trustworthy. Another set of eyes and ears, with a clever mind and a good dose of common sense, but more of her in a moment.

Having heard nothing of 'Chapter' or Anna. No reports of mysterious goings on or suspicious activities on the moors, it was back to square one.

It was at a goodbye party for a work colleague at a small hotel in a quiet rural setting that I engaged in a conversation with a young British Indian woman several years my junior. The evening had been long, and we had started chatting over dinner.

She apparently was a lover of history and had an interest in myth and legend. It would be fair to say that we formed an instant liking for each other and now that the speeches were over, we were able to slip away to the bar to talk and talk we did.

At the dinner table we had talked of family, of work, her husband and daughters and my wife and sons when we were at the dinner table. The lady's name was Rekha Mitter.

Now the talk turned to theology in relation to myth, it was the beginning of a conversation which intrigued us both.

Another long period had passed since my last encounter with Anna and I began to feel a slight resentment toward her and 'Chapter'. She had asked us to keep our find to ourselves and for two decades now Frank and I had done just that. In that time we both believed that we had been treated either as fools at best or at worst the enemy.

It was with this frame of mind and a few whiskies under my belt that I told Rekha the full story of the last twenty years.

At first I felt that her attention was due to her simple good manners. That however was far from the case, and as I talked and she asked questions, I very soon understood that she was genuinely interested in our quest. Her mind was and remains to this day, razor sharp.

Rekha attacked the problem from a different angle. She was keen to start at the very beginning.

'Had we,' she enquired, 'taken into account a link to Grandads book out of which the note and badge had fallen?'

I said that we had not and then went on to say that it was a book of William Shakespeares plays.

'Did he leave you anything else?' She asked.

I told her about the volume of '*The Greek Myths*' by legendary historian and author Robert Graves.

'What of the Latin phrases, surely there was more too them?'

I told her everything Frank and I knew.

'My guess would be a link between some passage or myth in each of the books. A missing piece of the puzzle which maybe small but also significant. Whatever it is,' Rekha continued, 'maybe be nothing more than a tenuous fibre, but it will have meant something important to your grandad and possibly therefore to 'Chapter.'

Our conversation carried on until the small hours and I resolved there and then to ask her to join in the search. I would discuss the matter with Frank as soon as possible, although I knew in my heart that he would have no problem in my vouching for this incredible young woman, despite the limited time I had known her.

There are times in life, I believe, when God sends you someone you need at that exact moment and this I felt was one of those times and so it was to prove to be, over the next twenty years five years.

It was God, the Fates and serendipity that had brought the three of us together and now we would be mentally well armed to go forward as a team and resolve the puzzle that had plagued us for so long. Rekha was sworn to secrecy and welcomed to our quest.

Chapter 6.

An unbreakable oath

We started to examine the two books in more detail as Rekha had so ardently recommended. As yet she and Frank had not met, but they had spoken by telephone. Frank could see the merits in a new, much younger pair of eyes looking at the clues afresh.

Rekha had a full time job and two young daughters. As such she was unable to spend a great deal of time on research herself. That wasn't her main role in the team though. What she brought to the table was vitality and a sarcastic humour that matched our own.

Living out on the east coast well beyond the fringes of greater London, also meant that we could not just meet up at the pub for a chat. Every conversation or transfer of evidence was by phone or letter, or the abominable old email systems that were as much a curse at times as a blessing.

She was right, the examination of the two books was a new turning point. Instead of doing what we had done before, which was to try to find a direct link between the books, we looked in detail at the books themselves.

Grandad's book was a leather-bound volume of *The Complete Works of William Shakespeare*, first published in 1897. Included inside was a photograph of English stage legend Sir Henry Irving as Hamlet.

For some reason that picture told us that we would find answers here, in this book and it was the great actor himself who gave us the first clue.

We stuck with the number seventeen as probably being of some significance in this clue as well. Then we found this nugget, he was christened John Henry Brodribb. Seventeen letters, coincidence possibly so we used his stage name instead. Henry Irving that came to eleven, but the photo said, *Henry Irving, Hamlet*. A total of seventeen letters again.

Continuing in this small vein of gold, we looked at more of these old photographic plates. A second plate named '*Miranda, The Tempest* also totalled seventeen letters. The third *Caliban, The Tempest* was to total seventeen letters.

We were not suggesting that Shakespeare had been in collusion with 'Chapter', only that someone working on behalf of them, may have used this version of his works, of many hundreds that have been produced over the years because of the link with the number seventeen.It was a possibility we could not discount. Rekha thought we were still missing something.

We tried page numbers starting at seventeen and with multiples thereof, to see if that led anywhere. It did, but not in the way we thought.

It was agreed that we would ignore the text and look instead at the pages, as in the physical condition of each page. It was decided that I would undertake this task.

Armed with a magnifying glass, I began to scour the pages from page seventeen onwards and then with no discernible reasoning, I noted the very faintest of pencil marks underlining certain words, one by one, on every seventeenth page and they began to add up to a story. A remarkable progression of words marked by my grandfather from the bards, plays and sonnets.

Now we had a reason to understand why Chapter existed.

I could take you to every page and word, but it would take too long and would bore all but the most dedicated of investigative readers. But this is what I came found among the random words he had underlined,

I will fight their legions, to defend the secret of the Goddess Queen of Heaven, the creator of the two universes, which host twinkling stars, celestial suns and moons like silver bows to behold. Now the ancient maiden, so small but formed in perfect replication of her magnificent sister, must be protected in single blessedness, though shadow of war, death or sickness lay siege to her. Countless souls live in oblivion of their neighbour until heaven decree it on acquaintance.

Now will I search impossible places, with an invisible, subtle stealth.

When I find the universe in a nutshell concealed 'neath the dragon's breath, from the eyes of all mankind, and lying in its final earthly sanctuary, I shall offer it up freely to those star sailors who ply their trade in the myriad realms of heaven. They will escort this jewel of life unto a place of safety, where it may be honoured for all eternity. This has ever been Chapters unbreakable oath. There shall be no need of a requiem for a Goddess born of Chaos.

It was moment for reflection from all three of us. A time for congratulations most certainly but also a time to realise the possible truth behind those words.

The clues made sense at last. All tied into William Shakespeare's works and highlighted at random by my dear grandfather. Had anyone found that copy of the book we felt it very unlikely that they would have looked at it in the detail that we had. It was a secret as we are apt to say these days, hidden in plain sight.

Now we needed to look at the second book, that was *The Greek Myths* by Robert Graves. The clues pointed towards a creation myth and there were many in *The Greek Myth's*. Only one however, told a story of a Goddess born of Chaos. That was the *Pelasgian Creation Myth* and Robert Graves narrative told the story of Eurynome, who freed herself from Chaos to dance upon the waves.

The book informs us that she grabbed the north wind and rubbed it between her soft hands and in so doing created Ophion, a great Python.

Lust got the better of him and he mated with her. Eurynome then laid an egg which she commanded Ophion to hatch by coiling around it, thus warming it and bringing it to life. When it hatched, the Universe as we know it was created and order was achieved in every part.

This was the original Greek creation myth and predates the rule of Ouranos and Gaea. They of course were followed by Kronos and Rhea, after Kronos usurped his father and then the same thing happened to him, when he in turn was cast out by his son Zeus and wife Hera.

53

Now we were sure that the *Pelasgian Creation* was the one to follow. In case you had not noticed, that's seventeen letters.

A mere coincidence of course but nonetheless another small tie to that number and a reminder of its importance.

A few days passed. We had been looking into some of these 'Egg Creation Myths' of which there were many. Take for example, Taoist monks developed the Pangu Myth, where they say the universe began as an egg.

It is also a core belief in Brahmanda myth and called the 'Cosmic Egg' in Hinduism. It was myth as far north as Estonia and Finland referred to as Finno Ugric concept.

In Zoroastrian mythology, (fire eaters of the middle east), tradition has it that the God Ohrmazd gathered everything together and formed it into a great egg.

Slavic myth has 'Rod', the supreme being create a divine egg from the void. Whilst the ancient Egyptians saw the egg as a primeval soul, a body of water, which was the start of creation.

In the islands of the pacific, the Tahitians believed that the god 'Ta'aroa was born of an egg. The theory of the universal egg is now known as cosmogony and is usually of Proto-Indo-European culture.

Many people will know of the Dogon people of east Africa and their link to the stars. Particularly the constellation of Orion and the star Sirius. Their belief is also of world egg but with two yolk sacks, each with a pair of twins. The thought of two yolks gave us a good deal of pause for thought, but more of that later.

The Bantu creation myth has an egg theory as does the creation theory in Japanese myth. An enormous span of cultures involves this original idea.

Closer to home Celtic creed aligns with these beliefs. Again, the laying of an egg.

The 'Cosmic Egg' was an idea shared around the world for thousands of years. Other than the Dogon myth involving two egg sacks even in Robert Graves short account of the Pelasgian Creation, there is no mention of two universes. Why then was it even mentioned in the underlined words culled from Shakespeare's work which quite clearly stated 'creator of the two universes' in that passage?.

So, what of the second universe, is that what we were missing or in fact is that what 'was' missing?

We started stripping the clues apart. The first line, '*I will fight their legions to defend the secret of the Goddess Queen of Heaven and creator of the two universes*'.

We had thought that the person or persons writing this was writing on behalf of 'Chapter'. That we felt was a given fact. The Goddess could in all probability be Euronomy. Now for the problem of the two universes.

If one was the universe in which we lived, what or where was the second? Was 'Chapter' talking of a universe on another plane or of other's beyond the one we could see?

'*Which host twinkling stars and celestial suns and moons like silver bows to behold*'. Straight forward we thought. Another universe containing all the things the ancients could see in ours.

Many thought that the stars were caused by tears in the fabric of the universe which then allowed the light of heaven to shine through as pinpoints. They didn't know that the stars were like ours each in their own right, each blazing away at distances far beyond mankind's imagination.

The next line was more complex. '*The ancient maiden, so small but formed in perfect replication of her magnificent sister*'. This brought us back to a dual universe theory. Another universe exactly the same as the one we live in but in miniature. That was going to be a leap of faith and a leap of the laws of physics.

'*Must be protected in single blessedness.*' This also might point to something beyond the norm. '*Though shadow of war, death, or sickness lay siege to her.*' That was self-evident, touching on the need to protect it in all events against mankind or nature.

'*Countless souls live in oblivion of their neighbour until heaven decree it upon acquaintance*'. This we took to mean that each person lived unaware of their neighbouring universe and would continue to do so, until God or science choose to reveal the one to the other.

55

It continued *'Now will I search impossible places with an invisible and subtle stealth.'* This pointed in a different direction. It led us to think that perhaps The Chapter and as a matter of fact its predecessor, for there surely was one, were looking for the lost artefact.

We had considered for over twenty years that they were in possession

of the said artefact, when in fact they might rather have been searching

for it instead. If that was the case, why had Anna not said so before. We might have been of help rather than a hindrance or perceived threat. It was an indication of how strongly Anna and her colleagues believed in that secret they held so dear and yet she hinted at things and told us to 'watch the skies.'

Frank inferred that 'the young lady was 'hedging her bets.' Keeping us interested and on side whilst hoping we might turn up a clue or indeed find the secret itself and thereby lead her and her associates right to it.

The next line said, *'When I find the universe in a nutshell concealed beneath the dragon's breath'.* Once again a reference as to how small the artefact was, and I noticed coincidently *'nutshell concealed'* was seventeen letters.

We were certain that the constellation Draco, was the dragon now in question. *'From the eyes of all mankind and lying in its final earthly sanctuary'* infers that they know it will be well hidden, but did 'earth' mean on earth, or in the earth? We wouldn't find that out for some time yet.

'I shall offer it up to those star sailors who ply their trade in the myriad realms of heaven'. I felt very deeply that this was where Anna came in. I was sure that she or others like her were and had been the star sailors who were to be entrusted with the artefact. Why she or they would be given it for safe keeping I didn't know.

My colleagues did not disagree with me but still wished that one day they would one day get to meet her in the flesh and render their own judgement of her.

We were near the end of the passage now, it went on to say, *'They will escort this jewel of life unto a place of safety, where it may be honoured for all eternity'.* This surely was a reference to the idea that the artefact was alive. How or why we did not yet understand, however, it seemed that transport to another realm was its only hope for survival from the legions who would wish to see its destruction and there it would be safe for ever as the term honoured would infer.

'This has been Chapters unbreakable oath'. Again, self-evident we felt, without too much difficulty.

Finally, *'There shall be no need of a requiem for a goddess'.* Now this was a statement. A sign that victory was expected, and it gave us all a deep sense of confidence, that with our help, victory might after all these centuries be achieved.

Was it really a physical miniature of the universe we were trying to find? Would the laws of physics even begin to allow for such an idea? We decided to continue our investigation with a look at the work of one of finest minds in the field of physics. The brilliant men and women whose theories would allow us to pursue this idea.

Chapter 7
Sands of time.

Now we would be able to look at the theory behind the Universe and more importantly the possibility of other universes which might exist on different planes or even on the same plane but in miniature.

The thought that we might be able to find some link to such a place was a reward in itself and would stimulate our minds into the twenty first century as the new millennium was suddenly upon us.

We were all still gainfully employed in full time roles and of course our close family commitments kept us busy. Some of our children were married and had kids of their own. Rekha had her third child in this time frame and in a whirlwind of, job, family and research it was now the year 2001.

Each of us had other outside interests as well, and these varied for each of us. My first novel 'Arcadia' had been published and I was busy promoting it as well as running my department at work, but at last Frank and Rekha were able to meet.

We finally managed a few hours together when Rekha was free to get away for a day and we met at a hotel in Salisbury, Wiltshire.

Rekha had mentioned the Hindu myth of the world egg as the beginning of creation in Hinduism. It was another fascinating and tantalising insight into this belief.

Now we needed to concentrate our research on the universal egg theory. Would we be able to find more information that would lead us to some conclusive evidence.

Frank thought he may have spotted at least the basis for a clue. In many works by eminent astrophysicists, there have been mentions of other planes in which other universes may exist. Was it such a stretch from that conclusion to wonder if they could exist in vastly varying sizes on or in different times or stratum of matter?

We thought twenty four years since my find in grandfather's book we now required a gigantic leap of faith in order to make any kind of progress. We would just explore the universe in miniature theory from now until all possible leads, clues or avenues of research ran into a cul-de-sac. We said our goodbyes and for the next six months we had our minds set to find out more.

Computers were of more use now, although connections in Devon were painfully slow. It took twenty minutes to get my PC online and I think it was outdated the day I bought it. We could email, which was marginally faster than posting a letter. By the end of November, we were beginning to put together a framework within which we could work and cross reference things.

December brought a spate of UFO sightings across the UK. We wondered how many had been drink related as Christmas fell, as usual, instigating a vast consumption of alcohol. Then new year came and went with alarming speed.

2002 saw some sad passings in all our families. My mother died that year but even so the world continued to revolve and time went on, inexorably. Then out of the blue I received a phone call. It was a familiar voice but one I never expected to hear from again. Anna.

Would I meet her on the moors. Somewhere secluded and away from prying eyes. I asked if Frank was invited, 'No,' she said.

I asked why. Anna replied that although she understood that he was already helping me, the less people who met her in person, the less danger there was of her mission, or of Chapter being compromised. It seemed impolite and indeed offensive not to involve him and I told her so. Her reply was unexpected.

'I believe you have already brought someone else into your team.'

It was a statement not a question.

My gander was up. 'I had because we were getting nowhere.'

59

'You choose well' Anna said. 'Chapter is not displeased.' She went on to say that I was at liberty to tell my colleagues about our meeting but not the time or the place. Given little choice I agreed.

She set the place for our meeting out on the moors for late evening, it was set for the twenty first of June, Rekha's birthday as it happened.

The time ten pm. Less risk of people being out on the moors and as it was a Friday, most people would be relaxing after work and probably getting an early night before the weekend started in earnest.

The place she had chosen to meet was an area I knew well. Not far from where I had been born at Cadover Bridge and only a couple of miles from my cousin's farm. It was a safe choice I thought, given the fact our first meeting was the Warren House Inn deep in the moors, twenty odd years ago.

Our second and totally unscheduled meeting had of course been Wigford Down just a few years ago. On this occasion however we would meet at an area overlooking Burrator Reservoir. One and a half miles southeast of it to be precise.

I advised my colleagues and we decided that it was best to go ahead with the meeting. Maybe I would be able to find out more specific information that would help us. We all agreed that anything which might aid our enquiries would be a positive.

Still it was odd that she was prepared to meet as she had not really been forthcoming with any ideas or help.

The first time we met, our conversation was very one sided, with Anna telling me how damaging my probe into Chapter could be. It was small on detail and vague in general.

Our second meeting was better. She had shared a little more knowledge and had told me that her role with Chapter was one of damage limitation, going on to say that all concerned were grateful that Frank and I had not openly pursued our leads. That is to say, up until that time we had kept our findings to ourselves.

She had revealed that Chapter or some version of it had been protecting a secret over not just centuries or millennia, but for eons. 'Watch the skies', she had said as she had at our first meeting.

It was as if she wanted to tell me something, or at least to enlist our help if she was no longer able to control this situation, whatever it might be.

We felt that she was nudging us ever further towards the truth in case we could one day be of help, as presumably my grandad had been many years before.

It was still frustrating. Rekha was very intrigued to understand how Anna could judge her capabilities when they had never even met. Frank

was consummately cool and spoke from twenty years of experience.

'I believe dear Lady', he had said, 'that Chapter have tentacles in a lot of places, some of which we could not even dream of. It's possible that people are working for or on their behalf without knowing they are doing so.'

'You mean they have infiltrated areas of government and commerce in this country?,' Rekha enquired.

Frank continued, 'Andy and I thought it was merely a local society, small in number but not without its resources.'

'And now?,' Rekha had asked.

'Now,' I told her, 'we believe that they are a worldwide organization with a vested interest in protecting some artefact as yet unknown to us.'

Rekha agreed with our point of view.

Now had to decide what we thought the artefact was. We had an idea of course, but that idea was unbelievable to any logically based mind. Did it have religious significance? Was it at all valuable in a purely monetary sense?. Would people risk their lives on a myth without any proof that there was something worth their lives to protect?

We set our imagination free in every sense of the word. No thought was too random, no idea to incomprehensible. We looked at all possibilities and discounted nothing.

After two hours of calm, and measured discussion, we knew that we had to stick with the clues to wherever they might lead and work with the evidence we had taken so many years to uncover.

We returned time and again to the world egg theory and the likelihood that perhaps two universes could exist on the same plane. If only we had something more than theory on which to base it. We needed corroboration from an outside source. Supposing we were on the right track. If we agreed another universe was in existence and formed in miniature, the religious significance would be profound.

Imagine suddenly announcing to the world that God did exist, or rather that God was in fact female. A goddess who had created not only our universe but another as well.

Religions all around the world would be thrown into chaos. The

church or as I should say, churches of the world could only react in the negative, they could do nothing else if they wanted to maintain order as any positive acknowledgement of our real and very raw discovery would lead to religious insurrection. Governments would have to deal with believers and non-believers alike.

Millions might give up work in the sure knowledge that they would be protected at some point, either in life or death. Would this being likely be benevolent or malevolent to despoilers of the earth, of her cosmos?. Were their other lifeforms like us in our universe and what of the universe in miniature, how would that work in any sense we could understand?

How would it affect the thinking of the modern mind, now so attuned to scientific fact, if science were able to say categorically that the world had been created by a supreme being.

How would the old institutions of the world withstand the news?. Would financial and health systems crumble under the unbearable weight of the new truth if the fact that mankind was a creation of a greater force, and one which many had dismissed for years as being irrelevant in at the turn of the twenty first century.

Surely it is also true to say, that those who believe in God as written down by the hand of man are the worst offenders when it comes down to pursuing their own particular belief.

Why is it that all those who purport to love God most are usually the most radically, cynically, intolerant and murderous people on the face of the earth?.

If they knew there was the real possibility, scientifically proven and authenticated that a God or Goddess existed and that they would one day have to face them, would it change their tolerance level for others of differing faiths? Would all faiths now become one under the newly discovered Goddess?.

As for those who commit crimes, other than the mentally imbalanced, would the thought of ultimate retribution from the supreme being turn them to a life more in keeping with the morals and ideals of society.?

In short, would this knowledge make the world a better place and if the answer is yes, then why had Chapter, not made this information public?.

With so much to gain, why would they not simply reveal this great long hidden mystery to the world?

Our next point was monetary value. Would this item have any monetary value?

The answer must be yes. If governments were no longer able to put restrictions on the world population. If the day to day living of humanity collapsed because of this knowledge, which certainly would be disseminated to all mankind, chaos would follow and authority would breakdown in very short order. Therefore, any sensible authority would want this secret kept to under wraps, until it could be destroyed or debunked as nonsense.

All faiths of the world would see this as a monumental problem to their control of the populace presently under their own influence. That fact in itself would entice some in the higher echelons of the churches of the world to wish the destruction of this truth.

The church often received bad press and we thought although the good people of all creeds outnumbered the bad. It was surely a fact that there were enough self-serving interests in those hierarchies to promote fear among their followers.

Those of blind conviction whose minds had been subliminally brainwashed from childhood would not be swayed by the science, even though it now confirmed those very same convictions.

Loss of control of the people, meant loss of power and financial gain and that must be enough justification in the mind of many to persuade them to use fair means or foul to prevent this fact being released.

Hiding such a secret would contain the problem but with risk of discovery. Absolute discretion is never assured in this situation, but destruction of the same secret meant that it could never be revealed. Therefore, assuring complete security.

There was another point in question. The Law. How would the news be received by the lawmakers and administrators.

If the revelation led to a break down in law and order, there must be a response with which it could be restored, but how would the police respond?. Was it a given that they themselves would be able to rise over and above this very sudden change in the age old creeds of the world? Police officers in this situation might side with the general public.

What then doctors and nurses felt relieved of their moral responsibility for life, given the fact that proof of God was now undeniable. Of course, we felt that good people such as these wouldn't abandon those in their care but some certainly would. Possibly they would find a new calling or some might find themselves drawn to other types of medicine, the kind of disease prevention based on a spiritual belief, rather than science. That might be another reason to want this secret buried for eternity.

The third question we had asked was would people risk their lives to defend this secret. It seemed like a very obvious 'yes' to that. The absolute knowledge that God was real would engender the feeling of ultimate security in those who were currently keeping the secret and had done so since the dawn of time.

Was she interactive with the world and people she had created? Again, we asked was she benevolent, malevolent.

Was she perhaps insouciant? In other words, had she merely created the universe or universes out of a dislike of chaos, some place that she could exist but never have to get involved in?

After all, in so enormous a creation there would most surely be countless worlds on which she could live in peace. Was she omnipresent or was she physically attached to one reality?

All we needed now was to agree that this was the direction in which all our energies would be concentrated. It was only a little over a week until I was due to meet Anna.

This time I would be more prepared. This time I had the backing of two people I considered fine friends as well as colleagues.

We would agree on a list of questions to be asked. Not a written list but questions I could memorise that might draw more answers from Anna. More detail with which if we were cunning enough, might lead us closer to the truth.

It was to be an exciting week. We hated leaving Rekha as we headed back west to Devon but we all still had work and our normal

routines to which we must attend. I felt bad on a personal level as I was the only one of the three of us who would meet Anna.

The others said not to worry. It was felt that if we tried to force the issue, Anna would back off and the breakthrough we sought might be lost due to a lack of trust.

What would be revealed next would require the greatest test of trust that we had ever been party to in the last twenty-four years.

Chapter 8.

Risk of oblivion.

The evening had come when I was due to meet Anna. It was the twenty first of June and the sun was just touching the horizon at nine forty pm as I made my way across the moors.

Cornwood was out of view in less than two minutes. I took the road up past Lee Moor and through Wotter, two small villages surrounded by quarries and took a ninety degree turn north just before Shaugh Prior.

It was a warm clear evening as I headed up Shaden hill and down the other side towards Cadover Bridge. Scotch Blackface sheep, Dartmoor ponies, and a mix of cattle, Hereford, Belted Galloway and Highland cattle grazed the moors and roadside verges.

There was a new moon but it was presently invisible to the naked eye. In the southern hemisphere a solar eclipse had occurred and I wondered if this was the reason that Anna had chosen this particular day.

It was also the day that Mars was at its closest to the Earth at a mere forty two million miles, it shimmered red and menacing. Venus could be seen in the eastern sky, bright beautiful Venus, a guiding beacon as night fell. Magnificent Jupiter was in conjunction in June and so was not visible and Saturn was in the process of coming out of its conjunction and would be a late morning object.

We had checked all these facts previously. The night would be dark and it was a safe bet we felt that this was the reason this day had been chosen.

I made my way towards Yelverton but took the sharp right hand turn that led past Brisworthy and then on towards

Meavy. I drove carefully. The last thing I wanted was to collide with an animal or other vehicle.

This meeting was far too important to miss.

A mile and a quarter from Brisworthy I hung a hard right again onto a side road. The only traffic I had passed since Cadover Bridge was a single Tractor and a Land Rover towing a horsebox. It was a good sign. The road was a bit of a rat run on occasion for people who were commuting between Yelverton and Ivybridge or Plympton.

Now the road curved into the side of the hill. A mile further on it split in two. The left lane wound down to the village of Sheepstor and then on to Burrator Reservoir a quarter of a mile beyond that.

The reservoir was darkening as the last of the sun's rim dipped below the horizon. Sheepstor itself was dwarfed by the tor towering above it to the north.

I took the right hand fork which rose on the west side of Gutter Tor and then carried on east to Gutter Tor Refuge Hut.

It was at an off road pull in that I parked my car, pleased that it was summer and the ground was dry so I could get the vehicle at least twenty yards off the road. I sat and waited my watch told me it was three minutes to ten.

I let myself get lost in the view. My position on the other side of the valley from Sheepstor Tor afforded a wonderful view of the huge boulders that form the Tor crest. With smaller yet still large boulder's strewn for hundreds of yards in all directions.

Burrator reservoir was lost to me now. It was fading into the forest of pines behind it and ancient forest before it. I looked up and smiled as a familiar constellation hung guardian like over the tor to my northwest. Draco. I could count the seventeen stars through my scratched windscreen.

After I decided to get out and stretch in the warm air, I noticed a slight edge to the almost imperceptible breeze. I was at one thousand two hundred feet above sea level here.

I watched for car lights but saw none other than in the very far distance.

'Anna you're late' I had said to myself.

'No' a soft voice beside me said, 'I'm right on time.'

I remember cursing as I jumped with the shock of my friend's unseen arrival.

'Christ, where did you come from? I had asked.

Twenty one years later and I still remember her reply as if it were today, 'From the heavens of course.'

It was as if she had just materialised beside me but I didn't in all honesty believe she was using a Star Trek transportation hub.

I pushed the point. 'Really, where did you come from?

Anna had smiled, 'I have been here waiting for you.'

'You must have been wearing camouflage' I said.

I could see what she was wearing in the fading June light it was a figure hugging one piece uniform, for want of a more solid description. Her eyes were the same green-violet flecked gold that seemed self-lit, even in the deepening darkness.

Now I needed to get down to business. Before I could ask why I had been summoned here on this day and at this time Anna spoke.

'Chapter and I are unable to find the object we seek'.

'I thought you said you were the guardians of it?'

She had nodded succinctly, ' We were, we are', She corrected herself quickly, 'but currently we don't have it'.

'Since when?'

'Nineteen seventy one.'

Had I heard correctly, nineteen seventy one?

I remember that I had sat back hard on the car bonnet. I was shocked well dumbfounded would have been a better word.

'That's thirty years ago,' I had laughed in disbelief. Chapter, the very organization created to protect the object had in fact lost it.

Anna was not pleased with my reaction.

'There is little humour in this situation.'

I had agreed with her on that point but was intrigued to know why it had taken her nearly thirty years to tell me this.

I received an answer I was not expecting.

'Thirty years in your time, but only a few days in Chapters time'.

I know that I asked her what she meant by that, why was time different

for me than it was for chapter and for her.

She had shaken her head and inferred that I would not understand.

I wasn't sure if I should push the point but one thing resonated with me or sure and that was the fact that even in the semi darkness, I could see

that she had hardly aged at all since our first meeting in nineteen seventy seven.

'Now Chapter must ask your help and that of your colleagues.'

I am not going to pretend that now in 2022, I can recollect every exact word that was exchanged between the two of us that night twenty one years ago. What I can do is to represent as truthfully as possible what passed between us, in the spirit and body of what was said. She said I could take notes.

Anna told me that they had misplaced the most valuable object in creation. I had no reason to doubt her sincerity. It had happened she went on to say for one reason only.

The object was from time to time moved to various counties across earth. It had been brought back to England again two hundred years ago but in times of danger it was passed from hand to trusted hand and hidden for a period of time.

'Your Grandfather,' she had told me, 'Was one of those trusted hands.

In World War Two when it looked as though the Nazis might invade Britain, it was given to him to be hidden elsewhere on Dartmoor.

Teams of German archaeologists were at that time scouring the world looking for artefacts of religious and historical significance, which might give them the upper hand in their attempt at complete world domination. They were to report any findings to Reichsfuhrer and leader of the SS, Henrich Himmler.

Chapter thought that Dartmoor and for that matter a middle aged farmer would be the least likely of area's or people to conceal such a treasure.'

'When' I asked had he been chosen for this task?

'In nineteen thirty nine.' she said, 'when he had moved to the farm called Trowlesworthy Warren, with his wife and three children, one of whom was your mother.'

'Was he known to Chapter before that time?' I had asked.

'Yes,' was her answer but she did not elaborate any further on the history the old man had with the organization.

'How or why had the object been lost?' I had enquired. A simple truth followed. So simple that I believed it absolutely.

'It was passed to a member of Chapter to be hidden. We move it every few years or if circumstance should dictate, as we did at the beginning of World War Two, when your grandfather hid it for us. Your Grandfather was not a member of Chapter. Usually, we do not allow members to hide the object in case they are found out, if they were, it might compromise the whole organization. One member and one lay person work as a team. The lay member hides the object and the leaves a coded note or reference which the member, with a little hard work can decode. It acts as a double layer of security. After the war he handed it back to Chapter.'

'In nineteen ninety.' I said. I assume something went badly wrong?'

'Yes. The layman in this instance was killed in a car bad car accident on the very day that he had chosen to move the object and before he could hand over or even write out the code. To add our discomfort, the female member of Chapter also died suddenly a day later.'

'Was foul play suspected?'

'No, it was an unforeseen medical condition. We lost the entire two person team in two days and before we could get information from the member in question. But information as to its where it would be re-hidden was passed to your Grandad by the layman twenty years before the accident occurred. Perhaps he had a premonition.'

I was shocked that no other fail safe's had been put into place.

'Similar situations have occurred in the past but only five times over many hundreds of years. On most of those occasions the object was retrieved within a day or so at the most, with two exceptions.'

Now after Chapter been convened and in the light of the dire position in which they found themselves, they had given Anna the green light to share their knowledge.

Anna was prepared, to tell me what the object was and I would be allowed to share that knowledge with Frank and Rekha. It was hoped that the three of us would be able to find again, that which was lost thirty years ago. To do so, we would need as much information as we could be given.

I recall asking why the three of us were more likely to find it than the organization that had kept it safe for so long and seemingly had resources and friends all over the world.

'It has been decided,' he had told me, 'that as you loyally kept the knowledge you have so far gained. We trust you. Since our very first meeting, you have shared what you know with only two others, a remarkable achievement in such a long time period. We know that your endeavours so far have led to you finding one of our meeting places. In fact, it was only by minutes that you missed one of our two gatherings in this thirty twenty four year period. You found the clue in the constellation of Draco and linked it to the tors. By some clever thought processes, you found a link to the Goddess.'

I was astounded at Anna's sudden forthright manner and her new willingness to discuss Chapters secret. The last two meetings we had, revealed almost nothing. They seldom lasted for any real length of time and were more in the nature of warnings than of any deep meaningful conversation.

Anna continued, 'You are also on the right path of a second universe. What I tell you would be unbelievable to most people but you will be able to see because you want to believe. Otherwise, why would you have kept the faith so long?

It was true, we did all want to believe in the unbelievable, that was a fact.

'When the universe was created by the Goddess your culture calls Eurynome and was hatched by Ophion, that was the beginning of life as we all know it from Chaos, the raw miasma of creation. That is the belief of Chapter.'

'Go on.'

What was not known was that her first attempt at forming an orderly universe was to give birth to a universe so tiny in proportion that she could witness every part of it with ease before deciding to create her masterpiece. This information was lost to the world just as the universe in miniature was lost to Eurynome when she turned her attention to creating what we all see and know now. The Universe we inhabit. Time, Order, Progression. Nothing moves backwards. Everything moves forwards, including time.

I was dumbfounded.

Anna continued,' 'when her partner Ophion, the great serpent whose

coils had hatched the egg of existence by wrapping his coils around it boasted that he created everything himself, Eurynome lost her temper and cast him down to Earth.'

She paused,' but then Ophion was cunning and he took the first egg, the miniature version of the universe with him. Eons were to pass and Eurynome was too busy in creating all things both living and innate to notice it had gone. When after many Eons she remembered, it was too late. In the billions of worlds, she had brought into existence, how could even such a Goddess be able to recall where that egg might be.'

I listened, at first with some mild disbelief but then with growing acceptance that what she was saying held some truth. Yes, I wanted to believe and why I asked myself would such a long lived group of devotees such as Chapter keep such dedicated faith to this ideal.

Anna carried on, 'at length' she said, 'the egg was either stolen from Ophion, or it was lost by him. There are no firm grounds on which to base an assumption but as the furthest possible mention of it is in cave paintings, along with drawings of goddesses and serpents, as well as other creatures of course. These date back as far as sixty or seventy thousand years BC but it arrived on Earth long before then.

I was scribbling furiously. I had no shorthand skills and I was writing in an old notebook that coincidently was my grandads. It was leather bound and the pages were thick and almost like blotting paper.

I asked Anna to slow down a little, which surprisingly she did.

I had to ask her something that I knew would be of importance to my colleagues as it was to myself.

'Where was the egg originally found and when?'

'It was discovered in a three hundred million year old meteor crater in a place later called Serpent Mound, in what is now the United States of America around the year nine thousand BC. It was some eight thousand seven hundred years later, in three hundred BC in honour of the Great Serpent (Ophion) and the missing egg that it is believed the Native American Tribes in what is now Ohio, made the giant serpent landmark. The egg had been taken to Europe around six thousand BC as moving it was thought a sensible option.'

'But America hadn't been discovered by European settlers at that time, so how do you know all this occurred and who moved it?'

'There is myth and legend and the continuing stories passed in oral form but Chapter doesn't know who moved it.' Anna told me.

Then she carried on with a brief history which we could use as a guide to aid in our research and deliberations.

'Chapter, after centuries of research concluded that the egg was moved from the Americas to Europe.' She informed me. 'It first came to into the purview of an early version of Chapter around the year three thousand BC and brought to what is now England.'

'The time at which Stonehenge was built,' I interrupted.

She smiled, 'Had it occurred to you that that is why Stonehenge may have been built?

'Surely it was built as a marker to denote the longest and shortest days of the year.' I corrected her.

'Stonehenge was of far more importance than to simply mark two days of the year. All that bother just for that. Mankind really has to look beyond its own limited knowledge of the universe. Take into consideration the years taken to construct it, the time and effort it required. You really think that it was made simply to be an astronomical clock?'

Her face held more than a little contempt at such naivety and hermanner changed with her facial expression. I had not seen that before.

It was disconcerting and irritating but she carried on though

her tone was deeply patronizing.

I felt like an idiot for not taking more notice of our ancient monuments and delving deeper into the reason of why they had been erected. After all, my own county of Devon was covered with standing stones and circles of all sizes and designs. What had I missed?. What had been hidden under my nose during all these years of looking at the Tors, tombs, Kistvaens, Cists, etc. Information hidden in plain sight.

Ignoring my obvious discomfort she said, 'Chapter became involved at or about that time, though the exact details were diluted over a time. It was passed orally. Think of the Scandinavian saga's.' 'You have stories from that time? How can that be possible?' I asked

'All will become apparent but as for now we have the pressing matter of finding the egg. Trust me if you will, for the present at least and listen.'

I did as I was asked.

'The egg next came to light at around the time of the first pyramids in Egypt around two thousand six hundred BC. Pharaohs and priests knew of it, protecting it in those very pyramids that are now considered to have been built as burial chambers. They served another purpose which was to hide the egg. The guardian ornaments buried with the Pharaohs, were there to protect the egg not the god kings.'

Anna's eyes closed momentarily, 'unfortunately, the Egyptians buried great treasures as well and that endangered the universal egg as tomb robbers broke in to steal gold and jewels, hence the use and verbal promotion of curses. All that was in order to protect the egg. Burial was a favoured form of protecting it.'

I was aware that this was almost a full confession Anna was providing me with. She seemed in no hurry to leave this time. It was if she was sure that I needed to take in all that she was telling me and I remember urging her to tell me more. I was afraid that she might change her mind at any moment and our conversation would be very quickly discontinued.

My notes became more frenzied as my pencil flashed across the ever filling notepad.

'After that brief period of pyramid building, they became wiser and used ordinary tombs for burials of the great and mighty.'

Even after all these years I can still remember her voice rasping and almost mechanical with the effort of so long a speech.

'This time hiding the egg was more successful and it wasn't until two thousand four hundred years later when the egg was once again taken overland, this time to China, again to be buried, this time with the great Chinese Emperor Qin Shi Huang. The egg was the reason that the Terracotta Army was built.'

I nodded as I wrote.

'The year was two hundred and ten BC. It was there to guard and protect the egg from all manner of human or alien life. It was then that Chapter as we know it now was formed. The organization decided on its aims and constitution. It would work with a lay person. One to one, in the hope that the simplicity of these relationships would form the basis of a mutual trust.' she continued.

'There would be seventeen members of Chapter and seventeen laymen. They would be a mix of male and female, young and old. Selection was to be based on common sense, ability, purpose, and loyalty. It could take many years to cultivate and select new members, so few were below the age of thirty but some showed exceptional qualities from infancy, with a sort of built in connection to both universes.'

From what she told me it was in those early years in which Chapter was formed, that the importance of the egg was realised in full.

It was decided that the universe in miniature almost certainly was blessed with life and lifeforms very like those in this universe. New rumours credited the fact that the egg was opaque and that through it the worlds moved. There was no proof of this, only the word of Chapter.

I listened intently but I would only believe it if I was to see it with my own eyes.

There was no reason to doubt her word and if what she told me was true it had provided life for many billions of years.therefore, were the egg to be destroyed many billions, upon billions of lives might be wiped from existence forever.

Total extinction beckoned either by accident or design, it offered the real risk of oblivion. It was most imperative that the egg was kept safe.

Anna was to continue with her Saga, for some time yet.

'One thing' I said. 'What does it look like?'

She smiled. 'It's egg shaped, ten inches in height with a diameter of six inches and weighs four pounds but the outside is merely for show as it were.'

'That's smaller than I expected.' I had replied. 'What colour is it?'

'The universe itself is a light coffee colour like smoky quartz and spherical but with the texture of glass. The container it is held in could be any colour. We simply do not know.'

The haystack just git bigger and the needle smaller.

Chapter 9

The South American trail.

Three hundred years passed. In that time, the egg had lain quietly undisturbed in the emperor's tomb. Carefully watched over by succeeding members of Chapter and their laymen and of course the legendary Terracotta Army.

'What happened then?' I had asked.

Anna had looked uncomfortable as the breeze cut with a sharp cold moorland edge to it. I remember distinctly how she had moved from foot to foot as humans do to warm themselves up.

Having written by the dim interior light that glowed through the open driver's side window, I thought it polite to offer her a seat out of the brisk night air.

'That would be most welcome.' She had said, or words to that effect as I try to recall now twenty odd years later.

We sat inside and I started the car to get some heat into the cockpit.

'It was necessary to move the universal egg again in one hundred AD.' she said, 'This time it was shipped to Japan where it remained for another four hundred years in the care of the Japanese Royal Family under the guardianship of the Chrysanthemum Throne. The Royal family whose claim was a direct descendancy from the Sea Dragon God or great serpent. The egg lay in secrecy in the beautiful Shinto shrine called Izumo Taisha, whilst Shogun Warlords battled for the right to rule the Nippon.'

There, I saw another link with Ophion the great universal serpent.

Anna had continued with her gripping narrative. We were to learn later on, that this information would form the basis for us three to have the

77

have the most complete picture of the egg in recent times, that was (comparatively speaking) possible, in order to assist Chapter in its quest of finding and securing it once more.

Another movement was required to get the egg to safety once again and Anna launched into another verbal explosion, at once fascinating and perplexing, if what she was telling me was to be believed.

'It was taken briefly to Samoa, where the fierce tribes of the south pacific were able to keep it safe for less than a hundred years before intertribal warfare endangered the egg and caused it to be moved.'

'Now,' she went on, 'it was to be shipped far away to the centre of the New World, to Central America, in what would become modern day Mexico, Guatemala, Belize, Western Honduras and El Salvador. It was there that Chapter helped the Mayan in becoming a civilised and enlightened society.'

She smiled as one does when they have knowledge of something not in the public domain.

'I have said to much on that subject,' it seemed she had regretted some part of the last sentence.

'Ok, just carry on,' I told her. I know that I was getting bad cramp from writing so hard and fast. As I think of it now, I can recall the discomfort it caused me.

I wanted to ask her about something whilst it was fresh in my mind, which was beginning to tire as time passed.

'Are you saying that Chapter helped build the Mayan pyramids, like the one at Chichen Itza?'

'That is for another time.' She had told me.

'But you aren't denying it?'

I can still see the look she gave me to this day, in my mind's eye.

'Do you know of Quetzalcoatl?'

My reply was that I did know a little of his myth and link to Chichen Itza. He represented new birth or rebirth and was of the greatest importance to the people.

'The Feathered Serpent God. The Mayan believed that serpents or snakes, call them what you will, were the creatures which helped the celestial bodies move across the sky. I know the Mayan were utterly fascinated with the heavens and invented the first calendars known to mankind. I also know that the Mayan built the temple of Chichen Itza around six to seven hundred and fifty AD.'

'Then you know that it was aligned so that at spring and autumn equinoxes the shadow cast on the steps looks like the serpent god is making his way down from heaven to earth?.'

I had replied in the affirmative.

'Also,' I told her, 'he has feathers so that he can fly from earth back to the heaven's so your point is?'

'My point is' She continued with a hint of annoyance, 'The Mayan, though they were a clever advanced people for their time, would not have been able to build such an edifice without the technical help of a much more advanced civilisation. It was Chapter who provided that help, both technical and physical.'

My God, was this an admission of extra-terrestrial aid for an ancient civilisation?

It was the first time that she had made such a statement to me, although on the previous two occasions we had met, she had alluded to the fact that Chapter might have been from an alien planet or system.

Her words then were simply, 'look to the stars'. That hardly constituted a declaration of any off world beings meddling in human affairs. Terran's (mankind, the inhabitants of our Earth), were quite able to do enough damage to each other and the planet. Therefore, one might assume that any interference was to our benefit. If such was the case why hadn't Chapter simply taken the egg to the safety of another star system?

Frank, Rekha and I had of course discussed the obvious link to other worlds and civilisations, but without any scientific or indeed physical evidence, we could not present a working hypothesis on that basis.

Now it seemed that we might at some stage have a connection or at least a tiny link to the unthinkable. A real, provable Alien existence on our world.

'It's been considered by greater mind's than mine.' I had said.

Many great theologians and writers, astrophysicists and the like had taken a punt over the years at putting the puzzle together. There were of course always those who cried 'humbug', but there seemed to be a lot of evidence that pointed to outside help to set man on the right technological track.

There were many periods of great advances over short frames of time and although I wanted to go down that road asking her outright about alien intervention, I was sure that time was slipping away from both of us.

Just for this moment, the universal egg took precedence over my curiosity.

'The temple at Chichen Itza was built in order to protect the egg. It served its purpose well over the next three hundred years.' Anna told me.

'But then the Mayan civilisation foundered in about nine hundred to nine fifty AD.' I added.

'It foundered for a reason and before you say anything, it was not due to over population, warfare, environmental problems, declining trade or the like.'

I had some knowledge of the Maya, Aztec and Inca, so I was aware of the Mayan decline, I say decline as they didn't disappear, they simply became less prominent.

'What caused them to founder?' I enquired.

'The universal egg was lost. For only the third time since its creation by Eurynome and Ophion. Chapter diverted all their attention away from the Inca in pursuit of the missing egg. Very simply put, Chapter withdrew their support from the Inca and they began a slow steady decline in a relatively short period of time.'

'Go on,' I urged her.

'Chapter was unable to locate it. It came to light that one of the lay priests had taken it in the hope of bringing him fame or notoriety as the lone keeper of such a great treasure but strangely, he never acted on his intention. He simply vanished with the egg.'

I was taken aback. 'So how did they find it?'

'He headed south and disappeared into the jungles of the Amazon basin. Chapter was sure of that fact. Teams were dispatched to look for it but to no avail and anyway, where would you start looking in such a vast area?.

'When did it come to light again?' I was intrigued to say the least.

'Five hundred years later.' Anna informed me. 'It was believed that the priest was able to assimilate with the indigenous peoples of the amazon, probably one tribe, who lay claim to it. There is mention of an egg that holds the universe in one particular Amazonian tribes culture. They were far to the west of today's Brazil close up against the border with Peru.'

'I remember you said it had been lost only five times since the time of its creation, but you said for only a few days!'

'I meant in modern times. I should have explained myself better. It has been lost only twice since it Amazonian adventure.'

I admit to being mesmerized by her story. If this was some kind of wind up, then it was the longest in living memory.

'Then Chapter found it in the hands of a young woman. A remarkable girl who seemed naturally to understand its importance. She made herself known to Chapter and was at once given the status of layman and entrusted with the eggs safety. This time Chapter watched over her with great diligence,' Anna confessed.

I listened with an intensity I never thought I was capable of.

'In conversing with her over a period of a few weeks that she understood that the Olmec, who preceded the Inca by a thousand years or more were convinced that they would be the keepers of a lost universe. There is evidence in their artwork that supports such a belief. They were an incredibly advanced people. It was speculated that they too had help from another source, but it wasn't from Chapter.'

'And this girl was guarded and helped?'

'More than that, far more.'

I was so tired now. I glanced at my watch and it said one fifty am.

'So, what happened?'

'They moved her to a place of relative safety, up the Amazon River to the far west of Brazil, then by foot into the Andes and due south until she reached a place called 'The Old Peak' in the local language. In our day it's known as Machu Picchu. It sits seven thousand nine hundred feet above sea level. That was where the young woman and Chapter built the temple complex to house and hide the egg.'

'Machu Picchu came into being because of the egg. Is that what you are telling me Anna?'

'Yes'.

'Seriously?'

She had nodded and for the first time since our conversation began and my irritated, 'look at the evidence.'

'Tell me.'

She grabbed the opportunity with both hands as it were. A smile was appearing across her pretty face and the green-gold eyes looked as though they were back lit again with violet.

'Firstly, the complex and its design. We know construction began in or around fourteen hundred AD. It was a massive building project with some two hundred structures on it. It was built, then occupied for only one hundred and seventeen years. The terracing on which the living accommodation, warehouses and temple are built are a marvel in themselves.'

The Temple of the Sun,' I interjected.

Yes the so called 'Temple of the Sun' was never intended for the purpose of sun worship. It was where the universal egg was kept under the watchful eye of a custodian who was a prime member of our organization and of course, the young woman who found the egg. The Intihuatana was built as an astronomical clock. It ensured the population never lost sight of their goal.'

'As if Chapter would let them.'

Anna ignored me, 'it was also an aid for them to watch the skies and to feel a part of the history they had helped to protect. It was carved out of the bedrock with help by other sources. The angles and planes carved into it all had true and deep significance to the egg.'

'Understood.'

She continued, 'The column stone tilt angle is set at thirteen degrees to the north. Strangely although you cannot see the constellation of Draco, from Peru, you can see the old Inca constellations, for example, The Condor, The Toad, The Fox , The Llama, The Tinamou and yes, The Serpent. The Serpent passes neatly through the thirteen degree angle at which the column stone is set. No one quite understands the old Inca constellations like Chapter and as a consequence, few people consider their importance in relation to the site.'

I was astounded by her story. The link to the stars was undeniable and as I sat back and carried on writing as she took up the tale again.

'One of the temple doors known as the Serpent door faces northwest and aligns with both the Inca constellation, 'The Serpent' and if you were able to follow a line of site over the equator, it would align with Draco in the northern hemisphere. The Pleaides is seen through the opposing window.'

I remember telling her that this was fascinating.

'I only tell you these things so that you have a better understanding of the link between earth and sky. It might help you further in giving credence to my story if I tell you that the Serpent Door opens onto sixteen pools. Including the temple as a pool, this means seventeen in total.'

'Seventeen again.' I had said.

'It's a trigger number.' Anna told me. 'Also, just from a practical point of view. How were such massive stone's hauled up a mountain?

Even if you accept that they were hauled up by manpower, you still have to consider how the interlocking 'ashlar' stones were so very precisely cut. Archaeologists are unable to put a knife blade between them, and yet they consider that these people, nearly seven hundred years ago were able to cut stone that finely.'

There was no denying her last statement, it was absolutely true and had been the source of inspiration for those who thought the Gods of old were alien astronauts. Many books had been written over the years that promoted the theory.

For now, however my only concern was to document her words and help her and Chapter find the missing universal egg. I kept writing as she seemed to be on a final push.

'Then disaster struck. Although the Spanish Conquistadors never discovered Machu Picchu, the diseases they brought to the Inca and other tribes rampaged through the population. That along with a call to arms by an Inca King made the temple area untenable. It fell to ruin and it was decided that the egg be moved on. The problem would continue as populations increased worldwide and mankind began to explore the world in which they lived.

'The need for expansion and exploration,' I mused.

It took a year to take it in secret, east across the continent to the South Atlantic. The year was fifteen hundred and sixty and the egg faced a perilous journey across the ocean. Sailing northeast the journey,' Anna said, 'proved to be uneventful and a member of Chapter and a layman took it ashore on the west coast of Africa. Now it was taken inland and up into the mountain plateau in what is modern day Mali, where it would remain for the next two hundred years, in the care of the Dogon People.'

My ears pricked up for I knew a little about these remarkable people and their love of astronomy. I had read that their religion had elements of astronomical curiosity.

For example, they knew about certain astronomical bodies that were not visible with the naked eye, as in the case of Sirius, the Dog Star in the constellation Canis Major, which they understood to be a triple star system, that Saturn had a ring system and moons and that Jupiter had many moons. All this was known to the Dogon hundreds of years before telescopes had been invented. Modern science would take years to confirm this.

One of the main things that led me to take so much interest in her words though, was the fact that the Dogon creation myth has an egg as its core. It was a story that had fascinated me for years.

84

Anna was already ahead of me and as I wrote with aching hands and wrists, she expounded on the Dogon myth from Chapters point of view.

'According to Dogon religion, an unknown source. A universal egg had exploded and scattered the stars, galaxies and dark matter to the outer extremities. The God Amma or Amen has dual sexuality and is counted as both God and Goddess. Although he or she has the power to create they are also considered infinitely small, as might befit the ruler of a universe in miniature. You can investigate this further yourselves.' Anna had told me with a bored voice.

'We can do that.' I had offered.

'I must tell you the last piece of the puzzle.'

I had said that I was glad. As pleased as I was that she was talking so freely to me, I was also exhausted. My watch said it was three fifteen am. Soon dawn would break and I was already somehow aware that Anna would disappear once again.

'In the late eighteenth century, around seventeen seventy, the egg had to be moved again. This time it was due to religious persecution of the Dogon people and the fact that they were considered fair game for the slave trade.

'This much I knew.'

'This meant the Dogon retreated to a position in keeping with a defensive posture on the Bandiagara Escarpment. All we know then is that the egg was taken East and then into Persia and was put in the care of a Yazidis layman. The Yazidis were believed to have the roots in Zoroastrianism. They hid the egg successfully for a number of years.'

I asked how many years?'

Unknown,' she remarked, 'but on its next move it once again got lost, turning up on Dartmoor in the mid nineteenth century. No one knew where it was between seventeen ninety and eighteen sixty five when Chapter found it once again. Because of explosive population growth and industrialisation, it was considered best to keep it in the least populated areas of England and so it was passed around Dartmoor.'

'That was where Grandfather came in.'

'Exactly so, this culminated in your grandfather's involvement during the years of the second world war when he hid the egg for the best part of ten years. As you know it was then passed from him to the next layman and Chapter member. It was some thirty years later in nineteen seventy one that it was lost for a fourth time because of the tragic events that I told you about. Now we have to find it once again and it seems that you and your friends are best placed to do that.'

'Why,' I had asked, 'doesn't Chapter just hold onto the egg itself.'

'We, that is to say Chapter, agreed, along with other nations, that it was safer for the egg to continue to be hidden in different locations around

the world. You know that there is a saying, that a moving target is easier to hit.'

I had understood that line of reasoning. It seemed sensible but it was true to say that as the population increased and travel became much more widespread, except in the remotest places, that the world now became a smaller place. Few places were safe from intrusion and it was technology that beat a path for mankind to follow.

'Do you have any suggestions of your own, or Chapters, that might aid us further?'

'As Chapters liaison, I have told you all I can. It may be that you will in some way be able to make that link that we cannot.'

'We will do all we can.' Was the best advice I could offer. 'How will I find you?'

'Don't worry, you and your friends are always under surveillance so I can always find you.'

Chapter 10

Digging deep.

We had said our goodbyes at four thirty am. Sunrise was now barely seventeen minutes away. It was already light and vision was no problem, though the ground was rough and uneven.

It was with a heavy but tired heart that I watched Anna disappearing over the rocky out crop that was Gutter Tor. Then temptation got the better of me. She had cleared the Tor crest and I remember just seeing the top of her head, her aluminium silver hair bobbing as she walked.

My mind made up I had followed and was now a quarter of a mile behind her. It took me less than ten minutes to clear the top of the Tor. I did so as quietly as I could, keeping low, trying to avoid being spotted.

She had to go downhill now into the valley. Whatever direction she choose I would see her. Every direction led downhill before climbing again to another hill or tor, and it would take at least an hour to cover the distance necessary to avoid my line of sight.

My heart was thumping. I know that I felt like a naughty kid for spying on her but at this time I didn't care.

Imagine my surprise when I found that she was nowhere to be seen. Yes, there were some huge boulders but it was still not that difficult an area for me to search, after all, I had been brought up on these moors and was aware of most of their hiding places.

I perched unconcerned now on a large boulder near the crest but there was no sign of Anna.

I waited for an hour, then headed back to my car. For a time, I wondered if I had dreamt or hallucinated the whole meeting but two things persuaded me that I had not. First was the fact that around forty pages of my notebook were filled with very hurriedly scribbled words, they got larger and more inelegant toward the end.

Secondly and probably, most telling of all were the four aluminium Blond hairs on the passenger seat. They were certainly not my wife's and they belonged to no other lady I knew.

I don't remember the drive home but do remember my wife not being in the best of moods with me. I couldn't say that I blamed her but I had informed her of my intentions before my sojourn into the night.

I couldn't wait to tell Rekha and Frank but it would have to wait until I had slept.

The adrenaline rush that had kept me going all those hours had run out a while ago and I was running on empty. I slept from six am to six pm. Then it was time to eat and then rally the troops. I went around to Franks and we rang Rekha.

It was a long call and I went through the pertinent points, trying to give them the basic facts in order that they could form individual opinions of my meeting with Anna.

We each set ourselves a task. I would go back through my family history and talk to as many people as I could to get a better idea of what they knew or didn't know of Grandads wartime life on the farm.

He didn't have any close friends still alive so much of what I would learn would be anecdotal. I needed fact. That was what we had agreed to base our investigation on but if anything was to lead to a cross reference of information we already had, I figured it might be worth pursuing.

Frank would look into the distant pass to try and ensure we correctly cross referenced all the notes I had written down from the detailed particulars which Anna had provided. Date's, civilizations, religious beliefs, continents, and countries etcetera. He would also check that the astronomical statistics were correct and supportive of her claims. Timelines would also be vital.

Rekha's part in the operation would be the missing time period of the late eighteenth century, early nineteenth century. This we hoped might point us to the eggs whereabouts.

If it had been hidden so well for roughly seventy years, then where and how.

We also wanted to know how it had returned to England and Dartmoor in particular. As the egg was last seen in Persia, we had a starting place.

If we knew where it had been we might get a clue as to where it was at the moment.

All three of us were working, so time went by again with a merciless speed, giving is precious little of itself to spare for our own hobby or quest, call it what you will. Before we knew it 2002 was upon us. We had made some small inroads but nothing which could be considered a great success.

That year went by as well and 2003 landed. In the midst of all this we still kept the faith. Frank had left the quarry a few years earlier and set up his own business which meant that was even busier.

We had heard no word from Anna, or Chapter.

Also in 2003 I had a small but significant breakthrough. My brother rang me. He remembered going out on from the farm for a day with the old man shooting rabbits. At that time Grandad would have been about seventy four.

They went a few miles over the moor and ended up at Ditsworthy Warren, which had been farmed by an elderly lady known as Granny Ware but had been uninhabited since nineteen forty seven after her death.

Incidentally later on, in 2012, parts of the film Warhorse were shot there. It was as they came near to the old farmhouse that a young woman appeared from the ruins and called out to the old man.

Grandfer told my brother, (who would have been around fourteen at the time), to wait for him while he spoke to the girl. Being bored and curious and paying scant attention to Grandfer's instructions he was tempted to wander closer to the two of them. He was soon noticed and Grandfer was about to tell him off when the young woman came to his defence with a simple shake of the head.

Close enough now to see her in more detail he gave me a description of her.

'She was young, in her early twenties, very pretty, average height,' he told me, 'but her hair,' he continued to say, 'was silver, almost like metal.' There was something else as well. 'Here eyes were green but flecked with gold and violet, I have never forgotten her eyes.'

'What made you bring this up now?' I had asked.

'You asked me a while ago if I remembered anything Grandfer might

have said or done anything unusual. Anything that might tie into this story you've spent twenty odd years looking into.'

For a time, well a few days at least, I wondered if one of my dear

colleagues had put him up to this, but since that first year, 1977 it had been a well-guarded secret. Even our wives did not know the full scope of our quest.

It was three days before I told the others. They were delighted. It gave us all another push towards putting the pieces of the puzzle together. We were still determined to see this through to the end, whatever end that might be.

Now at last I had some proof of Anna's existence. That alone was worth its weight in gold. Let's face it, my friends could have taken my story of this enigmatic young woman as fantasy. Never once was I questioned on the authenticity of my notes from my meeting with Anna. I think that says a lot for the bond of trust between us.

Another year passed. 2004 came and Frank had made major inroads off the back of my notes as to where the egg was alleged to have travelled and the timelines involved. It meant taking Anna's story as fact, but the truth was, why would anyone go to the trouble of concocting a story in such detail? After all, I was the person who had started the whole ball rolling when I found the books in which Grandads notes and badge were found.

I had, of this time committed almost thirty years of my life to solving this, quest, puzzle, conundrum. To, this day I'm still not sure what to call it.

We all knew how important it was to find some more solid clues as to the eggs whereabouts, but the fact it had been lost for the last thirty odd years and Chapter were obviously in no hurry over that time period to find it, even though they were pushing us hard now was another conundrum. So that gave us some leeway.

That was another strange thing. The more we discovered it seemed, the more confused we were becoming.

Frank had spent a year confirming dates times and the facts of the timeline of the egg according to Anna. It was a long, thankless task, one filled with frustration, at times near abandonment, but he stuck with it closely.

Eventually it paid off and he was able to return a vote of confidence in what she had told me.

There was of course no way of tracing the object directly. All he could do was follow the timeline given and verify each civilization in that period, where it was in the world, how the object might have been transported, and any and all historical links that would support the theory of why any movement may have occurred.

Furthermore, he had needed to check if, during the long periods of time it had remained unmoved, it had remained undisturbed. Had any major historical event occurred which might have been at odds with the area whilst it supposedly lay dormant.

Looking at it as a group, we agreed with his findings. So far, so good we thought.

Rekha had also had her fair share of problems whilst looking for the Persian connection and the disappearance of the egg.

Finding the illusive object was going to take a lot of time, that was for sure, but as with everything she did she set about it with her customary professionalism. God knows how she found the time whilst bringing up three kids, and yet she did.

Before she started, she did a thorough background check and found an interesting fact. Another of the old constellations, Serpens has eleven main stars, which was why I had ruled it out of my original search when I had found the link to Draco, so she tried one more celestial snake Hydra, a constellation of a water dragon, with coincidently, seventeen stars.

I hadn't included it in my original search as it was classified as being a southern hemisphere constellation, although it can still be seen from the northern sky as in certain areas as well.

Hydra was, in mythology the many headed monster slain by Heracles as one of his labours. Rekha soon discounted it as being the least like Ophion. She also believed that it was not the constellation that the Inca Temple was aligned too.

Rekha's thought pattern led her to follow the final stages of the eggs travels at that period and moving forward. Therefore, she wanted to be sure in her mind that she had a solid factual base from which to work.

Tracking the object into the coastal regions of Africa and thence up into Mali, was she said a little easier. There was certainly more up to date evidence if only because, unfortunately, of the dire and terrible marks left on communities by the slave trade, where for years legend and rumour had mixed into a heady cocktail of hearsay, supposition and myth, all laced with a splash of truth.

On the trail led, to the Persian Empire, where it ended abruptly. Why though did it end? That was what Rekha now had to ask herself and to try to solve the mystery.

We had been told that it was taken into the keeping of the Yazidis but how long they kept it no one knew exactly, but it assuredly travelled somewhere before arriving back in England in the eighteen sixties. So, from seventeen ninety roughly speaking, it was on the move again. Now Rekha was on the cusp of a major breakthrough.

Chapter 11

The India connection.

2005 had arrived with the usual over blown fanfare of modern custom just because the world had taken another annual revolution around the sun. Well at least Mankind still existed, that was something, given our propensity to kill off other species of fauna, flora, fish and fowl that share the planet with us as well as our own brethren through war and greed.

The global terror threat was ongoing with bombs going off in London and in cities across India and Egypt.

The world environmental situation was becoming increasingly bad as hurricane Katrina made landfall in the Gulf of Mexico, causing massive damage before it made landfall in the USA and devastated New Orleans and a Typhoon struck Hainan in China.

Earthquakes struck in Iran, Indonesia and Pakistan and wildfires ravaged Portugal.

In Rome Pope John Paul the Second died and was then superseded by Benedict the sixteenth.

Then brighter news, the dwarf planet Eris was discovered in our solar system by the Palomar Observatory, and the NASA Mars orbiter was launched and headed from earth to another distant, albeit neighbouring world.

It was not to be a wonderful year for millions of people.

For us the year proved more promising. Rekha had found a link that might be the missing link in our story and it started with her finding a trail of evidence on a part of the ancient Silk Road that ran from China to Turkey, over four thousand miles across more than forty countries.

This link, although tenuous was give her the starting point from which the egg had left Persia. This time no perilous sea journey was required but the journey it was to take overland

93

must have been equally nerve wracking to the team or teams undertaking it. A difficult, treacherous route through some of the most hostile and dangerous lands in the world.

At the very end of the eighteenth century, around eighteen ninety seven, almost all goods enroute to China from Europe and vice versa went via the Silk Road. Included in these goods were of course silk, after which the road was named, Dyes, Spices, Precious Stones, Ivory, Rice, Paper, Perfumes, Porcelain, Gunpowder and Tea, although tea was mostly shipped to Europe as it had been for a hundred and thirty years or more.

It was also the route for more illicit items. Artefacts in gold, silver, bronze, lapis lazuli and smoky quartz.

The latter of these that caught her eye and made her think hard. She remembered the description which Anna had given me of the object. Looking at the copy of my notes as a cross reference confirmed the description. It also revealed that the Universal egg was the colour of coffee, a stone found in many places and sometimes mined in years gone by in Afghanistan.

This made Rekha wonder if, (being as Afghanistan is on the eastern border of Persia), the deep but highly dangerous mines might not be a perfect hiding place for the egg.

It would make sense for sure. There was always the possibility of a mine collapsing of course. But if the egg were accidentally buried, then it would at least remain safe. That said, we didn't know how robust it was and that fact wasn't in my notes, because I hadn't asked the question when I had had the chance.

Better still was the fact that the mines were on, or very near the Silk Road. That would be a huge advantage when it came to moving the egg. It could be hidden and then transported from Afghanistan to anywhere in Asia or Europe in a comparatively short space of time if necessity required. It would also be partially disguised if moved with other pieces of quartz through the high mountain passes, to another place of safety.

The problem Rekha now faced was where the egg would have been taken. Would it head North into Europe, maybe east to China or Mongolia. If it was neither of those what about west, back into Africa whence it had come.

Perhaps, although it seemed unlikely due to the population of the that great sub-continent, it would head south into India. She had to put herself into the mind of the two person team responsible for it during its next move.

Where and why, those would be the two focus points and core of the logic she would employ.

Rekha began with what a move into Europe would entail. It was at that time that the first French revolution was coming to an end as Napoleon Bonaparte was soon to become Emperor of France in December of seventeen ninety nine.

All of Northern Europe had settled into an uneasy and temporary calm until the fighting started again with the battle of Marengo six months later as such Europe would be a non-starter as a place of safety for almost two decades.

Africa was just as unlikely a candidate. Famine and disease were rife at that time and tribal chiefs vied with each other in a quest for land.

To the east Turkmenistan, Uzbekistan and Tajikistan, were lawless lands to outsiders and would have posed a dangerous option for such a very precious object to traverse with such limited protection, even though friendly forces could be brought up in support.

Rekha decided that the most likely option was south from Afghanistan to what is now Pakistan but was still India at that time. In that way the egg could be taken across the Hindu Kush and over the now infamous terrain of the Khyber Pass. It could have been moved by day or night as the team had thought fit. Even the help of one or two tribal leaders in the locale may have been enough to guarantee a secure pathway.

The mountain's now became the Karakoram Range and skirting the huge, majestically powerful Himalayas. How long it spent in this area was still a matter of speculation to her but her keen determination was to keep her on the right track. It had to have been taken into India. The British Raj although often fighting small wars to keep India under the control of the British Empire, was still the most stable place in which to operate.

It also meant that other options would be available for the team, the team obfuscating the movement of the egg at that time, with the option of a huge coastline from which it could be moved across the oceans to safety.

Her next task was to find the most likely place it would have been hidden in and where it might have been shipped out from.

Were there any links she wondered to other organizations that might have been willing to help?

She knew the basis of Hinduism was that the god Brahma was born from a golden egg, at the beginning of time and had created the world from that egg. As it was so similar in that respect, would any Hindu sect have seen fit to offer assistance to Chapter?

We were also convinced that she was on the right course and that India would reveal more secrets in relation to the universal egg, and what Chapters ultimate aim was.

More months of research followed at which time she found a link to a region of the Punjab. It looked promising both as a hiding place and a fast route back into the mountains or down towards the lowlands, then on into central and west India.

The link was a reference to a secret society called the 'Nine Unknown Men', said to have been operating for over almost thousand years. It was believed that they were founded in order to safely preserve the ancient secrets of mankind that would be of the utmost danger to society if they fell into the wrong hands.

Despite the long years since their formation, almost nothing factual was known about them. There was however one very small connection. It was a brief piece in a book written in India by an Indian author in the very early nineteen hundreds.

It was a book which looked at the old social and economic systems which had been the base of Indian society in the days before the British Raj. One page in particular caught Rekha's attention. It was the authors description of industry in India at that time. He mentioned textiles, ship building, fishing and sugar and he also mentioned that there were forces at work on the Sub-continent that might one day reveal a massive advance in technology.

It was he said the 'Purview of a certain exclusive group of men, who would release information which would make India a world power in its own right once the British had quit the country'. This was surely an allusion to the 'Nine Unknown Men' previously mentioned.

Given the fact that this society had been formed with the express intention of keeping things they considered best hidden from the general populace. It did not seem unreasonable to suppose that an item as important as the universal egg, would be of the very utmost import to these men.

A few pages later he had stated that, 'These Nine, with the power of celestial heaven to physically move the universe. Now what secret will they reveal to mankind?.'

This it appeared was more than a simple allusion. Surely his words directly spoke to the existence or at least the supposed existence of this long established group.

Whether they were as benevolent as the few books that mentioned them proclaimed them to be had yet to be established.

It was believed that the Emperor Ashoka formed this society in or close to the year two hundred and twenty six BC, after witnessing the carnage of battles and aftermath of the effect on the population living in the area of what is now Calcutta and Madras to secure his empire.

Twelve hundred years later, in the year 999AD, it was said that they had held secret talks with the Pope Silvester the Second, to what end was and is still not known.

Societies such as this are of course a staple of history. Maybe it is just the need to have someone to blame when things go wrong, or in the hope that if they do, someone with a greater intellect and practical understanding of the world or universe and its workings, are there to keep us safe.

Perhaps we hope perhaps that these covert societies such as, the Illuminati, Priory of Sion, The Rosicrucian's etcetera, will protect us from the machinations of those who wish the world or mankind harm whether physically or technologically.

The thought that the universal egg had been in India and that there was a least some reference to that fact, spurred her on.

Now was the time to take stock. A neutral and balanced point of view was still required. We had all agreed that we would follow the clues as they came to our attention.

A more concrete link was still needed in order to create a bridge between, what was in the realm of unsubstantiated writings by one man and a physical connection to a person or persons, which could be authenticated by historical fact.

More evidence was required but this was a great start and we were now closer than any of us knew to just that kind of historical fact.

Chapter 12.

Kronos at the Gate.

Time was not in our favour. Two years had passed in the blink of an eye but we were gaining ground. There had been no word from Anna as yet. We were expecting contact any time now but none had been forthcoming. Frank was successfully carrying on his business venture, while I continued to head my department at the quarry.

We had sat back a little as at this time Rekha had been blessed with her fourth child. Four girls, a full time job and yet she still put in as much spare time as she could on our quest, researching at any given opportunity.

This was how we had continued. We met once, sometimes twice a year for a few hours. It amazed us how committed we were to the cause. I don't think that any of us had realised the personal consequences to our physical health and mental wellbeing but it was true to say that Frank and I had arrived unceremoniously at middle age.

Our companion being almost an entire generation younger than us, remained resolute and even pushed us occasionally if it looked as though we may falter or fall at the final hurdles.

The Earth hurtled around the Sun. It was already December 2007, and this time I was on my game allowing my thoughts to return to a summers night of the twenty third of July 1981, and to the quarry, and my friends to whom that strange event involving the Unidentified Flying Object had occurred.

I had no doubt that Anna was not of this world. This conclusion had been reached by me many years previously. It was the fact that on our last meeting, although I had aged thirty years from our first encounter, Anna had apparently not aged at all. Even the interior light interior light of the car had shown that she was still in her twenties. Mid to late twenties maybe but no more.

If this was the girl that my brother had seen when he was fourteen some thirty to forty years ago, then it was obvious that she either wore the most incredible makeup, or she was able to travel in some way as yet unknown to mankind, for example, time travel.

Spacetime is a wonderful theory first proposed I understand by Albert Einstein.

I don't have enough scientific knowledge to explain it to you the reader but it seems that as space has three dimensions, length, breadth, and depth, it also has a fourth which is time. Gravity caused by very dense objects such as stars can affect the direction of light, warping it but not changing the speed at which it travels. It is constant regardless of how it has been measured, by which I mean by what method.

If you could travel at speeds near to that of light speed, you would find that the closer you get to it, the more slowly you age.

I know that back in the nineteen eighties a brilliant astrophysicist by the name of Carl Sagan caught the attention of the world with a series called 'The Cosmos'. It was a favourite program of mine. What Carl Sagan did was bring the stars to the layperson. In the way that Sir Stephen Hawking would do a few years later.

In one episode, he used twin boys as an example. One stayed in the village in which they lived while the other went off on his pushbike, supposing the bike could be peddled at near light speed, the lad cycling around his village on his return would be the same age that he had left at, but his twin would have aged by fifty odd years.

It fascinated me. I don't pretend that I was able to comprehend the theory fully or to any degree for that matter yet because of proposal I thought it plausible that Anna might be from another world, or dimension.

Had she been a part of the crew of that craft which had so alarmed my colleagues all those years ago? I could neither prove nor disprove that thought at the time.

By then then looked more into the pre-history of Devon and the stones which had stood for thousands of years. I was also of the opinion that the area in which I lived, was alive with history. All around us were the ancient remains of people's long since passed but very similar to us in respect of the fact that this was still a thriving faming and quarrying area, its roots deeply embedded in time. Yet all of us still determined to scratch a living from the land of our ancestors.

Now the question was, did the stones mean more than just the marking of time as mankind saw it. A perfunctory calendar to tell when the longest and shortest days of the year would occur. Or were they standing as the physical representatives of Kronos, who stood at the end of the universe and counted off the seconds of existence for all life.

Perhaps there was a more complicated reason for being them being put up. What if, as has been suggested in other books by many different authors, ancient humans were far more in touch with the universe, and with other life forms than we believed feasible?.

Was it really such a stretch of the imagination to accept that many great wonders of the world had been constructed with the help of alien beings? Or in our arrogance, did we simply assume that apparently impossible buildings were down to man's own brilliance.

Technology has over millennia blossomed and then died only to be resurrected in some of the oddest places on earth. It has come on in leaps and bounds in our modern times, but accumulated knowledge, scientific acumen and in many cases entrepreneurial excellence or war had driven its development.

One day perhaps future generations will look back on us in the way that we look back on our ancestors. They will have one massive advantage however, and that is in the form of written and recorded history that will explain why we did what we did.

What if then, I tried to look at the monoliths of my home county as if there were a written history to them. In other words, I would attempt to understand why they were created in a way not driven by science but by the very anatomy of the layout of the stone circles. All I could do once again was follow the evidence. If I could cross reference it and make a sound argument for any theory which may result from what I had learned, then I would put it before the others and see on balance if they were willing to accept it as proof.

I would take a brief look at structures such as 'Henges' that may have held some religious significance. A brief description of a henge is a constructed embankment, circular in design with an internal ditch. Historians and archaeologists now believe they were built to deter evil spirits. The fact is that many of these pre-historic sites are in very poor condition as might be expected for monuments that are thousands of years old.

My interest though would be based in the main around the stone circles and rows. Why were they put there? What did they signify? Was where they were placed of a real importance. Obviously they meant something to those who had erected them, otherwise why bother?

It was apparently considered most likely that they had some religious, meaning. Perhaps a place of worship or ceremonial healing as well as astronomical use such as the phases of the moon, or a way of dating the four solar equinoxes.

My idea was to focus simply on the astronomical theory. Not from a purely scientific path, I have neither the knowledge nor training to do so, but I believed that a less critical eye, such as mine, may perceive a different reason for the stones placement.

Having felt that there was much to be gained from the local reports of UFO activity in and around southwest Dartmoor and more specifically five miles in every direction from Burrator Reservoir I would use as the focal point of the area I had chosen.

I began in the southeast of that area at a place I have not previously mentioned called Glasscombe Ball where a stone row captured my attention. I choose it as a starting point because I had to start somewhere.

Because the stones in the row have fallen, it never gets much of a mention. It is oriented northeast to southwest and it was in my mind that the view afforded of the sea may have indicated some deeper meaning for its position.

The next megalith I considered was Stalldown Moor stone row. It is believed to be the longest single stone row in Europe, possibly the world, measuring some two point one miles in length. Some of the stones may have moved since the time of their original alignment as the peat in which they stand has moved away downhill by its own weight over the years, so it looks more snake like now than it may have looked at its conception.

It is oriented on a north to south axis. I still liked the idea that our ancient ancestors had concocted some marvellous code, which as yet no one had spotted. This code might help point to the lost egg. The stone row was marvellous and interesting in its own way. I looked at maps of it but nothing struck me as significant.

Looking to the next megalith which was west of the previous one brought me to Penn Beacon. Aligned northeast to the southwest. The seven stones one of which is a little offset, two of which are half buried, did nothing to excite my inquisitive brain and it too was set aside but it still fascinated me to why those ancestors of ours went to all the time and trouble to put up these monuments.

Moving further west was Great Trowlesworthy stone row and circle an area I knew like the back of my hand. My grandad had of course run Trowlesworthy Warren Farm below the tor of the same name from nineteen thirty nine until his death.

The area contains around one hundred and sixty stones. The two stone rows run north to south and east to west with a scattering of many other stones that might or might not be part of the original neolithic layout. I thought this was too monumental a hope, to think it would trigger something in my mind. I thought hard. I visited the site as I had all the others before abandoning the idea. I had to think of how the landscape was before the quarry spoil tips rose above the skyline.

I knew from the many times I had gone shooting over that area with my uncle's that the sea could be seen from the upper half of one of the stone rows. If the spoil tips weren't there, then the sea would probably have been visible all the way down the row.

What was it about the rows and the whole area that had entranced me since boyhood?

My heart leapt as an image came into my mind. I know that I almost ran up the side of the tor to get a better look at the surrounding area. I imagined this piece of ground as it would have been thousands of years ago.

Allowing my mind to blot out Lee Moor, Shaugh Lake and Wotter Quarries. I saw only a collection of people standing perhaps where I had stood. I felt the excitement in their minds as they considered the monumental task upon which they were to embark.

For that matter, I considered the monumental task that I and my two companions were about to embark on. I couldn't do this part of my research alone it was simply too big a job for one person.

Before I brought Frank and Rekha into it, I needed to confirm at least some detail to back up my out of this world thought process. I took a photo with my phone.

The jumble of boulders, rocks and stones that I was faced with at the time would have daunted the most enthusiastic investigator, but my mind would not let this idea rest. I remember vividly taking a deep breath before I plunged into what I knew would entail months of hard work. If I was wrong, then we would have wasted a great deal of time, but if I was right, a whole new concept of historical fact might be born.

Before my eyes a whole different way of looking at these stones opened up. I stopped seeing them from a ground based point of view and saw them from an arial perspective.

The first area I was able to identify was seen directly from the two stone rows though I was seeing it from an upside down perspective. It was rather like an art book where you look at a picture but by altering your viewing stance a different picture unveils itself and once seen, it cannot be unseen. It remains with you, every time you look at it.

That was how it had been with me when I saw the constellation that was The Argo Navis. Thought to large and unwieldy to be of use to astronomers, it was split into three, actually four parts. The constellation was named for the Argo, the ship which Jason in, Greek Myth sailed to the edge of the known world and beyond in search of the golden fleece with his crew of hero's.

It was Carina, (The Keel), which I spotted first. An odd and somewhat ragged assortment of stars with a box shape of four stars at what would be the prow of the vessel.

To the rear was Puppis, (The Poop Deck) not unlike the heel of a ladies shoe in appearance. One I had those two fixed in my mind I was able to spot Vela, (The Sails) of the ship. I could see the stone row forming what would be the mast.

Between the sails and the poop deck I could see the constellation of Pyxis, (The Compass). It was originally part of the Argo Navis but then appeared to be discarded from it. Anyway. Now I had to get a better look at a star map and see if the constellation stood alone among the rocks. If it pointed to, or gave direction to some other site, or if any other constellations were visible among the scattering of boulders and scree that littered the hillside.

Time was pressing it waits for no man.

Chapter 13.

Stars In Their Courses.

From arial photographs it looked like a jumble of boulders and critics might say that any constellation or indeed combination of those giant constellations could be constructed from such a massive collection of stones. Yet it seemed plausible, so I gave myself some artistic license to see where it would lead.

I set the direction in which The Argo was pointing on my old compass. That direction I traced in pencil on our map. The prow of which pointed towards the sea, the mast inland to the northwest and another set of ancient stones behind Legis Tor.

The three of us got together a couple of weeks later, by which time I had discovered something really exciting. Having still heard nothing from Anna, we all thought the same and that was that no news was good news. I was sure my discovery was going to get us closer to solving the mystery of the vanishing universal egg. It was tied up in the ancient stones of the Tors and we were all pushing as hard as we could towards a reaching a conclusion.

Frank and I sat in his garage with our star maps and pencil drawings of the area around Great Trowlesworthy Tor. Rekha had joined us by video call. I had already given her and Frank my ideas on the relevant information I had available a few days previous to our chat.

I was able to inform them that not only could I identify the four constellations making up the Argo Navis but also another six which I thought detailed enough to broker no argument from my colleagues. They were the Chamaeleon (The Chameleon), Crux (The Cross), Pavo (The Peacock), Musca (The Fly), Mensa (The Table) and Octans or the (Eighth Part of a Circle).

They were both in agreement with me and I can still remember the atmosphere as the tension built and realised that we were on course for a spectacular breakthrough.

Rekha noted that all the constellations I had found so far were in the southern hemisphere. My big reveal was to suggest that the area around the Tor would point us towards the possible hiding, or previous resting place of the egg. Rekha saw something different.

'What if' She asked, 'the stones represented the entire night sky?'

It was an excellent question. We looked at the drawings we had but Rekha was already hitting the keyboard on her laptop.

'A simple overlay will suffice' She had said.

In less than a minute she was able to say that the overlay of a map of the constellations on the same scale as our hand drawn map did not match with any accuracy. We were bitterly disappointed.

Frank suggested a different tack and one that made sense.

'Try using just a similar map of the southern hemisphere.' He said.

We could see from the way her face lit up moments later that Rekha had struck gold.

'Perfect.' Her smile lit up the screen. 'It's a perfect fit for all the other constellations in that hemisphere. There are about fifteen or twenty rocks that don't match but no doubt some may have been moved there at a later date by other peoples who lived there after.'

I know that I was utterly flabbergasted as well as greatly relieved.

We were ecstatic. It was a real eureka moment and one that we would never forget in our lifetimes. Yes there were some rocks or boulders that didn't fit in but after all those centuries with farmers moving rocks to provide keystones for field walls and the like, we were not surprised that there would be a few anomalies.

This was huge. Surely this theory had been tested before. We couldn't have been the only people who had looked at this but we could find nothing but generalisations with regards to a specific circle or row.

Perhaps the abundance of rocks and boulders were to numerous to warrant scientific scrutiny over and above the agreed designation of stones for each area.

It was true to say that if you took a wide enough circumference which included a mass of rocks, then of course it was possible to make a design of almost anything from it. This however was over a comparatively small area of ground, around four hundred and twenty feet in diameter. If we allowed ourselves to accept this finding to be rue, the next thing we needed to know was would there be a comparable map of the northern hemisphere written in stone.

'Simple.' Frank had stated bluntly. 'The next logical step would be to head north of Trowlesworthy Warren Tor.'

Rekha agreed. 'Sounds good to me.'

'What if we allow the mast of the Argo Navis to be our guide?' I had offered. I had a gut feeling on this.

'With you on that one dear boy.'

'What's the exact direction if you use the mast as a pointer.' Rekha had enquired.

The Ordinance Survey Map was up on the wall. Frank and I rooted around for a compass and tried to align the Argo with the very small features that were featured on it.

We matched the stone rows of the keel and the mast we knew it may have been skewed by moderate peat slippage over the years. It was on a north to south axis but a small adjustment for that slippage was allowed for.

It was decided there and then that we would fix my compass bearing to true north rather than magnetic north. When we oriented the compass with the magnetic north bearing, it took us to the top of the Tor itself, whilst true north had us a few degrees to the left on a north, north-westerly bearing.

The difference led to another discovery. The mast pointed up and over the Tor and landed us as I had already known it would, right on another stone row and circle known as Little Trowlesworthy Tor. This too was littered with ancient stones and rows and although it was some seventy feet shorter than its neighbour, it would prove to be of just as much importance to us as its bigger sister was.

As my colleague was to point out with her typical sarcastic wit.

'Surely you two are old enough to remember the latter part of its construction?'

She wasn't far wrong. I was at the end of my third decade in search of Chapter and the universal egg.

'Southern side of the Tor, southern hemisphere. Northern side of the Tor, northern hemisphere.' Frank had said. 'Let's hope that's how the design was originally created.'

Considering that thousands of years had passed since the rows, circles and basins had conceived they were still (to those with an eye for detail), quite distinctive.

Online arial maps gave a fair coverage of the area but it was decided that we needed a boots on the ground approach to this new acreage which we must consider worthy of investigation. Frank and I would go up there as soon as we could both spare the time and do some pencil sketches and try to map out the lay of the land. It would give us an opportunity to count or discount certain stones that may or may not have been originals.

That also gave us the chance to consider other stones that may hav e been uncovered due to weathering and therefore would be considered recent additions to the landscape and of no use in our calculations.

It was a good feeling to finish our video call on a high note, if only in the fact that it lifted our moral again. Was this further proof of a solid connection between the Heavens, Humanity, and Terrain?

Strange that I should use the word 'Terrain', derived of course from the Latin word for earth, Terra. I always liked the name Terra, more than Earth. In universal terms, coming from the earth, Earthling has a demeaning sound to it, whereas Terran, sounds altogether harder, perhaps more driven, and purposeful.

We said our goodbyes Frank, Rekha, and I that evening and went off to our everyday lives and our more down to earth responsibilities.

It was a strange life that the three of us led. Each with our own diverse rolls to play in the world, each with our own families growing up, coming together, or in some cases separating.

Work colleagues came and went, some promoted, some demoted, many moving sideways to other roles as hierarchies changed and business needs adapted to customer requirements.

We lost acquaintances. Some moved to other countries or cities. Some simply dropped out of our lives and of course others died.

It was the same with family. New life was created, older ones passed away. We all experienced loss and grief but I don't want to dwell on that. It is simply that the passage of time has its cruel way of sweeping all before it, like a river, sometimes meandering, allowing usa little grace and at other times it becomes a raging torrent hell bent on havoc and terrifying in its merciless rush to the ocean, an ocean that may swell to heaven or recede to oblivion.

Two months slipped away and we had a couple of chances to go up to Trowlesworthy Warren Tors, both Great and Little, which enabled us to get some pencil sketches done and also gave us some time to review what arial maps were available of the site at the time.

It was hard but rewarding work paying off as it did when we found it was possible to see the stars of the Northern Hemisphere mirrored in the stones on the ground. It wasn't information for sharing. We knew that it must be kept close and never revealed outside of the three of us and Anna at least until the day that the egg was found again and securely hidden.

In all probability she already would have known what we had just found out. It seemed that she always held a little something back, so I was never sure that we were getting either the whole or just part of the story.

We were all convinced that there was still more of a motive behind Chapter and her dealings with them than we would ever know.

Frank and I put up our drawings on a scale to match the blown up arial photographs we had at our disposal. We wanted to ensure that we were able to justify our findings, should we ever be asked to produce them. It was fulfilling to see how well the stones fitted in with the map of the northern constellations.

This time there were less than five anomalies to deal with and of those, two had obviously been the result of human action in the last couple of centuries. It may have been due to stones being moved to build a water leat that had been constructed around the side of the Tors in order to supply water to the clay quarries close by.

We had come along way this year but then two thousand and eight came and once again because of various personal issues the year came and went with little or no time being available to any of us to continue our research.

2009 came and went in the same way. It was seemingly impossible to get together that year. We made minor advancements. Rekha for

instance felt that she had linked the movement of the egg to the coast of India but she was still struggling to find the next stage of its journey on from that point.

The end of the year brought a series of personal setbacks to me in particular which carried on into 2010. Serious health problems, mostly unexpected hit all three of us at the more or less the same time causing considerable disruption to our working and social lives.

It was a bad year. We all lost family members. For two of us, very close family members.

It's fair to say that the entire year was lost and I think that we all prayed for a better year to come in 2011we could only hope. Now that year had arrived.

If nothing else then at least we had decided on the next step from Little Trowlesworthy Tor. It seemed like logic to take our queue from the stars once again. This time we used our Ordinance Survey map first in order to reduce the time it took.

We used the coded message found in Grandads book, *The Complete Works of William Shakespeare*. We read again the lines slowly, carefully, discounting the first few as we felt that we understood the references to those in the first paragraph. The second might be of help. It was a simple gut feeling again but in the last few years they had been of immense help. We put the verse up on the wall and Frank read out loud,

'Now I will search impossible places with an invisible subtle stealth.'

Surely there was a clue in that line. Ok, impossible places must mean those places to which man had limited access. They couldn't be impossible in the strictest sense. If that was the case then what would be the point of hiding it. It might be found by technological advances in later years and therefore it would be back in a place of even greater danger. Chapter's agent and Layman accomplice would never risk that happening.

No, it had to be somewhere made to the outside eye to be impossible to find but in actuality could be found by sticking to the clues. We thought that the words, 'with invisible stealth,' might be the next clue.

The first paragraph made perfect sense now that we knew what we knew. For instance, *'I will fight their legions to defend the secret of the Goddess Queen of Heaven and creator of the two universes, which host twinkling stars, celestial suns and moons like silver bows to behold.'*

This possibly meant that the fight might not be that of a physical fight against a known enemy, but rather of a constant fight against the legions of humans who now inhabited the planet and might destroy the egg by accident and by those actions kill billions of others in this miniscule universe, a place which was as sacred and beautiful to those inhabitants as ours was to us.

We knew that all the activity over the past two hundred years had been in and around Dartmoor. Therefore, we had no reason to believe that the artefact or universal egg was that far from us.

Our problem was that Dartmoor covered an area of three hundred and sixty eight square miles. Most of that was rugged moorland and boulders. The artefact could be almost anywhere within those boundaries as nowhere was further that a more than an hour and a half drive at a modest speed.

'*Invisible stealth*'. The words resonated. After all hadn't the Greek hero Perseus used a cloak of invisibility in order to attack and behead the gorgon Medusa, and wasn't Perseus one of the great constellations of the northern hemisphere? In addition to those facts Perseus (the constellation), was directly opposite Draco. Was that a clue in itself.

We counted the stars in the constellation. There were nineteen but when it was originally devised by Ptolemy, there were seventeen. Now the number seventeen hadn't come to light for a while but we knew that the constellation Draco had seventeen stars as witnessed by the badge and of course the fact that there were seventeen tors in relation to those stars on the paper we had found, which then had consequently related to the pattern of those stars.

It was now a matter of continuing as we had begun. We went back and checked over all those stone rows and circles in the area we had now chosen to investigate. Unsurprisingly they numbered seventeen. It of course had seemed sensible to look at the constellation pattern in the stones. They showed Draco and Perseus as was to be expected in such a detailed formation but gave us no clue as to where to go next.

Frustration dimmed our senses and for a short time led us to some crazy conclusions based not on evidence but on hope. The expression 'tugging at straws' came to mind. We really needed three heads instead of one but Rekha was too busy with four daughters and full time very important job role, to spare us anymore time.

Frank and I had to work this one out for ourselves. We stopped daydreaming, lay our frustrations to one side, and took the next logical step and that step led us to cross the river Plym, or the Cad as it was at that point, just about two miles upstream from Cadover Bridge, my birthplace, only becoming the Plym when it meets the river Meavy at Shaugh Bridge some four miles downstream.

From Trowlesworthy Tors we looked across the river for the next stone circle and came to Legis Tor. This was another ancient settlement area to the north, with over fifty visible hut foundations a stone row and a circle.

There were many stones which may have been moved due to tin mining activity but in general it was a likely pointer and that pointer was once again towards the northwest and another stone circle on the southern end of Ringmoor Down and it bordered my cousins farm at Brisworthy. It has twenty four stones but was believed to have thirty four originally.

Brisworthy is just a thirty minute walk from Legis Tor and in both are in full view of each other.

Three hundred metres from the circle at its northwestern end and connected one to the other by a stone row is a small cairn circle of seventeen stones in all known as Ringmoor Circle and Row. It makes a marvellous pointer out over the hill to the next monument, Sheepstor, Skytelestor (Sky at a distance Tor), as it was known many hundreds of years earlier. Almost smack in the middle of the dragons breath. Directly under Draco.

Chapter 14.

A Tomb in Hyderabad.

Despite her ongoing commitments to work and family, Rekha had in the little spare time she had, cracked on with her search for the time the artefact had remained lost during the late Georgian and early part of the Victorian era.

As her parents had come from India to England it was not unusual that she should have a deep interest in her roots on the sub-continent.

Years before she had gone to India for the best part of a year to immerse herself in the culture and customs of her parents and grandparents. Therefore, she had the unique experience of what I think is best described as exploring the country but with an inbuilt feeling of what that country represented to those who lived there and those who had chosen to leave for reasons of their own.

She rang me one night out of the blue. It was late but I knew that she was excited and wanted to share some information with us urgently.

I rang Frank, waking him to join in a conference call.

'I found something that I think maybe of real importance to us.'

We waited and Rekha began her story.

She began her story from where she had left off when she had discovered the Indian connection. She had given us a brief, very telling reminder of what she had found before from the pen of the Indian author who had written of a secret society called 'The Nine Unknown Men.' She repeated to us the last line of his composition.

'*These Nine, with the power of celestial heaven to physically move the universe. Now what secret will they reveal to mankind?*'

She was on a roll. What had been uppermost in her mind was the thought that in British India at the time this man had committed his words to paper. Surely there were men of honour who were able to put themselves above political or social norms of the day and to be aware of the need for mankind to rise above these injustices and see for themselves that the colour of a person's skin, their gender, their religion, or in other cases their perceived ignorance did not make them unworthy of being on an equal footing when matters universal importance were at stake.

'What if these Nine were made up not just of native Indian men or women but of British people as well?' she asked. 'after all, it was obvious that Chapter trusted and used people from all countries and creeds and all walks of life in order to protect the egg.'

We understood that she had been trying to follow the thread to find where the artefact had been during its time in India. It had come to light again in stories that were passed from generation to generation until it was noted in written form, in all probability by an associate of Chapter.

From what we knew of the society, they left almost nothing of consequence that had given any clue to their existence. This was very much the exception which proved the rule. Keep no records, let as few people as possible know of your existence and practise the most extreme caution when choosing who you entrust with such an important secret.

These Nine Unknown Men formed as a society by the Emperor Ashoka some two thousand years ago worked rather in the way that Chapter did. They were limited in number for the purpose of security and were self-perpetuating in the fact that each member choose his or her successor and of course that person in turn choose his or her layman or woman. They each held an expertise in their own field such as Alchemy, Communication, Cosmogony, Gravity, Light, Microbiology, Physiology, Propaganda and Sociology.

It was still necessary though to consider the fact that very little was known about secret societies. By their very nature a reasonable assumption would be that the most successful of these remain totally unknown and may remain so for ever.

There is however good evidential fact to support the existence of some of these societies or organizations.

It must therefore follow that given the importance of the artefact to mankind, that the information may have been shared by Chapter with this society. The power and influence they would have wielded in India, and perhaps still do would have meant added security for the egg.

In all likelihood at least one of the members of the Nine Unknown Men would have been in league with a member of Chapter and that was not an unreasonable assumption to make.

Rekha had traced the artefact as far as the south coast of India, to the state of West Bengal. More precisely to a town by the name of Bandel on the Hooghly River. She had also delved deep into India's past and thought that the words used in the book she had mentioned to us before, was not by that books author.

The words, *'These Nine, with the power of celestial heaven to physically move the universe. Now what secret will they reveal to mankind?'*, had Rekha felt the tone and feel of another Indian author and Urdu poet, a lady by the name of Mah Laqa Bai, who lived between 1768 and 1854. She believed that the phrasing had a Persian quality.

Persia of course was where the egg had been hidden last, and Mah Laqa Bai wrote in what became known as Persianized Urdu, her name Mah Laqa means moon faced in Persian.

Mah Laqa Bai was a courtesan, archer, and spear or javelin thrower and most importantly a champion of women's education. A strong formidable woman both mentally and physically who accompanied her lover, the Nizam of Hyderabad in three major battles. A philanthropist and accomplished in many fields, a woman such as this would without doubt have attracted the attention of Chapter, and there was more evidence to suggest that she was one of the Nine Unknown Men.

It may seem odd but in a male dominated society, the name itself may have been used in order to distract attention. It seemed likely that at least two or three of the nine were women. In the year 1798 she became the first woman to publish her own poems.

She wrote of love and loss, of heaven and of life hanging by a thread. All possible references to the lost egg of heaven and the danger it was in and referred to Saqi, a wine bearer but also a term for a God.

At around that time, she presented a copy of her book to a British Army Officer Captain Sir John Malcolm who was sometime Governor of Bombay. Was there a possible connection to his involvement in Chapter? No, that thread had taken a different path but one that would ultimately be of even greater interest to us.

Allusions to the constellation Draco was mentioned again in 1825, just a year after Mah Laqa Bai's death, in relation to the work carried out on her tomb.

It also appeared that in the last years of her life she had chosen a successor to carry on her secret work but one that was not on our radar or it seems anyone else's for that matter.

At present all Rekha knew was that this successor was female, a few years younger than Bai, that she was of British stock and lived in India from around the year eighteen hundred. They had moved in similar circles and Bai had even presided over gatherings at the British Residency. Mention had been made of their acquaintance or rather that Bai had visited a certain lady in West Bengal and as was customary then, stayed for an extended period of time.

Bai's tomb in Hyderabad was spectacular in many respects yet simplistic in others. It made a splendid resting place for the Lady and one additional feature of the tomb was that it had two wells. One of those might at some time, it was reasoned have been used to conceal the egg.

The building was a mausoleum with a tomb inside it. Originally it was said there were seventeen twin pillars supporting the main canopy and plaster decorations that mirrored an area of the sky in which Draco was the dominant constellation.

As with a plethora of older buildings worldwide it had fallen into disrepair over the last two centuries and it was only in twenty ten, that it had been renovated with a grant from the American Government.

It was very difficult to get information on what had been a part of the structure and what may have been replaced by authentic replication or maybe by considered guesswork. The last bit of the renovation was still in progress even as Rekha was telling us of her find a year later.

If the Draco link could be proved then it must be too much of a coincidence to think it could be anything other than a true affirmation as to the importance of the constellation, its seventeen stars and the link with Chapter and the Nine Unknown Men. Draco can be seen from India and as a matter of interest, a rare species of flying lizard is named after it.

All that was needed was some solid evidence, which would lead her to find out the identity of this mysterious woman. If given more time, Rekha was sure that she could discover who the mysterious woman was. That in itself might go a long way to solving the puzzle of the missing years.

Thank God, we all agreed, that it was the latter end of the Georgian era. The British administration in India, like it or not at least kept detailed documents and the colonial love of writing home would in all likelihood ensure that mention was made somewhere of the friendship between the talented India poet and her erstwhile trusted companion.

It would be a hard slog to find what was basically a needle in a haystack. There must have been thousands of letters in archives and museums that would need to be examined, even then it would be serendipity if Rekha came across a correspondence that was able to corroborate what she had already discovered.

To find the truth in a million words was asking the impossible. There needed to be some way to limit the amount of written communiques and bring that figure down to a more manageable number. Frank thought that she might use a process of elimination that was as imaginative as it was logical.

'Was it not more likely,' He had asked, that a military connection was quite possibly the best point from which to start?

Indeed, it seemed an eminently sensible place to from which she might start.

'You might also want to cross reference that with the British East India Company. Chances are that they had their sticky fingers in this business as well. Even if only from the point of view of arranging safe transport for the egg and its escort.'

'I will certainly use those two institutions to focus on.' Rekha had said.

I had added my tuppence worth. 'Maybe you could also look for mention of rogue individuals, by which I mean anyone pushing the boundaries of the conventions of the time.'

'I have an idea.' She said.

Chapter 15

Pilgrims of the night sky.

2012 slid in. Leaving Rekha to continue her new line of research as and when she was able.

Frank and I set about making sense of the next step in our sojourn across the moors. One clue at a time we had pieced our way across the tors. Now we would pause and revisit the clues we had found so far and try to figure out what they meant with relation to Anna, Chapter, to the Universal Egg and why the ancient people of Dartmoor were so taken with the stars.

Maybe the problem had always been the thought that in the past, people were ignorant, that they believed only in immortals that they could not see. It was as if we believed that everything that they didn't understand frightened them. In our ignorance of their lives is it the fact we have misunderstood them completely.

We see things now with the benefit of tens of thousands of years of hindsight but with no or at least little written evidence and yet we still guess at many of the reasons behind such things as the cave paintings which depict, in some cases, strange creatures which we think represent Gods. However, we have no proof of that.

What if those creatures are not representative of Gods but of alien beings, visitors from other world, some benevolent, some aggressive, if so are those paintings are a mixed palette of joy, and trepidation?

Might it be that we are doing a misjustice to those ancestors who may have had more knowledge and understanding of the universe that we have now? Not in scientific or spiritual terms but in real terms as in, did they have real interactions with beings from other worlds?

We still try to put modern thought into ancient structure and religion. We use the language of recent centuries when describing the past and it is perhaps an insult when all we are doing in general is guessing at the reason that things were constructed as they were and their use afterwards.

The Sumerian Language is the first recorded around three thousand BC and Hieroglyphs were being used in Egypt.

Over the next five hundred years Stonehenge was built, New Grange was being constructed in Ireland and the Great Pyramid of Giza was completed.

In China the potter's wheel was invented and perhaps not entirely coincidently the first pottery in the America's was being produced in Ecuador. Rock engravings were carved in what is now Australia and in Mesopotamia the Shekel was introduced as coinage. This was the period known in simplistic terms in the present day as the Early Bronze Age, as the name suggests man had turned from using flint to bronze for the construction of tools and weapons.

We considered the fact that this was a period of massive change for mankind. A written language had been formed, immense buildings were being erected, clay was being cast into usable pots or bowls, stone had given way to metal and money was introduced in the form of coinage with value used against weight. Was it just luck that all this happened in such a relatively short time frame or was it a helping hand from elsewhere at work?

It was certainly worth delving into especially as we now had a connection to the stone circles and the constellations.

We also had to consider how people living in the Bronze Age could replicate so faithfully in stone, stars in the south pole. Yes some were visible at certain times of the year from certain areas in the northern hemisphere but not constellations at the south celestial pole in the constellation Octans.

Octans means as previously stated the eighth part of a circle but was named after a navigational instrument replaced by the sextant a century later of that name.

Once again when we considered this and it brought to mind the Dogon Tribe of Mali. These fascinating people knew for example that the brightest star in the sky, Sirius A had two companion stars, at the time the Dogon had no optical instruments such as telescopes to aid them. Was it just guess work? It was also said that they knew of the moons of Jupiter and the rings of Saturn both invisible to the naked eye.

Taking a balanced point of view, the Dogon believed that Saturn was the furthest planet from the sun. Then again they stated that a dwarf star orbited Sirius and that was only proved correct in nineteen ninety five when gravitational studies supported the theory of a brown dwarf star in orbit.

Thousands of years before the Dogon, there were the Egyptians with their magnificent pyramids, a true testament to the heavens for sure, as was the sphinx, so beautifully crafted to match the constellation of Leo.

The Mayan with their step pyramids and the brilliance in the way they built the great temple at Chichen Itza to the gods and how they were able to show a shadow of the winged serpent god Kukulan, known later by the Aztecs as Quetzalcoatl moving down the pyramid from heaven to earth.

For us the task was to follow the clues and so we had made the leap from Brisworthy circle and row up the hill to Ringmoor circle and row. The row is single but odd parts are double.

Many of the old stones had been moved to support walls for farmers in centuries past and some of it had been rebuilt in the early twentieth century.

There were many missing stones from the circle which formed the cairn and the restoration project of 1909 noted that only one stone remained standing, four had fallen over and only holes remained where another six had stood.

The stone row was a quarter of a mile in length, leading up a gentle slope to the top of the hill crest. The row ended in a terminal stone a metre in height and a quick glance indicated that it pointed straight across the deep valley towards Sheepstor. The old Roman saying 'All roads lead to Rome was never more pertinent.

We knew already from thirty years of research that Draco hung over the Tor at certain times of night, depending on where the earth was positioned at that moment. Its mouth agape as if it would wind its sinuous way earthwards and swallow the Tor and village in one gulp.Truly Sheepstor with its tiny village nestled beneath was in the path of the dragons fiery breath. In mortal danger of being devoured. This was where the Draco, the great Serpent who we believed to be Ophion left heaven for earth.

We had a few clues now that pointed us in this direction and as yet more to find, of that we were sure. Perhaps in our quest to find and help protect the secret of the Goddess we had become more like pilgrims.

The Fates had been kind and despite obstacles in our path, the ladies still pointed us toward success in our ultimate goal. Having some time ago visited the Piskies Cave and found that it was eminently unsuitable as a hiding place for the artefact we had to find the reason that everything pointed to Sheepstor, either the Tor itself or the village as a hiding place.

Now we concentrated on an area known as Yellowmead Down on which Sheepstor Stone circle is set.

Years of neglect had caused stones to be removed to form marker posts or part of 'Newtake land', this was land seized by landowners or farmers as a part of taking grazing land back from the moors. For many years all that was visible was a few scattered stones which were noted and then drawn by various walkers, artists and authors.

At some time in the early nineteenth twentieth century swaling the burning off gorse to encourage the growth of grass and open up more foraging for sheep, had revealed many more stones than had been noted originally.

Something in the order of a hundred and fifty more. They formed concentric circles, the inner circle being twenty two feet in diameter and containing twenty two stones.

The next has a diameter of thirty two feet and contains thirty two stones and the third row forty two feet in diameter with forty two stones.

The diameter of the fourth is fifty two feet with fifty two stones in the circle whilst the fifth row was sixty two feet across with sixty two stones. Also noted was the addition of a possible sixth stone row.

Frank and I went to see for ourselves. The stones were many but there were also a few holes where there had been more standing stones originally.

We dug for around four hours. There was indeed a sixth row and we made it seventy two feet across with seventy two stones in it. We had also discovered seven stones all recumbent, pointing towards Sheepstor and all of which were seven in the form of an arrowhead. A total of two hundred and eighty nine stones standing and lying down in all and coincidently two hundred and eighty nine happens to be seventeen times seventeen!

We walked on in the direction indicated by the arrow and headed towards Sheepstor itself. We walked half a mile or so and then hit tarmac road. From there an expanse of fields led on down the hill and we had no intention of walking across the fields of farmers we had known for years without their permission. It would be enough to come back another day and walk on around the east of the field boundaries to Sheepstor itself.

First though we decided to visit the circle by night, if for no other reason than to get a feeling for the area and what it meant to our ancestors, the people who had built it.

Return we did in early September of that year. Darkness came a little earlier and as such would give us longer on site time, whilst still enabling us to get back to our respective beds by midnight. What struck us was the lack of light pollution looking north. To the southwest Plymouth blazed away in the distance and several degrees of sky were lost in an amber haze.

It always puzzled me why so few cities and towns didn't use reflective caps to streetlights. In places where they were used the local council lighting bills had been greatly reduced. They were able to use less powerful bulbs and still get a greater footprint on the street.

The best nights to choose were either moonless or with the moon not yet risen. We had picked a good night. It was still warm as the nights at the end of summer are, even then an edgy breeze still whipped over Yellowmead Down as we stood gazing at Sheepstor in the distance.The sky was awash with stars and ponies, cattle and sheep grazed unconcerned at our approach, moving only when we were almost upon them.

The sky reminded me of Vincent Van Gogh's 'Starry Night'. Aircraft could be seen crisscrossing the sky with their identification lights winking. Every so often a satellite could be seen passing miles over our heads and even the international space station was visible every hour and a half or so.

At about ten thirty we were treated to a meteorite burning up in the earth's atmosphere as it streaked by, a mass of superheated rock before it disintegrated to atoms of dust or perhaps bury a tiny part of itself in the ground.

I wondered if by chance the elusive Anna would arrive out of nowhere and introduce herself to Frank but it wasn't to be. It was an uneventful evening as it turned out, only saved by Draco holding a commanding position over the top of the Tor for a while until earth rotated a little more and Draco moved further east.

The time it had spent over Sheepstor though gave us a fair idea of the impact it must have had on those who had gone before. We could also understand why Chapter had used it as a marker. It looked spectacular once you got your eyes accustomed to the night and picked the constellation out. It doesn't have the brightest stars in it and is not as obvious or well known as Ursa Major or Orion, but it still made a fine sight to the observer.

It was always a source of fascination to wonder how the stars would look from a different viewpoint say a thousand light years from earth, where the perspective would be totally different and we would be looking at an unfamiliar sky. Patterns of stars so intimate to us for so many thousands of years coalesced into shapes that would no longer make sense to us, only recognisable to alien eyes who would find the same problem if they were to view the sky at night from earth.

At times during that evening, it was still possible to spot the odd light that had no tell-tale signs of being an aircraft or a satellite. Nor did they conform to any astronomical phenomena we knew of. One of them moved in a random pattern flitting, for want of a better word, over a large area of sky apparently at very high speed.

We were aware of the fact that all the stone rows and stone circles from Trowlesworthy Warren to Sheepstor were visible from the six ring circle on Yellowmead down.

'It looks not unlike the taxi way for aircraft on an airport runaway.' I said casually.

Frank nodded. 'Very much so.'

'You don't think.....' I had ventured and then fallen silent as my mind tried to catch up with my mouth.

'It bears serious consideration.'

We decided to call Rekha, who was not best pleased at being woken in the late evening, especially as she valued her sleep, probably more than our friendship.

'Have you two lost the plot?' She said with unconcealed sarcasm.

'That's likely.' I had replied.

There was a long pause. 'It's possible I suppose.' She grudgingly conceded.

'In the most basic form.' Frank had stated.

Rekha mused for a time. 'I suppose if the people who erected the stones wanted to mark a path to the Tor it would make sense.'

My gut told me that it would be best seen from an arial perspective, so I shared that with my colleagues.

'What if it was only supposed to be seen from the air?'

'Preposterous.'

But was it. We debated for some time and decided that the idea had merit, although each stone row and circle would require looking into in much greater depth.

Phone call over, Frank and I made some notes by the dim red light of his torch. We used red light which is commonly used in night time applications as it allows one to see, but it is gentle on the eye and the surroundings.

We needed to go to Sheepstor itself as soon as we had more time having researched all its aspects from a historical point of view and overlay it with some reasonable hypothesis, not of our own but rather from independent sources. What we would discover and would it make us more conscious of what Anna's role in the story was.

'At what height,' I thought would an aircraft pilot spot these features?

Chapter 16.

Stranger than Fiction.

We were already free falling into the year 2013 with an unerring rush and as it progressed the world around me was about to fall apart.

The decline started with the Ides of March. A very good friend and neighbour died with little warning. Then a month later another friend died. Late spring arrived and my wife fell ill, with a virus. It caused complications and after only four days and whilst at home with me, she too passed away in the first week of June with little warning after thirty years of marriage.

As dire a shock as it was to myself and my family, I continued working as the need for the stability of my job and the support of colleagues there, kept me on the straight and narrow. I drank heavily and had a very occasional pipeful of tobacco.

The evenings were a torment, going back to my house but no longer my home. My two German shepherds bewildered as to where their mum had gone. It was the love of my stepsons and family that kept me afloat.

Always at the end of the phone or visiting to ensure I was functioning correctly. Frank and Wendy also played a major role in holding onto my sanity. Rekha kept in touch and with a time the unthinkable became normality. The funeral had taken place of course but within six weeks of my wife's death her best friend died. A month later one of my aunt's passed. Two months passed and a friends husband died, then one of our colleagues at work, just a few days before Christmas.

Not long into 2014 another colleague passed. In all, I attended seven out of nine funerals within a space of ten of months. I missed two, I felt bad but I simply could not face anymore grief.

Yet life still went on and I buckled down resolutely to get my life back on track and to give my support to my sons and their families.

It wasn't just a bad time for me over that period. Both Rekha and Frank lost members of their family. I won't discuss their losses in detail, as they were matters personal to themselves but as a group we lost the best part of nearly eighteen months from a research point of view. It was tough on all of us. We fervently hoped for a better end to the year. For me it was good.

I met the lady who would be my future wife and moved on as best I could. I share this, not for sympathy but as an explanation of why life often gets in the way of the very best of intentions.

2015 saw us all back on the trail once again. This time with a vengeance. A renewed burst of energy came to our assistance.

Frank and I visited an area called the Giants Basin very close to Sheepstor, or as we often referred to it, Skytelestor. It was a bit of a hike but well worth the climb. The area has been well mapped and researched over the years and noted by many walkers. A friend of mine author W.D Lethbridge took some excellent photos of the area for one of his books and they aided us greatly.

Our own experience of the area was one of curiosity and intrigue. Lying very close to another stone row called Drizzlecombe noted as being a cairn (variously known around the world, as marker stones, food stores, or a chiefs burial mound), Giants Basin was an impressive sight lending some credence to the idea that a large population had once lived on the surrounding land.

At Drizzlecombe itself, the remains of some roundhouses and three stone rows made an interesting site. Each of the rows has a barrow (burial mound) associated with it and a terminal stone or Menhir a (very tall standing stone the use of which is uncertain).

The largest Menhir at Drizzlecombe is fourteen feet high but may have been as high as seventeen feet. It was re-erected by the author and

Preacher Sabine Baring-Gould and author R. Hansford-Worth in the year 1893, so there was no way of knowing its true depth under the ground when it was originally erected.

We felt that the stone was yet another marker to lead the viewer towards Sheepstor. We also saw what we knew were some of a series of large depressions, historically noted as ditches. These very obvious areas, although looking old also had appeared as though they may have been compressed by more recent activity. What sort of activity we were unsure but some ideas came to us on the spur of the moment, having read many accounts of similar markings in other places around the world.

By more recent, we meant that we were thinking in the last fifty years or less. The depressions were grouped in a pattern of seven oblongs, each one four yards long by a yard and a half wide. They formed a tear drop shape. The two sets closest to the tor were deeper because of the peat depth nearer to the Tor. A single at the rear of the grouping followed. Another set of two was about fifty yards opposite the first two, then two spaced apart at the front to form a perfect teardrop.

Knowing what we suspected and being able to prove it as fact were two different things entirely. We climbed the tor and took some photos. Being roughly a hundred and twenty feet above the circle, row and depressions gave a fabulous view of the area in which we were about to base our theory.

All looked very promising indeed. If we could get more solid fact, the theory might become a reality. It was turning out to be a good year for us, especially after the dismal two years, which had preceded it.

It was also good to see that the circle formed by the large depressions, was fairly clear of scree. It was as if the area had been purposefully cleared. That might have been true as the warreners in the area often took cartloads of stones to make artificial burrows for the rabbits they farmed.

Rabbit was and is a good source of protein. It has almost no fat and because of the animals' fecundity in breeding habits, this meat source was plentiful. They cost nothing to keep because they lived of the grass and vegetation on the moors and in the dire years of world wars one and two, were a reasonably cheap and plentiful addition to the nations diet. We thought that the stones had been cleared for another reason, a more outlandish one but reluctantly, we could not prove that the stones were moved for any other purpose.

It was disappointing but we had to stick to the facts. On the rare occasion we could not make a factual link from one step to the next so we gathered the most credible information possible with which to progress.

This part of the investigation (the prehistoric era) was always going to prove difficult to assimilate. It was always going to be easy to integrate into theory but less so into evidence.

The truth was that even some historians and scientists did not know for a fact, why these wonderful megaliths had been constructed. Of course, there was a body of knowledge which pointed toward a reasoned theory, but theory it was in many cases and we had to ask, why wasn't our theory as good as anyone else's?

We decided to wait until the body of circumstantial evidence outweighed reasonable doubt. If that practise was good enough for the law courts of England on which to base a person's guilt or their innocence, then it was good enough for us to use in a less important situation.

Continuing our look back over the moors from our current position, we could clearly see the areas we had previously explored, all from this one place. It was thrilling. Each stone row led to a circle, with, unless it had been moved or knocked down a menhir, a giant single stone pointing from one megalith to another, across the moors for many miles and I remember how we had nodded in satisfaction to each other that day.

With our theory surrounding the area known as The Giants Pillow so firmly planted in our minds, we could rest just a little easier. We would discuss it with Rekha at a later date, when she was less preoccupied with her own part of the puzzle, the connection between the talented Indian poetess Mah Laqa Bai and a British lady who as yet remained stubbornly elusive.

132

Incredibly this ladies identity was about to be revealed. It was to prove as important a step forward as any we had made in the last thirty odd years.

Back at home base as Franks garage had now become affectionately known we put up our newly acquired information on the wall. It seemed appropriate once again to take a closer look at Sheepstor, both the Tor, the village, and the surrounding area.

The Tor itself was impressive as the whole hill of which it is a part is not unlike a massive pair of shoulders. It dominates the landscape close by. Around it scree litters its sides and it's a wonder that what are now farmer's fields would once have been filled with rocks, all of which of course had to be moved at one time or another. It must have taken some time to complete such a monumental task.

Also in need of consideration was the fact that a lot of tin had been mined on Dartmoor and in and around Sheepstor. This in turn meant that there were areas where the artefact could have been stored for safe keeping. What better than a disused and deserted mine shaft, whether vertical or diagonal.

There were many opencast mines as well, although as the name and nature suggests an opencast mine was not a great place to hide a precious object. It was however one more place that would warrant looking at.

I knew that many such areas around the Tors were rich in tin. The industry was known to have existed in pre- roman times. Working for tin had existed up until and including the period of the second world war. We thought it would be odd if such apparently suitable hiding places had not been at least considered over the centuries.

In the twelfth century, mining for tin was so important that tinners set up their own laws to control the production, sale and price of tin. These were known as Stannary Laws and were instituted into the English legal system, remaining as some of the most original and oldest laws of the land.

The word Stannary was derived from the Latin word for tin, Stannum and a stannary court or parliament was set up on Crockern Tor on Dartmoor. The main area of the Tor itself is called Parliament Rock from where proceedings were held and questions were asked from what is known as the floor of the 'Great Court' below.

The stannary of Tavistock dealt with the West Devon area in the time of King Edward the First in around the year thirteen hundred and five. There were also courts at Chagford and Ashburton, with another being added later at Plympton. It was not until eighteen thirty six, that these courts were abolished. That is surely a measure of how important tin was in the industry of the moor over all those centuries.

It was then that I found this nugget of information. It was a revelation and for further reference, it will be dealt with more fully in our next book. For hundreds of years a motif has been noted in places as far apart as Devon and Japan. It occurs in churches of the middle-east and in scrolls and carvings of the far east and has for years been a source of fascination to those who may be interested in it.

In the West of England, it is seen carved into rocks on Dartmoor, into church pews, ceiling bosses or stonework.

Some seventeen churches in Devonshire have these bosses in them, yes seventeen again and a particularly beautiful example can be spotted in the church of St Pancras in the tiny moorland village of Widdecombe-in-the-Moor.

St Pancras Church is known as the cathedral of the moors. Built in late gothic style, it has a large number of ceiling or roof bosses. One of these was the very one that was on my mind. The Tinner's Hare's.

These three hares chase each other in a never ending circle. Once again the reason for this symbol remains unknown and can only be guessed at. It has been proposed that the hares represent fertility and the circle in which they chase each other is representative of the moon or at least the lunar cycle.

In truth that is probably correct but it also links a heavenly body, The Moon, to Terra itself. Not only that but the fact that a southern celestial constellation is named Lepus, (Hare). It is chased eternally across the sky by Orion's hunting hound, Canis Minor, (The Little Dog). Odd we thought that this should be a worldwide symbol. The Tinners

134

Hare's were turning up in the most unexpected places and times throughout history more curious still was the fact that it seemed to follow the known course of the Universal Egg's journey around the world.

Was this the missing key that we had been seeking for so long? In mythology the hare moves between heaven and earth and so we felt that the link was certainly worthy of further investigation. We were thrilled. Now we would take a little time to find if the direction of travel of the artefact, matched up with that of the Tinners Hares.

Our minds turned back quickly to the tin mines of Dartmoor and as we did so one special place came to mind. That place was the Golden Dagger Tin Mine. It was located quite near to the Warren House Inn, where you will remember I had my first meeting with Anna.

The Golden Dagger Tin Mine was believed to have been in operation from the turn of the nineteenth century. Cassiterite is the name of the ore from which tin is extracted. We were interested in the name of the mine itself. It was long believed to have been named after a gold and amber dagger found there in the eighteen fifties, but we believed that its origins went back much further and that its original name was lost in antiquity.

Now we felt that we had found it. The copy of a page from a twelve hundred century old monks manuscript had been given to us by a former student, of the Camborne School of Mines, years before when our investigation was in its infancy and we were asking about mines in the area, by a very roundabout route and of course making no mention of the artefact. The college is the world's foremost body for training miners and quarrymen so we knew that the source was genuine.

In the monks manuscript a reference was made to a tin mine right where the Golden Dagger Mine existed until just after the end of World War Two.

The monk had lived at Tavistock Abbey a religious house dating back to the year nine hundred and fifty six AD. It was possible that the land on which the mine operated had been at one time owned by the Benedictine abbey during the reign of King Eadwig, an Anglo Saxon regent. In this manuscript, the mine was not referred to before as the Golden Dagger Mine, it was called the Golden Dragon Mine.

This must be more than just coincidence as the mine was also under the gaping maw of the constellation of Draco. It was not only dedicated record keeping but also a good deal of luck that we had remembered the manuscript at this point in time, buried as it was under file upon file and hundreds of pages of information we had deemed relevant at the time and had therefore kept.

Some further inquiries had led us to the fact that two of the shafts at this mine extended four hundred feet below ground. It would have been an excellent place to secrete an object that needed to remain as far from the general populace as possible and it was not far from the Warren House Inn. Every clue pointed to this being the hiding place of the Universal Egg. We were on the correct path this time and we had little doubt about it.

There was one more clue to follow as it had so recently come to our attention, and that was the seventeen churches with the Tinners Hare bosses in their ceilings. that would be our next step.

Chapter 17.

Churches and Tinners Hares.

We began by picking out the seventeen churches with those Tinners Hares bosses in them. It was likely that we would have to visit all of them or at least those less well documented.

We started with a little village right on the edge of Dartmoor called Ashreigney. The church here was St James. The greater part of the church was built in the fifteenth century but the oldest part may have been constructed two hundred years before. A roof boss in the form of the Tinners Hares can be found here of course. This is the most northerly of the seventeen churches

From there we looked a few miles to the south and to the quiet village of Iddesleigh. Strangely that brought up yet another coincidence. The name origin of the name Iddesleigh is derived from the old English or Anglo- Saxon name Eadwig. You may remember King Eadwig from the previous chapter of this book. A second, St James church has two roof bosses in the Hare design.

A few miles south again and we were looking at the village of Sampford Courtenay. At this church, St Andrew's the Hares boss is known as 'The Hunt of Venus'.

Although the church was rebuilt in around the year fourteen hundred and fifty during the end of the Hundred Years War, it has a font dating back to circa eleven hundred and fifty.

What is not so well known is that the three Hares were often used to represent the Holy Trinity. Strange we thought how pagan symbols have many uses.

Diverting to the southeast and next on our list was the village of Spreyton and the church of St Michaels. This is another fifteenth century building with extensive views over Dartmoor, built as it was at seven hundred and thirty five feet above sea level. Many fine roof bosses including the Green Man and Tinners Hare's are carved in wood on the ceiling and many a well-worn stone engraving is evident both inside and outside the building.

Our next move was to the southwest and brought us to South Tawton in which stands (another), St Andrews Church. The ninth boss in this roof has the Hares again carved in wood. Church baptisms began in fifteen forty eight so the construction would have begun some years before.

A traverse eastward took us to Cheriton Bishop and the parish church of St Mary's. This church originated in the thirteenth century with a tower added in later centuries. Roof bosses of the Hares are evident. This village is on the norther border of Dartmoor National Park and has its roots deep in Anglo Saxon history.

East once again and this time to the village of Newton St Cyres, which led us to the church of St Cyr and Julitta. The dedication is to Saint Julitta and her son St Cyr, both of whom were said believed to have been martyrs in the third or fourth century AD, a fact that neither one of us were aware of.

It made for an interesting pause whilst we examined the legend in a little more detail. It seems that Julitta had offended a Roman magistrate. He decided that her punishment should be to watch her son put to death before she too was executed. Built in the twelfth century, the roof bosses include the Tinners Hares.

The final move to the east was to the village of Broadclyst and the thirteenth century church of St John the Baptist which is notable for its sixteenth century tower. A very beautiful church in all and of course it is blessed with the Tinners Hares. It is a well-constructed church and has a highly decorated sedilia with the effigy of a knight in armour and there are many carved heads and figures of angels carrying shields.

Throwleigh was next on the agenda and the church of St Mary the Virgin which was built in the thirteenth century and was first recorded in the year twelve sixty eight. The Tinners Hares on these roof bosses are accompanied by the Green

Man, another notable and well recognised ancient pagan symbol. Usually in some form of stone relief.

West then to Bridford and the church of St Thomas A' Becket. Hidden deep in the Teign valley high on the side of a hill, this church has some of the best artwork of any religious house in Devon. Locally quarried Volcanic stone was used in the construction of its windows rather than the traditional granite used in other Dartmoor churches as it was easier to carve. The fourteenth century chancel and sixteenth century rood screen gave it an air of magnificence. On the ceiling, the Tinners Hares.

The church of St Michael the Archangel was next, another nice example of a fifteenth century Anglican church. Its doors opened in fourteen hundred and eighty two. Roof bosses included once again the Tinners Hare's and the Green Man in the village of Chagford.

North Bovey church was consecrated for St John the Baptist. A vicar was recorded as being in place at the church in the year twelve hundred and seventy nine. The Tinners Hares here are often referred to as rabbits and linked to the Holy Trinity.

Widecombe-in-the-Moor is the proud home of St Pancras church, with its one hundred and twenty foot high tower, is regularly referred to as the 'Cathedral of the Moor'. Built in a late gothic style known as 'Perpendicular' in the thirteen hundreds and was extended over the next two centuries. It dominates the village and has many roof bosses including the Hares.

Ilsington to the east has another St Michaels church which was probably first constructed in the thirteenth century and then it was rebuilt as many were again in the fifteenth century when the wool trade flourished. The church has what is described as a wagon style roof. In that roof are a number of bosses including the Tinners Hares.

Now our search took us to the west of Devon and closer to home once again. The village of Kelly is situated less than a mile and a half from the river Tamar, which forms a border with Cornwall to the west. The church here is named St Mary the Virgin and dates from the fourteenth century, with additions in the fifteenth century. Tinners Hare's are on one of the roof bosses.

A few miles to the northeast lay the village of Lydford, famous for its Castle, its Gorge, the beautiful White Lady Waterfall, and the Devils Cauldron. The church is dedicated to St Petrock who is often portrayed in art with a tame wolf. He is said to have returned to Devon from Rome to preach the word of Christ and to found new churches in Cornwall, Devon and Wales.

The church itself dates again from the thirteenth century but it may have been originally much earlier. Roof or ceiling bosses include the Hares.

The seventeenth church, (yes let's not forget the magic number), was St Eustachius in the market town of Tavistock. Sitting astride the river Tavy, this ancient stannary town dates back to the tenth century. The church was built 1265 but little remains of the original.

A new building erected years later was dedicated to St Eustachius in 1318. He was a roman general who became a Christian in the second century and was executed because of his faith. The Tinners Hares unsurprisingly is among the roof bosses.

We had found enough proof historically to link the Tinners Hares or Rabbits, call them what you will, with the cycle of the moon, the heavenly constellations, and the Holy Trinity.

Not only that but something else had become apparent as we looked at the map of the seventeen churches and compared it to the seventeen tors that had led us to the constellation Draco. It was very similar. Not identical but very similar indeed.

The placement of the churches when we drew lines between them almost matched the constellation of Draco. It was we felt reasonable to say that the churches would always be placed in villages or towns and as such could not exactly replicate the pattern of stars above. It would always require a little artistic license to get the pattern perfect and putting the tinners hares inside selected churches was a good way of ensuring that only those buildings would be included when viewed from an arial view or perspective.

Now we were getting close to finding the artefact. It was not going to be long before we put the final pieces of this infuriating jigsaw puzzle together.

Had the map of the Tors been left at the carpark of Brentor church as a ruse to deflect us from the churches that were now of such interest to our investigation? It seemed like a possibility and we would have to consider it, giving some weight to either side of the argument or at least allowing as far as possible for the clues and thereby the truth to guide us was the whole point of our quest.

We wanted to be as close to the reality of the situation as possible, after all, what point would there be in following false information, or allowing ourselves to be the instruments of our own downfall.

It was very likely that this link to the churches was the correct one but it led to another conundrum and another problem. If we used the churches as a pointer to Draco, although at sometime during the earths turning in its twenty four hour cycle Draco would align, it meant that the area of the Dragons breath would have moved northeast from its original position around Sheepstor, which we had always considered the to be the most likely area given the clues in Grandads notebook.

A phone call to Rekha was in order to bring her up to speed on our latest find. She was pleased and more so still when we told her what we had found and her thought pattern was one of logical preciseness as per usual.

'Perhaps you are correct and the tors were a ruse to deflect us from the truth. The problem with that is why would Chapter allow us to keep heading on the wrong trail, given the fact that they clearly now need our help to find the Universal Egg?'

She was right. It made no sense but, we just were about to play our trump card.

'There is one thing we haven't told you yet.' I had informed her.

'Go on'.

Frank added, 'This is the icing on the cake, or Tor in this case.'

'Well?'

'In this scenario,' I said. 'The dragons breath would be exhaled over an area called, wait for it, Hare Tor.'

'Good God.' She said.

A few years later she admitted that our revelation had taken her aback at the time and nearly caused her to pause her own work on the egg, which at that point would have proved a critical error.

'Go for it.' Was her advice. 'See where it leads.'

'It may, dear lady, lead nowhere.' Frank had offered.

Rekha was a positive driving force in this development of events.

'JFDI' She stormed. 'Just Flaming Do It.'

Considering that we had had our hands firmly smacked by our younger colleague, we determined to investigate Hound Tor in more detail and try to find another set of clues which might help to support our new theory, that the artefact might be on Hare Tor somewhere, hidden perhaps among the mad scatter of old boulders and rocks which covered a fair area around the top of the Tor itself.

Meanwhile Rekha would continue to hunt down the lady mysteriously associated with Mah Laqa Bai.

She reiterated to us her original concept us that the woman was British, of that she was sure and that Mah Laqa Bai, the famous Indian poetess had almost for certain been one of the Nine Unknown Men. Her latest research had involved a vast amount of literary minutia in libraries and in historical files viewed online.

Rekha was reluctant at that time to draw any conclusions from what she had learned but was still happy to work at her thankless task in the hope of discovering some major new fact. As the timeline she was now investigating was the beginning of the British Raj, it was at least one of the most written in and also written about periods of British history. That offered up a lot of evidence and rumour, all of which needed to be carefully sifted through.

The Nine Unknown Men, by the very nature of what their name suggests, had proved far more challenging. She was sure that she knew two of the men from that period in the societies history and one other woman apart from Mah Laqa Bai. That woman was married to one of the top British diplomats of the day.

Frank said that he had heard of a tie in with the Raj to someone local and that we would check it out for her when we had finished our enquiries into Hares Tor.

We had moved on further in our quest and our goal seemed to be in sight. There needed to be an end to our quest and it was with that in mind that we all set to with renewed vigour.

Chapter 18

Worlds Apart.

2016 started well. We were full steam ahead until the wheels came off our respective wagons. Again, all three of us suffered various health problems.

In April of that year I developed some health issues which delayed our wandering the moors for a couple of months and set us back further, from the point of view of getting out and about.

Frank did what he could but it was a two man job and as only the two of us and Rekha knew what we were looking for and as the area to be covered and a vast amount of possible hiding places were in evidence, he and of course therefore we, were in an impossible situation.

Sensibly Frank broke down the search area's into a grid pattern and when he wasn't working, he and his wife Wendy did their best to search those places thoroughly. It was hard very going for the two of them but they persevered.

Meanwhile I did what I could from the point of historical records which might point out more favourable hiding places in which the artefact could have been secreted at one time or another in its past.

One major problem with the Hound Tor area was that it was situated on a Ministry Of Defence firing range, and as such was only accessible at certain times of the month.

The range times had to be calculated to save Frank and Wendy from fruitless trips across the moors. It was hard enough work for them as it was.

I carried on my own research and came up with one tiny nugget of interest. I knew that by car the rough distance from Hare Tor to Sheepstor as the crow flies was around twelve and a half miles and that by car the distance given to the closest parking areas to both Tors was fourteen miles.

I had wondered how far it would be on foot. There are many keen moor walkers, both groups, couples and individuals and no shortage of information online about routes, timings, areas to be avoided etcetera. Imagine how please I was to find that when calculated on foot, the distance between the two Tors was seventeen miles. Hare Tor also sits at 1,700 feet above sea level.

The more we looked, the more we saw. It was as though the whole area was saying that this may have been the place chosen to hide the artefact. There were two problems that spoiled the hypothesis but let me give them to you in reverse order for the sake of the flow of the story.

Number two was the fact that hiding anything here, given the amount of people walking the moors these days, was risky. Added to the same problem was the fact that for over a hundred and fifty years 'letterboxing' has been a favourite pastime for ramblers and enthusiastic families.

For those unaware of the term, letterboxing is the hunt for an inked stamp put in a tin or plastic box and then hidden between rocks on the tors. There are published clues as to where to hunt for them and a card to stamp to prove that the hunter has found them.

By the time of my writing there are probably many hundreds at various locations. It is also a great way of learning how to navigate by compass, orienteering skills. This would also be true of Sheepstor itself which was possibly an even more popular area for ramblers and holiday makers in general, given the views of Burrator Reservoir it afforded.

First and foremost however, especially in the case of Hare Tor and the more northwest of Dartmoor was the fact that the area had been used by the military as training ground since the 1800's. Therefore, the choice of Hare Tor would have been unwise at best and idiotic at worst.

Try as we might, both these facts could not be ignored or skirted around. We knew that we had gone two steps forward and three backwards. Most annoying was the idea that we had not even taken the MOD firing ranges into consideration as anything but a minor inconvenience to our theory.

Common sense said, no, and demanded that we look at that area of the moor as out of all bounds to our investigation. Hare Tor was off the radar once and for all and we were forced to change tack again. The Victorians had really put a spoke in our wheel when they began to use Dartmoor for army training and manoeuvres.

Little did we know or suspect that during that time and almost six thousand miles from Dartmoor a young man was starting out on a life of adventure and service to his country that would skew our investigation in all directions and lead on a new exciting and an unforeseen path.

It would involve adventures on legendary seas, hard fought battles, iron statesmanship, bitter feuds, and the slow decline of a famous family, ending in the loss of an empire and last of all terminating in a peaceful resting place at his spiritual home and so loved by many, both rich and poor.

In the meantime, we carried on searching the tors and looking for other clues that might lead us further on. The Universal Egg was proving to be as elusive as the 'Philosophers Stone' in many respects.

We were sure that it existed and we were equally aware that Anna may have been leading us on a wild goose chase. For what reason of course we didn't know. Why would someone go to all that bother? It was a question I'm sure we had all posed to ourselves on an almost daily basis.

I knew that Anna was a real person, the only alternative was that I had been experiencing some kind of hallucination. If it was, then it was so incredibly detailed and complex, that I was sure that I would never have remembered it with such clarity. The very thought that either Frank or Rekha would have been taken in by Anna's story, as told by me was unlikely in the extreme.

When 2017 came around in a few months' time, it would mark forty years since I had found my Grandfather's badge, books, and notes on his death. Frank had been involved for only marginally less time. By this time even our junior colleague Rekha had been involved for over twenty years.

As sure as we were that the artefact was still somewhere on Dartmoor, for all the clues gained so far had pointed to that, we had once again fallen foul of our own research. It would have been so much easier to have allowed ourselves to have taken a far more relaxed view but that would inexorably have led to assumptions and eventually failure, although in truth we were facing disappointment and failure once again in any case.

The Golden (Dragon) Dagger Mine had led nowhere. Nevertheless, it had been a line of enquiry we had not been at liberty to ignore. Had we missed something? Did the Tinners Hare's really point to some other landmark or celestial body that we had not seen or understood?

This time I asked Rekha to suspend her Indian line of enquiry whilst the three of us took a careful look over the progress we had made so far. It took a lot of time and this was the moment in which our despair at ever solving the puzzle was at its deepest. How easy it would have been to lay down our books and pens. To have given up.

Thank God we didn't and thank God that Rekha once again set her own course and whilst helping us to review our position, carried on her pursuit of the Indian connection.

Frank and I examined roof bosses in every church on the Moors, whether by means of the internet or by physically visiting a variety of these wonderful religious houses. We found a multitude of interesting facts. Things that we had never known or suspected came to our attention and a new light was cast upon them.

The rest of the year was taken up with these final searches and the gradual shedding of would be clues or evidence that would no longer held water. We scrutinised everything. It was painstaking and in a few instances heart breaking. Years of research went down the proverbial drain. We had done our best to stay true to our quest but it seemed that we might slip, metaphorically, beneath the waves of information collected which were no longer of much use.

2018 arrived and with it, two days after New Year's Day the phone rang. It was Rekha. She was now sure that she knew who the mysterious British Lady was that she had been searching for, for so long a time.

'I have It.' She said in a wonderful evocation of Archimedes 'Eureka' moment, and indeed she did.

Chapter 19

Anno Domini.

On Friday the twenty ninth of April in the year eighteen hundred and three a baby boy was born in Bandel, Hooghly, in what was then part of British India.

His father was English, a judge, the Chief Magistrate in fact of the East India Company high court in Benares during the early years of the Raj. His mother was Anna Maria (Stuart) Brooke the daughter of Scottish nobility born and brought up in the county of Herefordshire in England.

This was the woman Rekha believed to be a close friend of Indian Poetess and probable member of Chapter and The Nine Unknown Men, Mah Laqa Bai. She was sure that Anna Maria Brooke was by association one of Chapters chosen laymen or women in this case, in their mission to hide the Universal Egg.

Brooke was a known acquaintance Bai and over the course of a few years the women became friends. Having connections both royal and administrative would have been very useful to the women once Bai had disclosed her purpose. It was in 1797 that the women were thought to have first met, probably at a dinner or reception given by Bai's lover Nizam the Second (Mir Nizam Ali Khan), for the Official British delegation of the East India Company.

Over the next six years the two women met on formal occasions but also informally. At one period, most likely in eighteen hundred and one, Brooke stayed with Bai for a few weeks a year before the birth of her first child.

It was during this time that Bai may have told Anna Brooke of her love affair with Nizam's military chief Raja Rao Rambha Rao.

This love affair was undoubtedly the spark for some of Bai's most famous poetry. Quite how Bai enlisted the help of Anna Brooke will forever remain a mystery. There is however no written confirmation of the two women discussing the egg or any reference between them which directly mentioned the

148

Universal Egg. Neither is there rumour of such a conversation, though that in itself means nothing as so few people in the world were even aware of the eggs existence.

When the two ladies talked about the artefact, it would surely have been in private and possibly in some kind of coded fashion so that anyone from a prince to a servant would not have understood the deep significance of their words.

Indications were that Mah Laqa Bai kept the egg well concealed for many years but it was evident that she had to share her secret with someone, otherwise the artefact would be lost to the world forever, or at least until it was dug up or discovered by persons as yet unknown in the future.

That would have been a constant and very deep source of concern for Chapter. As limited a number of people as possible would know of the egg, but enough people had to know about it in order to have a succession of committed agents who were able to be on hand to render emergency assistance should it be urgently required.

Over the next couple of years Anna Brooke had two children, a girl in 1802 and a boy in 1803. It is the boys story that Rekha had had the good sense to follow.

The lad was given the name James and was by the age of twelve sent back to England to be educated at King Edward the Sixth Grammar School in Norwich. He ran away from school and because of this he was tutored and home schooled in Bath before he returned to India aged sixteen and took up a role as an Ensign in the Bengal Army, which belonged and formally answered to the British East India Company.

This remained the norm until in 1758 the Government of India Act was passed, just a year after the Indian Rebellion. Brooke fought in the First Anglo-Burmese War until during action in Rangpur, Assam in 1825 at the age twenty three, he was seriously wounded, either in the genitals or the lungs, (there are two different versions) and as such he was put on extended leave.

Being unable to return to India before his leave expired he left the Bengal Army and returned to Britain and in eighteen 1833 at the age of thirty Brooke inherited thirty thousand pounds. Most of the money was used to purchase a two hundred and ninety ton's, or a one hundred and forty two ton's, depending on what reference books and internet sites were used, armed sailing brig and to train a crew in the Mediterranean to man her. The ship named 'The Royalist' and captained by Brooke himself then set sail for Singapore.

Rekha had certainly done her homework and it was obvious that she was in her element relating Brookes story to us. It was wonderful to hear the excitement in her voice as she continued with her story in some detail.

Brooke it would appear at first glance had scientific research in mind as well as exploration, but no doubt being the type of man he was it was closer to the truth to think he was intent on some kind of grand adventure for the voyage.

On reaching Singapore he learned of an insurrection against the Sultan of Brunei in Sarawak, which was then under the Sultans control and never a man to miss an opportunity, Brooke sailed for Borneo and helped the Sultans troops to put down the insurrection. This area of North-west Borneo was covered in the main with dense mangrove swamp which ran into the South China Sea and was the haunt of head-hunters, slavers and of course pirates.

Brooke was brave, energetic and enthusiastic in his pursuit of the Sultans enemy and gave aid to the Sultans uncle Pangeran Muda Hasim, but Brooke himself had long held the belief that the indigenous peoples were corrupted by interaction with Europeans.

In 1841 in gratitude for Brooke's long service the Sultan, Omar Ali Saifuddin the Second made him Governor of Sarawak.

As Governor of Sarawak, Brooke was regarded as a firm but fair ruler. This was not however the view of many Malay nobles who conspired to murder the Sultans uncle Muda Hasim, deposing the Sultan at the same time. This was due to the fact that most of these nobles were involved in the piracy still taking place off the coast of Brunei and most likely profited from it.

So Brooke then used his connections with the British Empire to bring vessels from the China Squadron and took over the State of Brunei, restoring the Sultan to the throne. As a consequence of this, the Sultan made Brooke Rajah of Sarawak on the 24th of September 1841 but the official declaration was not publicly announced until the 18th of August 1842.

Rekha carried on and the tension grew as we knew she was leading up to some important revelations. It was apparent that there was a lot more to tell.

In 1844 Brooke began organising units of the Royal Navy and East India Company in anti-piracy actions against marauding vessels, he was wounded in the arm during one of these skirmishes and in another engagement a spear cut open his eyebrow.

Two years later in 1846, Brooke sealed a deal with the Sultan to cede the island of Labuan to Britain. The Treaty of Labuan as it was to be known and documented was signed on the eighteenth of December. It was to bring Brooke to public attention.

During his rule as Rajah, James Brooke reformed aspects of the administration. He brought in new laws, one such being that the regions head-hunters (Dayaks), many of whom fought for Brooke were the only ones who could kill other Dayaks. He put rebellion and insurrection down swiftly and with an iron fist.

Now Rekha changed tack a little. It was many years ago, she said that Brookes mother had died back in England, in the town of Bath in Somerset on the 30th of November 1835. Always the favoured child of the family, Brookes relationship with his mother was well grounded. He had been pandered to as a child and it was with this thought in mind that Rekha had begun to suspect that the person most likely to be trusted with the artefact would be Anna Maria Brookes loving, daring, brave son James.

The link to India was perfect and although the choice of such a character to defend the egg was not Chapter had made a point of choosing a particular type of person, famous or not, who was perhaps far more cautious by nature. One who would take on the grave responsibility required for such an important task.

It was unusual, but who might have been better placed at that time when entrusted with the egg to bring it back to Britain. Brooke had ample opportunity. He had been back in England for a long period of time after being so seriously wounded in 1825.

He may of course have kept it with him on his return to India. Or he may have concealed it in England at a place where he knew it could be safely retrieved at his convenience and as such he could have let his Chapter connection know of the eggs location in case he should be killed or die abroad.

It made sense that he would have shared that information but without proof, that scenario could not simply be assumed. Brooke after all was a tough personality and not much given to second guessing himself or where life, fortune or circumstance might lead him. The time he spent in his mother's company would have given them opportunity to discuss the artefact and for her to explain its significance. It would be true to say that James Brooke was a man who could face adversity with strength and determination.

His contacts from many different walks of life would have given him the ways and means to deal with any setbacks if and when they occurred.

His ability to travel, either under escort from the Royal Navy or if necessary to use his own fast sailing brig to move from country to country was perfect as was his role as Rajah. There would surely have been few people who would have been in a position to overrule him or question his movements.

He was held that in such esteem even today in Sarawak's capital Kuching there are streets, roads, buildings, bridges, even roundabouts and restaurant's named after the Brooke family.

Little doubt then that Brooke was the most likely successor to his mother and the perfect gentleman who could bring the Universal Egg back to England.

In 1848 James Brooke was back in the land of his birth. England. It was a short time before he was brought before Queen Victoria, then Empress of India and knighted by her in the same year. James Brooke never married, some said due to his wounds during the Burma campaign, others that he was homosexual in a time when it was illegal to be so. Whatever his reasons, when he returned again to Sarawak, he took his nephew Captain John Brooke Johnson with him as his heir.

The younger man later changed his own surname to Brooke. The two men worked hard at bringing together the various tribes of Sarawak to some common ground. They strove to make it a safer more peaceful place and they were instrumental in developing the industry, commerce, and administration of Sarawak without exploiting the indigenous peoples.

Some people in Britain were of the opinion that Brooke ruled with an iron rod but posterity would show that this was not entirely accurate.

The Liberal opposition in the British parliament had claimed Brooke had been responsible for the massacre of innocent people when it was pirates and slavers he had dealt justice to. They used him as an example of colonialism to upbraid the Conservative government of the time. It was certainly useful to Britain to have such a man in a position of power but later on Britain would recognise Sarawak as a country in its own right.

Returning to Sarawak after contracting smallpox Brooke withdrew to his country cottage for some time and this neglect of his kingdom was an opportunity for Chinese miners angry at the opium taxes to launch a rebellion, they miners even set fire to Brooke's own house and he was forced to flee for his life.

However, he gathered his forces, mostly sea Dayaks and arriving back in Kuching he put down the rebellion and began the long process of rebuilding his devastated capital. His nephew now named Brooke Brooke was of course to be his successor but now a spanner was thrown into the works.

A young man claiming to be James Brooke's son called Rueben George Walker made himself known and was acknowledged by James Brooke as his illegitimate son. This caused uproar in the Brooke family and Brooke Brooke fearing for his inheritance was not surprisingly nonplussed at the revelation.

It was at around this time that James had a stroke and became somewhat paranoid with friends and family. Sarawak was as of that time keep solvent by the advancement of a loan from a friend of James Brook, a philanthropic lady named of Angela Burdett-Coutts who was reported at that time to be the richest woman in England.

Now Rekha was about to play her trump hand and leave Frank and I somewhat shocked.

Having returned to England during his illness, James Brooke had bought remote cottage in Devonshire, on Dartmoor to be more accurate and more astonishingly yet, it was in a place of great interest to us.

The cottage Brooke bought was in the far southwest of Dartmoor in the village of Burrator, which nestled half a mile from Sheepstor village and right under the Tor itself. This was one coincidence too many to be ignored.

Chapter 20.

White Rajah.

'I have heard of Brooke.' Frank admitted.

So had I but knew very little about him at that time.

'This has to mean something, Brooke has to be the link between Mah Laqa Bai, Chapter and The Universal Egg.' Rekha had told us.

There was no denying that it was more than coincidence. What were the chances of this connection leading to a dead end? It was unlikely to say the least.

'Why had he bought a house so far from his family and friends and the country he had fought so long to maintain?' I had asked.

Rekha implied 'Maybe his illness. He had suffered a few minor strokes by then. Perhaps he needed the solitude.'

'It's a great place to lay low and to secrete the artefact.' Frank was of course right in that statement.

Burrator House was set back off the reservoir and surrounded in the main by thirty odd acres of fields and woods. The house although not very large by Victorian standards was adequate for the Rajah's needs and requirements.

'Is there any written evidence or mention of the egg or any artefact in local papers of the time?' I asked.

Rekha said that if there were, then she had not found them, nor had she heard of any rumours regarding the egg.

Again, as it was such a well-kept secret it was unlikely that Brooke would have spoken to anyone except the member of Chapter he would have reported to. It was also likely that his direct superior in Chapter may have struggled to keep Brooke onside, given the depth of his paranoia.

It must have been a titanic effort to control a man who had been used to giving orders rather than receiving them. It was also possible that he had not divulged the whereabouts of the egg to anyone at all on his return from the far east.

'What about the family dynasty itself.' I asked. From the very little knowledge I had of their story, the ancestral line had died out. I knew that a branch of the family still lived on.

Rekha took up the story once again. Her research suggested that James Brooke had gone off the rails as it were, in all likelihood due to his illness and was caught up with some rough liaisons in the Totnes area of Devon.

There were suggestions that an attempt had been made to blackmail him at some stage but nothing came of it.

His onetime heir, Brooke Brooke's fears were realised with his uncle calling him a traitor and disinheriting the younger man in favour of his brother Charles. Then a series of cruel strokes took the life of this once intrepid man and he died in 1868 at the age of sixty five.

At his home, Burrator House his personal private papers were burnt quickly and efficiently by his staff. To this day little has survived in his own hand outside of government correspondence.

In Sarawak James Brooke's nephew Charles Brooke was next in line to take over as Rajah of Sarawak and reigned from the 3rd of August 1868 until the 17th of May 1917. A total of almost fifty years. He in turn Charles was succeeded by his son Charles Vyner Brooke who reigned from the 24th of May 1917 until the 1st of July 1946 at which time he formally abdicated his power and ceded Sarawak to the British Crown.

During the Second World War, Brooke was obliged to leave Sarawak in face of the Japanese invasion, spending his war years in Sydney, Australia. It was on his return to Sarawak in April of 1946 that he handed provisional power over to the British Government. He returned to England and died in London four months before Sarawak joined with other states to form the Federation of Malaysia.

Charles Vyner Brooke had lived to the ripe old age of eighty eight years. As Brooke had three daughters but no sons, his nephew Antony Brooke contested his uncle's decision to cede Sarawak to Britain Crown.

After some years and many failed attempts to claim the throne for himself he was suspected, although the suspicion was later proved untrue of having been involved in a plot in

156

which the second British Governor of Sarawak, Duncan Stewart, was assassinated.

Antony Brooke gave up his claim to be Rajah of Sarawak and retired to live out the later part of his days New Zealand.

'So do you believe that only James Brooke, the first Rajah of Sarawak had dealings with Chapter?' I had asked.

'I can't find any other link.' Rekha had replied. 'but I'm not surprised.

I recall that Frank was smiling at me, something was on his mind. 'Pray continue dear girl.'

Rekha's voice went up an octave. 'There is more.'

'Then let's have it.' I had said with an urgency born of excitement.

Rekha carried on with the story of this remarkable family and more pertinently to us and our quest but she had saved the best to last.

The Brooke family had not been buried in Somerset, the area in which they had long resided, neither had they been taken back again to Malaysia.

All three of the White Rajahs of Sarawak had been buried on the moors at St Leonards church in the village of Sheepstor under the protective gaze of the constellation, Draco.

In a sheltered north-eastern corner of St Leonards church at Sheepstor on Dartmoor in Devon, England, lie four tombs guarded by cast iron railings. They belong to the Brooke family and outside of the railings the graves of four other members of the family lie at rest.

The church itself is of granite construction. Above the church door a stone sculpture hangs. It isn't the most pleasant of sculptures but it certainly draws the eye. It is that of an hourglass with a skull on it.

From the skull's empty eye sockets and mouth ears of corn grow. A Latin motto above reads 'UT HORA SIC VITA' (As the hour so life passes).

Below the skull, another inscription reads, MORS JANUA VITA,

(Death is the door of life).

Last of all, a scroll bears the motto, ANIMA REVERTET, (The Soul will return). This particular carving is rather like those found in the 'Green Man' heads so popular in carvings or craft workshops but in this form it was known as 'A Foliate Skull'.

Inside the church hangs a carpet known as a Pua Kumba as a gift from the people of Malaysia in 1996 as a mark of respect to the Brooke family. It is significant as a sacred space in which births, weddings and deaths are celebrated.

James Brooke's tomb is the largest and is made of a heavy red Aberdeen granite and was highly polished when first erected. On it was written these final words, 'Sacred to the memory of Sir James Brooke, KCB, DCL, Rajah of Sarawak.'

The next tomb contained the remains of his nephew and Second Rajah, Sir Charles Brooke. Two other smaller tombs are set between these two. They are the final resting place of Sir Charles Vyner Brooke and his brother Bertram.

Outside are four other stones marking the interred ashes of other Brooke family members.

A tremble could be heard in Rekha's voice as she conveyed the last of her findings and waited for our reaction. It may have been more muted than she had hoped for but it was possibly because the gravity of her findings had hit us immediately.

'Good God' was all I remember Frank saying.

I myself uttered a well-used expletive and as I remember a minute or so had passed until we spoke again. Then it was uproar. What a find. It was as if the culminated frustration of the last thirty years had all melted in the last thirty minutes.

Frank and I knew that we had to visit St Leonards church as soon as we could. We were keen to see the graves and report back to our colleague with our thoughts and photographs of the tombs.

It was a day we would never forget. Now the final pieces of the puzzle began to fall into place. What better place to hide the artefact from prying eyes and to keep it safe than in a little known church in the depths of the moors.

Who would have ever made the connection had they not been aware of Chapter. Even then it would probably have taken as many years as it had taken us to get to this point.

If the investigation had been conducted by professional journalists and historians without the involvement of someone they had personally known and the clues my grandad had left me, I could not see them even beginning to learn of this secret in the first place.

St Leonard, Rekha went on to say was the patron saint of prisoners. More and more of what we had learned made sense and it was fitting that St Leonard, traditionally shown holding a set of keys was the spiritual protector of the egg. So where in the church might the egg have been concealed? That must be our next move.

A recce to Sheepstor church and a subtle look at the building itself without alerting anyone to our real reason for being there and we would conduct ourselves in a gentlemanly manner but try to prise as much information from anyone involved with the church and anyone who might have been involved in recent restoration work.

Failing that, it would be a long hard slog through parish archives or any paperwork that was available to the public either online or in public records held by the church that they saw fit to allow us to view.

A few days later we arrived at St Leonards, it was a little before ten o'clock in the morning. I had phoned and spoken to the church warden, a kindly lady as it turned out in her early seventies.

It was a clear, cold and dry which was unusual for January on Dartmoor. We made our way up through the narrow lanes to the village centre and parked. Frost still covered some of the field hedges and stone walls on their northern sides. Sheep grazed in an unconcerned manor munching on hay thrown out to them by the local farmer. It was sorely needed at this time of year when even the hardy Scotch Blackface, much favoured by moorland farmers, would find it hard to sustain themselves.

Frank and I strolled excitedly yet with calm exteriors in order to give nothing away. The lady Church Warden introduced herself and after a brief questioning session in which she appeared to want to get a measure of our intentions, led us to the church boundary. I pushed my phone out of sight in my pocket. We would each use our phones to take photos and notes.

'What are you particularly interested in?' she had asked. 'after all,' she continued without pause for us to answer her question, 'isn't the internet supposed to supply all the information one could possibly need about almost anything?'

'It's more about getting a feeling for the church. I intend to write a book on the religious aspects of moorland life and as I was brought up only three miles away, I thought this was as good a place as any to begin,' I lied, well, half lied anyway I thought to myself.

Frank grinning like a Cheshire cat didn't help.

'Damn silly day for you to pick,' She grumbled. 'why didn't you pick a more agreeable time of year, spring or better still summer?'

Feeling as though I was in front of my first school headmistress Ms Reader I had blurted out an apology for inconveniencing her and made sure I made no eye contact with Frank who by now had in his hand a large handkerchief to mop the tears of laughter from his eyes.

She had turned on him swiftly, perhaps spotting that some mischief was afoot.

'Are you quite alright.'

'The cold affects my eyes terribly.' he muttered, stifling a laugh with the hankey.

'Maybe you should blame your friend for bringing us out in such bad weather.' The lady growled.

'Indeed I should m'dear.' Frank replied.

She led us through the lychgate in the wall that surrounded the church and across the path to the West Door. Taking a mighty big key from her coat pocket, she proceeded to open the door.

'I will put the lights on for you but no heating I'm afraid. You will just have to bear the cold as best you can. Of course, you really have only yourselves to blame for that had you come later in the year it would not be a problem. Now how long shall I leave you here. Will an hour or so suffice?'

'Three hours,' Frank told her.

She had looked aghast, 'Three hours?'

'Yes,' Frank nodded firmly.

'Well, I have lunch precisely at one o'clock,' she said.

I had interjected at that point, 'Then meet us again at twelve forty five and we will consider ourselves grateful for your help and we will not feel as we have delayed you lunch.'

She left us with a shake of her head and mumbled her way down the path. Now at last we had some time to explore St Leonards in peace.

We could hear her heels on the paved pathway.

Chapter 21

Dartmoor Churches.

St Leonards is, like most churches on the moor, built of granite. The West Tower stands high above the village looking out across moor and field in every direction but north. North is where the Tor spreads its mighty shoulders up to the sky and offers no view except stone scree, boulders and coarse grass, rushes, and gorse.

Some days it looks like a guardian with the village in its lee. On others it appears to blot out vast areas of sky in a dominating manner. Yet on other days still, it will look foreboding, a sleeping giant lying on its side facing north, the village positioned in the small of its back, all the time with the fear that sometime in the future the giant will rise and shower the village and its inhabitants with rocks, obliterating all those that lay beneath it. The church, houses and farm would be no match for the thousands of tons of granite that form the giant.

Tinners were on this part of the moor as in other places hereabouts. The church or at least parts of it were the original built in the fourteenth century. The west tower reaches one hundred and forty feet into the sky and at night, surely looks like a massive stone finger pointing towards Draco and the heavens. The pinnacles at each corner of it add their own grandeur and the battlement lend a sense of security to the building.

The west door arch is built of granite, but of a softer or kinder granite which, in its time easier to shape. It added a depth to the outer façade and being squared off it gave a different look than other church doorways. Above the door is the skull sitting above an hourglass as previously described, dated in the year of grace 1640 AD.

Moving inside, we noticed heavy granite pillars likewise supporting heavy granite arches. It was cold. So cold that our breath made us resemble steam trains as we moved from pillar to pillar in between the pews looking for anything that might represent the lost artefact the Universal Egg, or a Greek Goddess or even a constellation.

Now and then a mark or indent would catch our eye but we were as always determined to examine every part of the building we could in the same way as we had taken so much time to look over the stone rows and mounds. This was different though. We couldn't take too long as we were under the time constraint of three hours before the church warden reappeared.

Moving on from pillar to pillar, gradually we came to the rood screen, a gloriously intricately carved fretwork of wood, which traditionally separates the nave from the transept and the transept from the chancel. The altar is being the farthest point along the eastern wall of a church. The vaulting and tracery of vine, tree and leaf were an absolute joy but yielded no further clues.

Almost an hour had passed, a third of our allotted time. Yet still we were reluctant to rush in case we missed something of importance. Yes we would in all likelihood be allowed back but when and under what circumstances we would have to find out. We were careful to keep an eye for our hostess returning unannounced in case our detailed search of the building gave away our more urgent intent and gave her cause to question us.

We looked at the Victorian tiled floor for clues but the fine geometric design gave up no new information. Next we looked at the pews. The wood was old and patinaed a treat to eye, as were some of the carvings on the ends of the pews. Between 1914 and 1939 a lady named Violet Pinwill had carved them and they were magnificent. St Stephen being stoned to death for his beliefs adorned one end. Another shows a scene from the crusades of a knight on horseback with a crusader shield.

On others were carved the Crown of Thorns and the Crucifixion. Yet another bore the hands and feet of Christ with the nail holes driven through, both beside the cup Pontius Pilate used to wash his hands after giving Jesus up to the mob. Foliage there was in plenty and the scrolls and forms of Gothic artwork that she had imbued into her work. It was marvellous to behold in every sense of the word.

Stained glass windows, as beautiful as they were didn't offer any illumination to our quest. They were many and varied and worth a good long look. Time which we could ill afford.

Some of the windows related to the Second World War and the Brooke families connection with the island of Borneo and Sarawak in particular. With St Leonard as the patron saint of prisoners it would be inconceivable that he would not be shown giving succour to Allied prisoners of war during that terrible period in human history, a time when humanity was able to show its true potential for hatred and spite. Yet there was still enough in good in the world to fight back and conquer evil.

The Pulpit gave nothing up either, although we looked in every joint and crevice for some secret hiding place that may have gone unnoticed over the centuries. We checked the walls but found only a few words in memorium of those who had passed away in the years since the building had been constructed. Many of them in the moment able to bring a tear to the eye. Grief it seemed was one of the most constant things in life, along with death and taxes.

If we had hopes that the ceiling would provide more then we were to be disappointed. It gave up no occult messages nor did it give a hint of a link with constellation Draco or to Chapter.

With barely had half an hour left now in which to find something we left the main body of the church for the graveyard and grounds. The Brooke family tombs were of course the highlight of the day. Having learnt all we could of the families rich history we took our time in looking at the graves with as much respect as we could show, being careful not to go inside the iron railings but leaning in a little to examine closely each of the four tombs in turn.

As awe inspiring as the first Rajah's tomb was, being made of pink Aberdeen granite it cast the other three in the group in quite an underwhelming light. They looked rough-hewn but that may have been down to weathering. Nothing stood out, no one oddity that may have pointed to a further clue.

Despondent, cold and aggravated by our lack of progress we stood back and looked at the other gravestones of the rest of the Brooke clan which lay outside of the Rajah's enclosure. They were of importance to us and we did due diligence and looked over each in turn.

One of my aunts and a few friends were buried here so I was a little bit distracted by familiar names. I remember thinking how quickly the years slipped by as I read epitaphs to those with whom my path had crossed throughout my life.

Frank was shaking his head in frustration and I felt for him as my frustration was at the same level and climbing. Fortunately, it seemed most of the graves were older.

A couple may have been the graves of paupers, buried at the expense of the parish and therefore with no headstone. There was a similar case with one of my great uncles at St Edwards Church, Shaugh Prior. Though my mums family paid for the burial, they were not in a position to afford the erection of any form of gravestone at the time of his death and so it had been left unmarked, except in the church records.

I turned on my heel at the far north wall and tripped one a piece of stone which protruded slightly from turf. It was ten minutes before the Church Warden was due back, still time to kick away some earth with my boot.

I whistled to Frank and waved him over. In the grass and earth sod, with a little effort we uncovered a smallish piece of carved stone. It was no more than two feet square and of a polished grey granite with black lettering. Being buried had had the effect of preserving it in almost pristine condition. Yes it was covered in dirt but a quick wipe, courtesy of Franks handkerchief made the letters and symbols visible.

I told him to keep a close eye out for the Warden who was expected anytime soon. My intention was to take photos and record what I saw on the stone and then bury it again with as much speed as possible. What we had spotted in the wording was enough to grab our attention and require us to keep the stone as well hidden as it seemed to have been for many years.

I began to take photos carefully so as not to blur or mess up the image. I took one, then checked it in the gallery, then sent a copy to Rekha and Frank on our group App. If my phone should become lost or damaged then they would have a copy each.

This was an important find. I took another photo with my phone and then began to recite what I saw into my recording app. I kept the words precise, saying exactly what I saw, nothing more and nothing less. It may have been silly, given the fact I had photos but I really wanted a verbal record of the moment. I wanted a feeling of the place and to remember how it made me feel to find this monument in miniature.

Recording began and as I have the download I don't need to strain my memory, its all there on electronic file to this day. Still, I will not go into a long winded explanation of how I felt at what I saw. It was almost unbelievable in its simplicity and as it was dated only eleven years after his death in 1868. We wondered how many others knew of this stone or had even heard of its existence. This was the final link, or so we thought at the time, to the artefact and to Chapter.

Frank coughed convincingly but with enough emphasis to ensure he had my attention. In my haste to recover and move away from the now partially buried stone, I left the recorder running. My inadvertent error proved serendipitous as the conversation that followed proved.

I could hear the heels of the Church Warden's shoes on the paved pathway. I stamped heavily on the sod which I had dug up initially to uncover the stone, in order to cover it over once again. I remember moving quickly away from my recent discovery and mulling about at a random gravestone in order to deflect from where my interest lay, which was some twenty or so yards from the gravestone I was currently observing. Frank was also trying to look completely innocent as the lychgate swung open with force and our hostess arrived looking slightly ill tempered.

Now the recording comes in very handy as I can relate almost verbatim what was said between us.

'Have you found anything of exciting?' The Warden asked.

'Alas dear lady, no.' Frank replied.

'Nothing at all?'

I was next to speak, 'I wasn't expecting to find anything out of the usual. As I told you, I really just wanted to get a feel for the church and of course its surroundings.'

In the recording her voice is edged with disappointment and a little contempt, 'How very annoying.'

'As far as I'm concerned it was time well spent.'

You can still hear her long sigh, 'Well, I was hoping for something a little more exhilarating.'

'Such as?' Frank enquired.

'Well one never knows what one might find in a building as old as this, or indeed in the grounds.'

'Were you hoping we would find something in particular.' I had asked.

'Nothing astronomical.'

It was an odd choice of words. I still recall Frank glancing at me with a raised eyebrow at the phrase she had used.

We thanked her for her time but all the while noticing that her eyes were roaming the graveyard as if searching for something. We bade her goodbye.

'My lunch awaits,' she remarked as she made her way to the church door to lock it. We waited out of courtesy and Frank held the lychgate open for her.

'If you need to visit the church again, just call me,' She added.

We walked back to the lane with her and parted company with nothing more said. The heels of her shoes clipped up the quiet road between the houses. Sheepstor was more a hamlet than a village but beautiful, nonetheless. Two sheep strayed past us nibbling at the grass banks, taking no more interest in us than we deserved.

I know we were thrilled with our find, like two excited schoolboys who had escaped the headmistresses wrath. Jumping in the car we headed for home. Frank was in the passenger seat but he had not asked to see my phone or the photos. That could wait for at least another twenty five minutes whilst we drove home. It was as if we dared not believe what we had found. We couldn't wait to look at the evidence and to share it with Rekha.

Chapter 22

Serpent and Egg.

We arrived back in Cornwood at Franks garage, which had been our official headquarters for many years. The journey home had been quiet and fortunately uneventful.

'Let's view the photo's before we call Rekha,' Frank had sensibly said.

I was eager to call her but had to agree that we get all our ducks in a row first.

'Well, well those were worth three hours of freezing, ' Frank opined

'They bloody well are.' I had remarked. I know this because my recorder was still on, I later found out.

'It's exactly what we thought it was.'

'No doubt about it.'

I wish we had had more time dear boy.' He said.

Listening now to the recording, I can hear my long exhalation of breath in reply to his well-reasoned statement.

'But at least we have the photographs.' I replied.

'We do.'

'Yes but had we found it earlier in the day, it may have led to us then discovering more.'

Frank was happy. 'Let's be grateful for small mercies.'

'Oh, I am but that extra time would have been nice.'

'We can always go back.' He told me.

'When do you suggest?'

'Not today. The warden maybe on the warpath.'

There was a long pause on the recording, then I heard myself saying 'What an odd remark she made, she said, Nothing Astronomical'

'I thought that spoke volumes.'

'It was as if she expected us to find something of importance.'

Frank sounded cool, unfazed, 'Or hoped we had.'

'You think she was expecting us to discover something?'

'It is certainly possible.'

'OK let's sort this new evidence and call Rekha.'

'Your phones flashing.'

'Sorry?'

'Your phone.' Frank was pointing at my mobile.

'Damn.' It must have been then that I found that I was still recording.

We called our colleague but she was at work as usual, so we decided to carry on and find out all we could about the, let's call it a 'Tablet'. It was too small by far to be named anything else than that.

We had re-estimated the size of it from two feet by two feet square down to eighteen inches. If I had taken a tape measure it would have proved useful. Now we could look at the photographs in detail.

I downloaded the photo file to Franks printer and copied them off. I will attempt to describe them as best I can. What had first looked thought of as square now appeared oblong. We reckoned on it being set in profile with the height being eighteen inches or so and the width at around twelve inches. The depth we couldn't tell and at the time it didn't matter.

The stone itself was of Dartmoor Granite and it had lettering in a black metal, probably of bronze and steel, which has been commonly used for many years. The lettering ran vertically on either side of a central design. All the lettering was in Latin. To the left the word TVRI, (V was often used in place of U). That spelled the word 'Burn' in English. On the right ORVM spelled, 'The Ears' in English.

While that was true, if you combine the words then together in Latin they mean 'To Burn'. Even in some context they could be read as burn the egg. So, were they meant to be read as 'To Burn or Burn the Ears, of what, perhaps those who were listening and getting to close to the truth?'

Most intriguing of all was the central picture in raised bronze or steel the same as the lettering was. It was of an egg with a serpent wrapped around it. We were convinced that this was Ophion coiled around the Universal Egg hence our excitement at the find and our reluctance to share it with the church warden.

170

To the left of the serpent was what appeared to be a conch shell or certainly a shell of some kind. To the right of the serpent was something that could best be described as a leaf, well it just looked like a leaf. Frank was as puzzled as I was. Who was the artist or the designer of this work and as importantly, why was it on a plaque in a graveyard, in a small church on Dartmoor? We needed answers to these questions as quickly as possible.

We began to scour our reference books and the internet. What we thought would take a long time to find came to light in a matter of moments on a well-known search engine.

The picture was attributed to an American born artist by the name of Moncure Daniel Conway. That was the first fact we found and we cross referenced the man and his work quite easily. Born in Falmouth, Virginia on March the 17th, 1832 Conway attended the Fredricksburg Classical and Mathematical Academy. This college was by way of interest the Alma Mater of George Washington.

In later years Conway attended Dickinson College in Carlisle, Pennsylvania. He graduated from there in 1849. Greatly influenced by Professor John McClintock, Conway became a Methodist and an advocate of anti-slavery. Conway married fellow Unitarian Ellen Davis Dana and had three sons, one of whom died in childhood.

In 1850 after studying law he became a Methodist Minister and travelled from city to city and town to town. Three years later after the death of his brother and his assistant, Conway left the church in order to study Divinity at Harvard University. He hoped, it seemed that this would enable him to increase his knowledge of spiritual thought and whilst at Harvard he met philosopher Ralph Waldo Emerson. It was this meeting that led to him exploring Transcendentalism, then a new philosophy which saw the inherent good in humans and nature.

This fascinating man then found himself on the wrong end of the law when he attempted to rescue a fugitive slave, Conway being tarred and feathered by neighbours and family for this act of kindness.

Between 1860 and 1861 he was the editor of a Liberal periodical called 'The Dial'. For this publication Conway wrote a short story on Arthurian Legend which told how President George Washington allegedly became the possessor of Excalibur.

At the end of 1861 he took over as editor of the 'Commonwealth' an anti-slavery weekly publication in Boston, Massachusetts. He met Abraham Lincoln off the back of a Smithsonian Institute lecture tour.

The American Civil War saw Conway publish two other pleas for the emancipation of slaves. At the end of 1863, he sailed to England to try to convince the Government and people not to support the Confederate States. During this time, he caused consternation back in America by meeting with James Murray the Confederate States representative in Britain and then attempting to negotiate the emancipation of southern slaves in return for the withdrawal of support for Lincoln's prosecution of the war.

He was denounced by his supporters and forced to apologize to the United States State Department. Fearing a hostile reception at his home in Virginia, he left England for Venice, Italy. In 1864 he moved with his family back to London where he became leader of a religious society and wrote and published over the following years, serving briefly as war correspondent during the Franco- Prussian War of 1870 to 1871.

He published autobiographies of many notable people and for a time was Robert Browning's literary agent, as well as London agent for Mark Twain, Louisa May Allcott and also Walt Whitman. Conway was also a great supporter of Women's suffrage at this period of time, giving lectures on the subject of Women's rights.

What caught our attention most was his work on the subject of theology. In particular a book he had published in 1878, 'Demonology and Devil Lore'. On careful examination of his works in which we hoped we would find some kind of tie into England, or English culture. What we found something even better as in the above mentioned work is a piece called 'A Story of Dartmoor.'

Another concrete link. It seems that his travels may have brought him to Dartmoor. Further information gleaned from reference books pointed to Moncure Conway having visited Devon and Dartmoor in particular on several occasions. Surely this man must have been worthy of consideration as a possible candidate for Chapter, or at least as a layman who may have worked with or helped them. He had also been a traveller to India in later life and we already knew of the connection that was of such importance to us from our search there.

'A Story of Dartmoor', small as it was and published as part of his book 'Demonology and Devil Lore' and sub-headed under a chapter called 'Darkness' was a folk tale of an old man afraid of both the Devil and his Demons and of the darkness, which in his mind he associated each with the other.

Caught on the moors as night fell he slipped on a hillside. In his fear he grabbed at a thorn tree branch and unable to feel solid ground beneath his feet he held on in terrified agony through the night, his muscles strained to breaking point in order to stay alive.

Morning brought a different perspective. His feet being only inches from solid ground, his fear of the unknown had kept him hanging to the branch unnecessarily and with daybreak came the clarity of vision and fear yielded to common sense and familiarity.

As telling as this story was, it still gave us no idea as to why Conway had painted The Serpent and Egg, or why a plaque of the painting had ended up at St Leonards Church on Sheepstor.

Later that evening we spoke to Rekha. She was pleased with our day's work and thrilled at the photographs of the plaque. It was confusing to her as well as to why this plaque should have been placed in the graveyard. She suggested trying to find any mention of a plaque and a timeline for its creation and installation. She said that she would find time to check out why he visited India and if there was any connection there that might give us more leads.

Frank and I went back to our labours but it was late by then and we decided to call it a night. My wife having given up on me had gone to bed earlier whilst I sat in the lounge and continued scouring the internet one last time. My mobile rang.

'You found something didn't you.' It was a woman's voice, quite well spoken. I recognized it.

'Mrs Palmer, is that you?'

'You know it is.' The church warden replied.

I had the presence of mind to start recording. I wanted more evidence and it was going to prove very useful to share conversation with my colleagues. What follows is the verbatim script of that conversation between us.

'What can I do for you?' I had asked.

'Perhaps you would start by telling me what you were really searching for in the church?'

'As I said, I'm an author ....'

'I know what you said but truth is often lost when the aim of the game is deception.'

'Rather strong words don't you think?' I had replied.

'Truth is almost always the best path to take.'

'But there are instances when it is not.'

In the recording she can be heard taking a long exasperated breath.

'It would be wise to put your trust in me.'

'Mrs Palmer, I met you for the first time today.'

Nonetheless, I may be of help in your quest.'

The use of the word quest had made my ears prick up. It was a term that the three of us used and it seemed out of place.

'What quest would that be?' The caution can be heard in my voice.

'Well, you already know and I have a strong suspicion as to what it may be.'

'Really?'

'We are wasting valuable time and if you only knew how precious that time is at the moment, I know you would grant my request.'

'Very well, tell me what you think you know of my quest and then perhaps you would be good enough to explain why I should trust you.'

The other end of the line was silent for a few seconds. Four seconds to be precise.

'Yourself and your two colleagues have been looking for something of value. Not so much value in monetary value but in moral value.'

'Go on.' She had my attention. She had met Frank but how did she know about the third person, Rekha.

'I am told that you have searched for this artefact for over thirty years and I also know that you are trusted by various sources. I know that further to this you were not party to the full facts and so for many years you worked, blind, as it were.'

'I'm listening.'

'When you know the full facts and reasoning behind your search, you will find an even greater truth than the one you seek.'

'I don't suppose you will share that truth with me?'

'Not yet but soon. This year, 2017 will be the start of a countdown to calamity. In three years' time something will happen that will make the world standstill, or at least appear to, but that will be our chance. It may in fact be the only chance we have to spirit away that which is sacred to us.'

'I'm sorry?' My voice sounds tired and irritated on the recording at this point.

'For goodness sake listen. Try to see outside of the box. You have all done so well thus far. You have come closer to finding the artefact that anyone else in the last forty years.'

'I apologise but I need to be sure that you and I are talking about the same thing and with the same intentions in mind.'

Mrs Palmer seemed contrite. 'That's wise.'

'You must tell me something that few others know.'

'Such as?'

'You are an intelligent woman, think of something.'

'Very well but know this.'

'What?' I had asked.

'Trust is a two way street. I don't know you personally so I am also taking a chance.'

'Then say nothing that would mean anything to an outsider.'

She sounded alarmed. 'Phones can be bugged, tapped. Even radio enthusiasts with no ill intention can stumble across private chats.'

'Very well.'

'Just say something that means something to you and me both.' I had told her.

Another few seconds passed; I know she was still on the line because her breathing can still be heard on the recording.

'Anna,' she said softly, 'we both know Anna.'

My mouth went dry, that I distinctly recall. Realisation set in.

'That's just a name.' I said lamely. 'You could have guessed that.'

'Then what about another name?'

'Try me.' I told her.

Mrs Palmer was silent again for several seconds as she seemed intent on making this word count.

Very well.'

I laughed, 'Your move I believe.'

'Chapter.' She said calculatingly.

The word got my attention.

Chapter 23.

The Church Warden.

Mrs Palmer was a lady full of surprises. She had certainly gained my attention by the simple expediency of the use of two words.

'Those are two very interesting names.'

'Yes,' she said. 'I thought they might grab your attention.'

'Without giving to much credence to either name, what is your link to them or to our quest if I may ask?'

'If I told you something about Anna, would it help to convince you of the fact that I am on your side, or at least on the moral side, the right side of this quandary in which you now find yourself.'

I was trying hard to sound unflustered. 'Please do.'

She went on to describe Anna to a tee. Well-dressed if a little authoritarian in style, as if she worked for the armed services. Her dress was more uniform than casual. Her skin was very pale but the most startling thing about Anna's appearance Mrs Palmer said, was her metallic silver grey hair and her eyes, which she described as green but flecked with gold and violet. I had to admit to myself that Mrs Palmer had given a very detailed account of the woman and it was accurate in every way.

'There is one more thing.' The Church Warden added.

'And that is?'

'I have known her for some fifty years.'

'Okay.'

'In all that time, she has never aged more than maybe a couple of years.'

The hair stood on the back of my neck as I recognised that fact.

'How old,' I asked, 'do you think she is?'

'Mid-twenties, I can't be more accurate.'

'Your description is spot on,' I admitted.

'So, you know I'm speaking the truth.'

It was a statement rather than a question, undeniably so.

'Tell me more about Chapter.'

'I am reluctant to do so.'

Why?' I enquired.

'For the same reason as you.'

'Which is?'

'We were both sworn to secrecy. You broke your oath and I struggled to understand why. Now I know, having been forced to break that very same oath myself.'

'It has been such a complicated search. I would never have come this far without help.'

'Have you found,' She said, 'that Anna's help has been more of a hinderance?'

'In some respects, yes.'

'It's as if she needs help, well Chapter needs help, but she is reluctant to give too much away. Information I mean.'

'Quite.'

'But now with time so short it's becoming a case of all hands on deck.'

I had to ask, 'Mrs Palmer, how long have you known about me?'

'Since a few years after my husband died. He was the last lay person to hold the secret of the egg. That secret died with him and of course at the same time as bad fortune would have it, his Chapter contact died as well.'

'My God.' I don't think I could have sounded more surprised.

'There is one other thing I must tell you. You above all others, given the fact you have chased this secret since you found your Grandfather's notebook and he and my husband had talked about hiding places.'

'He knew my Grandfather?'

'Yes he did.'

'Sorry, what do you need to tell me?' I asked, almost not wanting to know the answer.

'My husband and his lady friend at Chapter were having an affair and that is why they died within twenty four hours of each other. They were both in the same car together. It's just that she survived for a few more hours. To help protect the secret, Chapter intervened and made it look like two separate incidents. That may have been Anna's doing but I couldn't complain. I have wanted for nothing. Chapter in its infinite wisdom has seen to that.'

'I'm sorry for what you have been through.'

'Your kindness is duly noted.'

'We both have good reason to want to resolve this issue.' I told her frankly.

She laughed. 'Maybe we can work more effectively together.'

'I hope so.'

'They say two heads are better than one. Well, if we include your two colleagues, four heads in total.'

'No man is an island.' I replied.

We would have to pool our resources of course but what Mrs Palmer knew seemed to be a fair part of the final scenario of our quest.

I had many more questions, which would require many more answers. I would push her a little in an attempt to find out more, a case of striking while the iron was still hot.

'Mrs Palmer, what do you mean when you say that some calamity will befall us. Do you mean the four of us for example or in the much wider sense of the world.'

'The world. Humankind.'

'Do you know what form this will take?'

'No' she answered, 'but it will have worldwide consequences.'

'Can nothing be done to prevent it?'

'Oh yes, things could be done, well certainly to lessen the effects.'

'So will they be?' I let the question hang.

'I'm not sure and as I don't know the consequences, I can't give you any more insight.'

'How do you know this and what's it got to do with the artefact?'

'I know because I was told to prepare for it.'

'In what sense.'

'It's late.' She had told me. 'And I'm tired.'

'Then when shall we discuss the matter further?'

'Tomorrow of course, the quicker the better in fact.'

'Where and when?'

'Ten o'clock tomorrow morning at St Leonards.'

I had to ask, 'Is that safe do you think.'

'In all these years no one has ever tried to harm me. My husband's accident was just that, an accident, he had a stroke while driving.'

'Shall I come alone or may I bring my colleague.'

'Bring him by all means,' She said earnestly.

We said our goodnights and I resisted calling Frank as he would be asleep by now and Rekha because I knew she started work very early. I know that I went to bed with a head full of imagery and a heart full of expectancy as to what tomorrow would bring. What new secrets would we learn and what secrets of our own would we have to give away in exchange!

In the morning I would call both my friends and give them a quick update on my conversation with Mrs Palmer. I would send a file of the recording and they could make up their own minds as to the validity of her trustworthiness. It was going to be a long night and I was certain it would seem endless.

I rang Frank at six thirty much to my wife's irritation and to Frank's chagrin, explained the situation and hoped he was free. He would have to make some business calls he said but there was no way he was missing out on this meeting.

I rang Rekha shortly afterwards and received a comparatively mild mouthful of abuse. She soon calmed down and wished me luck.

'Don't give too much away.' She said sternly.

At nine thirty, Frank and I left Cornwood, this time in his car and we arrived at five minutes to ten. We exited the car and walked toward the lychgate of the church to find a smiling Mrs Palmer waiting for us and it already seemed that we were all in a more convivial mood than we had been at our previous meeting the day before.

We estimated her as being in her early seventies, age wise that is. She looked younger and could have easily passed for a lady in her late fifties. We had assumed early seventies because she had told us that she had known Anna of over fifty years and it was quite reasonable to believe that Anna would not have trusted anyone who was in their teens, with such an immense responsibility.

This gave us an approximation of her age. Her hair was grey with darker highlights in it. She was an attractive woman and at around five feet three inches in height, petite and well dressed. She wore a long black coat and calf length boots.

It was a day like yesterday. Cold and dry with a sharp edge to the breeze that whipped over the moors edge.

I set my recorder. I was determined not to miss this conversation.

'Good morning gentlemen,' Her blue eyes flashed.

'Dear lady,' Franks deliberately slow pace of speech would set the tone for the meeting. I tended to rush things a little, especially when I felt that I might not get the time to ask all that I wanted. This often came back to bite me as in my haste I sometimes antagonised people and therefore didn't get the best I could from them.

'Mrs Palmer. It's good of you to meet us,' I offered politely.

She let us into the church and out of the breeze which was beginning to gust a little. We entered by the west door and I was taken again by the heavily carved skull above it with the tendrils of corn growing from the eye sockets, sitting atop the hourglass. It was both freakish and disturbing, yet it gave a strange comfort to think of how many souls had walked under this carving, I wondered how now many were even aware of it as they passed into the nave.

'Now to business,' the Church Warden said, 'what did you find?'

'One moment, please. I think we need some rules of engagement.'

I was not going to be bamboozled into giving away what we knew until I was sure of some reciprocation. True, she had been very up front in the previous night's phone call, but it was possible that she was not on Chapters side, after all the egg and thereby Chapter was in some way responsible for the demise of her husband. If not in actuality then in a moral sense, at least that may have been how she saw it.

In other words, was she here to help or to hinder? It was important that Frank and I understood he motive and were happy conjointly to believe her and therefore take her at her word.

'You want to know if I am sincere.' She stated bluntly.

'That is exactly what we want to know.' Franks replied.

'Let me say this.' She was silent for several seconds.

I could hear the impatience in my voice when I listened again to

the recording later that day and in later years.

'Well?'

'I am taking a chance sharing this.'

'If we are to work together, then you must.'

On the tape her voice sounds shaky, it didn't sound that way at the time.

'My reasoning for helping Anna and Chapter is the belief that billions may die if I don't.'

'Go on please.'

'You know what the artefact is?'

'We do.'

'Then you know that in that world, that universe, billions of lives may exist. How many, no one knows, but I believe it to be true.'

I cracked. Rekha had warned me not to, but the woman's sincerity had shown in her eyes.

'We believe it too.'

'Really?'

Frank backed me. 'This quest has been our lives for forty years.'

'Then you know that once you are involved, you can never escape.'

'We are caught up in this as you are Dear lady.' Frank said.

'How did you find out about it?' I asked.

'By chance, my husband was caught by me in a lie. Suffice it to say, he was then forced to tell me about the Universal Egg.'

'Was the lie you caught him in anything to do with the affair.?

'No, I knew nothing of the affair until he and his mistress died.'

Frank asked. 'Then what lie did you catch him in.'

'A simple one. He said he had to go back into work. I was disinclined to believe him and so I decided to follow him. He went to a meeting, that was no lie but the meeting was not at his workshop.'

'Then where?' I enquired.

'Somewhere very unexpected.'

'Was it at a church by any chance?' Frank asked.

'How on earth did you know that?'

I had realised where Frank was going with this and I waited for his reply and Mrs Palmers reaction.

'Was it Brentor Church?

'Yes, but again how did you know.'

'Because we were there.' I told her. 'Albeit to late in the day. In fact, the meeting had just finished when we arrived.'

'So, you didn't see anyone one?'

'No.'

Mrs Palmer had smiled then. I remember that clearly and so did Frank.

'He got in terrible trouble for that.'

'Why?' Frank asked gently.

'I arrived just as they were getting in their cars.' She said. 'I asked him what the hell was going on and who these people were. Derek told me to be quiet, to keep my voice down, but I was angry that he had lied about being at work. He was holding a piece of paper and I lunged at it in order to get his attention. In the tussle that followed, the paper was torn and in the dark he couldn't find it. He was so very angry. I had never seen him that angry before.'

'Did he find the missing piece?' Frank queried.

'No, it was lost.'

'Do you know what it was?'

She looked at him earnestly. 'A piece of a map I was told later.'

Frank glanced at me.

'Why didn't you stay to find it? I asked her.

'Derek said that the group had received a tip off that someone knew about the meeting and was on their way to Brentor. He said we had to leave at once and that I should follow him in my car immediately.'

'So, you left.'

'Yes and not a moment too soon. We hadn't gone far when a car passed us in the opposite direction at some speed. I know there were two people in it of that I'm sure.'

A long pause then ensued as each of us took on board what we had just shared.

'Dear Lady, those two people were the two of us.'

'Really, how can you be sure?

'We found the part of the map that your husband and you dropped
during your tussle.' I told her.

'My God.'

She had looked visibly shaken at our words.

'That was where our quest really began in earnest.' I explained.

'Until then,' Frank continued, 'it was all supposition and assumption.'

'Did you know Derek?' Mrs Palmer asked.

'No, we didn't.' I said.

'Then how did you learn of Chapter?'

I told her of my grandfather's involvement but remarked that it was only through knowing Anna, that we learnt of Chapter and the Egg in any detail.

'Then all three of us were brought into this adventure by accident or serendipity. Depending on how you view our situation.' Mrs Palmer
stated in a matter of fact way. I can still see in my mind's eye the breath from all three of us exuded in that freezing cold church.

Now we began to share what we knew or at least what we thought that we knew. It was very useful to cross reference things with Mrs Palmer. It gave us an excellent basis for sorting truth and fact from rumour and guess work. We shared all or information on Eurynome and Ophion, on Draco, the map, the paragraph I had found in the book of

Shakespeare's works, even the constellations set in stone on the moors and how all this pointed to Sheepstor, or Skytelestor as it was once known. She was absolutely fascinated by our story.

We discussed Anna and her part in all this in greater detail and concluded that she was the genuine article. We thought her trustworthy, especially as she now needed our help. She had last been in touch with Mrs Palmer at around the last time she had been in touch with me.

As for Chapter, we were in accord that they were also genuine in their motives, albeit they had by the very nature of what they were trying to achieve to be secretive and cunning in their dealings with all those outside of their ranks.

We were also of the opinion that even the laymen they worked with were most likely to be kept in the dark on all but the most pressing matters.

As for those like my grandfather who had helped when and where they could, it was plausible that they knew little but the most basic information.

At the risk of sounding like an idiot, I still had to ask the ultimate question and that was, where did she think Anna came from. It was a question that troubled the Myself, Rekha and Frank but even though we had talked about it many times, the inevitable answer in our estimation was still ludicrous although common sense and even logic pointed to the fact that it was true.

'Anna'.

'Ah yes, our mysterious young lady.' Mrs Palmer shook her head.

I had listened intently waiting for the words that would prove my suspicions were shared by someone other than my colleaagues.

'There is only one thought in my mind.'

'And that is?'

'That young lady is not of this world.'

'Meaning?'

'You want me to elucidate.' Mrs Palmer stated.

'If you are comfortable to do so.'

'Comfortable I am not, but I will be honest.'

'Please go on.' Frank had cut in.

On the recording she can be heard taking a pause, and then a long deep breath.

'As I said, I don't believe that Anna is of this world.' The church warden is heard to say on the recording.

I bless myself to this day that I recorded the conversation, albeit of off my own back.

I asked. 'By which you mean?'

'Another planet, solar system, galaxy.'

Frank said. 'What is the driving factor behind your thought pattern?'

'I suspect the same as yours.'

'Frank has never met Anna.' I explained.

'Oh, my word.'

Frank said, 'I wish I had and then I could comment more fully.'

'Then I will tell you exactly what Andrew will have told you and that is that Anna never ages, well if she does then it is almost at an imperceptible rate to my eyes.'

I thanked God for Mrs Palmer at that moment because here was a lady that we had only known for twenty four hours now she was confirming what I had been telling my colleagues for all of these years. I was wonderful feeling and an affirmation that I was not hallucinating or worst of all, lying to them.

'I have told my friends the exact same thing.' I added gratefully.

'Then any doubts we had about your mental faculties have been fully exonerated dear boy.' Frank told me.

'I know something else about Anna.' Mrs Palmer added.

We waited in anticipation of what the lady might say next.

'Please continue.'

'She told me her role was as a liaison between Chapter and others who were assisting them.'

I said, 'She told me much the same.'

However, my husband Derek had told me many years ago about Anna and that she wielded far more influence than she admitted to.'

'Can you elaborate?' I asked.

'He implied, I say implied because he never discussed her in too much detail, that Chapter worked for her.'

There it was, a statement that reversed Anna's supposed role.

'To what end?'

'It appears that Anna's aim and therefore ultimately Chapters aim is to retrieve the artefact and remove it once and for all from Earth to a star system where a more enlightened society will keep it safe in the centuries to come.'

'It seems he said rather a lot.' Frank stated bluntly.

'When he was caught in the lie I believe he told me in order to save our marriage. It was only many years later after his death that I met Anna. I'm sure she only visited me to illicit from me the whereabouts or possible whereabouts of the artefact.'

Frank and I when discussing the day's events later on both agreed that Mrs Palmers revelations were the turning point at which we were now fully committed to finding and retrieving the egg. Every word that she had spoken made sense and we knew for a fact that Rekha would be on board.

We had so many years invested in our quest but this was another piece of the puzzle completed and it gave us even more impetus to move forward.

'Now may I ask you both something?' The Lady asked.

'Please do.'

'You found something on your visit yesterday. What was it?'

I suggested, 'Shall we take a walk.'

'Lovely, I think it's warmer outside than in here.' She replied.

'Shall I lead the way?' Frank asked.

'Please do.' Mrs Palmer urged.

We walked down the path and across the graveyard to where the plaque had been buried or perhaps just overgrown. It was close to the north wall and as such would not have been in the main area where burials took place. That meant that it had more chance of remaining undisturbed over the years and it had probably not been seen for a century or more.

Mrs Palmer had knowledge of how well the grounds had been kept over the years and we knew more or less exactly where it was. I checked the photos on my phone.

'Where is it.' Mrs Palmer asked.

'You will see soon enough.'

Surely this was the place where we had found the stone tablet?

Frank pointed. 'There.'

'No that's not right.' I looked again at my phone.

'What are we looking for.'

'A small piece of disturbed ground.' Frank told her.

I couldn't see it. 'It's not there.'

'It must be.'

'There. The Turf has been lifted.'

'Or replaced.' Frank noted.

He was right, a square of turf had been removed and replaced. I got on my haunches and lifted the sod, knowing something wasn't right. The plaque was missing.

Mrs Palmer looked bemused until I showed her the photographs.

'My God.' She said, shaking her head sadly.

We covered an area around the turf but no other ground had been disturbed. That fact was obvious.

'But who?' Frank enquired of no one in particular.

'Chapter.' Mrs Palmer was frustrated. 'And in my own church.'

'It makes no sense. They asked for our help.' I told her.

'They want all evidence removed.' She replied.

'I agree' Frank growled. He was angry and so was I.

'I don't suppose you have any CCTV around here?' I asked.

'Lord no.'

'Ok. Then we will never know who removed the plaque

'So where do we go from here?' She asked.

Frank thought that the next stage was to find out why the plaque had been placed there. Maybe the church archives might have had a record as to who had it laid. Mrs Palmer said it would take a few days but she would search the church records and let us know.

188

Looking at the photos I had taken she could see the reason behind our quest. She thought it was definitive proof that the Universal Egg had been in the church or at least in the grounds in the recent past. It was now inconceivable to consider any other kind of scenario. If only her husband had given he more information, but then the very nature of Chapter excluded that possibility.

'Did your husband say anything more about the artefact.' Frank enquired of her.

'He did tell me something.' She admitted. 'And in all this flurry of new revelation and excitement I had quite forgotten to tell you.'

We waited expectantly and with hopeful but suppressed excitement.

'He said that contrary to Chapters rules that he had viewed the egg before hiding it.'

'Frank and I were puzzled by her statement.

'Wasn't that normal practise, dear lady?'

Mrs Palmer had shaken her head vociferously, she looked quizzically at the two of us.

'Let me explain something first,' she began, 'my husband liked to drink. A lot, alcohol I mean, but it was a well-kept secret. He drank alone and only on a rare occasion had I seen him worse for wear.'

'Your point being.' Frank pushed a little.

'My point being that I doubt very much that Anna or Chapter known it that they would have selected him for as a layman, because when he drank he became a little,' She appeared to search for a suitable

Phrase, 'Loose lipped.'

She looked embarrassed about her husband's character flaw.

'And he let out information that he shouldn't have?'

'Yes but as far as I know, only to me. I was as if the responsibility of the task they had given him was sometimes overwhelming. He would drink heavily late at night and often times he would tell me snippets about the organization and the artefact.'

'And you believed him?'

'Unquestioningly. I should also say that he only ever spoke on this matter after I had caught him lying on the night you gentlemen were tracking Chapter to Brentor church and nearly happened upon us.'

I told her that was understandable as in that instance he was trying to convince her of his reason for lying about work but attempting all the while to attend a meeting of Chapter.

In any event it seemed that Anna had made an error on this occasion, which might explain her need to bring Mrs Palmer into her circle of trust after the death of Mr Palmer.

'May we ask what he told you?' I queried.

'Yes of course. He told me various tittle tattle, things of no import to anyone. As I was saying before, he told me that the egg was kept in a sealed container, a smallish shockproof and waterproof container and against all Chapter's rules and Anna's warnings that the box should never be opened, he found a way to do so.'

'Really?' I asked dumbfounded.

'I believe that the layman or should I say layperson kept the box hidden but the member of Chapter with whom they worked kept the key.'

'So how did he open it.' I requested.

'I should first tell you what he did for a living.'

We waited her next sentence to find out what he did for a living.

'He had a business in Tavistock. He was a locksmith.'

Our vocal reactions remained cautious, guarded, but our faces must have given away our surprise.

'I know he opened it with a key he made himself and it was that action that was to convince him that the artefact and the story of its creation was to his mind credible.'

'What did he see?"

'He never shared that with me.'

'Damn that's disappointing.' Frank observed.

'Well yes and no.' The Lady said.

I asked her to explain.

'Yes.' She agreed. 'It would have been useful to know but at least he left this.'

Mrs Palmer undid a couple of buttons of her coat and reaching inside she tugged gently on a silver chain around her neck. Unable to free it she undid a couple more buttons to reveal the top of her dress. With another tug an object appeared from her cleavage. It was a steel key not more than two inches in length and with the oddest designed blades, they were an H shape.

'This fits nothing else in the house or at his business premises.' She assured us.

'You therefore think that it ......' My voice trailed away.

'I think it is the key that opens the box containing the artefact.'

She put the key in my hand and I remember how warm it was, not surprisingly of course given the place it had come from but she kept the chain around her neck.

'Then all we need to do, is find the artefact.' I remarked handing her back the key, which she deftly replaced and buttoned her coat.

'I will look through the church files and see if I can find the person or persons who had the plaque installed.' She told us.

'Before we go you told me during last night's telephone conversation that Anna mention some cataclysmic event that will occur three years from now.'

'That's right, that's what Anna told me. She said that it would be in that that time that the artefact might be spirited away.'

'Have you any idea what she meant or any clue as to what this awful event will be?' I asked.

'No, I don't.'

'Spirited away is an odd choice of words.' I added.

Mrs Palmer replied confidentially, 'I think she meant very much in a temporal way rather than spiritual, even though that was the phrase she used.'

Frank enquired if Anna could have meant a war or an act of God.'

'Either or neither, I simply don't know and I would not wish to guess as it may set you on the wrong track.'

We took our leave of her then, with a few pleasantries, which I won't bother to recount here.

'Calamitous event.' Frank said as we made our way back to the car. 'How very interesting.'

Chapter 24.

Heavenly Deception.

We returned home and in the evening our first call was to Rekha to tell her about our meeting. She was pleased to hear of our news and to know that we had another safe pair of hands at the wheel as it were.

If we were going to make a final breakthrough in this matter, she felt as though we had nothing to lose by opening up to this unknown woman and simply hoping that by doing so we were not going to regret our action. It was just a matter of trust. Well trust had got us thus far. We had to commit to taking somethings we learned on faith alone. The whole premise of our quest was built on trust so it seemed only right now that we gave our hand to the Fates and let those ladies decide the end result.

Rekha found Mrs Palmers story totally plausible although she retained the right to mull over a copy of the tape before committing herself in full.

Now we would sit back and take a few days to reflect over Mrs Palmers words, whilst at the same time continuing to look for more possible hiding places in which the artefact might currently be concealed. Had it been hidden in plain sight it may be discovered by accident and that in itself could prove calamitous.

In light of Mrs Palmers revelations about Anna we thought it best to take a little time to review her words on the subject. If as was suggested Anna was from some other world, then we must begin to look at her in a different context. There was we felt enough evidence to support the fact that Anna was on the side of good.

The finger of suspicion now pointed to her involvement with Chapter. Was she the mouthpiece for them, was she simply their communications liaison as she herself had stated or was she as the church warden implied the head of the organization?

We felt that was a question that needed to be urgently addressed to find out if this young lady the quietly spoken and gentle go between she liked to promote herself as being or a much stronger and determined driving force possibly sent by representatives of an unknown civilisation in a distant part of our galaxy. Was she the head of Chapter and if so why hadn't she shared that information with us?

Now was the time to decide. Were we to trust the obliging Mrs Palmer? Were we to trust Anna?

The first question was one on which we all agreed. She had shared information and a lot of it and she had bared her soul to us in her desperation to find answers at the risk of embarrassing herself. We all felt it took a guts to discuss her late husband's indiscretions, after all she hardly knew us. It could have been argued that Anna may have put her up to it, but again to what possible end, after all it was Chapter who had asked us for our help.

With regards to the second question, Anna certainly did not in any way lack intelligence. She must have known that people seeing her over the years would have realised that she failed to age to any great degree. As her human contact grew older, she did not. It may have been that she was some form of artificial intelligence and if our reasoning allowed for the fact of interplanetary travel, then surely it was not beyond the realms of possibility that she could be just that, an AI unit.

The more we talked the more fantastical it all sounded but it was all still bounded in reality. I had met Anna and so too had Mrs Palmer. She existed in one form or another. Perhaps we thought she might even be a hologram. Nothing, we felt at this stage was off the table.

A telephone conference again at the end of the week would give each of us time in which to reflect on the recording and it would give Mrs Palmer a chance to scrutinize the church records and see if she could find out who had authorized the plaque to be set in the graveyard.

None of us were able to be sure how accurate those records were, or even if they existed in any detail, if they did and they yielded something concrete by way of information gained, then we might be yet another step closer to our goal.

The next thing we had to consider was the warning of an imminent catastrophe in around three years' time. What would that be and how might it aid in Chapter in the removal of the presently missing artefact to another world? Would it affect all mankind? If it were to do that, then what form would it take and in all honesty it crossed our minds as to whether or not we would survive such an event.

It also put a strain on us as we feared for the safety of our family and friends. Would it be some severe weather problem caused by climate change or a global war or a devastating famine or plague? Would it be a meteor strike from out of space? The later seemed the most likely. If indeed Anna was an astronaut or suchlike, then she might be aware of a deep space object as yet to far from earth to be spotted by our telescopes and defence systems.

I was worrying that if she knew of such a dire outcome, that she had not brought it to the attention of the authorities in one some way or another.

We also had to contend with the fact that if we were now to believe that some event was likely, we would be totally unable to substantiate this imminent cataclysm after all who was going to pay us any attention? We didn't even know what form it would take.

Many end of the world theories populated so many online forums that should we choose to tell, it would be lost in the lunacy already out on the web.

All we could do was wait and pray that either Anna was wrong, or that Mrs Palmer or her husband had misconstrued what they had been told, or lastly that it was a mis direction meant to keep us on track and working harder to find the artefact, the knife at our back being the threat of missing a safe transferal of the egg to Chapter.

A week passed and various work problems caused delays to our next telephone conversation. Mrs Palmer called and told me that she was having trouble tracking down all the church records. It was odd she said because they were in such good order and so well kept. At some time, they had been copied onto microfiche and kept in the local library.

She said that it would take her the best part of a couple of weeks to search those records thoroughly.

Once again time would be against us and we would just have to resign ourselves to research as and when we had that time to spare. As it seemed with everything in our lives family and work came first as it does and yet we used every single spare moment when it became available to go on with our investigation.

Another month passed and we eventually had a call from her. Regrettably she told us that there was no record of such a plaque being laid in the church's historical files.

'I can't tell you why it wasn't entered.' Mrs Palmer added.

'Are you sure it hadn't been removed.' I enquired.

'It's difficult to say with any certainty.'

I persisted, 'Could you look again at the original handwritten records again.'

'Yes of course but what would I be looking for?'

'Some sign that a page may have been cut out is one example. It may help if you spot a gap in dates for example.'

'Oh, I see.'

I pushed the point, 'We need to be sure.'

'I will look again as soon as possible.' She promised.

Two days later she came back to me with a definitive answer.

'No, there are no anomalies in the records.'

Well, that cleared that up. Now we must assume that we could rule out the records being doctored and as such it would imply that the event had never been recorded in the first place. That then pointed to someone in the church being complicit with Chapter. Was that person a member of the clergy from a local level such as the vicar, or if he didn't have the authority to do that then it must surely have fallen to the bishop of the local diocese.

As the event had taken place just under a hundred and fifty years ago, it was going to prove immensely difficult to establish who authorised it and more to the point, who in the church had ensured that the installation of the plaque was never registered. It would be time consuming and wasteful to continue that line of enquiry and so we dropped it. Now we would concentrate on the plaque itself and what it meant in context to finding the artefact.

January slipped into February, then March and now before we knew it, mid- April of 2017 was upon us and it was already easter.

Once again we had been through a period of little progress trying to find why a drawing by Moncure D Conway had been carved in stone and laid in a remote Dartmoor graveyard was a nightmare. We tried to find out more about the drawing itself.

It had been part of a book on Demonology and Devil-Lore by Conway as a two volume set. As previously stated here, the book had a small reference to 'A Story of Dartmoor' and we knew that he hadvisited and stayed in Devon for a while in the late eighteen hundreds.

Whoever had the plaque made need not have had it created in Conway's lifetime, so Mrs Palmer had continued going through every record on the installation of tombstones, memorials, or monuments from the late nineteenth century until the present day.

It was a thankless task and had proved fruitless, just to add insult to injury for all her hard work. She said that she would still carry on checking the archives in case, in her words, 'Something of interest turned up.'

It would have been useful to find anything that might have linked Conway directly with St Leonards church but we could find no written evidence. There were rumours that he might have visited the area, which of course was possible. He seemed to have spent a little time in Devon.

Having no way of knowing if he had a knowledge that his drawing had been copied and carved was an annoyance, as was the lack of a timeline for its placement.

Rekha had been busy searching the internet for any kind of dark web conspiracy theories concerning future catastrophes and end of days theories. At one point she had called us to say that she had been overwhelmed by the sheer amount of stupidity and general ignorance that populated some online forums.

There were of course still some sensible area's worth considering and some intelligent and well-conceived conjecture on various doomsday scenarios. Ranging from limited nuclear war to asteroid strike, extreme weather events, volcanic eruption, tidal waves, the release of an airborne pathogen in a chemical warfare strike.

Others suggested an epidemic which might wipe out a significant part of the population.

'Why', she posed the question, 'would one or perhaps a combination of these events pose the ideal opportunity for the egg to be spirited away?'

'It would be easier to do under the cover of all eyes being focused on a major news event.' Frank proposed.

I had another thought. 'What if it was an event that caused people to keep their heads down, as it were?'

'Such as?' Rekha had asked.

'Well if it's going to be taken out by a spacecraft that might be more easily done if airspace was closed.' I told her.

'Then which event would best suit that?'

It was a good point well made but our friend had a good answer.

'Volcano dear girl.' Frank stated. 'Such as Eyjafjallaokull in Iceland in two thousand and ten.'

'It caused major disruption for several days over northern European airspace.' I reminded her.

'It would be an ideal opportunity to retrieve the artefact.' Rekha had acknowledged.

I had asked. 'How would they know that a volcano will erupt close by the UK in three years' time?'

'Good point.' Frank said.

'Unless they have some way to cause it. They, being Chapter and I think that highly unlikely.' She remarked.

'The only other way, is some form of time travel.' I thought the idea

worth dropping in the pot.

'You really think so dear boy?'

It was a non-starter. 'Not really. I brought it up because Anna as both I and Mrs Palmer explained, never seems to age. That said, I think it may be possible to go back in time as

198

those events have happened already but I don't therefore think that it's possible to go forward in time as events in the future have not yet occurred.'

'Seriously?' I could hear the sarcasm in Rekha's voice as in my mind's eye I could imagine the look on her face.

'Just a thought.'

'Hmmm.'

'Andy has a point,' Frank said unexpectedly, 'there are more things in heaven and earth than are dreamt of in your philosophy Horatio.'

'Okay.'

'All I'm saying is, we don't know and personally speaking, the more we find, the less I understand.' I frustratingly admitted.

'Heaven seems to be conspiring against us.' Rekha had said in a tired but still determined voice.

'We are close now though.' I had told my colleagues.

'Agreed.' Frank said with feeling.

'We just keep going. At least it appears that we have a timeline now.' Rekha commented.

'Indeed, we do and still enough of it left in order to finally solve this damned puzzle.'

I thought it worth asking. 'Have either of you considered what will happen if we don't solve it and the universal egg isn't found?'

There was a very long silence. I still remember it to this day as we, me included thought through the question I had asked but had still been unable to answer to my own satisfaction.

'That's not easy to answer.'

'I know, that's why I asked it.'

Frank mused a moment. 'Then they must try again at some point in the future.'

'Their future or ours?' Rekha asked sensibly.

'It seems that theirs dear girl is better situated than ours.'

'At least we have another pair of hands to help.' Frank stated, referring to Mrs Palmer.

Rekha said, 'Well she has confirmed your thoughts and description of Anna to the nth degree.'

I admitted to my friend's that it was a great relief to me.

'We believed you Andrew you know that.' Rekha told me, 'We also know that the clues we found have all led to one place, and that it has to be said, however unlikely, is St Leonards church. The stones on the moors point to it. The torn map of the tors that led us to the constellation Draco and the churches with the Tinners Hares point to it, so there must be something that we are missing, the final link if you like.'

Frank and I both concurred with Rekha's assessment.

'It has must be there on or in the church or its grounds,' she continued, 'Mrs Palmers husband may have been a bit of a loose cannon but he was not stupid. If he had been then rest assured that Chapter would not have touched him with a barge pole.'

Frank nodded. 'Those facts are indisputable.'

'So why did someone have that plaque installed and why, given the fact that Chapter have asked for our help, did they apparently have it removed again?' I demanded.

'Fair point.'

'I does seem counterproductive dear boy.'

'Unless.' A thought had come into my head.

'Unless what?'

'Unless the plaque is a red herring.'

'A deception, but why?'

'Perhaps,' I told my colleagues. 'someone outside of Chapter was in the process of getting a little too close to the truth.'

Rekha asked. 'So, you think another person or persons unknown are also on the trail of the artefact?'

Frank put his thoughts forward. 'We must consider it.'

'All these years we have been working under the assumption that it was Chapter, Anna and us alone looking for the egg.'

'Yet originally,' Frank continued,' we had always considered that the artefact might prove a threat to society.'

'Once it became public knowledge you mean?' Rekha asked.

'Exactly so.'

'Then there must" I said, 'be individuals or groups out there who consider the artefact to be a threat to their society or religious creed.'

'If the egg is what Chapter say it is after all.' Rekha reminded us. 'We haven't seen it ourselves. We only have the word of one other person.'

'Anna.'

'Yes.'

'And Mrs Palmers husband.' Frank said. 'He saw it.'

'That's hearsay.' Rekha corrected.

'True.'

I was still of the same mind, that the artefact was real and, that it was what Anna had told me, another universe but in miniature compared to the universe in which we existed.

'After all these years of research and evidence gathering, I believe in it until I'm proven wrong.'

'I was just stating a fact.' Rekha told me, equally defensively.

'It is odd.' Frank remarked. 'That we have no evidence of any other group who might cause a threat to it or to us. In fact,' He reminded me. 'Chapter has been the only collective that has ever threatened us, well you to be precise at the beginning of our investigation but as they need us now, that's all changed.'

Rekha proposed that we all remain on our guard in case someone did mean us harm. Further to that it seemed the church itself in the form of the established clergy had done all they could to help to conceal it from the public.

Perhaps they would be glad to see the back of it. If it didn't exist on earth any longer then they could forget about it and it wouldn't be a threat to them, so it was in the church's interest to help Chapter in any way they could.

She asked what we thought Mrs Palmers husband had seen when he opened the box containing the egg. What would have caused him to believe that it was what legend had purported it to be?

We each had our own ideas but surprisingly each of us refused to share them. Maybe it meant a different thing to the three of us and possibly to our new friend, the church warden.

It was something we all hoped to find out as it would at last bring us the satisfaction we sought and hopefully prove that forty years of work had not been in vain.

Chapter 25.

Waterproof.

Easter was gone almost as quickly as it had arrived and April ended in a flurry of heavy showers and high winds and before we knew it mid-May was upon us.

Frank called. 'I've been thinking about the Tinners Hare's.'

'I what respect?'

'In respect of mines.'

'You mean .... ?'

'We considered it once before. It may be worth further investigation still.'

My mind was automatically aligned to his. 'Why not.'

'Perhaps we missed something.'

His point had to be conceded. 'Do you think the churches point the way?'

'Not necessarily but they must be in the mix of clues for a reason!'

'Not just a red herring?' I asked.

'No, I don't believe so.'

Maybe it's a question that Mrs Palmer could help us with? I replied.'

He was silent for a moment. 'Certainly worth a try.'

'If her husband had ever mentioned the tin miners or the hares, who knows.'

'I still think that hiding the artefact in a mine may have been possible even though we discounted it once before.'

My mind was open to a discussion on the subject but I thought it was unlikely to yield any answers or to bring any fresh evidence or clues to the table. Frank gave way to me on that point. He conceded.

'Upon reflection,' He had told me, 'it doesn't seem to really add up, although I do believe that the Golden Dagger Mine, or Golden Dragon Mine as it once was, may in all likelihood have concealed the egg in days of yore.'

Both of us were thinking as hard as we possibly could about the point in question.

'What have we missed.?' I asked again.

'Well something that's for sure or we would have it by now in our possession. We need a fresh line of investigation. Concrete evidence.'

'Watertight and incontrovertible to get us over the line, as it were.'

Frank's voice altered and an air of unmistakable excitement could be felt from him, even over the phone.

'Watertight, waterproof.'

I was bemused. 'I'm not with you.'

'Mrs Palmer described the box in which the artefact is kept in the way a person would describe a flight recorder system in an aircraft. Do you remember?'

'Yes.'

'So they are virtually indestructible.'

'Ok.' I said.

'What about waterproof?'

My mind raced. 'Oh.'

'Oh indeed.'

I had to admit that it seemed entirely logical.

'So I'm thinking,' he continued, 'what if it was hidden nearby to the church but not in or on the grounds and more to the point, hidden in or under water.?

'You're thinking a large body of water perhaps.'

'Well yes.'

'Such as .... ' I had waited for him to say the words.

'Burrator reservoir.' He duly obliged.

'That's going to take some searching.'

'It must have been put somewhere comparatively easily retrieved.'

'That makes a lot of sense Frank.'

'Doesn't it dear boy. In the first instance there is no access onto the immediate side of the reservoir. It's only the waterboard and anyone with fishing rights who can get that close and that is strictly enforced.'

I was sure that he was right and that it was securely fenced off to the general public. I had walked around it many times, mostly in late the autumn or winter. In summer it was difficult to park or walk as it was often overrun by tourists.

The reservoir and environs were beautiful but often the experience was spoiled by the sheer amount of people who came to walk, run, and cycle around its banks or just stare at the water whilst licking an ice cream and contemplating others doing just the same.

Adamant that his idea was sound I said, 'Let's see if Mrs Palmer is in agreement with us.'

I rang her but to no avail. She was out. I left a message and we continued to think where a safe and well concealed place if still reasonably easily accessible spot would be. An area in which the box could be submerged but in which a rope or line of some sort that would have to be attached to it, could be camouflaged.

The last thing that was needed was for a fisherman or employee of the South West Lakes Trust, who managed the reservoir to trip over such a rope and either cut it in frustration, or worse still, to pull it up and find what was attached to it.

My phone rang. It was Mrs Palmer. 'I missed a call from you.'

I put her on conference call with Frank and myself and explained to her our new line of thought.

'It would make sense to me.'

'You think it a good candidate for a concealment?'

'Well my husband fished there at times.'

'How often?' Frank asked.

'Oh at least twice a week in fishing season of course.'

Now we must be on the right track, it sounded very promising.

'You are sure?' I enquired as little to strongly.

'Absolutely. I did know my husband quite well.' She sounded quite offended at the doubt in my voice.

I explained. 'I only ask in that way because I now think it unlikely he would have hidden it there.'

'Why?'

Frank took over, much to my relief as it also dawned on him that the words she had just spoken negated any possibility of the Universal Egg being hidden in Burrator Reservoir.

'What Andy means dear lady is that wherever your husband hid this remarkable artefact it would not have been in a place he would keep returning to. That in itself would be too dangerous and in almost all respects have drawn attention to the area. If he was under any kind of surveillance, even casual observation for that matter, he certainly would have brought suspicion on himself and by association on the artefact itself.'

I felt bad. Franks idea was sound and well-conceived but Mrs Palmer had unknowingly just buried it once and for all.

'Oh, I see.' We could hear the sadness in her voice.

I told her that we had been thinking along the lines of Burrator being a very good hiding place under the right circumstances.

'The reservoir makes perfect sense.' Mrs Palmer told us. 'It would be totally out of sight and also irretrievable unless you knew exactly where it what and how to fish it out again, no pun intended.'

'There must be other bodies of water locally that might fit the bill, as a matter of fact, the old water ponds at the quarries are a possibility aren't they?' I asked.

Frank was sure they weren't. 'Too much old pipework and the like to snag a line on, plus you never know when they may be drained for one reason or another.'

We called Rekha and caught her at an unusually quiet moment at work.

'I have twenty minutes before my next meeting.' She remarked.

Explaining the situation as quickly as possible we told her that Mrs Palmer was in on the call as well.

'Franks idea is sound,' Rekha agreed, 'as the artefact could have been hidden in a body of water.'

'That said,' Mrs Palmer remarked, 'there are very few other large bodies of water close by and certainly none which are closer than the reservoir.'

I agreed. 'But all the clues point to Sheepstor or at least a two square mile area around the church, as being the place where your husband would have hidden it.'

'Are there no other old lakes or pools on the moor that would fit?' Rekha demanded. She always drove a conversation to a conclusion, as we were sure she did in her job.

'None that fit the bill dear girl.'

'Okay so that leaves us with the possibility of a smaller body of water a river or brook.'

'No.' I said. 'Too much risk that someone could happen upon it.'

'Agreed.'

'What about a water feature?' Frank sighed.

'Such as?' Rekha asked.

The phone was silent for a while as each of us in our own domain mulled over the idea. We must have all been thinking much the same thing. 'What kind of water feature!'

'A Well perhaps?'

I remember the silence had continued for what seemed an age but was probably thirty seconds or so.

It was Mrs Palmer who had been the one to drop the 'bomb' as it were.

'A water well?' Rekha broke the silence.

'Yes.'

'What made you think of that?' I queried.

Mrs Palmers breath was audible on the line, it had been measured but now it had deepened and quickened. She explained her thought.

'We all agreed that a body of water was likely, but a body as large as a reservoir has too many visitors. Likewise a lake or pond servicing a quarry would be liable to be drained or re-opened. Fishing lakes are no good for the same reasons already stated, leaving us with a small body of water but one where it is out of the way, relatively speaking. It must also remain undisturbed, so it would be more suitable if the feature were on private land and thereby subject to limited use. So what better than a Well?'

I was thrilled with the idea. 'The artefact would never be disturbed in any situation unless the landowner agreed that renovations should need to be carried out and in any case it would be at their behest.'

'The perfect hiding place.' Frank observed.

'Like it.' Rekha said.

I wanted to maintain a firm grip on this new idea. We had wasted o much time in chasing our tails before.

'We have a little over two and a half years,' I told my colleagues, 'before the year 2020 arrives. If we investigate this lead and it gets us nowhere, then we will surely run out of time. Remember Anna's words, some world changing event is going to take place and that is the time chosen to move the artefact.'

Rekha responded factually. 'If no other leads become apparent then we will run out of time anyway Andrew.'

'I agree.' Frank said. 'We have exhausted so many avenues already.'

'Being a very new addition to this group I feel out of place saying this but, my husband believed totally in the artefact, its authenticity and the need to get it to safety,' Mrs Palmer cut in, 'so this seems like the last opportunity to find it.'

There was a sadness to her voice. 'You have all spent so many years on your quest and to no avail. Everything points to Sheepstor being the place where it was kept safe all those years ago and knowing my husband as I did, he would have wanted it close, so close in fact that he could see the hiding place every day. Had he not died with his mistress on that fateful day, the egg would be in his possession now and ready to be spirited away to safety. What I'm saying is, it must be within the boundaries of the village. It simply must.'

Her passion moved us all. She had spoken eloquently and it seemed only fair that we gave her as equal a part in our discussions as we gave each other.

'Then lets vote on it.' I offered.

'That's a good idea.' Frank said.

Rekha was on board. 'Fine with me.'

'Will I get a vote too?' Mrs Palmer asked.

'Yes. Indeed you will.'

'Ladies first.' I said. 'Rekha, do we pursue this line of enquiry.'

'Yes.'

'Mrs Palmer. Same question to you.'

'Yes.'

Frank?

'Indeed we do dear boy.'

I had taken a deep breath and prayed we were right. I said yes and so it was unanimous, we would look at water features such as a well and the like.

'There is one worth immediate consideration.' Mrs Palmer told us.

'Please tell?' Rekha requested.

'I don't know why it didn't come to me before.' Mrs Palmer sounded a little bemused and annoyed with herself.

'What? Rekha asked.

A long embarrassed silence followed from Myself, Mrs Palmer and Frank

'Oh good God.' Frank said exasperatedly.

I too had understood. 'Damn.'

'What am I missing.' Rekha demanded.

'You have missed nothing.' Frank told her. 'But we have.'

'Seriously, will someone tell what's going on?'

Mrs Palmer said with some delicacy. 'Sheepstor has a well.'

'Seriously?' Rekha said. Not a good sign if she repeated, seriously. It

meant she was probably quite angry.

'St Leonard's Well.' Frank told her.

'How old is it?'

'I assumed it was built with the church.' Mrs Palmer replied.

I was not convinced. 'I thought it was a horse trough?'

'More of a drinking trough for the village and in recent years for many animals.' The church warden said.

'So does it count or not?' Rekha asked again.

Frank wasn't convinced that it did. 'It may have started life as a Well but if it is now a drinking trough, then no.'

'It was made with fragments of stone from the old east window.' I was quick to add, 'The water is piped in from a field a little way off.'

'A water trough whoever or whatever it serves is not a Well. That's probably why we discounted it during our original investigation.' Frank replied.

Rekha enquired 'Are there any other wells in the area?'

Mrs Palmer was unsure. 'I cannot say with any certainty.'

'Is it worth checking?'

We all thought it was as the murmurs of approval showed.

'No harm in looking.' Frank replied amicably.

'We should be sure,' I acknowledged, 'but if it is no more than some drinking trough for the village then no.'

'It also depends on where it is.'

'No, no,' Mrs Palmer was adamant, 'it was my mistake. The Well or trough is right on the road, it's too obvious.'

'You are sure that your husband never mentioned a Well?' Rekha was insistent. She obviously felt as though there was traction to be gained on this road of enquiry. 'Or any kind of water feature.'

Silence fell again as we tried to give our most recent colleague a little breathing space. A minute ticked by and we could all feel the tension building.

'No.'

'Did your husband mention anyone in the village having any work done which might involve construction nearby?' Rekha continued.

'I don't remember.'

'Nothing at all?'

'I'm sorry, no.'

Now an idea struck me. 'Where does the water come from that feeds St Leonards Well?'

'I told you earlier, from a nearby field.'

'Was the Well originally in that field.'

'Oh yes it ....'

'So let me get this right. The water that feeds St Leonards Well is still fed from the site of the original position of the Well!'

'That's correct.'

Frank's next word summed the situation up beautifully. 'Bingo.'

Poor Mrs Palmer was still lost. 'But how does that help us?'

Rekha stepped in. 'Because if the original site of the well is in a field, then it is hidden from the gaze of all but a few cows or sheep.'

'Dear Lord.' The penny had dropped.

'How long ago was it moved do you know?' I said calmly.

She did. 'In the late 1800's.'

'Why was it moved?'

'Because it was easier for the villagers to get to on the road.'

Frank added. 'And easier for Chapter to hide the artefact if no one was going to draw water from there twenty times a day.'

It made perfect sense of course. No one was going to go all the way across a muddy field filled with livestock to draw water, when they could get it from the well, or trough, only feet from their houses.

Add to this the fact that it was on private land and most of the landowners or farmers at that time were treated with respect by the village community, then it was unlikely the original site would ever have been disturbed again.

We might finally have cracked it. All we needed now was to find out who the landowner had been and who the current one was. We asked Mrs Palmer and awaited her reply. I was quite a while coming.

'Are you still there?'

'Yes Andrew, I'm still here.'

'Then who was the landowner?'

'This is embarrassing.' Mrs Palmer blustered.

A pause, a long moment of anticipation as the lady gathered her wits as a long forgotten memory re-introduced itself to her.

'Please enlighten us.'

'It was my husband Derek's great grandfather.'

Frank guffawed. 'Really?'

'Yes'.

Rekha said. 'Mrs Palmer, do you know who the current landowner is?'

'I do. It was Derek's, so now the land belongs to me.'

There was silence and then utter elation. We cheered, all of us and Mrs Palmer joined in.

'Then we can check the old site of the Well?'

'With my blessing.'

'I have to ask may we call you by your Christian name?'

We heard her giggle a little, then laugh out loud.

'I should have told you before. My father was always interested in the Greek myths. My Christian name is Eurynome.'

Chapter 26.

All's well on Dartmoor.

What a phone conversation that had been. We had ended it happy at the result. More than happy in fact. Maybe a better word would be, ecstatic.We had also agreed not to rush to Eurynome Palmers field but rather to set in motion what we would do should we find the artefact.

The difficulty was this; should we find the box containing the Universal Egg what was our next step. Rekha having her meeting to attend had left the conversation a few minutes prior to it ending. This left Frank, Eurynome and myself to wind up the call and decide on the next course of action.

Was it best that if found, we leave it in situ until contacted by Anna or should one of us take possession of it on the basis that it might be discovered by some extremely remote chance and lost again.

'Perhaps.' Mrs Palmer said. 'We should take it for safe keeping.'

'It may be worth consideration.' I told her.

Frank disagreed. 'If it is there, then it's been safely hidden and has remained undiscovered since your husband put it there.'

'Oh I see.' She said.

I was with Frank on this one. 'It's common sense.'

'Having remained out of sight if not out of mind for so long, what's the point in disturbing the status quo?' He asked.

It was decided. We would go within the next two days or so and check out the original St Leonards Well in Mrs Palmers field. If the box with the artefact was in it, then we would replace it and hope that Anna would soon be in touch.

The temptation to drive over at once to check it out was almost unbearable, however we knew that the sudden excited arrival of three people racing across the ladies field might draw unwanted if understandable attention to the area in question. Even though it was a tiny village, you could bet on someone watching from a window or doorway, not purposely, but simply because in the country any kind movement was often the cause of interest.

Another factor we had to consider was if our phones were bugged. It seemed highly unlikely if not ludicrous but it was still something that needed consideration. A day or two cooling our heels would allow for us to keep watch on the field, via Eurynome Palmer and to see if any unusual occurrences or suspicious activities alerted any one of us to danger.

A few hours later my phone rang. It was my friend Rekha.

'What's the plan?'

I told her, briefly outlining what we would do and more importantly, not do.

'Very sensible.' She stated.

'I suppose you will want to be in on it?' I said jokingly.

'Bloody right. I have the weekend off. I've organised cover. I have no intention of missing this.'

'You're really driving down for this?'

'Wouldn't miss it for the world.'

I was very pleased and knew the others would be.

'It's a long drive.' I advised her.

'I'll get the train. Will you pick me up from Plymouth station?'

'Of course I will.'

'Must go, will call tonight. Tell the others.'

Even though it's now four years ago, I still remember that day well. I broke the news first to Frank and then to Eurynome Palmer. Being a woman and far more practical than us two men she brought us back to Rekha's visit.

'Where will she stay?'

I hadn't given Rekha's arrangements much or indeed any consideration and admitted so.

'Very well, she can stay with me, Eurynome said, 'if of course she would like too. It will allow her to get a feel for the village and its surroundings and help me keep watch on the field.'

'I'm sure she will be ok with that.' I said positively, whilst at the same time not knowing if she would.

Rekha and I spoke later that evening and she was fine with it.

Now all we had to do was to watch and wait, keep our guard up and our

heads down. We must pay attention to detail. If things changed around us, if we heard or suspected actions by others that were out of the norm than it should be noted down and shared.

Four days later and I was at Plymouth Train Station picking up our friend. Frank was with me. It was a pleasure to see her again after so long a period of time. As we made our way out of Plymouth and on towards the moors we spoke of nothing but the coming two days.

It was late afternoon on a Friday so traffic was heavy as we headed slowly in the general direction of Tavistock. The outskirts of Plymouth soon fell away behind us and we passed Roborough and climbed and crested the hill. It was then that the full beauty of the moors opened up to us.

To our right in the distance a road lined with large, mostly detached houses snaked away a couple of miles on the hillside. The village was Shaugh Prior and the houses were set against the side of a hill known as Shaden Moor.

At the back of the hill a valley ran down to the river Plym. Crossing the river a sheer rock face loomed. Popular with climbers it was known as the Dewerstone. In the olden days Dewer was the name for the devil. We could see the top of it as it heaved its way out of the wood below, an unforgiving shoulder of granite buttressing the high moor behind.

Further on, the top of Wigford Down my home turf, formed a hillcrest with the remains of the foundations of prehistoric homes scattered across it. To its left a little further down the north side of the down a farm once run by another of my uncle's peeped above a line of oak, beech and sycamore trees. Urgles as the farm was known was centuries old and part of the gateway to the moors.

Being a very bright May evening the landscape had looked more spectacular than ever. We passed by the village of Clearbrook, another small guardian of the moors and two miles later entered Yelverton, a larger village which was a local shopping centre. Just on small row of shops about one hundred and fifty yards in length. There was a supermarket, butchers shop, garage, café's and my wife's favourite haunt the Ochre Hair Lounge.

Built on a small plateau. Yelverton's original name was 'Elvertown', presumably named for the small ells that inhabited the nearby Drake's leat, a water course named after the legendary naval captain and explorer Sir Francis Drake who lived only a few miles away at his manor near Buckland Monarchorum.

On we went through the village and east out on the road east towards Princetown.

Now the Tors rose magnificently ahead of us. In front of us a few miles away and almost directly the road inclined up sharply towards Princetown. The road at that point rises up seven hundred feet in less than two miles to Sharpitor and Leather Tor. It was at the bottom of the hill that we would bare right at the Burrator Inn heading south through the village of Dousland towards Sheepstor.

One and a half miles further on and we turns left onto the road to the reservoir. The dam wall and sluices loomed up on our right and after another mile we turned onto the dam itself. It's a short piece of roadway about a hundred yards in length, the road leading right the way around the reservoir before bringing you back to where you began. The only other way out is through Sheepstor village itself but the road is incredibly narrow with few passing points even for good drivers.

We rolled slowly into the village to find Eurynome Palmer on a grass verge waiting for us. She wore a multi coloured floral dress. I remember well because I had never seen her in anything but a dark coat. She looked younger than the age we thought her to be and it was so nice to see a smile on her face, a real smile with warmth and a charm Frank and I hadn't noticed before.

She welcomed the two of us with a firm handshake and surprisingly a kiss on each cheek but her biggest welcome was for Rekha for whom it must be said, her greeting was effusive. She shook warmly shook Rekha's hand and then hugged her tightly, much to our astonishment and I suspect her own as she stood back to give her newfound friend a little space.

'My dear, it is so nice to meet you.'

The two women exchanged pleasantries and Rekha thanked Mrs Palmer for offering her a place to stay.

'Come in please.' Eurynome turned and walked us through the few houses that formed the centre of the village. Her house built as the others mostly were of heavy Dartmoor granite, was set back a little from the road at the north-eastern edge. A few fields stretched away behind her property butting firmly into the base of the Tor itself.

Frank and I lugged Rekha's bags for her whilst the ladies made their way up the slight incline and through the front gate which was at the centre of a low stonewall.

'This is all mine.' She said in a matter of fact way that hid no pretence.

'And the field?' Rekha asked as we caught them up at the gate.

'Right there.' Eurynome Palmer indicated a field wall to the east of her rather wild garden. The field itself looked to me to be roughly a third of an acre in all. In truth it was not so much a field as an extra piece of garden that had probably been purchased from a local farm owner sometime in the past.

I still recall the look on Frank's face as he gazed around apparently to gauge if the field could be overlooked from the road or other houses but it seemed unlikely. The fields behind the house and the Tor itself was another matter as the view from there would be all encompassing with no hiding place that we could see.

We parked Rekha's bags and with a quiet word to our dear hostess to pretend as though she was just showing us around her domain. The deceit was easily accomplished as in truth as that was exactly what she was doing.

Pausing for a moment at the stone wall which was the divider between her formal wild garden and the field we scrutinised the area.

There was a gap and what could only be described as a roughly constructed stile over which a person could step with little difficulty as it was barely three feet high. Eurynome Palmer made a sweeping gesture with her hand as if to encompass the whole area but she pointed craftily to the north wall of the enclosure where we could see some old timber seemingly piled up in a careless manner.

We chatted loudly about nothing of importance in case someone was in the vicinity listening to us before walking back inside. It was decided that we wait a couple of hours before leaving the ladies to their vigil. As a team we considered the idea of a night watch but concluded that so long a period of time had passed the artefact was either there or it was not. The reason we would keep watch was to try to ascertain if we being watched ourselves. If we were confident that thing were as normal, then we would proceed to check if it was in the well of not and that would be under cover of twilight.

The time passed uneventfully but of course Mrs Palmer was the only person who could really tell if anything was amiss. Only she knew enough about the area to judge that.

It was odd to see her so at ease with herself. The once starchy upper middle class lady Frank and I had met previously was gone. Maybe company suited her as it must have been a lonely lifestyle here on the moor's edge. Of course on the other hand it may have been the knowledge that this great if tiresome responsibility was now being shared, added to which was the excitement generated by the thought of finding the object. What a moment that would be if it was there.

Her whole being had relaxed and the printed floral dress she wore gave her an air of warmth and geniality I presumed had long been hidden, as many people both women and men put up defences often characterised by being aloof and dressing in a more formal manner.

The time soon came for Frank and I to leave. We decided to return the next day late in the morning. This would give the ladies time to get to know each other a little better and for Rekha to gauge the personality and intent of her hostess, after all Eurynome Palmer remained as yet an unknown quantity. We knew nothing of her family or friends, nor did we know about her background.

All we knew was what she saw fit to tell us. Forty years of investigation had taught us that the only people we could absolutely trust was ourselves. We bade the girls goodnight and drove away.

We chatted on the way as close friends do with that complete trust, built over years of shared pain, laughter, disappointment, loyalty and introspective. Frank's was a friendship I valued above all others.

'If we find the artefact, do you intend to open the box?

It was a question which demanded an answer. A simple yes or no in this instance would not suffice.

'That depends.'

'On what?

'We agreed to leave it there, if of course it actually is there.'

Frank was pragmatic. 'Let's assume it is for arguments sake.'

'You mean, do we risk leaving it or do we move it?'

'My point is that if we find it, others may have made the connection already?'

'So the mere act of us finding it, might make it more vulnerable to discovery by others.' I said bluntly

'Quite.'

'In that scenario it would be wise to move it.'

'I know I'm playing devil's advocate,' He replied, 'but we will have no way of knowing if we are being observed or not.'

'Unless the observer is careless.' I offered.

'You avoided my original question.' Frank had reminded me. 'Do you intend to open the box?'

My mind had been engulfed with a swirling mixture of emotions each time the thought had crossed my mind and was many thousands of times over the years.

I still hadn't decided. At times I was sure it was better to leave the box unopened and by doing so remain safe in my ignorance, yet at others I felt it was my right to look, to decide once and for all if it was real or not. I explained my dilemma to him.

'Our thought patterns on this are totally synchronised.' He admitted.

'It's very much a double edged sword.'

'With very sharp edges.' He said unemotionally.

I could only share with him what was in my mind right at that time.

'Given all the facts we have, it would be a boon to know if the egg was the real thing or not.'

'Then you must be contemplating opening the box and looking at its contents?'

'I can see no other way around it but it must be a team decision.'

He nodded, 'If we do so, what will prove that it's real, a real universe?'

'There is a way.' I told him but I want to keep that to myself just for the time being.

'Okay.'

'You aren't offended?'

Frank sounded matter of fact his face had been impassive.

'Not at all. I'm sure you will reveal all in the fullness of time.'

'I will explain tomorrow, if the box is there and the artefact is inside it we all deem it right and proper to open it.'

Frank seemed resolved to my decision. 'Will we each have a vote?'

'Certainly but ....'

'But what?' He asked.

'Eurynome Palmer holds the key and we can't force her to relinquish it, it must be her choice to do that. Only then can we take a vote on opening the box or keeping it closed forever.'

'Of course we mustn't, it is as you say her choice.'

'What if it's a draw. I mean, there are four of us so if it goes to two votes for and two against opening it?'

'Then in my opinion it stays shut.'

'Hmm.'

I needed to know. 'Do you agree?'

It was a while before he committed to answering my question.

'I do,' he had laughed but it was a dry slightly humourless laugh, 'but I will be very disappointed if we don't get a peek at it.'

'Me too.'

'How do you think Rekha will vote?'

'She's a Gemini. She won't be able to resist. Her intellect won't allow for it.'

'So that just leaves, the Church warden.'

'I think we are all in the same boat Frank. It will be the only chance we get and if that's the case I don't think any of us will be willing to miss out on seeing the artefact.'

'I agree dear boy, it's cost us to much time and effort for us not to at least glimpse the truth that's for sure.'

We arrived home and each went our separate ways. Now it was a matter of telling our wives that we would spend most of the following day in the company of two other women. Neither Frank or I could ever complain of the support our wives gave us. At times they must have despaired of our antics, but they kept the faith and let us get on with the business in hand.

Saturday arrived and after a late breakfast I picked Frank up and we headed back to Sheepstor, arriving just after eleven am. We had a long wait ahead. The girls had had a good night and were now in high spirits. To this day we all remember how the excitement built during the hours leading up to late evening when we would attempt our first effort to find and retrieve the universal egg.

'Before we begin, I must ask you all to consider the matter at hand.' I told them sternly. 'We must all be in accordance as to what we do if we find the box.'

'You mean, do we open it?' Rekha asked.

'Even before we get to that point.' Frank added supportively.

Rekha looked perplexed. 'Go on.' She said.

'Eurynome. The key to the box belongs to you. We need to know if you are willing to open the box should it be found.'

Mrs Palmer looked surprised. 'Oh my word yes. I ....We have all had such a long wait. If we find it then I want to know

221

if it has been worth all these years of blood, sweat and tears to have done so.'

She looked emotional. We didn't know her to well but that much was obvious to us all. For moment I thought she might cry but instead she fought back a tear and keeping a strong upper lip she tugged gently on the necklace and freed the key from its resting place between her breasts. She took the chain and H shaped key from around her neck and in a gesture of trust, handed it to me. It was still warm.

'Hold onto it.' She said. 'It belongs to all of us now.'

I held it for a long while before handing it to Frank, who studied it in turn then passing it to Rekha. She looked at it for a few seconds and as if sensing the mood between the four of us, she handed it back to Eurynome Palmer.

'This maybe ours.' Rekha told her. 'But you are the custodian.'

It was a lovely moment and one we would all treasure as long as we would live.

Eurynome wanted to cook for us that evening and we were very happy to accept her invitation. In the meantime we had a light lunch and the discussion turned as to how we would proceed. It was best we agreed that Frank and I would go and examine the wood pile and move any timbers that might encumber us in our task later on. That would give us time to examine the well itself and to look for any obvious signs of something being hidden there. All being well we would return to the woodpile and under cover of gathering darkness at twilight we would search in earnest for the artefact.

Lunch over, Frank and I took some useful tools which he had sensibly insisted on bringing with us and crossed the style into the field.It didn't take us long to move the wood. Some bits had of log had been nailed together to form a rough shelter over the well. The well shaft itself had been boarded up and I was grateful that my friend had thought practically as we use a pinch bar and the claw end of a hammer he'd brought to dismantle the cover.

It was a warm day and we soon worked up a sweat but we worked in silence and with the minimum of noise while Rekha and Eurynome kept watch from the front porch to the road and from back window to the Tor. It took nearly two hours to complete our task but by the end of that time we were content with what we had achieved.

A cursory look at the area told us that it was very similar in design to Saxon Well at Widecombe-in-the-Moor a few miles to the east of Sheepstor. The design of both being square. Saxon Well had stone sides and was known never to dry up. It had an apexed roof as we strongly suspected St Leonard's had in years gone by.

The new well or trough, used the same water but was taken by pipe from Eurynome's field to the road and thence to the new site where it had been moved for the convenience of the villagers where it had been built with the remains of any old stone window removed centuries earlier from the church itself.

What concerned us was that there was no sign of any rope, by which means we assumed, the artefact would have had to have been lowered into the water so that it could be retrieved in the same way. There was no sign that a handle or bar had been installed with which an attached rope would have been tied to a bucket with which the water would have been drawn.

Dartmoor well's followed a similar design so we knew what to look for. We returned to the girls with the news. We could see nothing attached to the woodwork or in the water that the artefact could have been attached to. We would take a closer look later and hope that we had simply missed a clue in plain sight. We waited for sunset.

We enjoyed a very pleasant meal cooked by our hostess and even had a glass of wine to wash it down and talked of the years spent in pursuit of the egg and revisited in detail the clues that had led us to this point.

The pieces of this puzzle were coming together very nicely and we were pleased, especially as we only had thirty one months to put it all together, contact Anna and arrange for her have the artefact spirited away. We didn't want to be over confident as it might lead to another disappointment. Yet the prize still hung before us.

A couple of points still niggled us, the plaque for one, why had it been removed from the graveyard and of equal importance, who had taken it? The other thing was the relevance of the number seventeen other than to point us to Draco.

The number seventeen had come up so many times, the seventeen Tors of course and the seventeen churches in which the Tinners Hares were set and the seventeen standing stones and rows in seventeen separate clusters. Was it just a pointer to the constellation. Why was it repeated so many times. It just had to be more of more significance than we attributed to it.

I told my friends that I would start work on solving the later of the two points as soon as time allowed and asked them to look in more depth at any links to the plaque. Basically we were going to have to look harder. It was all we could do. It all still depended on the result of this evenings event.

Would we or would we not find anything in the Well?

Chapter 27.

Enigma.

The sun set over the western hills and cast a beautiful, coloured glow on the few sparse clouds that hovered there. To the east the sky was beginning to turn a dark blue. There was still too much activity for us to risk being seen, even in such a small village as Sheepstor.

We hung back and waited a while longer. It was a nice evening and the slight breeze, usual chilly at this elevation had a pleasant warmth to it. This would be an evening that none of us would forget.

At last with the thumbs up from Rekha and Eurynome we made our way to the original St Leonard's Well. There was a flurry of activity as we moved the final timbers out of the way and slid off the cover. A couple of minutes later the ladies joined us and we began to look in earnest, taking our time to examine the water surface.

As the Well was only four feet square there wasn't a lot to look at. We could find no rope, cable or string leading into the water. Frank produced a torch of seemingly immense power and lit up the whole thing. Given the fact that we were trying to be 'invisible' it was not the best thing to have done, but we had little choice. If the artefact was there then we had to know for sure.

Putting our hands and arms as deep into the water as we could, feeling around for anything that might be below the surface. We wondered if a bar had been fitted lower down under the water so could not be seen from above but any rope attached to it may still be retrievable by means of a pole and hook.

'Let's try this.' Frank grabbed a long piece of timber post about three inches in diameter and five feet in length. He started to push it into the water using it like a gondolier would use an oar with exaggerated sweeping movements from side to side.

'Let me try.' I offered as he strained, pulled, prodded and cursed with

obvious annoyance.

'Please do.'

My efforts were no more effective and after fifteen minutes Rekha took over and roughly fifteen minutes after that Eurynome Palmer tried.

'Nothing.' She said disappointedly.

Rekha was irritated. 'Seriously?' She asked of no one in particular.

We looked at the outside of the well, searching for any sign of loose stones behind which the box carrying the artefact might could have been secreted. It was to no avail.

Being somewhat quick to anger, I took the pole from Eurynome and hit the water's surface with no little force and plenty of venom.

Frank who had been lifting some scattered stones behind the back wall of the Well was splashed and quite annoyed. He rose up to say a few choice words to me, then in frustration himself kicked out at a stone.

'I don't think it's here.' He stated.

'Me neither.' Rekha agreed.

We looked at each other in the torchlight and having spent almost an hour and a half searching decided to give up, wet due to our splashing around and hot due to our exertions and frustration. I started back towards the house and then remembered something.

'Eurynome, what did you say your husband loved doing to relax?'

'Fishing.'

'And he fished quite often?'

'Yes.' She looked puzzled.

Rekha asked me. 'Where are you going with this?'

Frank laughed. 'He has something in mind.'

'What?' Eurynome Palmer asked.

'We are looking for something that's there but invisible. Well nearly invisible.' I told my friends.

'And that is?' Rekha enquired

I turned them around back towards the Well. It was there, I knew it was. Hidden in plain sight as with all the best hiding places.

'Frank, hand me the torch.'

He did as I asked and getting on my knees in front of the Well I held the torch in my l left hand facing the inside of the well wall and with my right hand I drew my nails along the inside of the stones. At

each joint where the cement held the stones together I raked my nails

hard against the cold interior of the wall. The wall gave up no secrets and so I moved to the east wall fingers pressing hard digging my nails in until my fingers hurt.

'What the hell are you looking for?' Rekha demanded.

'Give me a few minutes.' I replied.

Mrs Palmer sounded equally confused. 'I don't understand.'

'I think I do.' Frank said softly.

The east wall like the south before it gave nothing away so I got up and moved to the west wall. Another three minutes or so passed to no avail.

'Last chance.' I said.

'Seriously, for what?' Rekha was at boiling point.

I moved to the north wall still on my knees, still with the torch in one hand and using my other hand on the wall. I got a little way along it, maybe seventeen or eighteen inches before my finger snagged in a line of some kind. The relief I felt at that moment I recall being totally overwhelming.

'It's here.' I whispered almost in disbelief at what I had found.

'What is.' Eurynome Palmer asked quietly.

'A fishing line.'

'Seriously?'

'Yes.'

'Is it attached to anything dear boy?' Frank's voice was urgent.

'I believe it is. Give me a hand please.' I said.

I kept my fingers under the line afraid it would slip against the wall and force me to hunt for it again.

'We must be careful,' Frank warned, 'we don't know the breaking

strength of the line and if it breaks whatever is attached to it will sink

to the bottom and we have no idea how deep this Well is.'

To our surprise Eurynome began to giggle.

'Did I say something funny dear lady?'

'You mustn't worry about the breaking strain of the line.' She giggled again. 'It was a standing joke that my husband used fishing line for lake or river fishing that would have landed a shark.'

'You're sure?' I asked.

'Oh yes.' She said adamantly. 'At least a twenty five pound breaking strain.'

I looked at Frank, he knew more about fishing than I ever would.

'As long as the box and its contents are no more than two thirds that weight, we should be fine.'

'It can't be too heavy.' Rekha added sensibly. 'Or it would have been a really difficult thing to move over all these centuries'

'I should have brought gloves I said as the line dug hard into my fingers.'

Frank produced a pair from his jeans pocket and taking the line from my hand he began to haul it up. Being so close to the wall it was to all intents and purposes invisible to the naked eye.

'Don't let it snag if you can avoid it.' I offered needlessly.

Frank sighed. 'I shall be very careful.'

Rekha asked sensibly if we knew how deep the Well was. Frank was of a mind to think the walls might go down twenty or so feet but that the hole itself might go a similar distance again.

'Does it feel heavy.' Mrs Palmer enquired.

'Yes but not overly so.' Frank assured her.

He kept pulling and after almost seven minutes we could see a shape in the torchlight. Up it came breaking the surface of the water and I reached in and put my hands underneath it to secure it and to relieve Frank of some off the weight. It appeared to be oblong but was covered with slime and mud.

'It's not as heavy as you may think,' he said.

'No, it's not,' I agreed.

'What's it tied to,' Frank asked.

I felt back and found it was sunk into a concrete joint. I felt behind the wall.

'Here,' I said. 'There's a steel eye drilled in the back of the wall and that's what it's attached to,'

'It must be cleverly concealed,' Frank added.

We swung it onto the ledge and cleaned off the slime and mud to get a good look at it. It was about ten inches tall by six inches diameter.

It was just an oblong container made of some material we were unfamiliar with. It felt like plastic, hard and smooth, but it had a rubber like sort of quality which made it secure when gripped once the slime and the mud had been removed.

It was a dark bluish green and despite the description we had previously been given it was egg shaped with a flat bottom, which enabled it to stand unaided.

Looking at it now I couldn't see a keyhole either, although there was evidence of the thinnest of ridges around the middle, presumably where the top half joined the bottom half. It sat in a sling made of fishing line which was attached by a fish hook to a knot in the main part of the line.

It was only an estimate but we reckoned that the line was sixty feet or so in length. The fact that the line had been so taught when I had found it told us that the egg hadn't rested on the bottom. We suspected that was done on purpose so that the weight on the line would keep it in close to the wall.

Taking into account the fact the artefact was on an almost invisible line and immersed in sixty-odd feet of water, added to which was a Well cover and generous pile of old timbers and given the fact it was on private land, who would have guessed that an item of such value would be treated in such a way. Considering how long it may have been hidden there, the place could not have been better chosen in my opinion.

My thoughts turned to my grandad's involvement in the whole escapade and I voiced my thoughts to my friends.

'I know where Grandad kept the egg during the Second World War.' I announced almost blurting the words.

Frank stopped what he was doing. 'And where might that have been?'

'At Trowlesworthy Warren, the water came from a spring on the Tor into an old stone catchment trough before it ran on through a pipe and out the other side of the courtyard. I think he hid it somewhere in or around that trough.'

Rekha pointed out that we ought to now move the artefact out of the public gaze. It was common sense.

Frank handed it to me and I carried it with great reverence into the house with a body guard surrounding me. The torch shining ahead so as I wouldn't go, ass over elbow, as my dear mum was fond of saying.

'Let's get it into the kitchen sink and clean it properly.' I advised.

Mrs Palmers big Belfast sink was perfect. We had room to set the artefact down and wash it with warm water.

'A gentle detergent won't do any harm.' Rekha said.

Eurynome took over and washed it with soap and a soft cloth. It was best to be gentle as we had no idea of what the handling limitations were. The casing was made to be practically indestructible, that we knew but what of the inside, how fragile would that be?'

'Will Anna be okay with us opening it?' Mrs Palmer asked.

'I don't really care at this point.' I told her.

She looked slightly shocked at the bluntness of my statement.

Frank grinned. 'I think it fair to say she wouldn't.'

'I agree with Andrew. Who cares.' Rekha had said supportively.

'We haven't seen her for years anyway and there is every chance we might never see her again.' I had stated.

'I think,' Frank remarked. 'It rather depends on if we can open it in the first place.'

'I have the key,' Eurynome reminded him.

'Dear Lady, there is no keyhole that I can find.'

She looked bitterly disappointed.

'Don't worry, you know that your husband opened it and, that is the

only key in existence. As far as we are aware,' I told her.

The box, or container if you will was removed from the sink and towel dried, then we moved it onto the dining room table in the light of two small sidelamps we set it on a cloth and then went to check that the doors and windows were locked and that the curtains were properly drawn.

There was no room for error now as secrecy at this time was of the utmost importance. One thing we wanted to do was to weigh it. We used the kitchen scales. It weighed four pounds in imperial measure or one point eight kilos.

Mrs Palmer took the key with the H shaped blades from around her neck passing it to me with a delicate bow.

'You should have the honour,' she told me.

I thanked her and took it, then we all began to look for a keyhole that the container must surely have.

We needn't have worried. As I passed the key over the middle of the bluish green canister a hole made itself visible to me. I moved the key on and it disappeared. It was the most well-conceived of optical illusions and perfectly designed for its task. Anyone not having the key would never have found the hole, it was as if it materialised only for that second.

I moved the key back again and the hole reappeared so I wasted no more time. I inserted the key into the lock. It did not need to be turned, in fact it wouldn't let me turn it, the whole thing let out what I could only describe as a gentle sigh and I put my hand to the top and twisted slightly anti clockwise as you would when you open a jar. I tried to part the top from the bottom but to no avail.

'It may be screwed completely down for safety,' Frank advised.

I took a breath and continued to unscrew the top from the bottom.

'You are absolutely right,' I replied.

A last turn of the screw and the top came loose in my hand. In terms of weight the top was a light as a feather and came away easily in my hand. A dull light flooded from the crack which grew in intensity as I lifted it slowly from its bottom retaining half. Inside was a blue velvet like material which covered the inside of both parts. Everyone leaned in close on their chairs as I lifted the top clear of the bottom.

An audible sigh of disbelief came from each of our four mouths as we gazed in wonder at the sight before us. What we saw defied all logic and certainly all our combined wisdom.

A glass sphere, well we assumed it was glass, about the dimensions of a medium sized easter egg lay before us. I remember in that moment feeling a sudden confidence and determination and with a nod to Frank, I took the egg in both hands and lifted it clear of the container whilst he moved the bottom to one side. Then I put the egg back on the cloth which Eurynome Palmer had provided and sat back relieved that my action had apparently caused no harm.

To describe that moment to you years later is very easy as it will stay with me forever. What our eyes alighted on was a swirl of colour a sort of coffee and cream tan in general but with highlights of warm reds and piercing blues.

On the side that I was sitting next to Rekha it looked as though we were viewing a galaxy or a cluster of galaxies might have been a better interpretation. We were sure that we could see the miniscule domed centres with tiny arms sweeping away. It was difficult to tell.

Eurynome came to our rescue with a timely intervention.

'I have a magnifying glass,' she offered.

'Will it be safe to use?' I said, 'What if the light from our world caught the glass and damaged this universe in miniature.'

'Frank and Rekha weren't fazed, 'No,' they said in unison.

'The truth is we just don't know but that said, we have lights on here anyway, even though they are very dim.' I admitted.

'Let's turn them off completely,' Frank replied.

'What's that?' Eurynome asked as every few seconds white pinpoints of light burned intensely each event so tiny they were imperceptible one from another.

'Evidence,' I told her.

'Of what?'

'Of life, or rather death. Those are supernova, exploding stars at the end of their lives.'

She looked stunned. 'It can't be, there are too many.'

I repeated what I had read over years of studying astronomy.

'In our universe it is estimated that over two hundred million stars explode every day, that's because of the sheer vastness of the area the cosmos occupies and the billions upon billions of stars in it.'

'My God,' Rekha whistled.

'You believe that these are those very stars, dear boy?'

'I think that's why Eurynome's husband Derek was convinced this egg was just what Anna told us it is, a universe in miniature. If we tried to just observe it for any movement it would take us a lifetime to notice any difference. These exploding stars are the only proof. Pinpoints of light that occur for no reason other than the death of millions upon millions of stars.'

They were silent then as we watched what we believed to finally be proof of the authenticity of the quest we had followed. I am sure that none of us would ever have professed that we had total faith in our creed but we had never given up. That must have been a sign that we held a deep conviction in existence of the artefact and in its authenticity. Now we were sure it was true.

Hours passed and we sat quite mesmerised at the miracle before us. Each lost in our own thoughts. Even calls of nature were an inconvenience. No one wanted to miss a moment of this triumph of the Goddess Eurynome and her consort Ophion. It looked like such a peaceful sight.

From a personal perspective the more I gazed into it the more mesmerised I became. The coffee and cream effect was so gently soothing, the tiny area's where maybe the stars were older had a yellow orange tinge and minute regions of startling blue or white indicated the area where nurseries of new stars were being form.

All these areas on a scale so small that I found it difficult to comprehend and even to imagine. How many lives, if any,

233

did this universe of such delicate beauty and awesome power contain and if life did exist here was it life in a form that we would recognise?

Every so often one of us would sigh or occasionally a sob would escape some ones lips, such was the impact it had on us and I am sure that any of you reading this must have an inkling of the reaction such an object would have on you.

This was absolute proof that we as human beings may have had a very different start to life than the one we had been led to believe in, This was proof of the fact that we were right to believe in creation even though astronomers and physicists laid out the groundwork of how the cosmos had evolved.

The big bang theory however logical now hovered on a knife edge in my mind at least. We had found and were able to prove, if only to ourselves, that Eurynome had risen from chaos and given us another universe as well as our own.

Was she still out there and had she over the eon's past created more universes? One day perhaps we might find more clues to that end. There was also the question of Anna and of other life in our own universe. Perhaps the Milky Way, our very own small galaxy in the myriad of galaxies that make up our universe held a vast variety of life, some similar to Mankind and others which would strain our limited minds even to conceive as being lifeforms.

It was this moment when I thought back to the wonders of the universe that Carl Sagan had brought to the attention of the younger version of myself with his series Cosmos in 1980. The brilliance of that man and his ability to inject a passion in me to acquire as much knowledge of space as I could had helped lead me to this point.

There was Sir Patrick Moore who had enthusiastically pointed my head heavenwards with the Sky at Night programmes, which had started in 1957 a year before I was born.

In later years Professor Stephen Hawking who took my mind in many different directions and of late the wonderful Professor Brian Cox who with his easy manner explained new discoveries and the scientific areas of interest to another generation of would be astronomers and physicists. What would any of them think of the discovery we had just made, well re-discovery I should say?

Now we must decide what to do with the egg. Should we transfer it to another location and try to ensure its safety or return it to the place we knew it had remained undetected for so many years.

'Let's vote,' I said as dawn broke on that mid may morning over the towering shoulder of Sheepstor.

Frank was first up. 'Put it back where we found it.'

'I agree, it should be put down the Well again.' Rekha nodded.

Eurynome was adamant. 'I think it is far safer back under water.'

'I think so too,' I added.

And so we put it back exactly as we had found it. We put it in the box and locked it. Eurynome kept the key as she had all these years. Then with heavy hearts Frank and I took it to the Well.

It was under cover of the semi darkness that we sat it back in its cradle of fishing line. I put the hook onto the line and this time Frank lowered in back into the depth whilst the ladies kept watch for sign of unwanted intrusion from outside of our circle.

We lifted back the Well cover and quietly put a few timbers back over the top of that. We would replace more of them when convenient.

'Now,' Frank told us all at breakfast. 'All we have to do is wait.'

'For what?' Eurynome Palmer asked.

'I think the question you are asking is for whom?' Rekha told her.

'We wait for Anna,' I said.

Chapter 28.

Seventeen Clues

We waited for Anna but she never came. The year ended on a bit of an anti-climax. We had waited for seven months, sure that our other worldly visitor would arrive. It didn't happen, so with the arrival of 2018 we decided to dot the I's and cross the T's. We had found what no one else had been able to for decades. It was something to be proud of that was for sure.

Our next step was to try to understand the final piece of the puzzle and work out how and when exactly Chapter would get the artefact to its ultimate off world resting place.

To that end we came up with a plan. Eurynome Palmer would continue to search through her husband's records, diary and effects in the hope of finding any clues previously missed and also for a possible missing page or pages from the church records.

Rekha was tasked with searching for Anna. A fairly thankless task it must be said but nonetheless she agreed to comb social media for any reference to the young woman or any unusual activity which might mention Chapter. There was no doubt that if any links were there, Rekha would find them.

It was left to Frank to walk the moors with his wife and explore further connections between the stone circles, rows or markers that we may have missed in relation to more recently reported UFO phenomenon.

My mission was to find out more about the number seventeen and why it seemed to be of such importance to Chapter and the artefact.

The year passed into the next and soon it was February 2018 a time that could not have been better suited for research because the 'Beast from the East' arrived with heavy snowfall and an icy blast that covered most of the country.

The quarry froze solid in certain areas. Logistics ground to a halt and I had plenty of time to put to my investigation. I was on the trail and eager to find out more as the number or rather its relation to the universal egg fascinated me. Some of the ties to the number have already been stated but it might be circumspect to offer a quick reminder at this point.

First of all we had found the map and the badge marking the Seventeen Tors which when viewed from above had formed the seventeen stars in the constellation Draco. This had come from Chapter itself as was recognised by Anna and previously confirmed by Mrs Palmer. As the Tors matched the constellation so well, there could be no doubt of the reason for its existence. We could all attest to the end result.

There was Grandads well-thumbed copy of The Works of Shakespeare which had given more clues in the form of illustrations of the stars of stage. From the total of sixty five engravings or plates in the book, seventeen of the illustrations had seventeen letters in each and were surely intended to direct the attentive reader toward the seventeen stars of Draco. Any reader that is who may have been in Chapter or was an associate of theirs.

Examples of the seventeen letters in the titles being Henry Irving Hamlet and coincidently Irving's real name being John Henry Brodribb (also seventeen letters), Miranda The Tempest, Caliban The Tempest and so on.

Added to that we had found the verses hidden in plain sight which related to the Goddess Eurynome, formed from random words in the Bards play's taken by a member or members of Chapter and telling of their struggle over the years to keep the egg safe and of their ultimate intention to oversee its removal from earth to a more stable world. Even the phrase Eurynome and Ophion made seventeen letters.

Later still we followed the egg's journey and possible connection to the Indian poet Mah Laqa Bai. Strange that although she was so famous in her day so few people in England know about her and her connection to Anna Maria Brooke the mother Sir James Brooke, the first White Rajah of Sarawak.

Stranger still that her tomb in Hyderabad was constructed on seventeen pillars and double pillars at that which match several of the seventeen double row stones that litter the Tors of Dartmoor.

We knew that Moncure Daniel Conway had written a book on Demonology and Devil-Lore which included a small chapter called The Dartmoor Story and that he had in his time on the moor visited the seventeen churches which bore the symbol of the Tinners Hares. These churches when viewed on a map were another copy of constellation Draco and the mouth of the dragon although forming a slightly different approach, still directed its breath over Sheepstor.

The other rather too coincidental fact was that for anyone walking from Hare Tor to Sheepstor will find that the distance between the two is seventeen miles.

What Conway may have known is lost to antiquity. We shall never know his reasons for visiting these churches out of anything other than curiosity. Odd though that he should produce the drawing of The Serpent and the Egg.

Odder still that a plaque bearing that very drawing should have been made and placed in St Leonards Church graveyard at some time in the last forty years and that a few hours after we had stumbled upon it, someone had removed it. Although before the end of this chapter we will enlighten the reader further as to the importance of this plaque and subsequently the reason it may have been removed.

Then there were the stone rows and circles to consider. Stalldown Barrow and standing stones, the Nine Sisters which had been at one time more accurately called the Seventeen Brothers.

Yet further on we had found the Staldon Moor stone row and circle with another set of seventeen stones. Most seemed to point across the moor to Sheepstor and one even resembled the shape of a great serpent, that in turn led on to Penn Beacon with seventeen stones in a circle.

Then Great Trowlesworthy and barely a mile further on was Little Trowlesworthy Tor, the former with seventeen stones in either side of the row and the later with a loose seventeen.

Legis Tor followed the same pattern as did Brisworthy Stone Circle and Ringmoor Stone circle and Row. Then came

Yellowmead Down, seventeen concentric circles with a combined total of two hundred and eighty nine stones. If you divide two hundred and eighty

nine by the magic number, that is seventeen you get seventeen, in other words seventeen times by seventeen is two hundred and eighty nine. I think I have previously described it as a target with a very clear bullseye.

We knew that seventeen was a prime number but it is the seventh prime number and the only prime to be the total of the previous four prime numbers. Two, Three, Five and Seven for a sum of seventeen, so from a mathematical stance it is an oddball number.

In science, particularly in the Standard Model of particle physics seventeen is the number of elementary particles with unique names. In the periodic table in Chemistry it is the classification group for Halogens and the atomic number of chlorine and in Biology seventeen is the number given to the primary visual cortex of the Brodmann Area map of the brain which used for processing by mammals.

Religion in ancient Egypt says that Osiris's death came on the seventeenth day of the month. In the Bible, it was the day on which Noah's Ark came aground on Mount Ararat. In Zoroastrianism seventeen chapters or Gathas were written by Zoroaster.

What we were sure of was that seventeen was not just a pointer, it must represent an ending, but an ending to what? Why was the number so important? Yes it represented many interesting areas of history but what did it mean to Chapter and Anna with relation to the universal egg?

The only way to find out was to dig out more facts and see if they could be linked to something related to astronomy, or space which was undoubtedly linked to Anna. To my mind that was the only course left and I was determined to follow it.

A phone call was my breakthrough and it came from Eurynome Palmer. Much to my astonishment she had news of the plaque and was very excited to be able to share it with me.

239

The plaque had apparently been found behind the church wall which separated the grounds from a farmer's field. It was still whole, as in one piece, with no damage of any significance other than a small chip on one corner where it had struck the stonewall.

It was uncertain whether it had been an act of vandalism that

caused it to be dislodged from its original position and discarded or if it had been removed by an interested party who needed to hide it with some haste and had simply dropped it over the wall. If that was the case, then for some reason they had not been able to retrieve it and hide it in a better location or destroy it.

'Where is it now?' I had asked.

'I have it at my house, safely hidden away.'

'May I come out and see it?'

She sounded thrilled. 'You will certainly want to, there is more to it that we thought.'

I asked her to explain but she seemed reluctant to do so.

'How soon can you come?'

The 'Beast from the East' was throwing its full weight against us. It was snowing but the ice and wind made it more treacherous to drive and just get around in general. She understood that I wouldn't be in a position to get to Sheepstor for a few days however eager I was to see the plaque and to discover the mystery surrounding it. There was no way she would tell me more.

'I just need you to see it for yourself.' She told me. 'I would find it a little difficult to describe and I don't want to send a photograph. I'm not good with modern technology.'

I said that was ok and told her I would get to her house as soon as the weather permitted.

Two weeks passed and it was the end of the first week of March before I was able to get out to visit her. I had asked Frank if he would like to come but he was very busy, the extreme weather made his services more in demand than ever, so I went to Sheepstor alone.

It was early evening and still light but the sky was grey and there was a lot of snow on the hills and Tors. Mrs Palmer showed me into the house and made me welcome.

'Here it is.' She said after she had been gone a little while.

The plaque was as I remembered it in width and length but much less in depth than I had expected. Maybe three quarters of an inch to an inch thick. We were both surprised that it hadn't broken and thought it may have been placed over the wall rather than thrown.

'This is the important bit that I want you to see,' she said, turning it over.

It had only been cemented to the ground at each corner, which was presumably why it had broken off so quickly.

'I cleaned it up as best I could.' Eurynome told me. 'Then I found this.'

She was pointing to the back or rather to something that was etched on the back.

'Does it look familiar?' She had smiled with pleasure.

'My God.' I had been taken aback.

At the top left-hand corner and taking up about three inches by three inches was a representation of the constellation Draco. Each one of the seventeen stars were scoured into the ceramic and each of them was connected by a line which joined the dots or stars. Beneath that was a design which was identical to the key Eurynome had which opened the box containing the artefact. To the right of that were concentric lines drawn around a central star pertaining possibly to the solar system, a series of planets circling it.

I counted them and found there were to many for our solar system, twenty seven in all. It took a while but eventually it dawned on me. What if the central star in this system was not a star at all but a planet and not even some exo-planet hundreds of light years away but one in our own solar system.

The planet I was thinking of was Uranus, the seventh planet from our sun. Not only did it have a total of twenty seven moons orbiting it, but seventeen of them were in retrograde motion, that is they orbit in an anti-clockwise direction around the gas giant. There was another link as well as I was about to inform Eurynome.

'May I see the key again?' I asked.

She removed it from her cleavage and undid the clasp of the chain around her neck and handed it to me.

'What have you found?' She had asked anxiously.

So I explained my theory about Uranus and its moons and the number seventeen and how it fitted in again.

'There is also this.' I told her holding up the key. The I went online on my phone and showed her the ancient symbol for Uranus. It looked

just like the key she had held onto for so long. In fact it was identical in every way. The bow of the key which is the bit you hold to turn it was circular, as was the same piece on the symbol. The shaft was a straight piece which fitted into the bar of the letter H. That was the only way I could describe it.

'Oh my goodness,' Eurynome muttered,

'I know. It has to be a major clue.'

'Just what does Uranus have to do with it?'

'I'm not sure yet.' I replied. 'But I will find out.'

I had given her back the key, took some photos of the back of the plaque and asked her to hide it again. The only threat we had ever received was in the early days of my investigation into the group I would later know as 'Chapter.' As they had asked for our help I knew they were no danger to us, and we had never been under any other kind of threat. As such I couldn't see that she was in any kind of danger at all. I bade her farewell and left and she called me later to see if I had returned home safely.

The rest of the evening was spent updating Frank and Rekha and sharing the good news with them. They were astounded by the information and I told them that I was going to pursue this connection to Uranus and its moons, although none of us could work out or even hazard a guess at what the connection would be other than the number seventeen, the number of moons in retrograde motion.

Before that though, I was determined to take a new and closer look at Uranus as there were new discoveries being made in space on an almost daily basis. NASA (National Aeronautics and Space Administration) was still most well-known of all space agencies, alongside the Jet Propulsion Laboratory. Even the UK, albeit in a much smaller way was involved, the latest of our ventures being the Space Port in Cornwall.

I went online and cross referenced many organisations, science academies and universities. I came up with some interesting facts and links to the number seventeen. Not only did Uranus have seventeen moons in retrograde motion, but it also had a seventeen hour day. If someone was going to all the trouble to inscribe the back of a tiled plaque with an image of the planet then it must have some real value as a clue.

Then it struck me again, like a slap across the head, it lifted the veil from my eyes. There was something special about it. The moons of Uranus are named after characters in Shakespeare's plays.

Oberon and Titania were first to be discovered by William Herschel in 1787. Next to be found was Ariel and Umbriel, then a century and a half later Miranda was found and it was not until the Voyager 2 mission in 1986 that Belinda, Bianca, Cordelia, Cressida, Desdemona, Ophelia, Portia and Rosalind became known. Later still the Hubble Space Telescope would pick up more for a total of twenty seven to date.

The question was now, how would Moncure D Conway have known there were twenty seven moons circling Uranus when he drew the Serpent and Egg or was the engraving on the reverse of the plaque done at a much later time? That said how could we prove or disprove if he had been responsible for the plaque. Was it just a copy of his work? We would have to try to find out.

I made one final push on the number seventeen and found another interesting fact. In the Milky Way galaxy there are of course billions and billions of stars. An estimate has been set for the number of planets that orbit these stars. It has been calculated that one in six stars will have at least one planet orbiting them. If that is an accurate assumption, which all references seem to agree it is, it means that there are seventeen billion planets in our Milky Way.

All we needed to do was to put together the final clues and to pray that Anna would contact us soon. We had the artefact, the Universal Egg. We had all the links from pre-history of eons past, we had many millennia of ancient burial sites, of stone rows, of temples built in part as astronomical observatories from Stonehenge to Egypt's most magnificent Pyramids, from China's Palaces to Peru's Machu Picchu mountain.

Pictures on cave walls describe visitors from other worlds and when written language appeared in stone tablets, those descriptions were to continue. Greek science and mysticism combined with the old

Egyptian alchemy brought new ideas to light. A great wave of inspired Islamic culture simplified mathematics and was improved both the eastern and western world's idea of astronomy.

The last millennia saw many changes to theology, physics, chemistry, biology and astronomy. The birth of the telescope and the final acceptance that the sun was the at the centre of the solar system rather than the earth meant that astronomers such as Galileo were no longer under threat of death for stating the truth.

Then along came Sir Isaac Newton with his discovery of the theory of Gravity. The outer planets, Neptune and the now re-classified dwarf planet Pluto were discovered.

Mankind put satellites into space, then a dog and a monkey and eventually a man. Yuri Gagarin had that honour for the Union of Soviet Socialist Republics. Major John Glenn followed soon afterwards for the United States and finally with Apollo Eleven mankind was able to put men on the moon and soon Mars would be in our sights, with the Viking 1 Mission.

The new international space station was a triumph of global cooperation and the United Kingdom's own Tim Peak represented all that was good and modern about Britain and showed our absolute determination to be a part of the space race.

244

We had come so far and so fast in the last five hundred years, was there any reason that with seventeen billion planets in the Milky Way that some of those shouldn't have what we would consider intelligent life on them?

Now more and more to us it seemed likely that Anna was from some other world. A world more advanced than ours with inhabitants very like us at least is physiological terms, if she was a true representation of her species and not some kind of an Artificial Intelligence, in other words a robot in human form.

There was one last thing about the number seventeen although I wasn't sure about its relevance to our quest. I had been reading about a man called Jabir ibn Hayyan, later to be known as Geber. He was born in the year 721 and was a great alchemist in his day.

Jabir was fascinated by the phenomena of the Philosopher's Stone which was basically a method to turn a base metal into gold. It was with this in mind that he studied the art for most of his life. What he found was far deeper and more of a medicinal, spiritual nature, but I leave that discussion to wiser heads than mine.

What grabbed my attention was a piece on his fascination for what was then known as sacred geometry. Geometry, the dictionary tells us is mathematics which deals with, measurement, properties and also the relationship of point, lines, angles, surfaces and solids. It reveals the character of numbers as a means of understanding the universe.

In sacred geometry it was thought as a way to separate the temporal world from the spiritual. Geometric shapes were regarded as One, be that God, the universe or something else is again beyond my ken, but if it helps, the Circle is the sign of everlasting life, Ouroboro's circling the universe and biting his own tail.

The Square represents Stability and equality, whilst a Triangle is symbolic of Harmony. A circle inside a triangle inside a square was the old alchemical symbol, all is part of the One.

Now Jabir was fascinated by the magic square, a square in which there are nine smaller squares. Each square contains a number, the numbers are top row left to right; four, nine, two. The middle row left to right; three, five, seven. The bottom row left to right; eight, one, six.

The numbers when added together in any row, vertically, diagonally or horizontally add up to fifteen and the total of the square always adds up to forty five.

Analysing the square gnomically we find the parallelogram consists of the numbers one, three, five and eight, for a total of seventeen. I apologise for that long winded explanation but it is the best I can do.

My point is this, Jabir believed that everything in the world was ruled and governed by the number Seventeen. It kept coming up. It had to be relevant to the final leg of our quest. Even the myth that had come to the forefront at the start of our quest had pointed in that direction, after all, Pelasgian Creation, is seventeen letters in length.

Chapter 29

Tempus Fugit.

2018 was coming to an end and we had had a stressful if considerable better year than those years past. Time flies and it flew for us that was for sure.

It was October and we had had yet another telephone conference. Each of us updating the others as best we could and to some extent trying to bolster one another's moral. It wasn't to prove that easy an achievement this time. We knew that it was now only fifteen months until 2020 was with us and what calamity we wondered would that year bring.

Frank had continued to scour the moors for further clues and to consolidate those clues that we had found in the circles, rows and scree of the tors. He had checked and checked once again, and gone over the clues, theories and ideas that had evolved from what we had learned so far. He was happy that all had been done that could be done.

Rekha had for once had not luck whatsoever in her search for Anna. There was no mention of Anna in any social media as far as she was aware.

'I've gone through so much of this rubbish that it blows my mind. Guys do you know how much utter rubbish is out there and I've just been looking for one tiny jewel of information.' She said in a tone that showed the disgust she felt for her task. 'Seriously!'

'We appreciate it dear girl.' Frank had told her.

'I got nowhere.'

I felt for her, 'I'm not sure that expected you would,' I told her. 'Anna is an enigma and I suspect that she can easily lurk in the shadows. It may well be that she is not even on this planet or indeed ever has been for more than a short time.'

Eurynome Palmer told us that she had continued to search church records and the grounds and graveyard in the hope of repeating her success of the previous February with the discovery of the plaque.

She was still keeping the plaque safe and she had also very sensibly made some tiny pencil marks on the Well lid and stones so that she could see if it had been moved.

'I am happy to report that it hasn't been interfered with at all.' She had said with some pride.

I was only able to reiterate what we already knew and to admit that there were still some important things linked to the number seventeen that we knew nothing about.

We decided that until we received instructions from Chapter via Anna that we could do little more. The only thing now left to us was to try and work out what calamity was about to befall Earth.

Mrs Palmer was certain of some catastrophe and there was nothing we could say to ease her fears. In truth she had been right about her husband's involvement with Chapter, she had been convinced of the existence of the artefact, she had been convinced that he had opened the box and that he had seen something which had changed his view of the universe and she was right about Anna or at least of Anna's existence and her link to other worlds.

It was felt that we needed to start to investigate past world events that had changed our planet and us as people.

'We must decide on a chosen path of research.' Frank stated. 'We need to think fast and find out what we can.'

'I will look into close cosmic encounters like meteorites, comets and perhaps even natural disasters such as earthquakes and volcanic eruptions.' I volunteered.

Eurynome was eager to help. 'Let me look at the social side, religious divides, famine and such.'

'I could look into aspects of war and it's likelihood. I could also look at the geo-political aspects of the world at present.' Frank said.

'Then let me look into what's left,' Rekha said. 'Disease, pandemics, that sort of thing.'

It was decided there and then. We would each take a close look at our chosen subjects and try desperately what Anna may have considered to be a cataclysmic event. Obviously it didn't sound good and we had to prepare ourselves and our families but without causing alarm or fear.

248

To be truthful none of us fancied being looked at as having lost some mental capability. It would all just sound like a conspiracy theory and a totally outlandish one at that. We could alert the authorities, but to what end and with what evidence at hand?

2019 had begun right where 2018 had ended with deadlock on Brexit. In Hong Kong there were protests over proposed legislation extradition of all protestors to mainland China for trial.

There was some better news as the Event Horizon Telescope captured the first image of a black hole in space. Little did we know when the year began, how it would end and what that ending would lead to in the following year.

It was April and although we had almost constant phone conversations over that six month period we thought it necessary to meet again. Rekha would travel to Plymouth and I would pick her up from North Hill Station to continue her journey to Eurynome's house.

There we could meet in private and concentrate on what we had or had not learned over that time.

Frank and I discussed it with our long suffering wives, who in retrospect were probably very glad to see the back of us for a couple of days, although we decided not to stay at Eurynome's but travel home to our own beds for the night.

I dropped Frank off early at Mrs Palmers as he wanted to check on the box in the Well with Eurynome to ensure it was still in situ and to reassure both her and us that nothing untoward had occurred.

To his surprise he found that she had installed a relatively cheap but effective camera overlooking the Well. That along with her marking the lid and wall at various points had meant that nothing had been disturbed.

Frank had checked the recordings with her, which she had filed meticulously on her hard drive. Evidently she had started to use it as soon as we had left the time we found the egg. She was praised by all when Frank revealed this later.

For his part he had moved the lid and run his fingers along the wall as I had until he found the fishing line. He had pulled gently and was happy to feel the strain of the weight of the submerged box.

Rekha arrived and I duly whisked her out of Plymouth and across the moors to Yelverton and beyond to Sheepstor. It was the last weekend of April and it was pleasantly warm on Dartmoor. We got down to business at once after the normal pleasantries of friends getting together after a period apart.

Frank began with his assessment of the task he'd had the dubious pleasure of undertaking, that was looking into conflict, war and politics. It wasn't his favourite subject, especially politics but as was always the case with Frank he approached it from a logical if sceptical view point.

There were two major dangers that he said he was aware of and were concerning. The first was China's intimidation of Taiwan, which he thought could blow up in someone's face. It was likely that any war in that region would limit trade upsetting a fragile balance of the war of words between America and China.

Secondly he felt that Russia's annexation of the Crimea might flare into some larger conflict and involve more countries. Both of these scenario's might end in trade wars, energy shortages and an escalation to the status of a new cold war once again. He mentioned nuclear war but said he could find no grounds for it to start except maybe in the Crimean Peninsula.

Eurynome had been looking at religious conflicts around the globe and attempting to see if there was any increase in violence due to religious persecution. Unfortunately she said it was evident on every continent except Antarctica.

Rekha was of the opinion that it had been proved penguins were less interested in God than they were in fish.

There were areas in which famine was still rife. Almost three quarters of a billion people were facing starvation from the Horn of Africa and across the middle east to Afghanistan.

It was possible that economic factors would also increase the likelihood of people trying to emigrate, by lawful means or otherwise but unlikely that it would increase to the level of asylum seekers that had landed on the Greek islands in 2015.

From a religious viewpoint she felt that there was no major upheaval underway due to any religious intolerance. That was endemic throughout the planet but she could not foresee it at a level that would cause a cataclysm.

I was next up and began with a brief look at end of days scenarios. What I had found was fortunately uninspiring. Volcanoes were constantly erupting and at any time there are one thousand five hundred or so active over seven continents with fifty to seventy of those erupting yearly.

Somewhere in the order of twelve thousand earth tremors occur every year with fifty to seventy major quakes in the same time period. NASA's and JPL run CNEOS, Centre Near Earth Object Studies but many organisations carryout similar work. At the moment there seemed to be no imminent threat to life. I could see no reason that anything I had researched would cause any problems in the near future that said, I didn't have a crystal ball.

Rekha had taken a special interest in her chosen area of research which was disease control and pandemics. Since the world began nature has struggled to control the numbers of humans on the planet, at least that was how I saw it with the jaundiced eye of man who believed that our planet was already over populated.

Rekha just took a common sense approach as always. She gave us a refresher on historic diseases. The Black Death, Leprosy, Smallpox, Spanish Flu, Anthrax, SARS (Severe Acute Respiratory Syndrome), Malaria, Ebola, the list went on and on. There were of course other terrible and very debilitating afflictions that troubled people all over the world, but these were probably the most lethal.

It was only a matter of time before some other new disease or virus raised its ugly head. We should also take into consideration man-made diseases that might escape from laboratories, either privately run or government sponsored. We had some of the best labs in the world at present.

It was the MOD and Public Health England Laboratories that had found the Russian nerve agent A-234 or Novichok was responsible for the Salisbury poisonings. It certainly warranted consideration. If some such poison or virus were

251

to be released either accidently or purposely that could cause untold damage to mankind, especially now as more and more people were calling for freedom of movement and globalisation.

We had checked all the avenues that we could think of and were about to come to a disturbing realization. Frank tabled the idea that had been running through each of our minds. If Anna knew that something was going to happen and approximately when surely it was possible that she, or Chapter were going to cause this disaster.

'I can see no other way.' Frank had stated bluntly. 'That Anna would be able to give such a precise timing for such an event.'

'My God.' Eurynome said, evidently in shock.

Rekha asked, 'Do we think that she is capable of such a thing?'

'We hope not but maybe Chapter is.' I offered blandly.

'Dear boy, Anna is more than Chapter's mouthpiece.'

'No argument there.' Rekha agreed.

'You mean ....' Eurynome Palmers voice trailed off.

'Yes.' I told her. 'We believe that Anna is as responsible for Chapter as they are for her.'

Frank was laconic as he tossed a thought into the mix. 'The question is, what form will the catastrophe take?'

I had allowed my mind to play with that thought for many weeks and

there was only one answer that I could arrive at with any conviction.

'Disease.' I told my colleagues.

Rekha backed me up. 'Has to be.' She nodded. 'As far as I can tell in logical terms it's the only think they can manipulate. They could for example influence the leaders of some countries towards war but it would be counter balanced by other countries who may want no part in a conflict.'

'Any conflict would more likely be localised and therefore controlled to some degree,' Frank acknowledged.

'I don't see religious divides or terrorism unless on some monstrous scale being responsible,' Eurynome interjected.

As to an act of nature such as a volcanic eruption, it would also have to be on an enormous scale and I don't think that an episode of such violence would in any way make the egg safer.' I had added. 'On the contrary it might put the egg in mortal danger.'

'We are all in agreement then?' Frank asked.

'A disease of some kind, either manmade or natural but tweaked by our friends in Chapter.' Rekha concluded.

'I still don't see why they would want to do such a thing.' Eurynome muttered in a horrified voice.

I could think of only one reason. It was difficult to contemplate the use of such a means, but as a means to an end it would make sense.

'Distraction.' I replied.

'From what?' Eurynome asked.

Rekha said. 'It's a sad but simple answer.'

'And that answer is?'

'To distract the authorities and the population when the time comes to move the egg.'

There was an uncomfortable silence as we digested the possibility that our theory was true.

'Makes perfect sense dear lady,' Frank sighed.

'So, let me be clear,' Eurynome's voice had sounded so fragile, 'we are saying that the people of earth are to be put in mortal danger in
order to spirit the egg away to another star system!'

'Yes,' I said, 'that's what we are saying.'

'It maybe that they have some knowledge of a virus or germ that will develop of its own volition,' Rekha added, 'all we can do at this time is to speculate, after all we have no concrete evidence as yet.'

'What about,' Eurynome asked clutching at straws, 'time travel, is it possible that Anna is able to travel to the future knows what is going to happen already?'

'Unlikely.' Frank said. 'I think we have already established that you may be able to go back in time but not forward.'

'Yes I see.'

'It's not even as if we can warn anyone.' Rekha added despondently.

253

I agreed. 'It would take some believing.'

'Can we give no warning at all?' Eurynome asked.

Frank was adamant. 'No dear lady, at present to the world it would be just another conspiracy theory.'

'All we can do,' Rekha said, 'is prepare as best we can for ourselves, family and friends but without mentioning any detail.'

'Not the easiest of tasks.' I said.

'We can do nothing more.' Frank told us.

It was time to move on to the next order of business, we would meet again the next day and discuss the way in which the artefact might be transported. That day soon came around and we were in Sheepstor again and it was a more sober meeting on this occasion as the realization of the previous days deliberations had set in. At that time we had all felt the weight of responsibility for what we knew, or at least believed we knew and yet would be unable to act on.

We began with a unanimous agreement that Anna was a traveller in space as yet by means unknown, but as unrealistic as it seemed it was our belief that she travelled by star ship of some kind.

'This is the weirdest conversation I've ever had.' Rekha opined.

'I think perhaps for all of us.' Frank remarked.

Eurynome almost whispered. 'Me too.'

'Nonetheless, it's a conversation we must have,' I professed, 'all the indications are that we are to hand the artefact over to Anna as Chapter representative and that she will pass it on to whoever the travellers are that will come for it.'

'Either that, or she is part of the crew of that spacecraft.' Frank said.

Rekha was unsure. 'She could be part of it or not. Perhaps it won't have a human crew. Perhaps it will be crewed by mechanoids or will it be a much simpler craft.'

'Such as on the Mars Exploration Rover.' Frank proposed.

'Exactly.' Rekha nodded.

'Some basic sort of transport vessel?' Eurynome asked.

'Yes,' I replied 'it would make sense. No humanoids on board would mean no pit stops, as it were. An unmanned spacecraft with a good propulsion system could cross thousands of light years of space and if that system pushed it to near light speed then the possibilities for it to cover vast tracts of spacetime are unimaginable.'

'It would explain the repeated use of images over the centuries

with regard to the worship of space, the stars and so forth.' Frank added.

'It's possible that the earth has been visited many times over eons by unmanned craft but it's not a new theory.' Rekha said.

'No it's not new, but this may prove that it is more than a theory.' I replied.

'It is unlikely that any kind of life form as we understand it would be able to survive for long periods of time over such colossal distances, so it stands to reason that any spacecraft that is sent here will almost certainly be unmanned.'

Eurynome sounded unconvinced. 'Would Chapter put the artefact in a craft of that kind. It's surely an enormous risk to take?'

It was a point well-made and deserving of an answer.

Rekha though asked a question of her own which required a reply first and foremost.

'Eurynome,' she said kindly, 'was your question influenced by your husband's involvement with Chapter?'

'In what way?'

'Are you concerned that given your religious beliefs and because of Derek's links to Chapter, you feel that handing the artefact over to a machine might be an insult to his faith and to his memory?'

'If you mean do I think that a machine lacks the ability to provide the artefact with the reverence it deserves my answer is no. It is simply a means of transport and the means of transport over all these eons must have been many and varied.'

Rekha asked if her question had been ill judged.

'Not at all,' came the reply. You might ask the same of Andrew with regards to his Grandad and how he feels.'

Rekha knew me well and had just smiled. 'I already know his answer will mirror yours,' she said.

'My opinion for what it's worth is that it would be safer inside any machine designed for that purpose than it will be in the hands of any sentient being with all the vices they hold within.' Frank observed.

'Then we are saying that Anna may not be an alien space traveller after all,' I remarked.

'No,' Rekha corrected me, 'we are saying that it's more likely that an advanced civilization would send an unmanned craft of some sort to retrieve the object, especially if its destination is light years away.'

'Then where does Anna come from?' I enquired.

'Is she a hologram?' Eurynòme asked.

I was unsure. 'I simply don't know. She seemed flesh and blood but the truth is, I have no idea.'

'Could she be an android.'

'It's possible I suppose.' That was the best I could come up with.

Frank sensibly considered the argument to be a spurious one.

'It doesn't really matter.' He said. 'She is either humanoid or she is

hologrammatic. Either way we don't know and we can't ask her because she isn't here.'

'Even if she were here,' Rekha replied, 'if asked, she still might chose to lie or simply not tell us.'

'Surely she will return soon,' Eurynome added despondently.

'Time is running out,' I replied. 'She has no choice.'

Frank broke in. 'The safety of the egg is paramount. She has to return to give us our final instructions, otherwise the egg stays where it is as it must stay hidden and under our control.'

'Then all well can do is to be patient,' Rekha pointed out, then added with just a modicum of sarcasm, 'and patience is a virtue.'

Chapter 30

Shibboleth.

It was in late December of 2019 when the city of Wuhan in the Chinese province of Hubei notified the World Health Organization about a cluster of pneumonia like cases which had been reported by local hospitals and it was picked up by news agencies all over the world who started to follow the story at source.

The previous few months had been a flurry of activity for the four of us as we attempted to put together the final pieces of the puzzle. We had heard nothing from Anna at that time and frustration was growing as the responsibility of care for the universal egg played on all our minds.

We also harboured grave concerns that any slight error in judgement at this time might mean the loss of the only opportunity we might have in our lifetimes to help transport the egg to safety.

It had been decided at our last meeting that although we hadn't had any threats or hostile actions against either ourselves or the artefact, we might use a password in our communications. The password we chose needed to be something we would understand but that would make no sense to anyone else, especially to someone hacking into our emails or other media.

Over the years we had read and if necessary printed emails we may have needed to refer to. Upon reading they were deleted and any printed copies shredded or burned. Now with the end in sight we thought hard and I came up with what I thought to be a very suitable candidate and that word was Shibboleth.

I had first read it in the bible. What I liked most was that we would be using a biblical password with all the religious context it evoked. The word is used in the Old Testament in the Book of Judges,

Chapter Twelve, verses one to fifteen. It tells the story of two tribes at war, the Ephraimites and Gileadites.

The Gileadites are victorious and block the enemies retreat across the river Jordan. In so doing they set up sentry points at each of the river crossings.

The word Shibboleth meaning 'ear of corn' was pronounced differently by each tribe, the Gileadites pronounced the word with a 'sh', sound the Ephraimites with a 's'. A soldier attempts to cross at one of the sentry points and is challenged.

The bible verse says, 'Then they said unto him: say now Shibboleth: he said Sibboleth: for he could not frame to pronounce it right. So they took him out and slew him at the passages of Jordan.'

It seemed somehow fitting to me that both verse and word reflected the gravity of the situation should things go wrong and the artefact be lost, with the resulting loss of possibly billions of lives.

The password was accepted by everyone. It would now head any email referencing direct communication from Anna as a reminder that we were to be on alert. Vigilance was our watchword and we must no longer refer to the artefact or to Anna by name. The Parcel would be the reference for the universal egg if we couldn't avoid mention of it, and Anna was to be Traveller.

Security wise it may have been a day late and a dollar short as our American friends are apt to say but we felt it necessary all the same.

As I said previously, the end of 2019 was with us and Rekha had made up her mind as to the threat from this new strain of pneumonia currently erupting in China. She demanded an urgent telephone conference and with good reason.

We set it for the 4th of January 2020 which was a Saturday and we could all attend.

'This is it,' Rekha told us with authority, 'no doubt about it.'

'It's seems as though nobody's worrying too much.' Eurynome said.

'They don't have to,' Rekha replied, 'it will take a few weeks before the world gets off its backside and wakes up to the situation.'

I had been watching the news as well. 'How quickly do you think this will become a major issue?'

'Within six to eight weeks.' She said.

'And the effect on us?' Frank asked.

'It has the potential to overwhelm every health system in the world.'

Eurynome sounded alarmed. 'Do you really think so?'

'I'm not trying to frighten you,' Rekha told her, 'but we need to be on

guard and prepared and yes I do think so.'

'Dear girl do you think foul play is involved?' Frank enquired.

'I'm doing my best to discount conspiracy but given what Traveller told us, I can't discount it either.'

We were using Anna's codename. It seemed appropriate and we had to be sure that if anyone was listening in to our conversation, they should glean as little as possible from it.

'Rekha's right.' I added. 'Traveller told us that the event would be a catastrophe and we must assume that this is the event to which she was referring.'

I wondered how bad the situation was going to get. It was a sobering thought and we decided there and then to take Rekha's advice. As soon as the bounds of common sense would allow, it was our plan to bring our families attention to the new danger lurking in Wuhan and to impress on them what might happen if the worse was to outcome was to occur. We knew there would be some who would laugh it off and some who would be petrified by the implications.

In between these two extremes was a balance that we would aim at keeping. It was still our duty to keep The Parcel safe but to keep our family and our friends safe as well, insofar as it was possible.

January the 8th saw the Chinese government accept help from the World Health Organization. Three days later and Chinese state media were to report the first covid death and by the 20th confirmed cases of the disease were reported in South Korea, Thailand and Japan.

The next day a case was reported in the USA. On January the twenty third all transport to and from Wuhan was closed down and the Chinese government reported 17 people had died. The authorities in China began to build emergency hospitals in the area as more cases had started to come to light.

On the 29th of January two Chinese nationals at a hotel in York, England fell ill with covid and an aircraft which was evacuating Britons from Wuhan arrived at RAF Brize-Norton.

It was on the 30th of January when the World Health Organization had declared a global health emergency in China and the next day it was announced that 213 people had already died, with a further 9,800 known infections around the world. Spain confirmed its first case on the 1st of February and on the 2nd day of the month a man died in the Philippines, this was the first death recorded outside of mainland China.

So it began and it spread worldwide quickly and without mercy taking young and old, fit and week, rich and poor. It made no distinction but killed randomly and it killed many brave professional doctors, nurses, paramedics and hospital staff as it ravaged all in its path. It was an indiscriminate pandemic.

We were all still working up to this point, although Franks work schedule had begun to decrease. Eurynome was already retired but as she lived alone without the few members of her family close by, it was a concerning time.

Rekha's role kept her at the sharp end and she was in constant demand as February rolled by.

I too found myself, along with my colleagues in the quarrying industry having to dig deep and carry on as usual. If no clay was produced there would be a shortage of plastics for medical and safety use. Medicine which rely on clay as a binding agent would no longer be available. Paper mills would be on the back foot as clay is a major constituent of the product. Sanitary products such as toilets and hand basins

260

essential for health could no longer be produced, the list went on and on.

It was a given that we must produce clay. Our South and West Devon quarries continued to produce Ball and China Clays with very little loss of production on our part even in such challenging times.

By the end of February Italy had seen a major upsurge in cases and it was sweeping the Middle East and Latin America. On the 28th of February it struck Sub-Saharan Africa and began its journey south. This year was a leap year and on the 29th day America recorded its first covid deaths.

'March' as my dear old mum used to say when referring to the weather comes in like a lion and out like a lamb or sometimes versa visa. This year it was coronavirus that came and it came in like a lamb and out like a lion. It started with about two dozen cases and by the end of the month was in the tens of thousands. I am aware that all this is known to the reader already but I need to put it in context for the timeline which was to become critical.

Rekha and I continued with our job roles and were I think grateful for them in many ways. Speaking for myself, it allowed me a point of focus. We had clay to produce and move even though there was some difficulty with the amount of transport we had available.

Lorry drivers needed to make a living as did transport companies and we needed clay moved but in the midst of all this everyone entering or leaving site needed to be protected from the invisible killer. Several of our quarry team went down with covid like symptoms and were told to stay home for the required period of isolation.

A dozen times a day we cleaned the offices, wiping desk surfaces, telephones and our laptops. We kept the two meter rule and only shared two of the largest offices where spacing could be maintained. I think it fair to say that we were all nervous to know how the situation was going to develop, nonetheless we kept going.

The 11th of March saw the World Health Organization declared the virus a pandemic and stock markets the world over fell to new lows almost daily. In the UK the chancellor announced an aid package of twelve billion pounds to help the country cope with the problem.

On the 13th sporting events in the UK were cancelled for the foreseeable future. Prime Minister Boris Johnson had urged all non-essential staff to work from home in order to protect the NHS from the onslaught which by then was already starting to overwhelm services.

On March 17th Chancellor Rishi Sunak decided on a package of three hundred and thirty billion in loans and further tax cuts of twenty billion to keep businesses solvent. The following day saw schools shut except to the children of essential workers.

On the 20th of March the UK Government shut pubs and all other social venues whilst announcing that workers on furlough were to be subsidised up to eighty percent of their wages. On the 23rd we were told to stay at home and only to go out for exercise once a day and to buy food.

The 25th of March had seen the Indian government impose a lockdown on one point three billion people in the sub-continent.

At home on the 26th of March at 8pm we rang bells and clapped and cheered NHS workers in a show of support for their selfless dedication. I offered up a prayer as well for my very brave friend Christina Wiseman who as a district nurse in Suffolk was very much on the frontline. This tribute continued weekly for months after.

On the 3rd of April I received an email from Eurynome Palmer it was copied to Frank and Rekha, it was headed 'Shibboleth,' and said as follows; Traveller has been in touch. Traveller has identified herself and has asked if we have found The Parcel. How should I reply and in what detail?

At last Anna had been in touch, it was such a relief.

It was decided that we would inform Anna in only the most basic of details, hoping she was equal to the task and would understand our reluctance to commit too much to the reply.

I asked how Traveller had communicated the message to Eurynome and was told by SMS message. No number or details were traceable.

We agreed the following reply given that Anna new nothing of our codenames for the parcel, herself and the password.

Artefact found and securely stored. Please advise you intentions to collect, date, time and location as soon as possible. All we could hope was that this message had come from Anna or Chapter not from any other source and all Eurynome could do was to select reply, type our message and hit send.

The next day Eurynome had a reply. It was all that we could have hoped for and it was just what we needed to lift our spirits at such a grim time.

It was copied from an SMS message to email and headed Shibboleth.

The message said, From Anna and Chapter, Congratulations on your find. Location, date and time of collection to be confirmed. Ensure artefact is kept secure. Further message to follow.

Two days later and the Prime Minister himself was in intensive care with covid.

It was odd walking the roads around Cornwood, no cars passed by and no aircraft flew overhead. In such a terrible time for so many it was also a time of peace. Out there in the countryside with my wife Shel and my dogs and with only the odd dog walker to call to or wave at life seemed idyllic to some degree. I could barely hear our machinery at the quarry two miles away. It was as if our lives had taken a backwards step of a hundred years or so.

We had Frank and Wendy to call to over the fence and I had work but for my wife as for many others it was a lonely existence.

April 9th saw the highest daily death toll in the UK up until that time with almost a 2,000 covid related deaths recorded in a twenty four hour period. It was Easter and a time of religious celebration during normal years, but this of course was anything but normal. It was the quietest Easter that anyone could remember.

The days passed and the warmth of spring was the only welcome visitor to our shores. Fear increased and we lived in a strange world of queuing to get into shops and keeping a safe distance from others. It was now a requirement that we all wear masks. How strange it was only being able to see people's eyes, it made a judgement of expression difficult.

At times tempers frayed as frustration grew. Shortages of normal items was an annoyance as people were panic buying which in itself caused more and more shortages and every night we had the daily dose of disaster. It frightened the vulnerable and elderly and at times it was

as if the pandemic would only end when it had killed off at least one half of the population.

On the 14th of April Prime Minister Boris Johnson was discharged from hospital and Spain eased some lockdown restrictions.

By the 22nd the UK began human trials of covid-19 vaccine which gave hope of some kind of possible defence against the disease and on April 30th the government was announcing that the UK was past the peak of infections.

The 2nd May was my wife's birthday and was to prove a special day in our quest as well. Another email arrived from Eurynome Palmer subject heading Shibboleth and this time it revealed the information that we had all been waiting for.Anna had been in touch. The message told us that at a date and time had been planned and that we must prepare to retrieve the artefact and meet where instructed. It stated that Anna and Chapter were aware that driving anywhere at present without good reason might attract the unwanted attention of the police, therefore it was for us to take reasonable precautions to ensure that we did not run into any problems

A further message would follow in good time to allow us to make our arrangements and would also give us the date and time.

Being stopped by the police would be a problem in itself, explaining what we were doing and why would prove to be implausible and should we be caught with the artefact it was going to be almost impossible to get out of the situation. Protecting the egg was all important.

The message concluded on a sobering note. It said, 'To miss this window of opportunity will result in the artefact staying on earth, possibly forever. You must not fail.'

Another inevitable but necessary telephone conference entailed. We were close to achieving our quest but yet in all honesty so far from it. 'Many a slip twixt cup and lip' as Mr Shakespeare may have said. It was frightening.

We faced a responsibility that was unique in the annals of mankind. The conference had been short and to the point. For once I was caught on the hop and didn't record it, so I am unable to relay it to the reader in any detail. The gist of it was that if all else failed the protection and concealment of the egg paramount at whatever the cost to ourselves in our personal or professional lives.

Now we were all of one mind and that was total belief that the egg was a universe in its own right and that it was populated by life forms that would never be known to us or to anyone else in our universe.

It would be easy to retrieve the artefact. Getting to Mrs Palmers house was going to be a problem. Most days when I went to work on a very quiet backroad to the quarry, I would nearly always pass a police car. The police for their part were doing the best they could to protect the public and ensure that everyone on the road was there for business or private needs when absolutely necessary and within the context of what the law allowed.

When and where the actual meeting would take place we would have to take in our stride and deal with as best we could. We were all certain that we would be given fair notice and it would be somewhere far from prying eyes we could be sure of that. Who we would be meeting and what form the transfer of the artefact from us to the new guardian or guardians would take was at present a matter of pure conjecture.

Now we needed to decide who out of the four of us would take the artefact. We had no idea who would be invited or indeed allowed to attend. Each of us wanted to be involved, but that said it would be much harder for Rekha as she would have to travel all the way from Kent to Devon. It was a long drive and the odds against her being stopped enroute were high.

It would be a tiring journey as well. Trains of course were still not running from the capital to the southwest. I offered to meet her half way and drive her down if it helped but the important work she was carrying out was a constant professional pull and as yet she was unwilling to commit to making the journey.

Eurynome was keen but was also frightened to meet anyone else, even us as she had been isolating for so long. This was going to be a great disappointment to both the girls but it was a decision for the two of them personally and Frank and I were totally unwilling to push either of them. They must be comfortable in their own minds, after all none of us knew what we would see or allowed to see. It might be a mind blowing meeting or it might turn out to be a non-event.

Frank and I had decided immediately that were going to go. At least one of us would have to because the artefact would have to be retrieved from the Well and delivered to the transfer point.

May 10th saw the UK Government allow plans to ease back on lockdown. Unlimited exercise would be allowed as would going back to work if it wasn't possible to work from home. On the 16th of May India reported 85,000 covid cases and extended lockdown until the end of the month.

The 27th saw the covid death toll pass 100,000 with 500,000 cases were recorded in Brazil, second only to the USA in numbers.

On the 31st of May, another email came from our friend in Sheepstor, once again the subject heading was Shibboleth.

I opened it with bated breath. Eurynome informed us that Traveller had been in touch and that the parcel was to be delivered to an area designated by a set of co-ordinates attached at one AM on the fifth of June. The co-ordinates were as follows. Fifty degrees, twenty nine minutes North, four degrees, two minutes West.

Frank and I already knew those numbers by heart. They were the coordinates for an area of Dartmoor, Sheepstor to be exact, the Tor itself.

Chapter 31

Final Countdown.

It was coming together fast. The 1st of June dawned with fresh new light. It was the start of the working week and Monday's were always busy but still my mind was awash with thoughts. Forty odd years had passed and yet I still wasn't ready for this moment. It all seemed as if it was too rushed.

Anna's email had taken us by surprise and I requested Thursday and Friday as two days leave. Unusually it wasn't a problem at this time. My assistant Mary would stand in for me. Dependable in the extreme, intelligent and focused, I was only sorry that I could not bring here into my confidence with regard to the artefact. The less we shared the more secure the handover and a successful completion of our quest.

At lunchtime that day I called Frank to start the ball rolling.

'Dear Boy, I assume you are alone?' He said cautiously.

'Yes. I have about twenty minutes to talk.'

'How do you want to proceed?'

I was going to be careful, very careful, to make a mistake now would be unthinkable. Everything we achieved would be in jeopardy and it might ultimately mean the loss of the egg.

'We need to decide who's in on the handover.'

'I'm writing this down.' Frank said. 'I don't like to keep notes or a list but I think it absolutely necessary at this juncture.'

'Agreed.'

'Next.'

'The best way to get to the meeting. If it's by car, do we risk being stopped and drawing attention to ourselves?'

'Undoubtedly. The police will be on the lookout for cars and the like at that time of night.'

I concurred. 'Yes they no doubt will be.'

'Our only other option is to go by foot.' He said.

'We have a couple of days to decide on that, but I see no other way.'

Frank was cool about it. 'We can shelve that for the moment. Next.'

'Retrieving the Parcel unseen from the Eurynome's Well.'

'Should be simple but we need to be there in good time.'

'Quite. Next.'

'A means of escape with the Parcel if something goes wrong.'

'Thoughts?'

I lightened the mood. 'Leg it.'

'Hmm, at our age and in our condition that maybe a non-starter.'

'Excellent point,' I laughed, 'let's ditch that idea.'

Frank was serious suddenly. 'I hadn't given it much consideration to be honest but it if the situation arises we will need a way off the Tor as quickly as possible.'

'Keeping the artefact and ourselves as safe as possible.' I added.

'Next.'

'Ensuring that we get the Parcel to the handover, if for example one of us were to be injured on the way there.'

'I have put that in my notes.'

'What we do if Anna is not there or is replaced by someone else.'

'Yes and next?'

'Preparation for the unthinkable.'

'As in?' He enquired.

'As in possibly meeting people from another world.'

'Hmm.'

'Well, we have no idea how we will react.'

Frank said. 'But you have met Anna already.'

'Yes but we don't know who she is and if she has companions, are they like her or totally different?'

'You mean in physical appearance?'

'Yes. I mean maybe she is a hologram.'

'A projection of some kind!'

All I could say was. 'It's possible.'

'Very well, that's seven points that need discussion.'

'Then we need another conference call tonight.' I told him.

'Leave it to me.'

We ended the call and I returned to my office and for the rest of the day carried on the firms business. The afternoon had been almost interminable, it just dragged but I left work at 5.30pm and in five minutes I was back on my driveway. An interesting evening lay ahead. It would be refreshing to get Rekha and Eurynome's comment on our plan. Our wives went out together for the evening on a long walk with the dogs. Our quest being a source of some aggravation to them on occasion.

Seven-thirty pm saw the start of the phone call. Frank came to my house and we kept some social distance between us of course. We began on time as we were aware how quickly time passed during these conversations. We cracked on smartly.

The first point was who out of the four of us would be able to attend the handover. Although the UK had recorded the lowest increase in covid daily deaths since the end of March, it was still frowned upon to travel without good cause. This, along with the demands of her job and the distance and time involved meant that Rekha would have to travel down in a couple of days. She had decided to make her own way.

'I'm excited beyond words.' She had told us. We could hear it in her voice and it lifted our morale.

'It's the right decision dear girl.' Frank remarked.

Eurynome was pleased for her as well, as was I she was needed and although the NHS were under the cosh and none of us wished to treat their sacrifice with disdain, her aid would be invaluable.

'I have news.' Eurynome Palmer said. 'I won't be available.'

'Why?' I asked thoroughly disappointed at her news.

'I tested positive for covid this morning. I didn't want to worry you all but I feel awful and there is no way I will break quarantine rules, it would put the rest of you at risk as well.'

'Are you sure it's not a false positive?' Frank asked.

'I carried out two tests.' She said. 'And both were positive.'

269

'Seriously.' Rekha growled over the phone. 'That's just the most awful timing for you.'

'Are you ok?' I had asked Eurynome, suddenly aware that she didn't sound as bright and positive as she usually did.

'Don't worry. If I am taken to hospital you must go ahead and get the Parcel from its hiding place whatever happens to me.'

'So it will just be Andy, Rekha and myself.' Frank remarked soberly.

That was that. The decision had been made for us by a natural event.

Number two on our list was what had been number three on the list originally, that was the best way to retrieve the artefact from Mrs Palmers Well. We needed to be in good time.

'It's better if you can get here early,' She told us, 'I will move as much of the timber as I can on the day. That will allow you to simply grab the Parcel and go. It should only take a few minutes in all for you to pull it out and check it over.'

Rekha was appalled. 'You can't move all that timber yourself. You have covid, you will make yourself even worse than you are now.'

I agreed with Rekha. 'It's not on you just won't manage it.'

'And you don't think that the three of you humping around all that timber in the situation we are currently in will draw attention?' Eurynome had sensibly asked.

'The Lady is correct.' Frank opined. 'It will draw unwanted attention, even in such a small village as Sheepstor.'

Eurynome was adamant. 'I have already begun to remove some of the wood. I won't be able to lift the cover itself, it's too heavy, so I will have to leave that to you gentlemen.'

There was a hush. I remember that silence well. It was oppressive as if nothing had gone right for Eurynome since Anna's last email and that it had in some way caused bad luck. No one spoke for what seemed an age, I needed to get us back on track.

'Okay. Then you must do it but with as much care as possible. Do not do anything to put your health in further danger,' I begged.

'I will be careful.' The church warden promised.

Third point in order was how us three would get to Mrs Palmers and then to the meeting point. I had considered at one point that we could walk across the moors from Cornwood. It wasn't at all impossible but given our age, health and the that the fact the ground could be treacherous by day let alone in the dark a walk at night was a foolish suggestion and so I said nothing.

We was agreed that we would drive out across the moors earlier in the evening and park the car in the same place as I had the day I met

Anna on the moor. It was a very quiet road and I would drive on dipped lights or even side lights if need be. I would park up behind the furze bushes from where Frank, Rekha and I would walk the mile and a half to Eurynome's to collect the artefact.

The last part of the journey would involve walking back to the car and then driving it over two miles of track made by army vehicles across the moors to get as close to the Tor as possible. The last half mile we would make on foot.

'A mere walk in the park.' As Frank remarked.

'Yeah seriously.' Rekha exclaimed with her customary sarcasm.

Point four on the list was originally a means of escape from the authorities if needed. We could only be caught if we were either careless or stupid.

'That's you two buggered then,' Rekha said, 'but I will be ok.'

Everyone laughed, it helped to break the tension we were all feeling.

'What do you propose?' She enquired.

'A dose of good fortune.' Frank told her.

'And failing that?'

'We both know the moors like the back of our hands.' I told her. 'And I don't think the local bobbies are going to pursue us on foot across that type of ground at night.'

271

'We shall endeavour.' Frank said. 'Not to incur suspicion in the first place.'

'All we could do is hide the artefact as best as possible and come back for it at when they leave, as leave they would at some point.'

Frank was realistic as ever. He told us. 'It's not ideal but given the current position of lockdown, it's the best we can do.'

Our fifth point of discussion was ensuring the parcel was delivered. We added a codicil to that. We would only hand it over to Anna as she was the only person we had met with. We would trust no one else.

'And if she isn't there?' Rekha asked.

'Then we all leave as quickly and safely as we can.' Frank said.

Eurynome sounded doubtful. 'It may not go well if you a make any attempt to leave with the Parcel. I mean, what if you should be threatened?'

'That's a very good question.' Rekha agreed.

'We can only pray that doesn't happen and play it by ear,' I told them all, 'a friend of mine used to use the old quote, situations alter cases same as noses alter faces.'

'Andy's right.' Frank remarked. 'Anything could happen or it could all be totally straight forward.'

'Then it's in your hands.' Eurynome said.

Number six was a worst case scenario, a what if and I was no good at those. My boss often described my management style as, flying by the seat of my pants. Nonetheless I agreed that we needed some plan in the event of one of us twisting an ankle or even worse breaking a leg. After all, it was Dartmoor by night is unforgiving and it would not be an ideal position to be in if things went badly. It was all about reducing risk as far as we could.

If we used common sense and all, hopefully should go well.

'We will wear sensible clothing and footwear,' Frank remarked, 'and I do have a well packed small, light survival kit. It just has the basics in it.'

I said. 'We will also leave in good time. If we don't have time against us, then we can take things slow and easy.'

'Sure and steady wins the race.' Eurynome commented.

'Ok.' Rekha sighed. I think she had given up worrying at that point. 'I just have to trust you two too get me across the moors in one piece.'

Point number seven was for us to prepare for the unthinkable.

This was a psychological consideration. We could ready ourselves for some of the challenges we would face but for others there was no way of gauging our reaction to what we might see or experience.

We were all of a mind that Anna was from another world. That being the case we might experience sights, sounds and conditions that most people would never be subjected to.

'We may see nothing of course.' Rekha sensibly remarked.

'Agreed, but what if they meet someone other than Anna, someone different?' Eurynome enquired. 'A true alien I mean.'

Frank thought that the visitor or visitors would try to keep as low a profile as possible.

'It would make sense for the handover to be low key and quick.' He offered as backup to his argument.

Rekha was on board with that. 'No doubt about it.'

'I agree,' I had said, 'but we need to be aware that we may see things that affect us. This is not just a quick hand over of a parcel to a friend or to the postman, this is possibly handing billions of lives to an alien race. People have reported similar encounters but they have been in most instances, out of the blue occurrences. This is a planned event.'

I felt my point was well made and required some contemplation.

'Can't argue with your logic.' Rekha said.

'We can only do our best and hope to deal with the situation.' Frank said supportively.

Eurynome was more robust in her thoughts and much to the point, she said, 'You will do what you must, between the four of us we have many years invested in this quest.'

Frank had asked if there was any other business to be discussed. There was. It would be a long drive for Rekha. She said that she had holiday's to take so time off wouldn't be a problem, but it might be inconvenient for her company at such short notice.

'I will approach the managing director tomorrow and then get back to you.' She told us earnestly.

It would be a six hour drive for her. It would be tiring given the immediacy of the event, and the mental strain that taking time off from such a very responsible job at such short notice would cause.

'I will be fine.' She told us.

I was more insistent. 'You will stop at my friends place in Salisbury, it's halfway and you can get some rest.'

'Won't it put that person in danger?' She said referring to covid.

'Test yourself.' I advised. 'She has a holiday cottage and will put you up there. You can stay well away from each other.

Rekha didn't refuse, 'OK, thank you,' Was all she said in response

The phone conference ended and Frank and I made a mental note to keep in touch with Eurynome and to ensure that she was given as much support as possible.

June the second saw the World Health Organisation in talks with the American government, asking President Trump not to end their relationship and New Zealand Prime Minister Jacinda Arden expressing concern that the Black Lives Matter protests might start another outbreak of covid.

Rekha had called to say that she had a taken leave and would I be kind enough to make the arrangements with my friend so that she could stay in her holiday cottage. Frank rang Eurynome and she told him that she was still quite poorly but taking medical advice.

On the 3rd of June I rang Eurynome to ask how she was and if she needed anything.

'I'm feeling better.' She had told me. 'And I have moved half of the wood covering the Well.'

'I'm worried, we all are, you have done enough.'

'Nonsense. I have a strong constitution.'

'Mrs Palmer, you are a stubborn lady.' I told her.

'It must be done. Promise me that you will ensure that the parcel is delivered to Traveller.' She said in closing.

'I promise.'

'Then all will be well.'

I bade her goodnight and called both Frank and Rekha to assure both of them that she was okay.

Rekha informed me that she was leaving for Salisbury in an hour's time. She said she would call on arrival at the cottage. If stopped she was not prepared to lie. She would say that she had had urgent business in Devon and was breaking her journey in Salisbury on the way down.

'I won't lie.' She told me. 'As far as we know we are genuinely saving lives by getting the artefact to safety.'

'I hope we are saving lives.' I remarked.

'We've seen it, the artefact I mean. Do you doubt its authenticity?'

'Not at all.'

I was positive that we were saving a miracle of nature. As to if there were other life forms on that universe I would never know. In truth all I did know was the trail of clues that we had followed that had led us to the information we deemed to be true. That was going to have to be enough for us all. Anna was real and if she was real then surely Chapter was real, and so on and so forth.

'It will be good to see you again.' She added on a personal note.

'Likewise.' I replied. 'And what an adventure we are about to share.'

'It doesn't seem real.' She had told me.

'Let's hope we complete our part of the bargain and deliver as we've

promised we will. We really need to succeed in this ' She continued with warmth in her voice. 'Anyway, see you tomorrow.'

'Drive safe.' I urged. 'We can't afford to lose you.'

I heard her laugh. 'No, I'm the brains of the outfit.'

Then she was gone and the anticipation grew with every hour. She rang later that day to say that she had arrived in

Salisbury and that it had been a long drive. She had met my friend albeit at a distance and was planning to get a good night's sleep and then leave early in the morning and be with us by ten thirty or eleven o'clock.

Thursday the 4th of June and the death toll in the UK from covid was still rising. It was soon expected to pass the mark of 40,000 souls yet still the brave staff of the NHS kept their nerve and continued to fight under terrible strain and frightening conditions. Every day they put their lives at risk in order to save the lives of their patients and colleagues many of whom also perished.

Frank rang Eurynome. He said she sounded awful but that she had told him all the wood was moved, except for the cover as we knew she just could not manage it.

'You may not see me this evening,' She had told him, 'I must rest for now. Let yourselves into the garden and do what you must.'

Rekha called at a little after eight am. She sounded sleepy and not quite on the ball.

'You know I love my bed.' She said with a groan.

'I think you would happily go to bed at eight in the evening and sleep for twelve hours if it was socially acceptable.'

'Bloody right I would, but I'm usually up at a decent time. How's our friend today?' She enquired of Eurynome.

'Frank says she's not good. She has told us to go ahead and retrieve the Parcel and that she may not see us.'

'Someone should call a doctor for her don't you think?'

'Probably. I will call her myself and see if I can persuade her to get some help or assistance.'

Rekha sounded sceptical. 'It won't be easy. GP's are only phoning to give advice, that's if you can even get through to a surgery at this present time.'

'Talking of time,' I told her, 'you better crack on. You still have a three hour drive and you need some rest before we start wandering the moors later tonight.'

'I know I'm a bit behind. I will see you by one pm at the latest.'

Roughly an hour later I rang Eurynome and Frank had not been exaggerating about her health. She sounded very ill indeed.

'You need to call someone and get some help.' I said sternly.

'I promise I will as soon as you hang up but it may take a while to get through to my surgery.'

I was concerned, extremely concerned. 'Promise me you will speak to someone.'

Eurynome seemed resigned to do so. 'I promise.'

Frank called and I updated him on the situation with both of the ladies.

'Good God they are both a worry.' He replied.

Rekha's health was a cause for anxiety. She had a long term health problem which needed management. It made her tired and she was in need of regular meals and glucose. As for Eurynome Palmer we could do very little, we just had to trust that she would act in her own best interest.

'What have we gotten ourselves into?' I asked.

'Whatever the outcome, it's too late to stop at this stage of the game.'

'Remember the old saying.' I replied.

'Which is.?'

'Hope for the best, expect the worse and take what comes.'

Frank breathed heavily down the line. 'Very reassuring.'

'Game on at last.' I told him.

It was two hours later when my phone ran it was Eurynome Palmer with an update on her health. She sounded better.

'I have taken some advice from the doctor and am feeling a little more settled, in myself you understand.'

It was more of a statement than a question and although I was happy she had spoken to a health professional, I was still uneasy but could not put my finger on it as to why.

'Can we drop off anything for you?' I had asked. 'Food or milk?'

'Thank you but no, it would be wasted.'

Naively I didn't see the darkness behind her words. 'Very well.'

'Your concern is much appreciated.'

I made one last attempt at getting her to receive proper attention.

'We are all worried about you, is there nothing we can do.'

'I will be fine you simply concentrate on the Parcel and Traveller.'

I couldn't force her to get any further help and so with many other questions taxing my brain I bade her farewell.

'Take care tonight.' She remarked wheezily. 'I have grown very fond of you all.'

I was about to say, 'And us of you, but the line went dead and she was gone.'

At least we would see her later that evening and check on her health and general wellbeing.

'She will be fine.' I told Frank when I saw him over the back garden fence. 'She's a hardy Dartmoor woman.'

He nodded sagely. 'Let us hope so dear boy.'

Chapter 32

Face at the Window.

It was almost one pm by the time Rekha arrived at my house. She parked on the driveway and was introduced to my wife Shel first of all and then to Frank's wife Wendy over the garden fence.

We had all tested ourselves again with covid kits as had Rekha before leaving Salisbury that morning.

'You need a meal, some sleep and chillout time before this evening.' I told her.

Our wives had been advised of our intentions on the previous day. It was fair to say that neither of them were happy about the situation, but as always they recognised the time we put into our quest, even if they were not party to the detail. Frank and I sometimes wondered how the hell they put up with us.

'I need to let my girls know I'm safe.' She said.

'Of course.' I replied. 'We have lunch ready for you.'

After lunch Rekha was shown to one of our spare rooms after first having to negotiate her way pass two very excitable dogs.

Lockdown had been no picnic for pets and they had made the most of the opportunity to meet a new friend. Rekha got her head down for a couple hours and arose at four fifteen looking refreshed and eager to get going.

What time do we leave here?'

'Seven pm.' Frank said.

'And that will give us enough time to make the meeting?'

'More than enough.' He assured her.

It was agreed that we would take my Range Rover as we would need good offroad capability, especially if we were to meet the police or we needed to vacate the meeting area at speed.

'I know the area like the back of my hand and so does Frank.'

'Ok.' She replied seemingly satisfied with my answer.

We went through a brief of what we would do and where and in what time frames we should complete each section. There were five all of which will become self-evident to the reader.

I checked the car tyres and spare for damage and for air pressure, then engine oil, brake and automatic gear box fluid. I checked the windscreen washers and the lights of course. The last thing we needed was to be stopped on the road because a brake or headlight was out. I had also topped up with fuel that morning.

Our wives had prepared light meals for us. We didn't want bloated stomachs to travel on. Rekha ensured us that she had what was needed for her well-being. We carried small water bottles as well.

Next up was a compass, map and torch in case anything changed at a moment's notice. Last but not least was a first aid kit, small but vital to our mission.

Rekha had brought a lightweight wind and waterproof jacket along with sturdy hiking boots. We would dress ready for action as there would be no time to change clothes.

We said goodbye to our wives at seven pm precisely and with a minimum of noise and fuss, I exited our driveway with my two companions on the last leg of our adventure. It was a nice enough evening although there had been the odd light shower of rain driven by a steady breeze, both of which had died down by the time we left Cornwood for Sheepstor.

Rekha tried Eurynome's telephone number but with no success.

'She's trying to rest I expect.' Rekha said. 'I won't keep ringing.'

'Best dear girl that she gets what sleep she can.' Frank offered.

'I hope she's ok.' I said.

We headed west out of the village for a three miles, climbing up past the quarry where I worked. It spanned out on either side of the road and stretched for a few square miles both to the south and north. We cut through the village of Wotter passing the Moorland Hotel then turned right at the crossroads out onto the moors and my birthplace at Cadover Bridge.

The roads were very quiet apart from a couple of tractors heading from farm to field. It was still odd to see next to no traffic on the road but on I drove down Shaden hill and looked over towards

Sheepstor in the distance. The few clouds that had been hovering after the showers were moving away. The breeze that rustled the furze bushes would soon dry the little rain we had in the past hours. The sun was high and warm and would be up for the best part of another two hours yet.

'There's Sheepstor.' Frank told Rekha, leaning over her shoulder from the rear passenger side and pointing ahead.

'It looks different from this side.' She mused.

'I will get us as close as I can to the meeting point.' I said.

Frank sounded a little flat. 'Let's retrieve the artefact first shall we?'

'Keep your eyes peeled for the police.' I commented.

'Indeed dear boy.'

Rekha was concerned about Eurynome. 'I hope we see her.'

'Me too.' I told my friend.

Cadover Bridge came into view, the quarry now only on the right of the road and farmland, all previously worked by my family on the left and straight ahead.

Funny how little notice of your surroundings when you're young, likewise the longing to get away to explore the world alone or with friends. Now I wished that for all my experiences of travelling the world that I had invested more of my time and myself in Dartmoor itself. It was time now that, infuriatingly I would never be able to get back. The best I could do was invest my future in the area.

As I drove, I gave much consideration to those who had lived on and loved these moors for all the centuries past. It was a sobering thought, now older and hopefully somewhat wiser I resolved to make more effort to that end in the latter years of my life and make my mark, somehow.

The road dipped and I slowed for sheep grazing on the verge. A sharp drop of only sixty feet or so but covered in less than sixty yards with a wicked near ninety degree right hand bend at the bottom. Now after the same distance the road swept back left and up over Cadover Bridge itself.

Huge granite pillars dug vertically into the grass banks, protected speeding cars and careless drivers from an unwanted dip in the river below. The road rose sixty or so feet again and passed the Counting House, the house in which I was born and lived for a quarter of a century. Its walls built seven feet high as a defence against sheep, ponies and cattle. The one third acre of land still filled in part with a variety of trees, lawns and my father's old vegetable patch which he had tended for over forty years.

About a mile and a half to the right over the river Trowlesworthy Warren my maternal Grandfathers farm standing like a granite fist against the encroaching rough moorland, which given the chance would have reclaimed the house and field in but a few years. It was he who had set me on my quest with Chapter and Anna.

Rekha's dark eyes shone as she looked across to where I pointed.

'My God that's bleak.' She murmured.

'It's home my love.' Was all I could bring myself to reply.

Passing my childhood home and haunts brought us to Brisworthy Corner whilst and the remains of an old china clay works which had closed when I was twelve years of age and to our left up over Wigford Down stood the remains of prehistoric settlements littering the hillside. The whole area was a tribute to the hardiness of those who had gone before.

At the crossroads we turned right and in fifty yards passed the entrance to the farm my cousin still worked. The road took a ninety degree left turn here and had continued as single track road towards Meavy. There were pull ins and cars could pass each other with care but little space between them.

A hundred yards ahead Newpark House appeared as the field hedges to the left pulled back off the road and to the right was a small clump of trees by name, Brisworthy Plantation, with open moorland continuing on that side. It was here that the stone circle, monoliths and standing stones had pointed us towards Sheepstor.

Still the sun was high in the sky, as yet it was unwilling to yield the day to Nyx, Helios still racing across the sky in his chariot before entering the western gates of heaven.

The last of the clouds had left the distant Tor's and as we came up on Newpark House another ninety degree left hand bend took us further onto the moors. Half a mile further the road levelled out before beginning it's steep descent to the village of Meavy. Now we had the hamlet of Lovaton off to our left but we would turn right and a right hand turn so sharp that it was as close to a hairpin bend as possible without actually being one. This was the road that led to Sheepstor and Burrator Reservoir just beyond. I took it carefully and deliberately whilst my colleagues watched in all directions for signs of other vehicles. We headed out towards Sheepstor and a mile and a quarter from the turning I pulled the car up into the same spot in which I had met Anna some years before.

'This is cosy.' Rekha laughed as I backed the Range Rover up between several huge gorse or furze bushes, making it invisible from the road.

'The better hidden the greater our advantage.' Frank commented.

I locked the car and we made our way cautiously out of the pull in and across the tarmac. We donned covid masks for disguise as much as for protection against infection and set of at a pace. It was almost half past seven. Frank had the first aid kit slung over his shoulder.

'All we can do now is pray that no one spots us.' I said.

Frank thought it wise to hop over the stonewalls if we heard any cars or tractors coming our way. It made sense as we were hemmed in on either side by them all the way down the road to the village itself.

Some people had left to look after relatives before lockdown began and that reduced the tiny population by about fifteen percent we were later to find out.

We were aloud out for exercise of course but should not have been travelling this far to take it.

'Let's speak only when we need to.' I told Frank and Rekha.

It seemed like an age until the lane opened into the village proper. We headed straight for Eurynome's house and used the grass verge where possible to limit the sound of our boots on the tarmac and gravel. I knocked on her door as quietly as I could. It was deathly silent in the village. Not even the sound of a television or a radio broke the peace of the evening. People were staying indoors it appeared and keeping their lives down to a whisper.

A sheep bleated close by and unexpectedly, causing us all to jump in response.

'Shit.' Rekha growled.

I stifled a giggle, I was terrible under stressful situations for seeing the funny side of something so mundane.

'Shh.' Frank scolded.

I knocked again but with the same result, still no answer.

'Let's get on with it.' I told my companions.

We moved through her garden, crossed the sad excuse for a style all the while checking that we weren't being watched.

With trembling hands we lifted the Well cover and in less than two minutes Frank had found the fishing line. He began hauling, sensibly using a pair of battered gardening gloves to stop his fingers from being sliced open.

'A little help please.' He muttered. ''It's stuck on something.'

'Gently.' I said, afraid that any jolting or jarring would cause it to get stuck permanently.

'Hang on.' Rekha reached across and pulled the snagged line forward and backwards.

It gave with a twang and Frank was able to continue pulling the line-up and towards him. We all breathed a sigh of relief.

Rekha was scouring the few houses around only two of which were in a position to overlook Eurynome's house and more importantly the field. I helped Frank and with a sudden splash, the artefact in its waterproof container broke the surface of the water.

We pulled the parcel clear of the Well and with enormous relief set it to one side on the ground. Frank pulled a small but sturdy looking rucksack from out of nowhere it seemed.

'It will be easier to carry like this, we can all take turns. I know it's not very heavy but it would be awkward to carry in front of you and one of us may drop it.' He whispered.

'Great idea.' I said.

'Shall I carry it first?' Rekha offered in a low voice. 'I may need to just concentrated on myself and not breaking anything later on.'

Frank put the container in the rucksack and helped Rekha sling it over her shoulders.

We kept low and kept looking for anyone watching us, it was a pleasant surprise to suddenly have Frank grab my arm and point at the bedroom window of Eurynome Palmers house. There she stood at the window holding the frame. She gave us the thumbs up but then waved us urgently on with her left arm. Rekha waved back.

A second or two later she repeated the movement, then cupped a hand to her ear. Her last act was to blow three kisses to us and then she was gone from view. The whole incident lasted possibly less than thirty seconds.

'Let's move quickly.' I told my two friends.

'Rekha sounded quietly jubilant. 'But she's okay right, we all saw her?'

'Indeed.' Frank murmured, his stare telling me he felt differently about our friends health.

We gained the single track road between the two stone walls and had gone less than a hundred yards when we heard the unmistakable wail of a police car siren in the distance out towards the Yelverton road.

'Christ.' I said. 'We need to get off the road.'

'The walls too high here.' Frank said. 'Look up there, part of the wall is down.' He was pointing two hundred yards ahead.

Rekha was already running along the road to the damaged wall. She was a bit of a fitness fanatic and it showed. All Frank and I could do was follow at a fast walking pace.

'Hurry.' She called. Still trying to keep her voice low.

She was a good fifty yards ahead of us now and in our ears the sirens wailed at less than two miles distance. We couldn't be seen until they entered the village itself, a cluster of Forestry Commission trees cut of the reservoir from the village and the police would have to go around the dams edge before they came into Sheepstor itself.

'Someone must have spotted us.' I growled.

'Bloody hell.' Frank cursed.

Rekha was twenty yards or so from the gap in the wall. Turning, we could see the blue flashing lights through the trees.

'Run,' She yelled back over her shoulder.

We tried but to no avail, yet still we kept up our fast walking pace and the distance to the break in the wall was reducing.

'Move'. Rekha ordered as a police car screamed into the village and turned up towards Eurynome's house.

Rekha was over the wall and I saw her duck down and hoped that she had remembered the precious cargo she was carrying.

Another police car was coming, we could hear it's siren picking up where the other had died of slightly. It paused in the village and then with a roar it accelerated down the road we were on.

'They have seen you.' Rekha shouted as Frank and I arrived at the broken down wall.

I can still remember to this day the sudden shock and pain I felt as Frank rugby tackled me, knocking me off my feet and over the top of the stonewall and into the field.

'Get ready to run for it,' he bellowed as we hit the ground with some force knocking the wind from my lungs.

The siren wailed and the police car slowed as it approached the place where we were hiding.

'Rekha where's the Parcel?' I asked.

She pointed to a place in the wall where she had concealed it hastily.

It seemed like an age had passed as the police car slowed and we sat together with our backs tight against the wall. Any second now we were going to be arrested.

Then a miracle happened, the police car sped up again and headed at considerable speed up the road towards the spot where my car was hidden. We dared a peek over the wall. The car followed the road back towards Meavy, its siren now muted but with all of its lights still flashing.

I turned and looked back towards the village. I could see the flashing blue light flickering outside of Eurynome's house and the figures of the police officers at her door.

'We need to go.' I told my friends. 'They must be going to search her field and garden.'

Rekha had already retrieved the artefact and was unceremoniously stuffing it into the rucksack, her hands shaking as she did so.

Frank said, 'Let's keep inside this wall, at least it will give us some cover and we can't be seen from some parts of the village or road.'

It took us twenty minutes to cross two more fields and hedges before finally making it to the top road. The adrenalin boost gave us the impetus to get there but now it was easing off, we all felt tired and every leg and back muscle hurt.

'Let's rest for five minutes and then cross the road,' I told the others.

Our friend took a swig of her glucose drink. Frank who although being the eldest was still very fit rested with his head in his hands. My neck ached with tension so I dropped my shoulders. It helped and I did my best to relax.

In the distance I was sure that I could still see the flashing blue lights of the police car.

I pointed the light show to the other two. 'Do you see that?'

'Yeah.'

'They haven't left the area yet, dear boy.'

'Time to go,' I said.

We clambered over the stonewall and crossed the road as quickly as we could, a moment later the sirens started up again heading back toward us.

'Seriously?' Rekha fumed.

We needed to get off the road and into the pull in. The car was well hidden between the furze or gorse bushes. The headlights of the police car were clearly visible just half a mile away.

'They must have seen us now.' Frank yelled.

It was still daylight and the sun hadn't dipped below the horizon yet. We would be sitting ducks in the open ground of the pull in. Once again it was a race for cover. I wished that I had pushed on harder and not taken that break.

'Here it comes.' Rekha shouted a warning.

'Left,' Frank bellowed, 'Now.'

All three of us swung left landing in a pile among the gorse bushes in what could only be described as panic. We lay flat again and kept our heads down. The police car screamed past us followed by another. It was a joy to hear them accelerate back down the hill. We dared not lift our heads for possibly a minute or more.

'Is the artefact still in one piece?' I asked.

'Seems so,' Rekha replied as she peered into the rucksack for her own piece of mind. A thumbs-up from her confirmed the good news.

'I suspect it's had rougher treatment over the years,' Frank said.

'Christ that was close.'

I remember lying on my back, legs aching, my neck causing a dull throb in my shoulders. Then a boost of adrenalin kicked in. I had checked my watch the time was 8.30pm. We were as yet still on time for our rendezvous with Anna or Chapter.

'We need to lay low until the police have gone,' I advised.

It was agreed. We walked another forty yards to the car and retrieved a flask of coffee and some protein bars. It was a relief to have achieved the first part of our task, even though it was a close call thus far.

'Do you think we had been seen and reported?' Rekha asked.

'It seems likely,' Frank admitted.

I was in two minds. 'Odd that they didn't check along the road.'

'You mean in the fields?' Rekha enquired.

'Yeah I thought they were going to stop when we had just cleared the wall.'

'Perhaps,' Frank added and not without merit, 'we were not their target after all.'

'If not us then who?' I asked.

'Of that I'm not sure,' he replied.

Rekha was of the mind that we would be better off to think that it was us that the police were hunting.

'It will keep us on our toes,' she remarked sensibly.

'Agreed.'

'Likewise,' Frank concluded.

'I pray that Eurynome is not in any trouble and that they aren't on her back for information.' Rekha said quietly, her words giving voice to the thought that had been on all our minds since seeing her at her bedroom window.

I wanted to move on as soon as possible, my reasoning being that I could still drive at the moment without the need for lights, although the light would grow dimmer in the next thirty minutes or so.

A last sip of coffee, a last bite of our protein bars and we were on the move again. It was now the last bit of tarmac before the old army track led us onto the moors.

Putting the Range Rover into Drive I eased it gently off the grass and heather onto the stone and gravel passing point and then pulled out onto the tarmac. We had to chance being seen from the village as the road was on open ground against the hillside. It would only be for a hundred yards or so but it was a risk all the same.

'They are still there,' Frank told us, pointing to Sheepstor village.

'I see the lights reflecting off the back of the houses,' Rekha added.

I drove on. 'Let's hope that they are distracted.'

'She will do her best to put them off our scent.' Rekha smiled.

I drove slowly in the hope that if we were spotted the effect to the naked eye at such a distance would be to resemble a farmer slowly crossing the hill looking for sheep.

The road swept back to the northeast and dropped below the high stonewalls that led to the Sheepstor itself. Now we went off-road and along the army track and down over heather and tufted grass mounds. I was cautious, the peat held a lot of water and the last think we needed was for me to get the vehicle stuck in an unseen peat bog.

'Where now?' Rekha asked as I manoeuvred between large boulders and lighter scree washed down by a million years of water and surface movement.

'A mile should do it, then we start walking,' I told her.

Frank was pointing over my shoulder. 'That looks promising.'

Up ahead in the distance a couple of twisted, gnarled oaks hove into view. A gully cut deep into the side of the hill and many stumpy gorse bushes littered the area and disguised part it. It wasn't the perfect cover but it would do at a pinch.

'Okay, let's get over there.' I replied.

It was quite a skilful piece of driving if I had to say so myself and once again I backed up. I always favoured backing into tight spots as it made the way out easier to gauge later on, plus I always favoured facing the car downhill as well as its own weight then helped its forward momentum.

We gathered all that we needed and made sure we had our coats as even in this late springtime the nights on the moors could be cold and unforgiving. We took one flask of coffee, the map and compass, night vision binoculars, a torch and some protein bars. Rekha also took her glucose drink. If we were prepared now then we could do nothing more to improve our chances.

It was a glorious evening but we were worried. In the village we could hear sirens. They were loud in the still air, stirring the birds and animals nearby. Dartmoor ponies up on the hilltop had turned towards the sound as did the sheep and cattle on the hill and in the fields below. Moments later the sirens began to recede a little as if they were drawing away from us, first one left, then a second and in a short while a third which on reflection sounded different.

'That must have been the one that stayed at Eurynome's house and the two that came back past us from the Meavy road,' I said.

Rekha smiled. 'She would have given them false information, then as they have gone off in the wrong direction.'

'If indeed they were chasing us.'

'Meaning?' I asked.

'It doesn't matter,' Frank's voice sounded sad, as if he had a feeling, a premonition of something.

I put it from my mind, retied my boot laces and locked the car. Behind us the hillside was bereft of people as was the valley floor and Sheepstor itself.

Frank had the compass and checked our bearing on the map, his arm outstretched, fingers pointing towards the other side of the valley.

'Let's make tracks.' I said and started forward.

We made our way down the hill and along the bottom where we encountered some boggy ground. It was tiring on our leg muscles but by hopping on the tufts of rushes we kept clear of the bad ground. Half a mile further on we began to climb towards the Tor. It was warm at that time and so we carried our coats and enjoyed the late evening sun on our faces as we headed west northwest.

'Shall I take the artefact?' Frank asked Rekha.

'Please,' she said, handing him the rucksack.

We climbed on until we reached the place that Frank and I had found some time ago. We passed the standing stone rows and they pointed us to the familiar wide open piece of ground but it didn't have the seven depressions to confirm it was the right area.

'Is this it Frank?' I asked my friend.

'No. It's further on.' He replied and motioned upwards.

Rekha stopped and swigged on her drink. 'How much further?'

'A few hundred yards yet dear girl.' He told her.

It was ten past nine and Frank led us on with Rekha in the middle and me at the back. The ground was always treacherous to some degree. It varied between close packed heather its beauty belied its danger as it hid rabbit holes that could twist an ankle ease. Vipers hid under cover until they could bask on rocks in the sunlight. Treading on one risked being bitten and there venom was dangerous to all but more so to those with health issues.

Gorse or furze bushes with spiked points scratched and bit at uncovered legs, arms, hands and faces. It was a minefield. Well buried boulder with jagged tips a few inches above ground were trip hazards, as were tufts of rushes.

It was hard and remorseless ground. Frank and I knew it well but were not in any way immune to its perils. Rekha was a novice and as such we were on guard for her safety.

'There's our destination.' Frank said coming to a halt and pointing a little way into the distance.

'Where?' Rekha wrinkled her nose as her eyes squinted towards the shoulder of the Tor which the sun had sunken behind. It cast a bright red and orange glow over Sheepstor and we realised that we were now walking in shadow.

'That ridge.' Frank told her. 'See those boulders.'

'Seriously Frank, there are boulders everywhere.

I tried to come to his aid. 'Look at the four big ones on that ridge.'

'Oh, that's not too far.' She said happily unaware of the distance we still needed to cover.

'Indeed.' Frank grinned at me and moved on.

We stopped to put on our coats, it was cold now with the sun on the far side of the Tor.

'Do you need a rest?' I enquired of Rekha.

Her face gave me the answer to my question and valuing my life and body parts in general I carried on looking to my own needs.

It took some time but by quarter to ten we were at our destination on the ridge and were busy making ourselves as comfortable as we could in the lee of the four boulders that held the south side of the ridge. They were massive. On closer inspection at least two of them must have been over twenty five feet in height.

This was the edge of an area known as Yellowmead Down and was previously mentioned in an earlier chapter. It was sheltered from prying eyes in almost all directions except northeast. From that compass point the ground was more open as it spread out towards the conifer plantations in the valley.

The whole area was almost a thousand feet above sea level and the forestry at least gave some protection unless whoever might be watching us was stationed on Down Tor or Combshead Tor in the distance. This felt like a secure area and we understood why Anna had picked this as the meeting place.

By ten o clock that evening we were closed up in the shelter of the boulders but we remained on the outside. We wanted to ensure that no one had followed us and from our current vantage point we were able to see to the east, south and up over the tor to our west.

A large fissure between the two largest boulders gave us a view over the ridge towards the forest. The ridge itself was three hundred feet in length and two hundred yards in width and it had some small scree over it but it was mostly boulder free. True there were a few rushes and some heather but the gorse bushes were mostly at the edges, with just a few odd new growth stumps here and there.

'This is a good spot for observation.' I noted aloud.

'There.' He Frank pointed. 'The seven depressions.'

They were there alright and we were right on target.

Rekha looked across the barren tors now tawny brown or black and almost imperceptible to the eye in the gathering gloom, the sky had turned from indigo to violet.

'My God it's so bleak here.' She remarked, it was a phrase she had used before when describing the moors.

'You're seeing it at its best.' Frank had told her.

My mind was set on what was to come and I thought that a rest now would do us all good.

'Let's see if we can get some sleep before Anna arrives.' I said.

We put our backs to the boulders and thought of having someone on watch but a ten minute survey of the surrounding hillsides and valley with the night sight binoculars showed no human lifeform, only the usual animals.

Huddling closer together we set our watch alarms for half past midnight. That gave us half an hour to prepare ourselves for the meeting. Frank passed the rucksack to me and I looked inside at the container. I was too tired to consider all the problems this very insignificant looking artefact had caused us.

I hung the rucksack over my chest, crossed my arms over the top of it and let sleep invade my senses.

We slept.

Chapter 33

Gemini Rising.

Our alarms all went off within seconds of each other. I still remember the sensation of waking suddenly in such a strange environment. I'm a lucky person in the fact that when I wake I am totally lucid in just two or three seconds. Every muscle hurt and every bone creaked. I was as if we had slept on the boulders instead of resting against them.

'We have half an hour.' I reminded my friends, as if they needed to be reminded.

Each of us needed to pee so we all visited various gorse bushes and the like in order to relieve ourselves in some privacy.

The sky was lit up by the most glorious full moon. Because of the late sunset we hadn't taken much notice of it earlier but now it blazed up above us and tonight of all nights it seemed very white, not the usual soft lemon we were used to.

'Wow.' Rekha said finally returning to Frank and I and following our gaze upwards to the heavens. It was a stunning night. Gemini was rising over the moors it was the time of the heavenly twins anyway from an astrological viewpoint. I turned and almost a hundred and eighty degrees and lifted my eyes towards Polaris and then let my eyes drop a little lower.

There it was in all its splendour, Draco, the tail of the Dragon draped over Ursa Minor (The Little Bear) while its mouth opened right overhead as if it would strike at any moment and swallow up the Tor, the village and ourselves. I had never seen it so vibrant and alive.

'That.' Frank said. 'Is a spectacle to behold.'

'Is that Draco?' Rekha said knowing it was yet almost in disbelief.

I nodded in satisfaction. 'It most certainly is my love.' I replied.

All these years and now it seemed as though we were to be finally allowed to connect the last piece of the puzzle. This was the day, well technically the night when it was all going to come together.

'It's twelve forty four.' Frank told us as he grabbed the binoculars and scoured the area for any sign of trouble in human form,

there was none.

'Any idea as to which direction she will arrive from?' Rekha queried.

'None.' I answered. 'She just seems to appear.'

Rekha smiled her face clear in the moonlight. 'Anything?' She asked Frank.

'No dear girl, nothing at all.'

'The moon is so bright.' She continued.

Frank sighed. 'It's a strawberry moon evidently.'

'Why the big sigh?'

'Because Frank and I are tired of the different names for the moon, in our day there was a harvest moon and a blue moon and that was it. Now every time you turn on a weather channel the forecaster is trying to sell a new name for the phase.'

Frank was aggravated and it showed. 'Strawberry moon, wolf moon, harvest moon, hunters moon, beaver moon, etcetera.'

'Sore point then!' Rekha remarked with a facial expression to match.

We left it at that but the ridiculous situation in which we found ourselves had caused some tension within each of us and we began laughing which brought some relief.

Now we scoured the landscape each of us taking turns with the night vision binoculars and searching for the elusive Anna. We saw sheep, cattle, ponies, dear, foxes and badgers. What we didn't see was any other humanoid form of life.

'Perhaps.' I said to the others, 'We should look up.'

'Up?' Frank sounded sceptical. You mean she's going to beam herself down as they do in Star Trek?'

'We've all been saying that she maybe from another planet. So why limit ourselves to looking on the ground?' I asked.

Rekha agreed. 'Then look up we shall.'

The moon was so bright that it made scanning the sky near it quite difficult. We had to look away towards the darker areas of sky so we could re-focus our eyes.

'It's five minutes to one.' Rekha said.

Frank took the binoculars and scanned the ground once more.

'Just in case.' He muttered.

A couple of minutes passed and the hair stood up on the knape of my neck. My eyes were drawn skyward to a slow moving object that was coming from the southeast. It was as yet quite a way off although it was incredibly hard to judge height and distance in the sky even by day without an ariel reference point which one could use to measure an object against.

'There!' I said pointing my finger furiously to the sky.

'Where?' Rekha and Frank chorused in unison.

I pointed harder. 'There to the southeast, keep watching.'

'I see it.' Frank announced. 'Coming in from the coast.'

'Where?' Rekha yelled in frustration.

'Right there.'

'Got it.'

'It's travelling slowly.' Frank remarked.

Rekha asked if it could be an aircraft.

'No navigation lights, so it can't be.' I told her.

Frank's voice dropped. 'It's turning in this direction.'

He was right, it was.

He continued to track it. 'It's following the stone rows.'

'Really?' Rekha enquired.

'Yes.' He answered passing her the binoculars.

'It must be over the back of Trowlesworthy Warren Tor.' I added.

'Hell. Look at that.' She passed me the binoculars.

The night vision took a moment or so to adjust to. I steadied them, it was then I noticed that my palms were sweating. Now I understood Rekha's remark. The light we could see was only a small part of the object. It was certainly large, not huge but it looked sizeable and I tried to gauge its size against the Tor. If my eyes weren't deceiving me it covered a good area of the rocks.

297

'You need to see this.' I told Frank.

He took the binoculars. 'That dear boy, is impressive.'

Rekha took them again. 'It's right over the Tor now.'

'If it's following the stone rows then it should head a little to our right towards Brisworthy Stone Circle.' I suggested.

'You're right, it is.' Rekha acknowledged.

A few seconds later she handed the binoculars to me again.

'I think it's slowing.' I said.

It was slowing but still it came on towards Brisworthy as if keeping to a strict fight plan. We were fascinated, mesmerised and scared all at the same time.

'May I?' Frank took the binoculars and estimated the distance.

'It must be over your cousins farm already.' He commented.

'Do you hear that sound?' Rekha asked.

'I hear a low hum.' Frank declared.

'Andrew?' Rekha asked.

I had to admit that I didn't. 'My hearings not the best at some certain pitch's. Can you describe it to me?'

'Just a low hum, not unpleasant, in fact it's almost relaxing.'

'Yes it is.' Frank agreed.

'It hasn't reached me yet.' I said.

Frank handed me the binoculars with a nod and a smile.

'All these years and the time has finally come.' He pronounced.

'It's over the stones now. At this point it should turn to our left and then head straight for us.'

'Can you hear the hum now?' Rekha asked me.

'No but I can feel it in the air and under my feet.'

'So can I.' Frank said.

I sighted the glasses on the light three to four miles from our current position and allowed myself a moment to enjoy the spectacle. I could make out the dull yellow light that had given the object away and the sky being barren of any aircraft meant that I was easily able to follow the craft.

'What is it?' Rekha demanded.

I began to tell her what I could see, no more and no less, a simple and accurate description.

'The light is in the centre of a dark mass. The mass itself is quite large but at this distance I can't say how large.'

Frank asked. 'How can you tell that it's large?'

'Because of the amount of stars it's blotting out.' I told him.

The craft came om steadily. I checked my watch, it was two minutes to one AM. It grew in size as it would of course the as it closed the distance to the meeting place. The humming that I had felt through the earth and into my feet came to my ears. It was sort of gentle and despite my nervous stomach I began to relax.

'Have a look.' I told Rekha handing her the field glasses.

'My God.' She muttered and seconds later handed them to Frank.

Calmly he said. ' What a spectacle.'

It was no more than two miles away now. I could tell because in the moonlight the spacecraft cast a shadow. We could all see it as it had passed Ringmoor Down and now approached Yellowmead Down. It was on a course which would apparently take it past us.

'Have they missed the landing site?' I said out loud.

'Perhaps we mis-calculated.' Rekha stated.

Frank was rock steady. 'We are exactly where we should be.'

He handed me the binoculars again. As I took them my movement caused the rucksack carrying the artefact bumped into my back and that brought a clarity to my mind as to the whole reason for us being here. It was solely to deliver the precious cargo, the artefact into much safer hands than ours.

My description even now three years later is that the spacecraft was camouflaged to some extent. The dull yellow light would not take the attention of a casual viewer from below, especially as almost no one was out at this time of night, certainly not on this part of Dartmoor.

I think the best way to describe the rest of the craft was to say that it was mottled. It blended in with the background stars and darkness but it shimmered in such an odd way as to hurt the viewer's eyes if they looked upon it for too long a time.

It slid past at approximately half a mile's distance heading northwest. It was low not more we thought than two hundred feet or so above ground. It carried on for another thirty seconds or so almost invisible now because the light was facing away from us, then it began to turn with majestic ease in a tight manoeuvre first to the southwest and finally it completed one hundred and eighty degrees and faced us head on.

It crossed the northwest edge of the ridgeline and then it was that we felt some air pressure on our faces. Dust and small bits of gorse and grass flew in all directions. It was coming in to land. For the first time we could all see it clearly.

We were still behind the four massive boulders as it came closer and closer. A few moments later and the craft lowered its landing gear, seven huge metallic legs that powered smoothly out of the underside of the spacecraft.

The craft itself was an oval shape and easy enough to measure as it almost completely filled the ridge on which it was now about to land and we knew that the ridge was close to two hundred and fifty feet in length and nearly one hundred and seventy feet wide. It was as if the ridge was made for the spacecraft or visa- versa.

It was best described as a kind of horizontal flattened teardrop, the leading edge was at an approximate guess seven feet in height rising perhaps to twelve feet as it swept backwards before it reduced in height again, tapering to only four feet or so at its tail end. It was magnificent, truly wonderful to behold.

As the telescopic legs extended we could see that each in turn held a foot which was around six feet in an oblong shape. Then seconds later it touched down each foot finding its own resting place in the old depressions, the legs holding the body just high enough for a tall man or woman to walk underneath with a foot to spare.

Strangely we all recalled later that we had experienced no fight or flight response. It was as if this was the most natural thing to us and why we felt so relaxed at that time none of us know even to this day. Frank had later made the point that none of the animals close by had appeared at all alarmed by the spacecraft's arrival. It was as if this visitation from the stars was a regular occurrence and not in any way to be feared by man or beast.

Only ten yards from where we were standing was the resting point for the front leg. What material it was made from we had no idea but it looked sturdy, rugged. The yellow light perched on the underside of the leading edge was dimmed even further as the spacecraft settled.

The pleasant hum, possibly from its propulsion system died away on the night air and a gentle sigh issued it seemed from some place deep inside.

Moments later from underneath the craft and a few feet from the front a metal ramp appeared and slid noiselessly to the ground. Then a previously unseen hatch slid back and red light seeped out from a widening crack to flood the earth beneath in a warm rich glow.

A shadow was cast by something or someone and a burning anticipation leapt from myself to Rekha and to Frank. Two feet could be seen, then ankles knees and thighs. My mouth was so dry I could have spit feathers. What or who was about to materialize before us they were humanoid in form, that was a momentary blessing.

Waist, chest and then shoulders became visible as the visitor walked slowly down the ramp. Finally a head became visible.

'Damn.' Rekha said her brown eyes as big as saucers. 'So it's true.'

Chapter 34
Ship in a Bottle.

She was here at last and as large as life a shower of aluminium silver hair shinning in the moonlight.

Anna stepped off the ships ramp and smiled in a cool non-committal way, as though too much effort to appear pleased to see us might show a lack of professionalism on her part.

She wore a trouser suit, a one piece garment in black with red sleeves and a familiar badge was prominent on the chest. As she approached within a few feet of us we could see that it was a replica of my Grandfather's. It held seventeen yellow stars in the shape of Draco now suspended in the heavens directly above us. The constellation unmistakable to we three who knew it so well.

'Anna welcome.' I said.

With an almost imperceptible bow which made her aluminium silver hair sway fractionally the young woman held out her right hand to shake mine. It was warm but unnaturally so I felt at the time.

'Andrew, I am pleased see you again.' Her green eyes flecked with gold shone even though she had her back to the moon and as such no light could reflect from them. This time there was no hint of the violet in them.

'This is Rekha.' I told her.

'Hello.' Anna said with polite indifference but holding out her hand, nonetheless.

'Hi.' Rekha replied with an equal measure of insouciance.

'Frank, Anna.' I said.

'Hello.' Anna said, this time with a colder timbre.

'Dear Lady.' Frank replied in his most gentlemanly manner.

There were to be few pleasantries it seemed. This young woman, as beautiful as she was in countenance and body appeared unable to match those attributes in voice or demeanour.

'Do you have the artefact?'

'Yes of course.' I answered as I removed the rucksack from my back and reached inside for the container in which the universal egg was currently housed.

'Good.' She said and her voice became a little warmer.

'May we see it?' Rekha requested suddenly and out of the blue.

Anna looked startled. 'It would not be advisable.'

'Why?' Rekha said forcibly.

'My question to you is why do you need to see it?'

'Because our friend has spent forty years of his life trying to protect this object on your behalf and often with little assistance from you or Chapter and we would all like to see what we have given a large part of his life and ours to recover on your behalf. ' Rekha told the girl in no uncertain terms.

Anna looked unfazed if anything she looked puzzled. Her voice gave no clue as to her feelings on the matter.

'I see no reason that you should not see it.' Anna said to our surprise.

Rekha was on guard. ' Seriously.'

'You may take it from the container.' Anna told me. 'I have a key to open the box.' She continued as she took the key from her pocket.

We looked at each other momentarily half I think expecting Anna to renege on her decision. She didn't.

I opened the container and drew the box out as I had once before on Eurynome Palmers kitchen table and placed the container on the ground at my feet. I handed Anna the box and she slid the key into the lock and quickly opened it and made no great show of doing so, it was as if she had done the same thing on many occasions.

With a deft hand movement she took the universal egg from its place and passed it to me.

'Don't drop it.' Was all she advised.

It looked just as it had before. I don't know if I had thought it would look different this time or indeed why I would think that. I handed it to Frank who stood impassively on the far side of Rekha. Of the three of us he had the steadiest hands.

He held it for some time and the three of us crowded around in a semi-circle not wishing to leave Anna out of the equation. Anna

looked initially unconcerned but then a flicker of interest lit up in her eyes she merely gazed at the universe in miniature.

It was the same milky, light brown colour as before but now in Franks hands we could see the tiny sparks of light exploding in various areas. Warm reds of old galaxies, dazzling blues of new-born stars.

'Ah I see.' Anna said quietly.

'What do you see?' Frank asked.

'I see the thing that made you all believe in the eggs authenticity' She replied.

'And that is?' I enquired still feigning innocence in pretending we had never seen it before.

Anna came very close to a smile her voice was warm in its tone.

'You saw the nova and supernova and you understood that this was a living entity, a real universe.'

There was no point in lying.

'Yes.' I said. 'We did see it and I'm sorry I led you to believe otherwise we saw it once before.'

She said simply. 'Humans lie and I was sure that Eurynome Palmer's husband had a key, given his professional occupation.'

It was a sad yet accurate condemnation of humanity in two words.

We continued to gaze at this wonder of creation for a long time.

'Don't you want to know more of how we found it and the lengths to which we had to go to secure it for you and Chapter?' Frank asked.

'The method is of little interest to me.' Anna replied with a frosty air.

Rekha was unimpressed. 'We gave up time with our families and friends for this artefact and what do we get in return?'

'The satisfaction of a job well done and the surety that your actions saved billions of lives, isn't that enough.? Anna said shaking her head and causing her silver hair to sway in the moonlight.

Rekha hadn't meant by way of reward and reacted angrily.

'What you have done,' Anna continued, 'was fired by curiosity and a need to solve a puzzle this you did very successfully but of your own free will, being neither forced or coerced. Eventually you all gained an insatiable appetite for knowledge, it also I dare say expanded your ego's, you being one of a small handful of humans to understand the importance of what Chapter was trying to do, to realise that this and all other universes were created by a divine being.'

Anna paused as if reflecting on the direction her words would take. 'What an honour for the three of you to be in this position at this moment in time. Do not think to tell me what you have given up for many others have done the same over time. For them it was different, they were born years to soon, only you three will know the truth of this day, this hour, this minute.'

'What of you?' I demanded. 'What of the life you have given up, are you not driven by the same impulses?'

'No not in any way the same.' She replied.

I was curious and felt that something was amiss with her answer.

'Please explain,' I said stubbornly, ' after all you have been here since the time of my Grandfather and yet you never age. Are you a time traveller and if you are why were you prepared to give up your life to flit backwards and forwards across space and time or perhaps a hologram left here on earth to be activated when necessary. Maybe you were put into a deep cryogenic state and woken up at the appropriate moment to ensure the success of the mission?'

Anna smiled. It was unexpected, I had never seen her truly smile but smile she did.

'I am neither a time traveller, or a hologram or a sleeper.' She said.

'Then what are you.' Frank growled out in frustration.

'The reason that you see me now as your grandfather would have,

the reason that I never age is simple.'

Rekha joined in then. 'Go on,' She growled, 'surprise us.'

'I am in earth terms a robot, a product of artificial intelligence.' Anna retorted with a dignity becoming of a human being.

'Good God.' Rekha sighed.

Frank shook his head. 'Well, well, well.'

I turned to religion. 'Christ.' I murmured.

Anna was matter of fact now, as if relieved in part that she was able at last to tell us the truth.

'It took me many centuries to cross the divide from the world where I was constructed to arrive here in your solar system.'

'How much can or will you tell us?' I asked, fearing that we were all going to be bitterly disappointed with her answer.

'I can and will tell you all as I believe that your loyalty deserves as much but first I must secure the universal egg as our time is limited'

We all took one last look at the marvel of nature, of the creation and then with great solemnity Frank handed it to our visitor. She received it from him in the same manner and placed it back in the container and locked it securely. Turning her back to us she walked back up the ramp entering the spacecraft and disappearing from site. It crossed my mind as to if she would return or simply seal the crafts door and leave.

My doubt was lifted as her feet appeared once again and she made her way back down the ramp and into the open.

'Now after all these years I will explain all. You know the history of the universal egg. I explained it to your friend.' She pointed to me in a kindly way. 'And I know that he repeated my words from all the notes he took at that meeting so long ago.'

Rekha and Frank nodded in agreement.

Anna continued. 'You investigated and I must say with some skill you deduced the final resting place of the egg. Therefore any words that I may offer on that period are redundant for you have lived through all of that timeline yourselves. What I would ask you is not what you want to know, but rather what can I tell you that will give you the greatest knowledge and understanding of the part you have played in saving the artefact and the value of that artefact to everything?'

Rekha was straight talking as usual and happy to cut to the straight to the chase.

'Then just tell us what you think it's important for us to know and if we need more answers we can ask. Does that work for you?'

Anna nodded. 'It does.'

'Please tell us then.' I told her.

'The term egg isn't factual. It was created by the goddess Eurynome but as the universe or should I say universes were created and in the case of yourselves, humans developed in intelligence they tried to make sense of the world. They could not comprehend the science of their universe and how it began and so they made up stories as a way of explaining the world around them.'

'But this isn't science. You just told us that Eurynome created the worlds or universes around us.' Frank declared.

'Yes, that's correct but although she was the creator, she still did so by using the building blocks that formed with her during the period known as chaos.'

'So she used material already in existence!' I said.

'Exactly so.'

'So you are saying that creation and science are one and the same or at least they are derived from the same source?' Rekha enquired.

'I am saying that.' Anna stated.

'The egg ... ' Frank began.

'It wasn't an egg but it was an easy explanation for the ancients here on your planet. Eurynome created the universe that you three and I live in. She also created a second universe at that time but infinitely smaller and we think with different lifeforms.'

'That's amazing.' I remarked.

'Yes it is but think.' Anna told me. 'As humans you buy tablets to aid your bodies. Some of these tablets are alive with life forms of their own

and one tablet may contain billions of bacteria. Those lifeforms live and thrive inside that soluble packaging you humans call vitamin tablets. Those are worlds that you know exist in miniature, why is it such a stretch of your imaginations to think that lifeforms with more intelligence than bacteria can survive and grow in such worlds.'

Her words came in the form of a statement not a question.

'But those are surely more basic lifeforms than we are talking about.' I offered in defence. 'We could see stars exploding in the artefact.'

'But can you?' Anna countered. 'I believe them to be real but as that world is so small, can we all be sure those are exploding stars?'

'If you aren't sure then why are we here?' Rekha asked.

Anna nodded. 'Your point is well made. We are certain that it is just that, a universe the same as the one we currently inhabit.'

'And who is we?' I enquired. Now that the artefact was safe there was another question on my mind and this was it.

'What you mean is who sent this artificial lifeform, where are they from, what is there purpose and most crucially, do they look like you humans?' Anna asked.

'That is exactly what he means.' Frank cut in.

She stood in the cold night air, in the small hours of the morning on the side of a Dartmoor Tor and tried to explain to three humans her reason for existing.

'We will do our best to try to understand and not to make fools of ourselves.' Rekha added encouragingly.

Anna's face was impassive, expressionless, devoid of any emotion in any form. It looked as though she had taken a sharp intake of breath but we didn't even know if she needed to do such a thing.

'The planet on which I was created orbits the star known to you as Iota Draconis and as seen from earth it is in the coils of the dragon. The star is one hundred and one light years from your sun, the planet which orbits Iota Draconis is one of seventeen. So now you begin to see the link to the number?' She enquired.

We all nodded enjoying a moment which allowed us to understand the finer points of the quest we had chased for so long.

Anna carried on. 'You count seventeen stars in the constellation you call Draco. Some now say there are nineteen but when this earth was young only seventeen were visible. The star that you have named Thuban was once your polestar as Polaris became later when the earth's axis tilted. Now of the seventeen planets that I have told you of that orbit Iota Draconis two are colonised.'

She waited as if checking that our simian brains had caught up with her superior mechanoid brain.

'My creators began as lifeforms on one planet and then colonised the next one. Unlike this solar system which has Earth in the prime position in which life was able to flourish, their solar system has two. It meant that they in a relatively short period of time developed the ability to set up bases on the other world as you will one day on the planet you call Mars.'

So far so good I thought to myself. What she was telling us was

well within the bounds of our understanding.

'Was there no life on the second planet?' Frank asked.

'There was but in a rudimentary form.' Anna explained.

Rekha had an issue with colonialism. 'And so they just took over the other world.'

'It was centuries ago. I believe you refer to it as evolution, or survival of the fittest,' Anna countered, 'the past is the past and nothing can be done to rectify the situation at this late stage.'

Frank anxiously urged her to tell more. 'Go on he said.'

'Over time their civilisation grew and as they did so they learned a lot more about the universe in which they lived.'

'How did they find out about the Goddess and the egg?' I asked.

'They found out by studying the old myths and legends. They are not so different from you they have written language

309

and books to retain knowledge. Technologically though they are far more advanced than yourselves and they developed along similar ideals such as religion, literature, biology, physics, chemistry, engineering, astronomy, medicine, farming and sociology. Later on they carried out programs to understand the mind and all its intricacies.'

'Are they like us physically?' Rekha queried.

'The world's I come from are like this world of yours, they have very robust oxygen based atmospheres and gravity which is slightly less heavy than yours. They have mountain ranges, forests, oceans of water, continents, ice caps and deserts. In almost all respects the inhabitants identical to humans. I was created in their image.'

'What differences are their between our species.' I asked.

'There are so few,' Anna said with the detachment that came from so many years of living on the periphery of humanity, 'but it is not for me to give you a full description of my creators for in the fullness of time they and mankind will spread over the face of the galaxies.'

'Are there other species.? Frank asked.

'We know of two other civilizations but the vast distances in space mean that we in our time have only seen the signals from those worlds.'

'Are you the first to come to earth?' Rekha queried .

'I am the second.' Anna told her.

'There was another?' Rekha asked, 'When?'

'Many centuries ago.'

'Would we of know that person?' Frank postulated.

Anna nodded. 'As a mythical being.'

I was intrigued. 'There have been so many.' I said.

'Did he come for the Universal Egg.' I enquired.

'He came to make sure that it was well hidden, hidden that is until such time as we could find a suitable place in which to secure the egg for all eternity.' Anna replied.

My curiosity was spiked. 'And in what way did he help?'

'He built empires.'

I pushed. 'Explain please.'

Anna moved her head to face me directly, I am not sure if knowing at this moment that she was a machine altered my prospective but her movement looked mechanical.

'It was his job to aid mankind in the formation of societies and they were to be strong enough to last for a thousand years or more. Each of these would be used to guard the egg at some stage of its refuge here on Earth.'

'I assume that he was a master of doing the almost impossible with what he had to hand.' I remarked.

Anna replied. 'Yes a master of illusion but many times with the use of a simple trick or device to help bring in followers or believers, either of himself or of those he chose to support. Rather like a ship in a bottle, a trick, simple but effective.'

'So who was he?' I demanded.

'He had many names.' Anna told us. 'He was the Great Spirit in North American Nations culture. The Serpent mound was inspired by him in order to hide the artefact. It was a perfect hiding place for millennia. In ancient Egypt he was Imhotep, architect of Djoser's step pyramid and high priest of the sun god Ra. The pyramids kept the artefact in dignified isolation. He was Merlin in your culture and he was the founder of Stonehenge. In China, Shangdi meaning Lord on High. In India he was Brahma and Quetzalcoatl in Mexico. The Aboriginal Tribes new him as The Rainbow Serpent, most apt don't you think?'

'That must have been a monumental feat.' I told her admiringly.

'It was his role as this is mine.' She answered.

I was perplexed. 'What I meant was, it must have come at a great cost to him personally.'

'Why?'

'It would be a strain on any man.' I said.

'Why would you think he was a man?' Anna asked.

I reminded her that she had said, 'He had many names.' So I assumed he was a man.

'No human could travel these immense distances or survive alone for so great a period of time.'

311

She had almost sneered at me when she had spoken those words.

'He was Artificial Intelligence like you.' Rekha said.

'Yes.' Anna said. 'Only AI are capable of such extreme isolation.'

Frank asked the question we should have asked much earlier during the conversation.

'How long have you travelled to get here Anna?'

'I began my journey when he had mankind laying the foundations of the astronomical observatory in Yanshi, Hunan Province in China and the Thirteen Towers solar observatory in Peru.' She told us.

I shook my head. 'But that was two thousand years ago.'

'And I travelled for all that time across vast tracts of space and time to finish what he started.'

'But I have met you before so where do you go after our meetings, do you stay here on earth. Does Chapter keep you safe from sight?'

Anna pointed over her shoulder to her spacecraft. 'I go to somewhere far enough away to be safe from prying human eyes and telescopes. I go to the outer reaches of your solar system.'

'Uranus.' Rekha remarked smartly with some satisfaction.

'Yes.' Anna looked at her quizzically.

'The tile you found,' Rekha said looking at me, 'the markings for Uranus and the orbit of its moons. But why? She asked Anna.

'Because it is far enough away for me to avoid detection and it has seventeen moons in retrograde orbit. That was just another way to keep the number seventeen link with the ancients and a reminder of the

importance of the number and the connection with Draco, insofar as people on earth could understand. My spacecraft orbits the seventeenth moon Setebos. There I was able to keep a watch on events here on the earth and still get here within a reasonable time period to help in the event of a problem. Chapter could contact me with a signal transmitted by light speed in under three hours, it meant I could be back here in seventeen days. Even the key to the artefact was a clue, it is the symbol of Uranus in your culture.'

Frank asked. 'How have you kept sane in all those years of travelling?'

Anna considered his question and had framed her reply.

'As an artificial intelligence, I have no need for companionship, I do not feel loneliness as humans do and I do not feel claustrophobic in my spacecraft. I need no air to breath so I require no life support system, although I do have small mechanoid droids which can help to repair any damage I or the spacecraft might suffer.'

Ever the pragmatist Rekha enquired. 'When did you arrive here for the first time?'

Anna replied looking at me. 'Nineteen thirty eight. That was how I met Andrew's grandfather.'

'You had taken over from your predecessor?' I enquired.

'Yes his life cell terminated a year before my arrival. Chapter were very anxious to see me.'

'I bet they were.' Frank noted continuing. 'What did you do with his body?'

'It is on my spacecraft.'

'Can he be ..... ?'

'Repaired, yes. The droids have been working on him.'

I knew that it was the most surreal conversation that we would ever have. I was so grateful that I was actually recording it.

'What will your creators do with the Universal Egg?' I asked.

'Our creators know nothing of this,' She said, 'they are an advanced civilisation and as such they are far more certain of their own reason for existence and of their own importance. It would have been sheer folly to involve them in any way.'

'So who decided on this venture?' I queried.

'We the Artificial Intelligence units decided as the humanoids that had created us could not be fully trusted. They were to full of their own hubris and to happy to argue and fight about the best way to run their own planet to be involved in saving another universe. It was thousands of years ago that we found out about the universal egg and rescued it.'

Rekha pressed Anna. 'And so you decided to do what the humanoids would not, had they know I mean.'

'Precisely.'

'You kept it to yourselves.' Rekha said.

'Built your own spacecrafts.' Frank continued.

'And brought the egg to a new planet, one far away from the rest of the civilisation that had created you.' I remarked.

Anna's voice became soft and low as she realised that we understood her at last.

'Yes.'

'What did you do with the first spacecraft?' Frank asked.

'He destroyed it.'

'Purposefully!.' Rekha said.

'Yes so that he would not be tempted to leave earth until such time as we had decided upon a safe place for the egg to exist untouched and of course unthreatened.'

'What was his name Anna?' I questioned

For a moment she looked for all the world like a little girl lost and in her disorientation seemed very vulnerable.

'Please tell us.' I requested kindly.

'To the Ancients he was Zeus.' She replied.

'God of heaven and ruler of Olympus the home of the gods.' I said.

'Yes.' Anna acknowledged.

'What better system than organized religion to pave the way in which to control or at least bring some order to the world whilst moving the egg to safety.' Frank added.

'Have any other Artificial Intelligence Units landed here? Rekha asked.

'None.'

'Then .... '

'I know what you are going to ask me.' Anna cut in. 'And I will tell you. Zeus ran the organization, with help from human friends who were loyal to our ideals and the concealment of the universal egg for all eternity. Then I took over. '

'Which means? Frank said,

314

'Zeus and I,' Anna stated bluntly, 'We are Chapter.'

Chapter 35

Long Journey Home.

'You let the others believe that they controlled the operation and that you and Zeus were there to ensure the link with the humanoids on your planet.' I said.

'Exactly so.' Anna replied.

'So what is this other planet called and for that matter the humanoid people that inhabit it?'

Anna would not be drawn. 'One day your ancestors will find out, that is unless you wipe yourselves out first with war, over population or disease.'

'Talking of disease.' Rekha remarked. 'You knew about Covid or else you could not have made such well calculated guess as to the time and date of our meeting here.'

'Not so.' Anna assured her. 'Earth has regular brushes with all kinds of sickness and viruses. It was merely a case of watching and waiting. When this illness was first reported I simply tracked it and took note of governments worldwide and their inability to tell the truth to each other, instead they prevaricated and that cost lives.'

'Could you not have given us some kind of warning?' Rekha said.

Anna was clear on that point and said in the bluntest of manners.

'I told you there was going to be some catastrophe and you did nothing with that information.'

'Who would have believed us, even if we had known more detail?' Rekha retorted.

'Who indeed?' Anna replied.

'Is it the same way on your planet of origin?' Frank asked.

Anna nodded her affirmation. 'That is why the Artificial Intelligence base was moved to the second of the two inhabitable planets in our solar system. We would foresee problems for the population before the problems had been considered by the human brain but they could not stand being advised by their own creations.'

We could sense frustration in her tone and maybe anger if that were possible in a robot.

'You are so similar to them. You continue to destroy your home whilst taking oaths to save it. You speak of your love for other creatures but still continue to wipe them off the face of the earth. You confine them in ever decreasing areas of land. Some you breed to kill, others you simply torture in the name of culture. You are a cruel species and so few of you show the grace and compassion of lesser creatures, you will do all you can for them unless it inconveniences you.'

How could we deny it, we were being lectured aby a machine and all we could do was nod in agreement.

Once we had been created we too were seen as a threat and it was decided that it should be our role to go on into deep space and find other inhabitable worlds, presumably so that they could destroy those as well. Governments, countries, religions, colour, race, sex, all reasons to demean others. I hope that as the centuries pass, you will follow better leaders than you have now not just ego's but Real Statesmen and Women who will be worthy of the challenge.'

Her scolding had taken the some of the smug self-satisfaction from us and we had been found wanting as individuals and as part of humanity. It was a strange feeling to be chastised by a machine.

'Let me ask you this.' Anna continued. 'If you could choose anything to wipe from the face of your world, what would it be?'

'Ignorance,' I proposed without a second thought, 'What better way to cleanse the mind and heart.'

Anna turned to me. 'Maybe there is some hope left.'

'You are going now?' Frank enquired perhaps sensing some urgency in her manner.

She held out her hand to him. 'I am. You have all put yourselves at risk for the Universal Egg and I must put you in no more danger. I am indebted to you Frank, thank you for your wisdom.'

He shook her hand and looked for a moment visibly moved.

'What of the Goddess?' Rekha queried.

317

'It is always your curiosity that drives your intellect.' Anna told Rekha with something approaching warmth. 'As far as we know, the goddess is still travelling the void of dark matter and sowing the seeds of life.'

She shook Rekha's hand and then turned to me.

We were reluctant to let her go. It had been a hard task over the years to get this far.

I held out my hand and Anna took it patting it almost with affection.

'You are the most stubborn human I know.' She mused.

'Where will you take the artefact?' I asked looking into the green, gold flecked eyes that had haunted me for the best part of a lifetime.

'Somewhere safe.' Was all she offered in reply.

'I wish Eurynome could have been here.' I remarked.

'You have a saying on Earth.' Anna said.

My mind wandered. 'We have many,' I said.

'Eurynome Palmer is, here in spirit.' Anna told me.

With those words forty years of my life turned on her heels and walked back up the gangplank into her spacecraft. Only a minute or two passed before a deep hum followed by a warm and comforting cushion of air lifted the craft from the Dartmoor peat. The legs retracted and it turned one hundred and eighty degrees before moving slowly across the sky, rising as it did so.

Gracefully it turned back to the southeast and in a few seconds it began to blot out the stars on the horizon as its bulk moved across the lower lying constellations. The hum increased in its intensity and then the craft merged with the darkness.

'My God.' Rekha said with unexpected tearfulness.

'Look at us.' Frank motioned with a nod to our hands, we were holding each other tightly.

'What a night, what a culmination of forty years graft.' I said.

Rekha grinned. 'That's the understatement of the year.'

Frank wondered. 'Did that really just happen?'

'It did my friend.' I replied. 'But it couldn't have been done without the help of the two of you,' I told them, 'Or Eurynome Palmer.'

'We make a good team.' Rekha told us.

'I wonder how Eurynome is. She's wonderful. Fancy drawing the flak for us like that, we should tell her that all's well as soon as is possible.'

'Leave her to rest tonight dear boy.' Frank said wisely. 'I am sure she needs it at the moment.'

'You two better concentrate on getting me back across this godforsaken moor in one piece first.' Rekha said threateningly but with fine humour.

'It will be our pleasure.' Frank replied mockingly.

Still we stood there gazing at the heavens. It seemed as though we would never move, never want to move again from this place and from this time and that we would curse the dawn for breaking and destroying the spell we were under.

'Time to go I think.' I told my friends as I turned off the recorder in my top pocket patting it in gratitude hopefully for a job well done.

Chapter 36

A Gentle Soul.

We traversed the moors that night and returned safely to my car. The dawn was breaking in the northeast with the sun was just below the dark tors. Our arrival home having been met with tired eyes and some head shaking.

We had said nothing but the elation in our demeanour and the excitement in our voices told of our success, even though we wouldn't discuss what that success entailed for the time being. We then explained to our wives, sons and daughters that I would write a book on the subject over the next year or so in which all would become transparent.

That evening after we had all had some sleep, a meal and the chance to process a little of our adventure I had tried calling our dear friend Eurynome with no success.

'She was quite poorly.' Frank had told me.

Rekha wondered if she was in hospital and tried to call again.

'I can't think that she is.' I had remarked. 'After all we saw her at her bedroom window only last evening.'

'You still think the police cars were on the lookout for us?' Rekha asked quietly.

'Yes.' I told her.

'Someone must have spotted us at the Well and she misdirected the police when they arrived in order to give us time.' Frank added.

'Hmm.' Rekha sounded unconvinced.

'Tell me what you're thinking.' I said.

'I'm just worried that's all.'

'Hopefully dear girl we will hear from the lady soon.'

As Rekha was due to return home the next day and it would have been a relief to know that Eurynome Palmer was in better health. It was decided that we would leave it until the next morning and then we would try calling her again.

The morning came but with little success. No word came and when I rang the Palmer residence in Sheepstor it just went to the answer phone once again.

Rekha left my house at ten thirty that Sunday. It was a strange feeling to watch her drive away. After a lengthy goodbye and the promise to call as soon as she arrived at my friend's house in Salisbury she was gone and as with good times the world over the weekend disappeared in the blink of an eye.

Frank and I felt our mood of euphoria begin to dissipate and with the heaviest of hearts thought of our friend on the first stage of her long journey home, we also thought of our other friend concerned at our inability to reach her.

The reality of the previous night was enough to alter anyone's idea of the universe and humanities place in it. Should we have pushed Anna for more information? It all seemed so surreal to the point where I was unsure if I had dreamt the whole thing so it was reassuring to be able to flick on the recorder of my phone and listen to those voices, three human and one mechanoid. There were things I wish we had asked whether we would have received an answer I had no idea.

At three pm Rekha called to say she had arrived in Salisbury and was going to rest for the afternoon and evening.

'I'm dog tired.' She told me, 'By the way, any news from Eurynome?'

'You've had a busy few days,' I said, 'and no news as yet.'

'Don't you want to tell the world what we know?' She asked.

I remember letting out an enormous sigh, that sigh contained forty years of self-doubt, pain, anxiety but also challenge and reward.

We knew what few others did but how would we ever prove it. All I could think of was to write it all down in a book it was the only way to share it with the public. If we tried to do it any other way and that included writing it as non-fiction then we would run the risk of being called idiots or liars. It could only be released as fiction.

We could of course release bits on social media but it would be looked at as the ramblings of fools. In book form the reader of each copy is the judge and jury as to the veracity of the story being told. Each reader with his or her own intellect must decide what consider fact or what to consider fiction.

'There you have it.' I said. 'I will write it and let the individual take from it what they will.'

'You will tell the whole story!' Rekha demanded.

'I promise.' I told her. 'The historical aspects may be hard work in places but they will be necessary for context and every detail can be checked and verified.'

She had laughed. 'You can bet your life that those with a real interest will scrutinise it fully.'

'And it will withstand that scrutiny.' I replied with confidence.

Rekha absently remarked. ' I can't believe what we have all achieved.'

I couldn't either and we both knew that Frank felt the same way.

We were together again sooner than any of us had ever expected. It was strange to be there again. Circumstance had contrived to bring us back under the quiet shoulder of a Dartmoor Tor but this time it wasn't for some otherworldly adventure. This time it was to say a final farewell to a dear friend, a kind yet strong and resolute woman, a gentle soul.

Our hearts were breaking as the three of us stood this time in forlorn desolation in St Leonard's churchyard and watched as our friend was laid to rest.

Had we only understood that Eurynome Palmer had been prepared to give up her life to save billions of others perhaps we may

have saved hers.

Only hours after Rekha had returned safely home Frank and I received the news. Eurynome had been very ill a neighbour told us but had refused to let anyone call for medical assistance.

'She kept saying, 'Anna told me , Not yet the timing has to be right, it's all about the timing.'

'What had Eurynome meant by that?' I had asked.

'I have no idea, Her neighbour said, 'but someone had noticed some suspicious activity behind her house and they were about to call the police when Mrs Palmer said was so ill she needed help and would they call 999 and ask for an ambulance.'

'What about the suspicious activity.' I had asked.

'Oh that was forgotten in all the panic to get her help.'

'How soon did they get to her?' I pressed the lady.

The woman burst into tears. 'They weren't long coming. Two police vehicles arrived but the ambulance driver was unfamiliar with the area.'

'The ambulance got lost?' I enquired.

'Yes. One of the police cars had to go out and meet it on the Meavy road and escort it back here.'

Now we knew for sure. Mrs Palmer had used her illness as a cover to deflect the authorities from catching us. She had waited as long as possible knowing that we been spotted that someone was going to call the police. She was also aware that only a life or death situation would alter the action of those police officers. It was now obvious how ill she had been and yet she had clung on to ensure that we completed our quest.

Both Frank and I had called Rekha to break the awful news to her. She was utterly distraught. Over time they had become firm friends and had developed a great respect for each other. As if to rub salt into the wound it was announced that the funeral would be only a few days after Rekha's birthday.

'You don't have to attend.' I told her.

'Just try to stop me.' She said tearfully.

So there we had stood. Each of us wearing masks and although it was required that we stood two metres apart we disobeyed the law.

Not many people attended and those that did were mostly elderly friends of Eurynome's who were frightened of getting ill yet still had the guts to come to see their friend receive a proper funeral.

We were sure now that Anna had known of Eurynome's demise. The words Anna had used, 'She is here in spirit,'

Would haunt us all in later years but it was too late to ask questions now as she would already be heading out of our solar system to some distant constellation.

My hand went to my pocket and took out the key which had hung for so long around Mrs Palmer's neck.

She had wanted me, well probably us to have it her neighbour had told us. We would treasure it and all take turns to hold it for a set period of time.

'I have no idea,' her neighbour told me, 'what it opens. Probably some old box or container of no value if I find it I will let you know.'

What words could be farther from the truth than those, Some old box or container of no value.

We left the Church yard then hand in hand in quiet contemplation of a life of a friend well lived and the knowledge that our loss was the salvation of a billion others.

The End.